Effigies in Ashes

A Comedy

By

Robert Joseph Dagney

xulon PRESS

To the priests, religious and lay people of the Catholic Church
who kept the faith while I was wandering in the wilderness

Table of Contents

I watched a man
against whose throat a sudden serpent bit,
More swiftly than the shortest word is writ
Take fire, and burn, and in his place there came
A little heap of ashes. As the flame
In cinders sank, a sight most marvelous
Was mine - the calcined heap reversed the wrong,
Arising to its human form.

Dante
The Divine Comedy
The Inferno
Canto XXIV

"If it be awful to tell another in our own way what we are; what will be the awfulness of that Day when the secrets of all hearts shall be disclosed! Let us bear this in mind when we fear that others should know what we are really; whether we are right or wrong in hiding our sins now, it is a vain notion if we suppose they will always be hidden. The Lord will come in judgment and 'he will bring to light what is hidden in darkness and will manifest the motives of our hearts....'"

John Henry Newman
Christian Sympathy
Parochial and Plain Sermons

1.

A Twitch upon the Thread

The chimes at the Shrine were playing the Ave Maria as Father Joseph Gallagher C.M. limped slowly down the corridor toward the community chapel. His feet were killing him but he had to spend some time in front of the Blessed Sacrament. He had just received a phone call that troubled him and he wanted to talk with the Lord about it. The eight o'clock novena was just finishing and the chapel was empty. Vespers were long over and the other priests were either in their rooms or over at the novena. He made his way slowly up to the prie-dieu in front of the tabernacle and knelt down. He made the sign of the cross slowly and reverently.

'My Lord,' he prayed, 'An old friend called me on the phone and asked if he could see me. He said that he needed some help. Bill Casey. I had to sit down when he told me who was calling. I haven't talked to him in years. I've heard such strange stories about him that I don't know what to believe. I'm going to meet with him tomorrow night. I know he's one of the ones you came for: one of the lost. He told me that he has nowhere else to go. He needed to talk with a priest. Something happened to him that he doesn't understand. I told him that I would be more than happy to meet with him but he asked me to do something for him that I don't feel capable of doing. Please, Lord, tell me what to do.'

After listening for a few minutes, Father Joe nodded and smiled.

'Yes, Lord. I'll talk this over with my spiritual advisor. Father Mike has been a great help to me.'

Feeling much better, Father Joe struggled up from the kneeler, slowly genuflected and limped out of the chapel.

When he passed by the library, he saw Father Michael McDonald himself sitting in an easy chair reading a book: **Brideshead Revisited** by Evelyn Waugh. Father Mike was always reading: books, magazines, newspapers, left wing and right wing, orthodox and heterodox, those with us and those against us. 'We can't be like the ostrich, hiding our heads in the sand,' he liked to say. 'We need to know what our adversary is thinking and doing.' Father Mike was eighty years old but his mind was as agile and active as the computer he had in his cell. 'Got to keep up with the times,' he said whenever he was teased about it. 'If Saint Paul or Saint Maximilian Kolbe were alive today, they'd be using a computer and the world wide web.'

Father Mike looked up and saw his confrere coming. He put down his book and waved Father Joe into a chair next to him. They chatted for a few minutes before Father Joe told his mentor about his problem.

"I got a call from a guy I grew up with in the Falls."

"The Falls? Niagara?"

Father Joe shook his head.

"East Falls. Saint Bridget's parish. Right here in Philly. We went to the same schools together: Saint Bridget's, Roman Catholic and LaSalle College. I was a philosophy major. He was in political science, I think. He kept changing majors. We knew each other growing up but we weren't really friends. I remember him as basically a good kid in grammar school, an altar boy, an honor student, but then in high school he got in with a bad crowd. He started drinking and fighting. He even got locked up a couple of times. One of the mysteries of life, a tragedy, a good kid gone bad. Why?"

Father Joe shrugged.

"He only got worse in college, although he did graduate. Somehow. His mother's prayers, probably. To me he seemed self-centered, shallow, a party guy. The last time I saw him must have been in May of '68. Twenty four years ago. He went into the army in June, only a few days after graduation. Volunteered for the draft, he told me. He wanted to be part of the crusade against Communism. Can you believe that? Most young people were trying to avoid the draft at that time. But he was really nervous about going in. Afraid. He looked so young, still a boy, really. He looked like a lamb going to the slaughter. I told him I would pray for him. I went into the seminary when he went into the army. Every time I would read about Vietnam or see it on the news, I would think of him and pray for him. He did go to Vietnam, I know, but I don't know what he did over there or what his experience was. Although I do remember hearing stories about how he was always coming home, sometimes illegally, you know, going AWOL. I don't know how much trouble he got into over that. Over the years, once in a while, when I talked with my parents, his name would come up. They said he became a writer. Had a couple of novels published. When I talked with him tonight, he told me he's writing some short stories about growing up in the Falls. He asked me if I had read his novels. I had to admit that I hadn't. I don't read novels. Most of them are pretty poison as far as I'm concerned."

Father Mike smiled. He disagreed. He had taught literature at Saint John's University for many years and had a Ph.D in English Literature. There were many novels worth reading. He had written his master's thesis on the expiation of guilt in Lord Jim and his doctoral thesis on the loss of youth and innocence in the Yoknapatawpha series by William Faulkner. He pointed to the book he held in his hand and asked Father Joe if he had read it.

He hadn't.

"There's literature and there's entertainments, diversions and especially today: a lot of trash," said Father Mike as he held up the book as if it were a standard to rally around.

"This is literature. Art is the universal in the particular. All true literature is concerned with the struggle between good and evil, between God and the Devil. Did you know that Emerson believed that literature was a part of theology? Who believes that today? But all stories should be concerned with reconciliation and conversion. Just a twitch upon the thread, a tiny whisper, is all it takes to bring sinners back to God and to see Him as he truly is, as far as our feeble minds are capable, of course. Truly great literature reflects the mysteries of life and merely hints at the marvels we can make happen. As Dorothy Sayers observed: all creative literature reflects the Trinity in some way; it has to, for we are made in the image and likeness of God."

Father Mike stopped there and lowered the book to his lap. He had to remember that he was no longer in front of a class, teaching students, giving lectures.

"So what's our writer's name?"

"'The Case' we used to call him. Casey. Bill Casey."

Father Mike thought for a moment. The name was not familiar to him but he knew that there were thousands of books published every year, most of them not worth a tinker's damn.

"I heard about him and his books," said Father Joe, "From my father. My parents still live in the old neighborhood. Casey moved back there a few years ago, I believe, to live with his mother."

Father Mike was surprised.

"With his mother? This guy is either a real loser or a good Christian man."

Father Joe shrugged.

"I don't know about that: being a good Christian man, that is. Not from what I've heard. The word is that Casey went off the deep end after coming home from Vietnam. He turned against the war, against America from what I heard. Became a radical, a rebel. Maybe even a communist. It's as if he became the enemy. Apparently, he was down in Nicaragua with the Sandinistas a few years ago, cutting coffee. Before that, he went to Ireland a few times during the '70's. My father remembers him going around in the bars boasting about how he was recruited by the IRA and had been hanging out with gun runners and drug smugglers and bank robbers. I know. It sounds far fetched to me, too. But according to my father, one of his buddies, Mad Dog Daily, vouches for him. One of Casey's books is set in Ireland and is about his experiences with the IRA, his supposed experiences anyway."

"Really?" said Father Mike. "Do you know the title?"

"**The Circle of Stones**," said Father Joe. "Strange stuff from what my father heard. Has goddesses in it or some such nonsense."

Father Mike sat back in his chair, thinking that the title had a pagan ring to it. Some scholars thought that the Druids used stone circles for their rituals, for human sacrifice, supposedly.

There was a few moments of silence before Father Joe spoke again.

"But they say he's been good to his mother. She's a widow on limited income."

Father Mike shrugged.

"He seems like a very contradictory sort of person but let's hope he's a paradox, instead. He doesn't seem like the sort of person who would live with his mother: Vietnam, Nicaragua, the IRA. I hope he's not mistreating her."

Father Joe shook his head.

"No, I don't think so. The old folks in the neighborhood think highly of him despite his history. He's a nurse, now, a pediatrics nurse of all things. When I heard that I thought that maybe he had gotten himself straight. But then there were rumors going around that he was involved in this New Age nonsense, that he was practicing some sort of sorcery. I don't know what that's all about. His other book is based on his experiences as a pediatrics nurse. It's called **The Story of a Swallow**. Casey told me it was set in a seaside house."

"A swallow? In a seaside house?" exclaimed Father Mike. "Sounds like it should be called the story of a seagull."

They laughed.

"He hasn't been very successful," said Father Joe. "I don't think many people have read his books. For good reason, I'm sure. Weird stuff, poorly written, probably. I'm surprised he wants to see me. I haven't seen him in years."

Father Mike shrugged.

"So what does this, eh, character want with you?"

Father Joe smiled.

"He's thinking about coming back to the Church."

Father Mike leaned forward in his chair. He was always interested in people coming back to the Church.

"You're going to meet with him, of course."

Father Joe nodded.

"Yes. But that's not all he wants. He asked me if I would read his books. I told him that I don't read fiction. That's not my field."

Father Mike put his hands together as if he were praying.

"That's strange. Why does he want you to do that?"

Father Joe hesitated, trying to remember what Casey had said. He had talked in such short, cryptic sentences that it was difficult to understand what was being said. It was almost as if he thought the phone was being tapped.

"His books are a record of his sins and crimes. No, crimes and misdemeanors was the way he put it. 'And the names have been changed to protect the guilty,' he said. But he was laughing when he said it, so I don't know how serious he is about that. But get this: He thinks that when he was in Ireland he had some sort of religious experience. Until recently, he had believed he had met some triple goddess of Ireland, whoever that is, but now, he's beginning to think it had something to do with the Blessed Mother. Not an apparition, he made that clear. He didn't see anything or hear any voices. Only that some woman came to him in a mysterious way and prevented him from making a terrible mistake while he was there."

Father Mike banged the arms of his chair and exclaimed, "You're kidding me! The triple goddess of Ireland! The Blessed Mother!"

Father Joe laughed.

"I don't know what to make of it either. He also said something about wanting me to show him where he had gone wrong in his books. But I don't feel capable of that. I can hear his confession or talk with him about his spiritual life but I can't critique his books. I was hoping you would give them a glance."

Father Mike had to think about that. He had no interest in **The Circle of Stones**. Goddesses and gunmen! It seemed like a mish-mash of phony feminism and pulp fiction, flea market material, a comic book with stock characters all talking like New York City Irish gangsters and the hero a clone of the Jimmy Cagney character in the movie **Shake Hands with the Devil.** No thanks. He would bet that this guy Casey never met any gunrunners or drug smugglers and never went to any circle of stones. The guy was probably having delusions or living in a fantasy world. A wanna be. He had a little interest in the other book. It wasn't often that you read about a man taking care of sick children. But sorcery? The New Age? He had heard about the New Age. Shirley MacLaine, that poor deluded woman, was part of it. He had glanced through one of her books: pure drivel. The last time he had been in New York he had walked into a New Age bookstore and wandered through it for a little while. Hypnotic music: flutes and harps. Incense. Crystals. Connected to the occult somehow. He hadn't stayed in there long.

"I'm sorry," said Father Joe. "Forget it. I shouldn't have asked. It was just that I feel sorry for him. He thinks that he has something important to say in his books and no one will read them."

Father Mike sighed. He didn't feel like wasting his time reading an amateur but he could do it as a spiritual work of mercy for Lent.

"I'll look at them if he wants me to."

Father Joe was relieved.

"I'll ask him. He's coming tomorrow night."

With that resolved, the two priests talked for a few minutes about what was going on in their community and then went to their cells upstairs, Father Mike to finish reading his novel and his younger confrere to do some spiritual reading. He was reading **Immaculate Conception and the Holy Spirit: the Marian Teachings of Saint Maximilian Kolbe** by Father Manteau-Bonamy, O.P.

2.

Not Death but Love

As Casey rode the K bus through Germantown on his way to the Shrine, he remembered riding that bus to LaSalle College so many years before, a naïve young man, totally unaware of the trial his life was to become. He could never be that young man again, too much had happened. All part of growing up, he thought, but nonetheless, he felt that familiar emptiness inside, something he felt whenever he thought of his past. He wished he knew what caused it. He remembered carrying his lunch in a brown paper bag his mother had packed. He had started college with such hope, such anticipation. College. It was like a magic word to his father, who had not been able to go further than high school. He would learn so much there. It was going to open the door to a better life. That's what his father had wanted for him: a better life than working in the factory at Budd's. But it hadn't worked out that way. There he was: forty-six years old, riding the bus, living at home. A failure.

He had liked at LaSalle, hanging out in the cafeteria with the guys, going to the Big 5 basketball games at the Palestra, even going to class, some of the classes, that is, the English classes. But after the war, he had trashed the school and the education he had received. What had he learned there? 'Nothing,' he used to say, 'If I had learned anything, I wouldn't have gone to Vietnam.' But over the years, his views had mellowed. LaSalle was a good school. It wasn't their fault that they hadn't understood the Vietnam War. Who did? But his degree had enabled him to get jobs with the government after his discharge from the army and the money he made took him to Ireland three times. And college had brought him into contact with the intellectual world: with literature and history and political science but now he realized how little he knew. He also had thirty-six credits in theology and philosophy but the more he thought about God and metaphysics the less he understood. What was the point of learning if there was no Truth?

How could he hope to learn about the real world when he didn't know who he was. Who was Bill Casey? He would hear himself saying things he didn't mean, or doing things he didn't want to do. It was as if a stranger was saying them or doing them and he was off in the distance, watching, like a spectator at a shadow play, watching images of himself thrown up on a screen.

If whatever he did, whoever he was, had no ultimate meaning, then why do anything but party? Eat, drink and be merry, for tomorrow we die. Then: nothing? Or back to the circle? The eternal recurrence? No, he couldn't believe that; if he did, he would wind up like Nietzsche howling at the stars: no, no, not again, not another life like this: more lies, more pain, more death, over and over again. But then the thought came to him: what if instead of returning to the circle he became a new person in a new life instead? In a new heaven and a new earth with no lies, no pain and no death. That would be a different story.

He had devoted years of his life to writing about his experiences in Ireland and at Seaside House, trying to see them as episodes in something larger than themselves: a metadrama. But they remained pieces of a puzzle that would not fit together. It was as if a malevolent being had stolen a key piece and had hidden it away somewhere. He had looked for it everywhere: in books, in mythology, in experiences, in politics and pipe dreams but he was like a little boy trying to fit a square piece in a round hole. But recently he had started thinking that perhaps he had been looking for it in the wrong places. Maybe the key was right before his eyes. He knew one thing: He had to find it. Everything had to fit together, somehow or else it was as

Mick had said, 'Life, a weary puzzle past finding out by mahn.' Something significant had happened in Ireland; he was convinced of it. But what? He had to find out. His life depended on it.

As the bus slowly weaved its way through the chaotic street which was blocked by heavy traffic and double-parked cars, horns honking and people shouting, jaywalking, oblivious, or not caring about the danger around them, stores boarded up or changed beyond recognition, Casey remembered Chelten Avenue as it had been when he was a boy: the Orpheum Theater with its red carpets and large ornate pillars, the balcony, the plush seats; Allen's Department Store where his mother had worked, selling candy; Adam's, the clothing store where he had gotten his first suit. He remembered walking over to Woolworth's with Larry O'Donnell and Bobby Perry and Jimmy Myers, all dead now, to buy some rock and roll and to have a hot dog and an ice cream soda at the lunch counter. All that was not there anymore. The person he had been wasn't there anymore either.

Germantown was mostly black now, not the mixed neighborhood he remembered. The bus was almost full and he was the only white person on it. That didn't bother him. Over the years, as a nurse, he had worked with many black people and he always got along with them. But that hadn't always been the case. He dipped into his gas mask bag and took out his manuscript: **Falls**. He flipped through the pages until he came to the story, **It ain't them** and began to read.

It was a warm night in November and we were hanging on Rowland's corner, spitting and smoking and telling lies. Not all of the gang was there. The girls weren't there, only Quell'heure, Lurch, Packy and myself. We had talked about trying to pick up a few quarts of beer but all of the bars were closed on Sunday because of the blue laws. Only the Benny and the Dago club were open and they didn't have take out. Besides, we didn't have anyone to go in for us. Phil the Bum was our usual runner but he wasn't around. We had the usual end of the weekend blues. Another week of school. What a drag! We were in a bad mad mood. The Eagles had lost another game, their fifth in a row:27 to 20 to Dallas. King Hill had almost brought them back but Timmy Brown had fumbled a lateral pass and Dallas recovered and won the game. Roman had just lost their third straight game. We were 1 and 4 with the Saint Joe Prep game coming up. We were tired of being losers. So we had gone out looking for trouble; they did, anyway, not me. I just wanted to go home. As usual, we had lost the game but had won the fight.

Lurch shadowboxed as he told us what he had done.

"I gave this punk the old one-two. I said Bam, Bam and he just stood there with his head thrown back, seeing stars and hearing ole Tweety Bird, his legs shaking like he was doing the Mashed Potato at The Dance. Then he went to his knees like a holy roller saying his prayers."

Lurch laughed as he took a few steps backward and held his arms and legs like a kicker lining up a field goal.

"I was about to kick his teeth in when the cops came and we had to split."

Then Packy testified.

"I punched out this cat with a Tommy More pennant. He was waving at me like some fruit and laughing at me. I gave him a couple of line drives to the head and he went down. And he stayed down."

"Yeah, sure," said Quell'heure. "I saw the cat. He was this little guy with glasses. Dangme here would tower over him. Now me, I duked it out with one of their linemen. Number 62. I sucker punched that big boy as he was coming off the field."

"Yeah, sure," said Lurch. "In your dreams. I saw you hiding behind Judy's skirts. Under her skirts. That's where you belong. With the girls. 'Cause that's all ya are. Nothing but a girl."

They faced each other for a few moments like two gunslingers at the OK Corral then Lurch took off his Camel's hair coat and handed to me like I was his servant. I threw it over the railing by the steps. I wasn't going to be nobody's servant.

Lurch and Quell'heure started slap fighting. They bobbed and weaved, ducked and dodged as Packy circled around them, shouting out their moves like an announcer on TV.

"It's Zale with a left and a right and another left and another right. Graciano is reeling now."

I sat on Rowland's steps and watched the fight. I really didn't like fights, not like those guys did. They liked to fight. Especially Lurch. He was always fighting somebody. He was the toughest guy in the neighborhood, one of the toughest, anyway. It was hard to say. There were a lot of tough guys in the Falls. He was the toughest guy in our gang. Maybe. I only fought if I had to. I had stayed out of the fighting that day after the game but I had been right there behind Lurch and I had helped keep the kid's friends from breaking it up. If the cops hadn't come, I would have gotten into it. I had to back up my friends.

Just a few months ago, I helped beat up some cat right up the street in front of the Hossy lots, near Bogie's house: me and Packy and The Bear. We cut him up pretty bad. We were walking up Scott's Lane that night after having cheese steaks at The Rack. When we got onto Indian Queen Lane, we saw this strange cat talking to one of the girls from the neighborhood. As soon as The Bear saw the cat, he snapped out. He didn't want nobody from some other neighborhood talking to the girls on his street. So he started yelling at the cat, telling him to slink on outta there or he was going to get his lights punched out. Now the cat was pretty big, an old head, eighteen or nineteen years old. He had muscles like an iron worker. He was no punk. He was from the Yunk and he wasn't taking no lip.

He came bouncing across the street and without saying a word sucker punched The Bear in the mouth, knocking him into the gutter. We couldn't let nobody beat up our buddy so me and Packy worked him over front and back. By the time we were done with him, he looked like Rocky Graciano after his fight with Tony Zale; there was so much blood on his face. As soon as we saw he was beat, we split.

We got into a lot of trouble over that. I had to stay in the house for a month. The girl's parents called our parents and told them what had happened. The cat had so many stitches on his face that he looked like Frankenstein coming off the table. The cat didn't press charges on us because he had thrown the first punch, but he told us that if we didn't pay his hospital bill he would take us to court, so we paid it. Our parents paid it, that is. We didn't have no money.

None of us were working. We were still in high school. My parents were real upset with me. My dad wasn't too bad. He had been in fights when he was a kid so he understood, but my mom, she was furious. I remember her yelling at me, 'Why did you do that? What happened to you? You never raised your hand to anyone before. I didn't bring you up to be a bully. That's not you.'

I knew she was right. I had changed. Something had happened to me but I didn't know what it was. After that fight, I really didn't want to hang out with those guys because it seemed like every time I did, I got into trouble, but I didn't want to be seen as a momma's boy either.

I wasn't going to go out that night after the game but I felt this powerful urge like a restless spirit within me that drove me out of the house. Something was going to happen and I had to be there. Besides, I didn't know what to do with myself. There was nowhere to go. The playground was closed. There was nothing good on TV. I didn't feel like watching **The Rifleman** or **Bonanza**, and I had already seen **Under the Yum Yum Tree**, the movie that was playing at the Alden. I had already done my homework. I did it as fast as I could. I hated doing homework. I hated school. Why did I have to study French? I was never going to France and I didn't know any French people. And trigonometry? What did I have to know that for? I flunked it last quarter, the only subject I ever flunked. Our teacher, Mr. McNulty said I cheated on a test. Not true. I did take a look at the answers of the kid next to me but only to see if they matched mine. I had no intention of copying from him. I was smarter than he was. I didn't do anything wrong and I was punished for it. I was guilty no matter what I did. But what else could I expect in a Catholic school? I hated religion. I didn't believe in any of that stuff anymore. The only class I liked even a little bit was English with Gyro. Father Daniel Maguire. He was all right for a priest. At least you could kid around with him and he didn't smack you around like Father Chewing Gum did. I felt my face get hot and red and tears came to my eyes like they did that day. I didn't want to think about it anymore. It only made me mad. I turned my attention back to the fight. Lurch had Quelle'heure on the ground in a scissors and a headlock and Packy was slapping his hand on the pavement like a referee counting the seconds. He announced Lurch as the winner.

Lurch got up and danced around, clenching his hands over his head like a champion then he brushed himself off and adjusted his clothes like a dandy going on a date. He donned his Camel's hair coat, pulled it forward and shot out his cuffs like a South Philly mafia man and preened in front of a car window until every hair was in place. Quelle'heure guffawed as he just took a moment to straighten himself out while me and Packy snickered. All of us were dressed in nice clothes, slacks and sweaters and wing tipped shoes but Lurch outdid us all. He always dressed well even if just to hang out on the corner.

I had an idea. I suggested that we take a ride and see where the Commodore Barry Club, the Irish Center was. Our Senior Prom was to be held there on Friday night and none of us knew exactly where it was. It was somewhere in Germantown or Mount Airy. I didn't want to get lost on Prom Night looking for it. It was the first time that the Prom had ever been held there and it was the first time that the Prom was to be in the Fall instead of the Spring. None of us knew why that was so. Apparently, one of the priests had taken it upon himself to arrange it that way, without asking us. That's another thing I hated about school. The priests were totally in charge of us. We didn't have no say.

"Do you know what street it's on, Dangme?" asked Lurch.

"Emlen Street, I think," I said. "It's just off Lincoln Drive. We can ask somebody for directions when we get over there."

"Who's going to drive?" asked Quell'heure. "I'll go as long as Dangme doesn't drive. I don't want to get racked up."

I shook my head and didn't say a word. The year before, I had totaled my father's car on Walnut Lane and Henry Avenue. I only had my driver's license a couple of weeks when it happened. It was my fault. I had been up Hacker's Hollow hitting golf balls with Bogie until it got too dark to see and we had to go. I was turning off Walnut Lane onto Henry and there was a car coming towards me. It was a strange experience. I could see the car coming and I knew I had to stop but it was as if I were paralyzed. I felt like I was in another world or something, zoned out. I wasn't drunk or anything. I wasn't going out tasting then. I smashed right into the other car. I banged my head on the steering wheel and cut my head at the elbow. There was blood all over my face. Bogie got his knees bruised up. The other driver broke one of his legs. I got a reckless driving ticket and lost my insurance for a year. I had it back now but I only drove once in a while. I made myself do it. I hated driving after that accident. I was so afraid of it happening again. I didn't want anymore people to get hurt because of me.

"I'll drive," said Lurch. "I got my little blue chariot over there by The Beverage."

We still called the place The Beverage even though it was empty now. It was a large brick building built in the 1890's. Kids had chalked it up with names and curses and most of the windows were broken or boarded up. It had been a brewery where they made Hohenedal's beer until it closed in the 1950's. It had been taken over by NiHi, a soda company that went out of business a few years ago. Guys from the neighborhood used to steal soda by case and drink it over in the playground. I didn't do any of that. I didn't like stealing. I knew it was wrong. But then one day last summer, Lurch and I stole a case of beer. I was helping him on his newspaper route when we saw a case of Ballantine beer on the back of a delivery truck. Lurch jumped up on the truck and stuffed it inside of his newspaper bag and we took it back Dutch Hollow and hid it. The delivery man suspected us and went to talk with my father. When my dad asked me about it, I lied right to his face. I told him we had nothing to do with it. He believed me and convinced the delivery man, a friend of his, that it wasn't us so we got away with it. I never did drink any of the beer. I couldn't. It was bad enough that I was not only a liar but now I was a thief and that my dad believed me made it even worse. I felt sick and sorry any time I thought about what I did that day.

We walked across Conrad Street and got into Lurch's car, a '56 Ford. I got into the back seat with Packy. Quell'heure took shotgun. As we rode up Conrad Street, I looked out the window at the dark stores and lit-up houses along the way. It was quiet now but in the morning, the street would be swarming with cars and people. There were three bars and a beer distributor, two barber shops, three grocery stores: Rowland's, Maxie's and Caldwell's, a butcher shop, a shoemakers, a variety store, a drug store and a sandwich shop were another gang of kids hung out. Mifflin School and the schoolyard where we played touch football was just down the hill It was my neighborhood. Parts of my family had lived there since before the Civil War. They had come to America from Ireland during the Famine. As my Aunt Marg used to say, 'We come from Donegal, we eat our taters skins and all.' I grew up in the Falls but now I felt like I didn't belong there anymore. It was as if I had become an alien or an outsider somehow. As we passed by McKeever's Beer Distributor's, I looked up at the window of our living room. We lived on top of a small store that my Aunt Marg rented out to The Evening Bulletin. The lights were on and I knew that my dad was sitting there, drinking a beer and reading a book. That's what he did every night. My Uncle John called him 'Warm Beer' because he drank so slowly. My mom was probably praying the rosary or doing some sort of church work and my brother, Richie, he was probably making stink bombs with his chemistry set or learning how to tie knots or something strange like that; he was a mystery to me. As we drove past, I had this sudden desire to tell Lurch to stop and let me out so I could go home. I had a terrible feeling that we were going to get into trouble again. I longed to be with my family but as I looked back towards them it was as if they were fading from my memory like smoke in the air and who I had been was a little heap of burning ashes.

"Hey man," I said. "I just remembered that I forgot to do my homework. Let me out here."

"Whaat?" said Lurch. "This was your idea, Dangme. We ain't stopping now."

The others turned and looked at me.

"What's the matter, man?" said Quell'heure. "You wanna be with your mommy?"

The others razzed me.

"The poor baby. He misses him mommy and daddy."

I couldn't let anyone think I was a punk.

"Ah, shut up" I said. "Never mind. I'll do it when we get back."

Lurch drove down Midvale Avenue and then turned on Wissahickon Avenue and went down past Alden Park to Lincoln Drive. He drove slowly, looking for Emlen Street.

"I think it's near here," said Packy. "I was here once, years ago, with Benny, my old man. He used to come here on Saint Patty's day and tie on a load. Emlen Street. There it is."

Lurch turned on the curving street and drove for a few moments, passing under a railroad bridge until we came upon a lit up building with a sign saying **Commodore Barry, the Irish Center.**

It sounded like there was a party going on inside. We could hear music playing and people talking and laughing. Cars were parked along both sides of the street. I didn't see any reason to stop but Lurch wanted to get a better look at the place. He found a parking place by the next corner where we got out and walked in front of the building.

As we stood there, talking about the Prom, we heard someone say, "What are you white boys doing in our neighborhood?"

We turned around and saw two black kids across the street.

"What did you say, black boy?" asked Lurch, walking towards them.

"You heard us, white boy," said the tall one. "This is our turf."

"Yeah, sure," said Quell'heure. "Here? At the Irish Center? You don't live around here. You'd better get back where you belong before you get hurt."

Racial epithets were hurled back and forth.

Lurch put up his fists like John L. Sullivan.

"Come on, boy. Let's see who's a boy and who's a man."

The rest of us put up our fists, crossed the street and walked towards the two black kids who back-stepped away from us. Then suddenly they whirled around and tore aerials off of cars and ran at us, slashing the air with them in front of our faces. They caught us by surprise. We turned and ran down the street, the black kids running after us, shouting and laughing.

After we ran a little way, Lurch shouted, "What are we doing running? We don't let nobody chase us around."

He stopped and tore off a car aerial and went after them like Zorro attacking bandits. I watched him duel with them for a few moments, then I tore off a car aerial and joined the fight. I was scared but I had no choice. I had to fight. A couple of times, I clashed aerials with one of the black kids, but for the most part, I kept crouched down, waving the aerial high above my head. I didn't want to get hit in the face with one of those and I didn't want to hurt anyone either. Meanwhile, Quell'heure had found a milk crate on the pavement and while we were dueling, he sneaked behind one of the black kids and smashed him on the back with it. The kid banged up against a car and started screaming. With that, a few people came out of the Irish Center to see what was going on and when they saw that we had torn off some car aerials, they started shouting for the cops. So we took off and ran down the street. As we got to the railroad bridge, it started raining cobblestones. We looked up and saw the black kids on the tracks lobbing down rocks which exploded around us like hand grenades. We ran as fast as we could to get out of their range and by the time we stopped running we were lost. We didn't know what to do. Our car was parked over by the Commodore Barry and we couldn't go back there, not yet. The cops were probably on the scene by now and all those people from the Irish Center had to be mad at us for tearing off their car aerials. As we walked along trying to figure out what to do, a red car pulled up beside us and a cop got out and called us over to him.

"C'mere, you punks. Youse are the guys that was in that fight over at the Irish Center, aren't ya.?"

We put on the act.

"Huh? Us? What are you talking about officer? We weren't in no fight."

"We wuz just taking a walk around the neighborhood. Seeing what it was like over here. What kind of trees they have. Looking at the bushes."

"We're from the Falls, see. Ya get tired of hanging on the same old streets all the time. We just needed a change of scenery."

"Ah, a bunch of wise guys," said the cop. "Then why are ya all breathing so hard if ya wuz just taking a walk?"

We looked at each other, trying to come up with a reason why we would be running.

"Yeah, yeah, now I remember. We heard some noise over by the Irish Center: some shouting and cursing like there was a fight going on. We don't want no trouble, see, so we just busted on out of there real fast."

"Yeah, that's what happened."

"Yeah, yeah. We were afraid we would get jumped by you know who. You know how it is, Officer."

But he wasn't buying it.

"Yeah, I know how it is. There's a black kid over on Emlen Street who says he just got hit on the back with a milk crate by a gang of white boys. Four of them, he says jumped him and his buddy. And one of them was wearing a Camel's hair coat. And a few people from the Irish Center saw four white kids running this way. They're very upset. They don't like losing their car aerials."

We looked at Lurch's coat.

"It wasn't us."

"It's just some coincidence."

"Yeah, we're being framed."

"Yeah, sure," said the cop. "Get into the car. I'll take you down there so they can eyeball ya."

I started feeling sick to my stomach. We were going to get into a lot of trouble over this. We had school the next day. Father Spike Dolan would find out about it and he would kick us out of Roman, a week before our senior Prom. We'd have to go to public school, a fate worse than death. I wouldn't get out of the house for a year over this.

When we pulled up in front of the Irish Center, the car got surrounded by a crowd of people like we were the Dalton gang being brought into jail.

We were doomed. I felt like I was going to throw up on myself.

The cop got out and brought one of the black kids to the window.

I was sitting next to the window. Lurch was sitting next to me in his Camel's hair coat. I looked up into the black kid's eyes and we stared at each other for a few moments. Something passed between us.

The kid shook his head and said, "Nah, those aren't the guys."

The cop couldn't believe it.

"What do you mean," he shouted. "These are the guys. They have to be the guys."

The kid shook his head.

"It ain't them."

The cop had no choice but to let us go. He was hot, his face the color of his car. He knew that we were the guys; the crowd knew that we were the guys; we knew what we were the guys. And so did that kid. But he said that we weren't. Why?

The cop walked us back to our car cursing at us all the way and told us never to come back there again.

As we drove back home, we couldn't stop talking about what had happened. We couldn't believe it. Why didn't that kid cop on us? Nobody could figure it out. I didn't say anything. I was thinking that kid saw how scared I was and had mercy on me.

The next Friday was Prom Night: November 22, 1963. What a night to have a prom. The day Kennedy got killed. I remember when he was elected in 1960. My parents voted for him. I was a freshman at Roman and everybody was happy that he beat Nixon. Kennedy was Irish like most of us were and he was Catholic like all of us were.

I was driving down Midvale on my way to the florist to pick up the corsages for the prom when I heard the news on the radio. I was shocked and I felt sad but that was about all. I didn't cry about him like some people did. I didn't cry about anything. I haven't cried since I was a little boy and even then I didn't cry much. I remember the first day of school at Saint Bridget's. All of the kids cried when they moms left but me.

We thought that maybe the prom would be cancelled but the priests decided to go ahead with it anyway. We were supposed to go down to Jersey afterwards to the Hawaiian Cottage for a midnight snack and we were afraid it would be closed but when we called, they said that they would be open. It was business as usual. Even the Eagles played that Sunday. On the way over, we told the girls about the fight and they were afraid that there would be trouble but there wasn't. As we went into the building we kept our heads down and peeked around for that cop but we didn't see him. Thank God. We were grateful for that. The prom was a little dead at first because of Kennedy. Father Kline said a few words in his memory and sang **Danny Boy**. Everybody choked up a little bit and some of the girls cried but after a while everyone loosened up and we had a good time: as good a time as we could have without any booze. We had promised the girls that we wouldn't drink. About 10 o'clock we decided to leave. When we got out in front of the place who did we see across the street but the two black kids that we had the fight with. I didn't think they would recognize us in our monkey suits but they did. They smiled and waved.

"You guys are okay, for white guys," they called out.

We smiled and waved back.

"And you guys are okay, too."

'It ain't them,' thought Casey. 'It wasn't me. It wasn't me acting like that, not the true me. I always hated fighting. It made me sick. I didn't want to get into trouble and yet, I did, over and over again. I was just a kid but I had already lost who I was. What happened? It was as if someone else was in control and I was helpless: paralyzed.

The word echoed in his mind.

He began reading the story again. As he read through the piece about the car accident, he put on the brakes this time. Something happened with that accident, something important. But what? He had tried writing about it as a separate story, for it was certainly a fall; his life had gone downhill after it but whenever he tried to envision it, a darkness fell over his eyes, blinding him. There must be some way he could open his eyes so he could see.

As the bus continued on its tortuous way up Chelten Avenue, he looked out the window. As he peered through the darkness, he began to recognize some of the sights: Bell Telephone, the old Rowells, the Presbyterian Church. Funny thing, though, he couldn't picture in his mind the Miraculous Medal Shrine. He had passed by it every day for four years on his way back and forth to LaSalle but he couldn't remember it. His mother had told him it was on the right-hand side a couple of blocks before Chew Avenue.

As the bus crossed Germantown Avenue, Casey's anxiety level rose. Chew was just a few blocks away. He had the impulse to jump off the bus and go home. He must be losing his mind. A few years ago, he had sat in a witches' circle in Vermont, feeling energy fields and envisioning auras and chakras. Rejecting that as pseudo-science, as smoke and mirrors, he had traveled to Central America for a dose of reality and had worked on a state farm in the war zone in mountains of Nicaragua near the town of Matagalpa, cutting coffee with the Sandinistas.

Suddenly, he remembered an experience that he had on his first trip to Nicaragua, one that had convinced him that the Sandinistas were involved in the drug trade. He had buried in the back of his mind because it had been too upsetting to think about but now it rose into his consciousness like a corpse come back from the dead. He had written about it in his journal of the trip but afterwards, in a moment of weakness and fear, he had ripped it out and burned it to ashes like a criminal covering up a crime. Now, he saw himself as a witness before a judge, giving testimony.

'I was with a group of veterans, mostly Vietnam veterans who were worried about the US foreign policy in Central America. We were afraid that American troops were going to be sent down there and we didn't want to see another generation go through what we had. We just didn't want to see a lot of people getting killed. We went there to find at least a piece of the truth.

The trip was sponsored and led by a left-wing religious organization, IFCO. Our first stop was in Guatemala City. The bus they took us around in was followed by an darkened SUV, the vehicle of choice for the death squads we were told. Talk about tense! We were all on edge. We went to this large government building that looked like a palace where we were welcomed by smiling and friendly politicians and generals whose hands were stained with the blood of thousands of Indians. All around us were these unsmiling and unfriendly sun glassed goons armed with Uzis. We were told that the Indians and the poor Guatemalans were being misled by communists like Rigoberta Menchu. Unfortunately, they told us, some people had to die. Freedom doesn't come free. When we came away from that brood of vipers, I was shaken and repulsed by them and angry with myself for actually shaking hands with those murderers. It was like shaking hands with the devil. However, a few years later, I found out that Rigoberta Menchu was a phony and that her book was a lie. Like most Marxists, she had come from an upper class family none of whom had been killed by the government as she claimed. Truth is not often what it seems to be.

Then we flew to Honduras, to Tegucigalpa, a spooky city if

there ever was one. From our hotel-we were advised to stay in at night-I could hear gunshots and shouts and screams. In the morning, we went by bus to a refugee camp in the war zone on the border of Nicaragua. A hairy, scary place. Most of the men were in the mountains fighting with the Contras but there were a few around: young toughs. They had no guns that we could see but we sensed that they had them hidden somewhere. Mostly woman and children were in the camp, all thin and poorly dressed. The children surrounded us begging for food and money.

They reminded me of the first time I was in Saigon: standing outside of MACV HQ's waiting for my lieutenant who was inside on a security matter concerning Long Binh, the base where we were stationed. I was paranoid as hell and packing a .45. Then all of a sudden I was surrounded by a gang of kids who were grabbing at my arms and legs: begging and pleading. At first I tried to be nice but they only got worse and more of them came. I shouted and pushed them away repeatedly but they wouldn't leave me alone. Their desperation was frightening. I had heard about the kids in Saigon who were called cowboys: criminals or VC who would kill Americans without warning. I began to panic and I was on the verge of pulling out my gun when the LT came out and we got out of there in our jeep. Thank God I didn't shoot any of them. If the LT hadn't come out when he did I might have. But we had no guns when we were in the refugee camp and the kids weren't as desperate. Nonetheless, I was glad to be out of there.

The next day, we went to Managua where we were escorted around to interview members of the Sandinista government, including Miguel D'Escoto, a catholic priest who was their Secretary of State, Tomas Borge, the Minister of the Interior and Humberto Ortega, the general in charge of the Army and the brother of President Daniel Ortega who was out of the country at the time. He was probably in the Soviet Union plotting with them or in New York buying hundred dollar sunglasses. One of the Sandinistas who had arranged the meeting with Humberto Ortega was a Nicaraguan national who had served in the US Marine Corps in Vietnam. Call him Raoul. One of the veterans in our group was also a marine veteran of Vietnam. Call him Ishmael. When we had gathered in

Miami preparing for the trip, Ishmael told everyone that he was in recovery from a long-time addiction to cocaine. After the war, he had become a pilot and worked for the lawyers of the drug cartels. He flew them back and forth from Central and South America whenever they had to defend any of their clients who had been arrested in the US. He let it slip that he had also smuggled "the white" and "the green" as he called cocaine and marijuana on his plane. He seemed to be friends with Raoul, the Nicaraguan marine. I figured that they had known each other in Vietnam or in the Corps.

At the end of the conference with Humberto Ortega, everyone started filing out of the room down one side of the long table where we had been sitting, but Ishmael went around the other way. I decided to follow him because there was more room the way he was going. Raoul was standing in the back of the room and Ishmael went up to him and began apologizing for this shipment that had not come through. There had been some problem with the plane, he said. I saw Raoul arch his eyes at me and Ishmael turned and gave me a menacing look. I wasn't sure of what I had just heard but I sensed that it was something that I wasn't meant to hear. I walked past the two marines with my head down and joined the others who were going through the door out of the room. As we rode the bus back to our motel, I kept going over what I had heard. What shipment? What plane? was he talking about? When I got back to my room, I kept pacing up and down trying to keep calm. I tried to convince myself that I had misunderstood what had just transpired. Suddenly, a knock came on the door. I hoped it was my roommate but when I opened the door, Ishmael was standing there with a pair of long white socks in his hand. I have to admit, when I saw him, I felt a wave of fear and nausea come over me. Another McCann. For a moment, I thought that he was going to strangle me with the socks. Killing meant nothing to him. He had told us that when he was in Vietnam, he had killed hundreds of people, including an old papa-san whom he had stabbed in the kidney and killed with his K-bar knife, for no other reason than the man had been a gook. He showed us pictures of himself holding up two VC heads by the hair. He also told us that he had an M-60 machine gun and 2000 rounds of ammunition in his house in Texas. Just in case, they came looking for him. He seemed to presume that we knew who they were. Back in the 70's, he had been shot in the chest by a DEA agent who he claimed was really an FBI man. Ishmael maintained they wanted him dead because of his anti-war activities. None of the other veterans believed that story. He had been wounded twice in Vietnam and so he seemed almost invincible, a superman. I closed my eyes for a moment and asked that woman for help and I felt a calming sensation come over me. I looked Ishmael right in the eye and asked him what he wanted. He asked me if I had gotten any of his socks from the laundry by mistake. He wore them with an old pair of combat boots. He had lost several pair and was asking around to see if anyone had gotten them in their bag. I told him, quietly, no, I was sorry I couldn't help him but if any turned up, I would let him know. We stared at each other for several moments and then he shrugged and nodded and thanked me, anyway. After he left, I had to sit down, my legs were shaking so badly. I knew that the socks were just a ruse that he was using to test me, to see if I would say anything to him or look scared so that he would know what I had heard. I thought about reporting the incident. But to who? I had no proof of anything. I knew without a doubt that he had been talking about a drug shipment. With Ismael's history, what else could it have been? The Right in the US had been saying for years that the Sandinistas and Castro were involved in the drug trade and I used to think that they were nuts. But then I knew that they were right. At first I thought, 'so what?' it was just a way for them to get money and all's fair in love and war. And I was still smoking marijuana myself, so I didn't care. But the more I thought about it, the more some pieces fell into place. I had found out a few years ago that it was the VC who had supplied us with dope in Vietnam, not the CIA, as people on the left had said. It made sense. Drugs were too widely spread and available for the CIA to be the supplier and it was to the advantage of the Communists to keep us stoned. I knew from McCann that the IRA also dealt in drugs. Now I knew that so did the Sandinistas. After all, Ishmael and Raoul were talking in a Sandinista government building and it had to be bugged so they couldn't have been mavericks or undercover CIA agents. Communism and drugs went hand in hand. Communism was the opium of the people not religion. Unfortunately, though, I'm a slow learner. Even after that experience, I went back to Nicaragua the following year to cut coffee in the mountains of Matagalpa and the following year, when the Sandinistas lost the election, I still didn't get it. I couldn't believe that the Nicaraguan people didn't want them in power. But they saw no future in the communist philosophy and they knew that the Sandinista leaders lived in luxury while the campasinos wallowed in poverty. They were smarter than I was. I persisted in my delusion. I even went to some meetings of the Socialist Workers Party and considered going to Cuba. That caused such severe anxiety attacks and tension headaches that it seemed as if there was a war being fought within me. Then last week something happened. I noticed that when I thought about going back to the Catholic Church, the anxiety and the headaches went away.'

With that thought, Casey sat back in his seat. Was he really going back to the Catholic Church? Thinking about going back,' he reminded himself. He hadn't made up his mind, yet. 'Mind? What mind?' He laughed into his hand. He had changed his mind about so many things over the years that he wondered sometimes whether he still had a mind. 'My mind is open' he liked to tell people, that being the wisdom of the day, but at times he wondered whether that was wisdom or foolishness. An open mouth was a good thing, too, but you also needed to close it to chew. Maybe he needed to close his mind on something solid and think for a change, instead of letting his thoughts and ideas flow through him like formula down a feeding tube.

Casey looked out the window and saw a large stone church and another large building next to it. That must be the seminary he thought. He had never been in a seminary before and the thought made him nervous. As he got off the bus, he noticed women standing on all four of the street corners. Though it had been a warm winter, it was a cold night with a raw wind and rain in the air. One of them, a tall woman in spiked heels wearing a thigh-high black dress, a short leather jacket, her breasts hanging out, her face painted red, came up to him and said, 'The hawk is out, tonight, honey. Why don't me and you go and get warmed up?"

He saw himself walking off with her to some filthy room in an abandoned house for a short time. He merely shook his head and kept walking.

"Am I that bad?" she called after him.

He didn't answer her. He didn't want to hurt her feelings. She had been hurt enough, already. He had been in brothels all over the world, so he knew the kind of life she led. Images of himself in sordid scenes passed through his mind: Fayetteville, North Carolina, Lawton, Oklahoma, Vicenza, Italy, Frankfurt, Germany, and Bangkok, Thailand and he felt ashamed of himself. For some reason, what had happened in Frankfurt come into his mind. As he walked toward the seminary, he told the story as he had done many times before.

'I had just flown into Frankfurt, Germany after being home on emergency leave from Italy. I had gone home to talk my brother out of going into the army. I had finagled my master sergeant into letting me go home for that purpose. But I had failed in my mission. I was depressed and I felt lonely, so when I got to Frankfurt, I decided to get drunk and find some comfort with a prostitute. So I asked one of the GI's at the base where the red light district was and I went there in the afternoon. I spent all the money I had on beer and prostitutes. By the evening, all I had was my train ticket. At midnight, I got on the train to go to my base in Vicenza and I fell asleep. I woke up when I heard the conductor call out for Mainz: that was where I had to switch trains to Italy. I got up and jumped off the train and I found myself standing on a lonely platform in the middle of the night. I had that empty feeling inside that told me I had made a big mistake. There was a ticket agent there who spoke a little English and I found out much to my dismay that I had gotten off at the wrong stop. I was in Mainz but it was as if I had gotten off at the East Falls station instead of 30th Street. The ticket agent told me that the main station was about two miles away and that I had a three hour wait for the next train. If I waited for that train, I would miss my connection to Italy so I decided to walk. I started down the tracks figuring they would take me right there. I was still drunk but sobering up fast. I remember going over a railroad bridge and I could see down through the tracks into the Rhine River below and thinking that if I fell in there no one would ever know what had happened to me. Well, after

I had walked about a half a mile, there was this railroad worker up in a tower who waved me off the tracks. So I went out on the road figuring I would pass by him and get back on the tracks but then I lost the tracks; they must have curved away from me. So there I was, lost in Germany in the middle of the night with no money and carrying my duffel bag and my AWOL bag. I had no idea where the train station was. I didn't know if I was walking toward it or away from it. There was nobody around to ask for directions and I couldn't speak any German. I hadn't been to church in a long time but that night I prayed. I felt sure that I was being punished for my behavior and I begged for forgiveness. I remember saying one Hail Mary after another and I promised God that if He got me out of this plight that I had gotten myself into that I would go to church every Sunday, every day if I could. As soon as I did that, the thought came to me to go straight ahead, so I did, and after walking for about a mile I could see these bright lights in the distance. It looked to me like the heavenly city. As I got closer I saw people going in and out and I heard the sounds of trains. It was the main station and I had made it on time for my connection. I was so relieved that I repeated my promises to God. After a long hungry and thirsty ride, I made back to Vicenza and as soon as I walked into the orderly room to sign in, they told me that my orders had come down for Vietnam. I meant to follow through on my promises but the bad news sent me off to Desolation Row. I was so bummed out that I had trouble getting out of bed. After a couple days of that, the First Sergeant, himself, had to come around and remind me that I still had my duty to do. I got up and went through the motions but then I went on a binge that lasted until it was time for me to ship out. But I didn't go to a prostitute again until I went on R&R in Bangkok, a year later.'

All of a sudden he realized why he been so miserable in Bangkok. He had suppressed that memory all these years. He had broken that promise too. He tried to keep it but he was too weak. Why didn't he have the strength to resist? The answer came to him: 'Because you didn't go to church on Sunday and every day if you could.'

He stopped outside the door of the seminary, paralyzed by guilt, shivering in the cold night air. What was he doing here at a shrine to the Blessed Virgin Mary? He couldn't go in there. He was too dirty and too ungrateful. There was nothing more hideous than an ungrateful child.

He paced up and down for a few minutes, trying to find the strength to go inside. Then he remembered that he had gone to confession before his father's funeral and he had confessed those sins and he hadn't been with a prostitute since that time. He had cleaned up that part of his act, anyway. It was time he fulfilled all of his promises.

He opened the front door and looked in the small side window where the telephone operator was supposed to be but there was no one there. He waited a few moments and knocked on the window. A tall, thin black man appeared in the room and asked what he wanted. He told him that he had an appointment to see Father Joseph Gallagher. With that, a buzzer sounded, and Casey opened the door and went into the seminary. The place smelled like an old musty museum. The floor was covered with worn carpets and the dusty walls had pious pictures of biblical scenes and portraits of Jesus and Mary and the angels and the saints.

Father Gal, dressed in black and wearing a Roman collar, was waiting for him in a side room. They shook hands and sat across from each other at a small desk. They asked about each other's families and talked about the Falls. They were both nervous and polite, feeling each other out. Having not seen each other for over twenty years, they were shocked by the other's appearance.

'Poor Father Gal,' thought Casey. 'Last I remember, he was tall and thin, with a full head of black hair, but now he's bald with a belly like a melon. He walks like a barefoot man on hot sand and his face looks like it just came out of a noose.'

'Casey looks good,' thought Father Joe. 'Not what I expected. Very fit. Very muscular. Short but not small. He must work out. Short hair, short beard. With that Irish cap and wire frame glasses, he looks like a revolutionary, like Lenin. Is he a Communist? Who is Casey, now? When I last saw him at LaSalle, in 1968, he wore horned-rimmed glasses and had the beginning of a beer belly. He dressed conservatively, as we all did in those days, usually in a sports coat and slacks. Now, he's wearing a dungaree jacket and jeans and has what looks like an army bag.'

He waited for Casey to begin.

"I called you, Father Gal, because I need to talk with someone: a priest. My mom told me that you were stationed here, that you had been in Panama for a long time in the missions but that you came back to Philly a few months ago."

Father Joe nodded.

"Eighteen years in Panama and a few years down South, in Alabama. But I started having problems with my health: high blood pressure and diabetes. So they sent me up here to be near our infirmary, Saint Catherine's. It's here in another building."

Casey was interested and they talked for a while about modern medicine and hospitals. Casey gave some advice about exercise and proper diet and Father Joe responded that he knew what to do; actually doing it was the problem.

Then, after a few moments of awkward silence, Father Joe said, "So, here we are. Why did you want to see a priest? And why me?'

Casey took a deep breath, trying to calm himself.

"I thought that since I knew you, I could talk to you easier than to a stranger. But now, I'm not sure. Maybe it was a mistake coming here."

Father Joe waited patiently as Casey fidgeted in his chair and looked everywhere around the room, then moved his chair sideways so he could look behind him like a gunman watching his back. Casey noticed a few priests dressed like Father Gal go in and out of the reception room and thought: 'I'm surrounded, deep in enemy territory. I got to be careful or they'll take me prisoner.'

"It's impossible," he said, almost in a whisper. "How could I come back to the Catholic Church?"

"Nothing is impossible with God," said Father Joe.

Casey snorted.

"How could I come back to the Catholic Church? It would take a total change in my way of thinking, of looking at reality, at history, at my past. Hell, Father Gal, I blamed the Church for all my problems, all the problems in the world, in fact. It was the Church's fault I went to Vietnam. It was the Church's fault I have problems with women, why women have problems with me".

Father Joe listened to him for a while as he ranted and raved about all the problems he had with the Church: its teaching on sexuality, the hierarchy, the Pope, its dogmas, the Crusades, the Inquisition, Galileo, the whole nine yards. Then he asked Casey, if he thought the way he did why was he even considering coming back to the Church.

"For my mother," he said. "It would make her happy. But is that a good reason? I was talking to her the other day and she was saying how she felt like a failure, that she and my father had brought me and my brother up in the Church, sent us to Catholic schools, prayed for us all the time and there we were, out of the Church".

Casey stopped talking for a few moments; despite himself, he felt tears come into his eyes.

"And it was if I saw my mother for the first time. As a person. And I thought of all she had done for me and how good she was to me, how good she is to everyone. So I started thinking that maybe I would go back to church for her. And after I thought that, I felt this calming sensation come over me, almost like a shadow over me, and a peacefulness that I had never felt before...."

Casey stopped talking for a moment as a thought hit him like a bolt from the blue.

"That's not true. I felt that way before. But the other day it didn't seem like it was that woman again. It was a male, no, neither male nor female. I couldn't tell."

"It may be the Holy Spirit," said Father Joe. "I leave you peace. My peace I give you."

Casey shook his head, took off his glasses and rubbed his face as if he were wiping off camouflage.

He stared hard at Father Joe, then stammered, 'The Holy Spirit? You think so? You mean the Holy Ghost?"

Father Joe smiled.

"There have been a lot of changes in the Church. I know when we were growing up no one talked about the Holy Spirit. But this is a new time, a new age in the Church."

Casey grimaced.

"A New Age? I've just been through the New Age. It embarrasses me to think that I used to believe in that nonsense."

Father Joe shook my head.

"I'm sorry. I misspoke. What you're talking about is the Counterfeit New Age. With the coming of Christ and the Church, we came into the true New Age. As we pray in the liturgy during Easter: 'In Christ a new age has dawned, the long reign of sin is ended, a broken world has been renewed and man is made whole again.'"

Casey arched his eyebrows, showing deep worry lines on his forehead as he remembered the story of a swallow. He thought that he had been made whole in Ireland but maybe he hadn't been.

"I hope so. I'm so tired of lies, illusions, confusions. All I know is that something happened the other day. I know that. And the thought came to me that I needed to talk to a priest. That surprised me since I haven't talked to a priest in years and had no interest in doing so."

He stopped talking for a few moments as he chewed on his nails. Then he sighed.

"I don't know if I would be allowed back in the church, even if I wanted to come back. I haven't made my Easter duty in almost twenty years. I must have been excommunicated or something"

Father Joe shrugged.

"Excommunication is a complicated issue. But you'd be allowed back, no matter what you've done. Forgiveness is what the Church is all about. Forgiveness for our sins is what Jesus accomplished on the Cross."

Casey rocked back and forth in his seat, bent over, grimacing, as if he had just been punched in the stomach.

"No matter what I've done? What I've said? Isn't there a sin that can never be forgiven? Doesn't Jesus say something about that in the Gospel somewhere?"

Father Joe knew he had to tread lightly here. He had to be careful. Casey had a guilty conscience about something.

"It's difficult to say what Jesus was referring to in that passage. The Holy Father tells us it is the refusal to accept forgiveness, to accept the salvation offered by God through the Holy Spirit. It's when a person insists on having the right to commit sin, any sin at all. But what I can tell you is this: there is no limit to the mercy of God."

"But what if you don't believe in God, the Christian God, that is?"

Father Joe thought about saying that there is only one God, the Christian God, if there was more than one God they wouldn't be God but instead he asked him what God he believed in, if he believed at all.

It took Casey several moments to answer.

"For a few years, I considered myself an atheist. I don't think I ever really was, though. I was always having a conversation in my mind with someone. My conscience? Someone told me that conscience is the voice of God."

Father Joe shook his head.

"Not exactly. It's the voice of our intellect. It reflects the voice of God, His natural law that's written in our hearts. When we go against that law and the teachings of the Church where our conscience is formed, our intellect revolts and our conscience troubles us. There is no pain like a guilty conscience. It can seem as if there were a war within us."

Casey took a deep breath and closed his eyes for a moment.

"Actually, I was more than an atheist. I was an anti-theist, if there is such a word. It was because of the war. Or at least that's what I told myself. How could God allow such things to happen? In fact, I thought it was because of God that there was war. I cursed God. Called him a murderer."

Father Joe had heard this before. It was a common argument. How could there be a good God and there be evil in the world? How could God allow war?

"God doesn't cause wars. We do. We and the Devil. No, God isn't a murderer. He doesn't thirst for blood but for self surrender. God is love. Do you know that's what Jesus called Satan: a murderer? 'You belong to your father the devil and you willingly carry out your father's desires. He was a murderer from the beginning and does not stand in truth, because he is a liar and the father of lies.' You have God confused with Satan."

Casey got hard around the jaws when he heard that.

"Have I? He approved of war. Didn't he tell the Israelites to kill all of the Canaanites: men, women and children. And to rape the women? And didn't he send his only Son to die on the Cross? What kind of father would send his son to die such a horrible death? And because of that fathers here on earth sacrifice their sons by sending their sons to die in war. I hated God. I hated Jesus. He was weak. He was a victim. I hated being a victim. "

Casey stood up and paced back and forth, holding his hands to his head. He acted agitated, like he was battling with demons.

Father Joe's heart hurt from what Casey said. 'Father, forgive him for he knows not what he says,' prayed Father Joe. He stayed calm and said a Hail Mary. Satan was afraid of the Mother of God and was impotent if she were around. Casey may not know it but what he was saying was based on a heresy, the first heresy, actually: Gnosticism. Not long after the Crucifixion, there were Gnostics who said that Yahweh, the Father, was evil and that He had killed Jesus. It didn't take Satan long to launch his counterattack.

After a few moments, Casey sat down and smiled.

"But then when I was in Ireland, something happened that convinced me that there was a god but that god was a woman, a god of healing and love, not of war and killing. And after I came home from Ireland, my life got better. I stopped drinking. I became a nurse. I had friends. I wrote books. I traveled. But it's all falling apart. I feel like I'm at a dead end again, at the end of my rope. I don't know what to believe, anymore. I have no context for my faith: no church, no prayers, no community. Nothing but my fantasies? Or maybe my best hope is the woman that came to me in Ireland. Maybe that woman wasn't God but someone sent by God. I don't know."

'Or maybe the Devil in disguise,' thought Father Joe.

"How did you know it was a woman that came to you?" asked Father Joe.

Casey shook his head.

"Like I told you on the phone. I didn't see any visions and I didn't hear any voices. I'm not crazy, not that crazy, anyway. Although at times, I do seem to hear voices, though maybe that's not the right word. Sometimes, they're the voices of people I've heard speaking or statements from books I've read. But then there are thoughts, voices that seem to come from nowhere. Who are they? Are they just ideas or thoughts that come from within my imagination, that have no external existence? I don't know. I just knew it was a woman, somehow. But I didn't know who she was. As I wrote the book **The Circle of Stones**, she became the triple goddess of Ireland. One of her names was Eire, the ancient name for Ireland. But now I'm beginning to believe it was the Blessed Mother."

"What makes you think that?"

Casey laughed.

"This is really weird stuff, I know. But I was reading a book a few weeks ago by the poet, Robert Bly: **Iron John**, It was about men bonding together and going out into the woods, pounding on drums and dancing around a fire to get back in touch with this ancient, archetypical, wild man. I got about halfway through the book and I was thinking: 'This isn't for me. I've had enough of being a wild man.' Then I came upon a strange statement: that the key to our problem lies under our mother's pillow. I don't know what Bly had in mind by that; he didn't elaborate. But it got me thinking. What was under my mother's pillow? The only thing I could think of was her rosary beads. I even went in there and looked and they were there. My mother always prayed the rosary in bed before she went to sleep and I know that she was praying for me when I was in Vietnam and when I was in Ireland, all my life really. So I started thinking. 'Was the Blessed Mother the woman who came to me in Ireland?' That had never occurred to me before. Is that possible?"

Father Joe smiled.

"I wouldn't be surprised. A mother's prayers, especially a good mother's, are very powerful. Over at the Shrine, people tell us every day about favors in response to the intercession of our Blessed Mother. In fact, while I was waiting for you, I read an interesting story in our Miraculous Medal Bulletin. Indulge me for a moment. Let me read it to you."

As Father Joe opened a small, blue book, Casey closed his eyes and thought, 'Oh no, he's going to bore me with a pious story.'

"Dear Father, A woman that I care for very much, JP, was turning fifty and I wanted to give her something special for her birthday, so I came to the Shrine to pray the novena. I asked the Blessed Mother to help me decide what to give her. (I don't think that any request is too small to ask of God. After all, I am a child of God and He is our Father. And Mary is Our Mother. We should be able to ask Our Mother for anything.) I knew that JP liked poetry so the thought came to me to give her a book of poetry. But what book? There are so many books of poetry. Then **The Sonnets from the Portuguese** by Elizabeth Barrett Browning came into my mind. I remember reading one of the poems in college but I really didn't know much about it and I hadn't thought about it in years. But since the thought came to me in prayer, I decided to go with it.

I found out that the poems were written by Elizabeth Barrett to the poet Robert Browning after they met and before they married. When she met Robert Browning, Elizabeth thought she was dying; she had been sick for many years and thought the end was coming. But it wasn't. It was love, the love she never expected. She was almost 40 years old and had never had a love affair in her life. But Robert Browning fell in love with her and they married and spent many years together, even had a child together.

She ended the first sonnet with this: 'A mystic shape did move behind me, and drew me backward by the hair; and a voice said in mastery, while I strove-''Guess now who holds thee' 'Death,' I said, but there - the silver answer rang. 'Not death, but love.'

I liked the book so I bought it. The next night, as I was getting ready to give the book to JP, she told me that she was having a biopsy done on a lump on her breast. I could see she was upset and we talked about that for a while. I gave her all the support I could and I almost forgot about the book of poetry but then I remembered it and gave it to her. It made her happy. It wasn't until after we parted that I thought of the message from the poem: 'Not death, but love.' It seemed to me that this was a message from the Blessed Mother that it was love that was coming, not death. For as Robert Browning loved Elizabeth Barrett so do I love JP. When I talked to her again, I told her not to worry, the biopsy would be normal. After all, when the thought came to me to give her that book, I didn't know about the circumstances around it and I didn't know about her biopsy, so there had to be a message there. And there was. A few weeks later, she got the result: it was normal. Thank you, Blessed Mother."

When Father Joe finished reading, he said, "As you can see by that story, the Blessed Mother knows what we need before we do."

Casey shrugged. He wasn't sure what to make of that story.

'That guy was at least going to church," he said to Father Joe.

"But why me? Why would the Blessed Mother help me? I was not what you would call a good person, Father Gal. I'm not a good person now if you want to know the truth."

Father Joe smiled.

"Maybe she did it for your mother. At least you're honest. Jesus came for sinners, not the righteous. He's the Good Shepherd looking for his lost sheep."

Casey laughed.

"Me, a sheep?"

Casey remembered going to Washington for a Pro-Choice demonstration a couple of years ago and ridiculing Pro-Lifers by baaing at them. 'Was he one of them, after all? Was he a sheep? Or a wolf? Which was he?' He opened up his gas mask bag and took out his two novels and looked at them for a few moments deciding what to do. He couldn't get anyone to read them. No one was interested. Even some of his family and friends wouldn't read them. He handed them to Father Joe. Then he took out his short stories, looked at them and put them back in his bag.

"I was going to give you these, too. My manuscripts of short stories about growing up in the Falls. But I think I'm going to work on them some more."

Father Joe looked at the books in his hands. One of them was a little green book with white lettering: **The Circle of Stones**; the other, a bright red one with yellow lettering: **The Story of a Swallow.**"

"Case, I'd like to give your books to one of our priests here, Father Michael McDonald. He taught literature for many years at Saint John's in New York. He has a Ph.D. in English. He'd be more competent to give you feedback than I would. I took the liberty of telling him about your books and he said he would read them. I'll give them to him if it's all right with you and he'll get back to you."

Casey shrugged. At least someone was interested.

"Okay. But tell him that I don't need him to tell me how bad my grammar is, or if I use punctuation properly, or if my figures of speech work. I want him to tell me where I went wrong in them, especially in **The Circle of Stones**. The book is a lie. But how did it become a lie? That's what I want to know. I wanted to tell the truth about what happened in Ireland but I didn't and I want to know why."

Father Joe agreed to pass that request along. Then he waited, hoping that Casey would want to make his confession and come back to the Church, but it didn't happen.

"Meanwhile, I'm here if you need to talk some more."

"I appreciate it," said Casey. "All you're doing for me, meeting with me, not giving me a hard time or pressuring me, having someone read my books."

Father Joe laughed." No problem. I'm here. We're here. I'll keep you in my prayers."

They shook hands and promised to keep in touch.

After Casey left, Father Joe took the books up to Father Mike's cell on the second floor. He told him about the conversation he had just had

Father Mike was puzzled." What did he mean by where he went wrong? In what way"

Father Joe shrugged.

"You'll have to ask him. I don't know if he knows himself. He's confused."

The two priests chatted for a few minutes before saying good night.

Father Joe went up to his cell on the fourth floor. He wanted to go to the chapel and pray, but his feet hurt too much to walk that far. He made a mental note to go over to the infirmary in the morning and have them checked out.

He sat at his desk and picked up the Kolbe book he was reading. It was a study of the intimate connection between Mary and the Third Person of the Blessed Trinity.

He thought of what Casey had said when he described the feeling that he had when he decided to come back to the Church: a peacefulness, like a shadow over him. Then he said that he felt the same thing a few times in his life before, but different. 'What was that about? Who did he mean by that woman? The Blessed Mother?'

In the book, Saint Maximilian teaches that Mary, the human Immaculate Conception and the Holy Spirit, the divine Immaculate Conception, are so intimately connected that the action of Mary is the action of the Holy Spirit. Nonetheless, Mary is a separate person, distinct from the Holy Spirit.

Father Joe thought for a few moments, then asked himself, 'Would someone be able to tell the difference between the descent of the Holy Spirit and the presence of Mary?'

Father Joe put the book back on the table. He was reading too much into it. It seemed to him that only a theologian or a true mystic could make such a discernment and Casey didn't seem like either to him.

He got into bed and turned off the light. He reached under his pillow and found his rosary beads. As he crossed himself, he thought of what Casey had said about his mother praying the rosary for him every night.

'It's a good thing she did,' thought Father Joe. 'You can never underestimate the power of the rosary. Casey needed someone to pray for him. He was one mixed-up man. He seemed almost demonic at times. Some of the things he had said - that he hated Jesus, that he hated God, that God approved of war, that it was the Church's fault he went to Vietnam, what kind of father would send his son to die on a Cross? - were such a hodgepodge of misconceptions and misunderstandings and downright ignorance that he did not have the energy to think about right now. It was too complicated and he was too tired. He would have to go over the Church's teaching on inspiration and inerrancy and biblical literary forms, plus, the theology of redemption. But that would have to wait until another time.

As he prayed the Sorrowful Mysteries, he kept Casey in his prayers and asked the Holy Spirit and the Blessed Mother to give Casey the grace he needed to go to confession, to repent and to believe in the Gospel.

Bill Casey sat at his desk in his bedroom and skimmed through his novels. He tried to see them through the eyes of a priest. He might like some of **The Story of a Swallow**: the healings. Maybe he won't believe what happened and how it was done. And who did it. Casey stopped. He had lied about that too. But the results were true. Those kids did get better. But there are other parts where he won't like what he's reading: the comments about the Church and about sex and abortion, and he won't like all the details about the kind of kids who are at Seaside House and how they live. And die.

Certainly, there was no way that a priest would like **The Circle of Stones**. He would be turned off by the bad language, the drugs, the guns, the blasphemies, especially against the Blessed Virgin. He wanted to tell the truth about what had happened in Ireland but the book was a lie and he knew it when he finished it. Not all of it. There was some truth in it: the part about Mick and McCann and the guns and the drugs, but the part about Madeleine and the circle of stones was a lie, a fiction. If he told the truth, he figured, no one would be interested. No one was, anyway, he realized now, so why not tell what really happened there. But what did happen? That was the problem. He wasn't sure himself. It was so nebulous and difficult to describe that he had written about it using myth and metaphor. But it wasn't myth or metaphor that he met in Ballinskelligs but someone he could talk to: a woman. Who was that woman? The Blessed Mother? The thought made him laugh. That couldn't be true. What was happening here? Was his life becoming a joke? A comedy? But it didn't feel like a comedy, more like a tragedy.

He looked at his watch. Ten p.m.. He stood up and looked out the window. It had just begun to rain. He had to do something; his mind was in a turmoil. He wished for a moment that he had some pot to smoke but he didn't smoke anymore. Just a few months ago, he had lost the desire to get high. He had started smoking pot in Vietnam, but now, after all these years, the habit was gone. He was out from under its spell somehow. He wondered how that had happened. It was as if someone had taken him by the shoulders and shook some sense into him. He noticed the difference. His mind was much clearer now. Thank God. Then he felt the urge for a beer but he hadn't had a drink in years and wasn't going to start again now. There was only one thing to do: run.

He looked into his mother's room. The light was out but he could hear her moving around in her bed. She was probably praying the rosary for him right now. He had told her that he was thinking about coming back to the Church and she had questioned him about his visit with Father Gal. To her credit, she hadn't pushed him about it but he could see the hope in her eyes. He knew how important it was to her that he come back to the Church but he couldn't do it just for her. He had to do it because he believed.

He went down to the basement and put on his gear, his Gortex suit and his running shoes. Then he went out the back door and jogged up the alley. Picking up the pace, he ran up Henry Avenue in the pouring rain. He thought of what the people who passed by him in their cars were thinking: That he was a fanatic, a crazy man, running in the rain, a cold rain at that, in the dark, alone. But he didn't care. He loved it. The air was so clear and the rain felt good on his face. He had been running for 18 years now. He had started running seriously in 1974 and hadn't stopped. It kept down his anxiety; it cleared his mind; it helped him sleep.

As he passed the Walnut Lane Golf Course, Hacker's Hollow, he thought of all the times he had played golf there with his father, so many years before. He missed his dad; the older he got the more he appreciated him. All the sacrifices he had made. He had gone to work every day in a boring job. Came home every night to be there with us. Put food on the table. Paid the bills. Helped us do homework. Read us books. A good dad.

As Casey came to Walnut Lane, the site of the accident he had as an adolescent, he stopped running and relived it again in his mind. But when he tried to remember what had happened afterwards, the darkness descended upon him once again and all he could see was his father's smashed-up car.

He had come home from Ireland just in time to make up with his dad before he died. His dad had forgiven him but somehow that didn't seem enough. He sensed that someone else had to forgive him too or maybe he had to learn to forgive himself. Or both.

"I'm so sorry, Dad, for smashing up your car," he whispered. "And I'm so sorry for the things I did after it: all the trouble I got into. How much I hurt you and let you down."

Immediately, he heard a voice objecting: 'Sorry for what! So you had an accident. Accidents happen. And so you went out and got drunk. So what? You were just a kid: a teenager. All teenagers get into trouble. It's part of growing up.'

Casey turned around and ran towards home. As he ran, he couldn't stop thinking that he needed forgiveness. He had turned bad after that accident for some reason. He tried to work it out in his mind.

'But who else has to forgive me? God? Do I need forgiveness from God? What God? The triple goddess of Ireland?'

He had to laugh at that. In his heart, he knew that there was no triple goddess. She wasn't real, even the feminists admitted that. The goddess was their own self-image, not a transcendent, omnipotent person who could forgive. Then he thought, 'maybe I need to go to Father Gal and ask God the Father for forgiveness.'

Then a chorus of voices began screaming in his ear.

'Not real! He's the one who's not real! He was created by men to keep women down! What about women? It's my body! No man can tell me what to do! It's a woman's right to choose! We have a right to abortion and birth control! The Inquisition! Nine million women burned at the stake! By the Church! The Vietnam War! They love the bloodbath! It was their fault! You know that!'

Like a man running from a swarm of horse flies, he flailed his hands around his head and began running faster and faster until the voices went away and left him alone. As he cooled off, he came to a decision. He didn't need to go to confession. He would go to church on Sunday and maybe even go to Communion. The whole thing was only symbolic, anyway; a communal meal, not something supernatural. That way, he would make his mom happy and would be accepted back in the community. But he wouldn't take it seriously.

When he was alone, Father Mike looked at the two books. He wished that he hadn't agreed to read them. He only did so to get Father Joe off the spot. He had so many books to read. Why waste time on an amateur? He was probably a product of one of those foolish creative writing programs like the one they had at Saint John's. Good writers were born not made. Neither Faulkner nor Conrad ever went to writing school. True, Flannery O'Connor did go to the one in Iowa but she wrote her worst short stories there. Despite its problems, he wished he could have stayed at Saint John's; he loved teaching the classics. But they didn't want him there anymore. They thought he was passé And he needed to be at Saint Vincent's. He had to accept the fact that he was eighty years old - a young eighty- that was true. His mind was still sharp but his body was breaking down. He had Parkinson's, a touch of arthritis, and his heart was failing. He was taking a lot of medicine, so he needed to be close to the infirmary. He continued to function as a priest. He said public Masses at the Shrine and heard confessions but other than that, he had a lot of free time to be with the Lord and to read and re-read the books he loved. He had just started re-reading King Lear so he regretted agreeing to read these books by Casey. They would certainly pale in comparison but he wouldn't spend much time on them. As he looked through the books, he realized that they were self-published. He felt a touch of sympathy for the man. So much time, so much effort and no one would publish them. He probably couldn't get anyone to even read them. He picked up **The Circle of Stones** by one corner like it was toxic material and then dropped it as if it were a send-up from **La`-Bas**. He'd skim through **The Story of a Swallow**, although he usually didn't like stories set in a hospital. They were usually about doctors and nurses falling in love and having sex in empty hospital rooms. This one had an unusual title. Why a swallow in a seaside house? He hoped it wasn't a silly, sentimental story told by a little birdie. A **Jonathon Livingston Seagull** clone.

He sat down at his desk, opened the book and began to read.

3.

The Story of a Swallow

"But then there are the children, and what am I to do about them?
It's beyond all comprehension why they should suffer."
Ivan Karamazov

2400

I sit rocking, holding baby Charles in the crook of my arm. I try to put the nipple in his mouth but he won't take it; he spits it out and cries, a spraying squeal that drives me crazy. He swings his fists like a bantam boxer in a frenzy, so I wrap the blanket tight around him, bundling him up like a peanut psychotic in a straight jacket. I bend him over and pat him on the back as if he were a tiny diner who swallowed a fish bone. I have already done his chest PT and suction and gave him his Theophylline, but he's still tachypneic, his belly bouncing like a baseball against my wrist.

I center myself, then put one of my hands on his chest and one on his back and send him some energy. I feel it shoot through me like jolts of electricity.

He stops crying and his breathing slows to once a second. I talk to him in my sweetest voice and stroke his face until he almost smiles. As I kiss him on the forehead, he grabs a fistful of my hair and yanks it. I curse him kindly as I push his hand away and put the nipple back in his mouth. Charles sucks for a few moments, then stops, frowning, his face purpling like an eggplant.

I feel a moment of panic. He's going to code. I'm not ready for this. But then he burps up what he just ate and cries and coughs a spray of secretions into my face. Refluxing again.

I sigh and wipe my face with my sleeve. I look at his lips. They're purple but they're always purple. I look inside his mouth. His tongue's pink. I check his fingers. His nail beds are the same color. I pull down his mist collar and look into his tracheostomy. His air hole's a black dot in a foaming white whirlpool. He needs suctioning badly. I reach up for the suction catheter that I have wrapped around the side rail, poke it into his trake and suction out the secretions. When he's clear, I put the nipple back into his mouth but he spits it out again. It doesn't work. I must be doing something wrong. I'm not concentrating enough. I'm too distracted. Healing requires concentration, a quiet, peaceful place like the circle of stones, not a hospital. It worked with Neil; he stopped having seizures. But, now, I think maybe that was just a fluke.

I put Charles back into bed on his belly, check the NG tube for placement, then run the feeding slowly into him. As it drips into his stomach, I pat him on the back until the feeding is finished. As soon as I disconnect the tube, he arches up like a fish on a hook and vomits an ounce of mucousy formula. I curse him unkindly as I wipe his face and dean the bed. I whisper how much I hate him, then I feel bad. The poor baby. Nobody wants him. He has no brain, bad lungs and one leg. And I hate him. Feeling guilty, I pick him up and sit in the rocking chair with him. I look into his shiny ebony face and talk to him.

"Hey, Charlie, hey, little man, you remind me of someone, a kid named Raheem. This was his crib, too. He was like you, except he had both his legs. No one thought he would live and he did."

He's alright. I guess. I hope. Raheem was one of the first children that I took care of when I came to Seaside House and he's one of the reasons I'm leaving. He and Richie Rich. I feel sad and angry when I think what about what happened with them. It's a disgrace.

The whole system is a disgrace. Over the last 3 years, I have seen an endless stream of sick and damaged children. Who don't have to be that way. Who cares? Only a few people. Mostly the nurses. Some of the doctors do. The hospital administration doesn't, not really; all they care about is the bottom line. The government doesn't, that's for sure; they're more concerned with killing people.

I am so depressed. Burned out. I'm lost again. I don't know what happened. When I first came here, I felt that I had come home. I had found my life's work. I was finally applying what I had learned in the circle of stones, after 8 years. But now I'm leaving. And I don't know where to go.

I look out the window at the snow as it falls softly from the dark sky. It is falling all over the city, softly falling on the streets, on the tall buildings and houses, on the river along Boathouse Row and to the west, on the hills and paths and trees of Fairmount Park.

It is the Cinderella hour, the graveyard shift, the time when most people die.

I look around the Baby Room. The rest of the children are asleep. The census is 12. I did rounds after report and everyone is stable, for now. But that could change in a hurry. There are two trakes on the unit, a coma kid, one baby with holes in her heart, a kid with Spina Bifida, another with JRA, twin 'Failures to Thrive', an asthmatic, a brain tumor kid who is going down the tubes, not tonight, I hope, not on my time, I've seen enough kids die, and two CP kids who are in for PT.

I hear Katie, the other night nurse, talking to someone in the next room. Probably Peewee; he was awake earlier. I look at my work sheet. I can hold Charles for a few minutes. After all, this is my last night at Seaside House. I think back to my first day here, 3 years ago last month, January 1981, the year Ronnie Raygun came and filled the hospitals with sick and hungry children.

Mother Goose welcomes you to Seaside House.

I paused by the glass door for a few moments, studying the chalk drawing of a smiling girl with a ponytail riding a fat goose toward the setting sun. It sent me back to Ballinskelligs, to Madeleine and the circle of stones. I thought of the faery that had escorted me to Ireland. Faery tales meant hope and happy endings. It was a sign. I had come to the right place.

I pushed open the door and stepped inside Seaside House. I walked past the dark kitchen and went around to the Nurses' Station. Two night nurses nodded awake behind a carousel containing charts. Their eyes heavy with sleep, they barely noticed me standing before them.

"Good morning," said one of them, finally.

She didn't seem surprised to see me on the unit. Probably, everyone knew that I was coming. I knew that my arrival would be an item of gossip among the staff. Everyone would be wondering what I was like and why I wanted to work there.

I took a tour around the unit. Seaside House Annex was on the fifth floor of The Holy Innocents Hospital of Philadelphia. Its main hospital was at Seaside Heights in New Jersey. The Annex was a subacute rehabilitation unit; the patients were less stable than those at the Heights. It was small, with a 15 bed capacity. There were three patient rooms in a semi-circle around the Nurses' Station, one for babies, one for toddlers and one for bigger kids. Across from the Nurses' Station was the Treatment Room, which was a combination med room, supply room, examination room and report room. There was a playroom in the corner by the fire escape. The Playroom was small, but it was painted in bright colors and good light came through the windows; it was filled with toys and games and beanbags and mats. There was wall suction and oxygen so even the sickest kids could come in and play.

I was excited about working at Seaside House. For the last year, I had worked as a staff nurse on an adult medical floor at MHP where I took care of people with cancer and heart and lung disease. On 3-11, I was usually the only RN for 16 to 18 patients, with a nurse's aide, maybe two, to help me. Here, they told me, the nurse to patient ratio was one nurse for every 2 or 3 children. But as I walked around the unit, I realized that there was no more night staff. They had only 2 night nurses for all these kids. I began to feel nervous. I hoped that they weren't lying to me. Hospitals lied all the time to nurses. But then I reminded myself that when I worked nights at MHP, I was the only RN for 30 to 40 patients, so even if they were, it was better here than there. Anything was better than that.

I looked into one of the dark rooms where I saw several babies sleeping. Beside one crib, I saw a monitor beeping the QRS complex across the screen in normal sinus rhythm. Suddenly, a child sat up and coughed large gobs of secretions from his trake. A monitor alarmed like a French police car, startling me. I ran over to his crib, calling out for help. I didn't know where anything was. I looked around for a suction machine but I couldn't see one. I watched the child vomit a long stream of milk.

"Good morning, Raheem," said one of the nurses, pushing me aside and lowering the side rail. "Don't worry," she said to me. "This is just his morning routine."

She took a catheter from a bag by his crib and, using the wall suction, began cleaning out his trake. Raheem gagged and coughed, his face changing colors from a light brown to a dark purple as she sucked secretions from his throat and mouth.

"What a way to wake up, huh?" said the nurse. "He does this every day of his life."

"What's wrong with him?" I asked. "Why does he have the trake?"

"BPD," she said. "Bronchopulmonary dysplasia. And sub-glottic stenosis. You'll find out about it soon enough. A lot of kids here have it."

"How old is he?" I asked, looking at his bloated face and his skinny body. With his barrel chest, he looked like an old man with advanced emphysema.

" Almost a year. He's been in the hospital all his life. 6 months over at 'The Holy' and another 6 months here."

"That long?"

"That's nothing. Richard was just transferred back to the ICU. He's been back and forth for 3 years. And there's a kid over at 'The Holy' who's been in the ICU for 4 years."

I had heard stories in nursing school about boarder babies who grew up in the hospital. I knew that some stayed for a long time in Seaside House but I didn't know it was for that long. How does growing up in the hospital affect their vision of themselves and of other people? What kind of life did they live? What future did they have? I wanted to ask her these questions but she was too busy with Raheem. He looked pathetic. I watched her as she cleaned his face, kissed him and gave him a hug, secretions spraying onto her blouse. I admired her ability to do that, to not care how he looked and love him anyway. As I watched him open his mouth wide with silent laughter and snuggle against her breast, I envied him. I could see why he would be happy in her arms. She was lovely, with wild black hair and blue eyes. She talked to him in a soft, lilting voice, rubbing his bony back as she rocked him back and forth. She seemed absorbed by the child, her attention focused on him, excluding me. As it should be, I thought, she had her work to do.

I walked around the room, looking at the other sleeping babies. They had apnea monitors connected to them, with blue lights blinking, one for respirations, the other for heartbeats. They were so tiny.

What was I doing here? I asked myself. Then I remembered the story of the swallow and recited it to myself. I was where I was supposed to be. I was with the women and children, finally.

I heard the sounds of many voices outside the room as the rest of the staff reported in for work. Feeling anxious, I walked out toward the Nurses' Station. As I did, everyone stopped talking and stared at me. I looked around for Cathy, the Head Nurse, but she hadn't come in yet. Finally, one of the nurses came over and introduced herself.

"My name's Lisa. You must be the new nurse. We heard all about you from Cathy. You've come from med-surg?"

I nodded, not feeling capable of speech with so many people staring at me.

She introduced me to the rest of the staff. Everyone seemed friendly, except Carol, who asked around the room, not looking at me, "Now why....would any man want to work in pediatrics? He won't stay long. Men never stay long here."

I looked at her and didn't say anything. I thought of a few answers I could give her: I had to get out of med-surg, the staffing is better here, I like kids, they need to have men in their lives. But I couldn't tell her the real reason: what had happened in Ireland, in the circle of stones. She would think that I was crazy.

As we stared at each other, Cathy walked through the door and waved to me.

"I'm glad to see you're here, Jim," she said. "I wasn't sure if you'd come. Come into my office after report and rounds and we'll start your orientation."

I listened to report by the night nurse, the one who had taken care of Raheem. Her name was Marianne. I liked the way she gave report: full of details and funny anecdotes about the children and the problems they caused. I liked her husky voice and her belly laugh. She seemed happy. I wondered how she could be happy in such a sad place, surrounded by such suffering. What gave her the strength to be happy?

I noticed the wooden crucifix around her neck and wondered if that could be the source of her strength. Her hands reminded me of Madeleine's hands, healer's hands, long and slender, with no rings or polish to mar their beauty. No makeup hid the lines around her eyes. I guessed her age to be about 30, a few years younger than I. She looked over at me a few times and smiled, lifting my spirits.

After report, I joined Lisa, the charge nurse for the day, as she made walking rounds with Diane, the resident. They tried to include me in their discussion, but I had trouble following what they were talking about; they moved too quickly from one child to the next and I didn't understand all of the jargon: RSV, E20, VSD, fundal plication. Everything seemed too confusing to me and beyond my ability to understand. And it was one sad story after another.

After rounds, I went into the tiny Head Nurse's office and told Cathy about my doubts and confusion.

"Everyone feels that way in the beginning," said Cathy. "After my first day, when I saw the kids that were here, I ran out of the place, crying."

I rubbed my forehead with my hand. What had I gotten myself into? I recited the story of the swallow to myself again and listened to its message. It reassured me. I was doing what I was supposed to do.

Cathy handed me a manual of nursing procedures as thick as two telephone books for me to read. I leafed through the pages until I came to the section on tracheostomy care. I had some experience with trakes from when I had worked in adult medicine, but I had never taken care of a child with one. As I read through the procedure, I began to sweat.

"Do the nurses change the trakes?" I asked.

Cathy smiled.

"Yes, we do. The nurses here know more about trakes than the doctors do. We teach them how to do trake care. Don't worry. It's easy, usually, unless there's stenosis or adhesions. And you don't do it yourself. We change them once a week and, of course, in emergencies. Sometimes, a kid'll cough one out."

"That kid, Raheem, he has BPD? Bronchopulmonary dysplasia? What is that?"

"It's a sequela to Respiratory Distress Syndrome."

"I know about that," I said. "When babies are born prematurely, their lungs aren't fully developed; they don't open all the way, so they have trouble breathing."

"That's right," said Cathy. "Raheem was 26 weeks. You should have seen him when he came here. He had had several brain infarcts. He wouldn't eat. Couldn't eat. He had a gastrostomy. He was a little vegetable. Now, he's cruising. He takes everything by mouth. Developmentally, he's almost normal. Except for the trake."

"Why does he have the trake.?" I asked.

"Sub-glottic stenosis. He was intubated after he was born and was put on a respirator. The tube irritated his throat and caused it to close up, stenose. Under his glottis. He has a critical airway. If that trake comes out, he could die."

I took a deep breath. I turned the pages until I came to the section on CPR.

"You don't have many codes, right?" I asked.

She smiled again.

"Not that many. Sometimes, a kid'll get apneic, but we can usually get him breathing again without calling the code. Most kids go into respiratory arrest, not cardiac. Once you open the airway, they're okay."

I took another deep breath. I didn't like codes. Some people did. They liked the excitement, being a hero, saving people's lives. Not me. I had been in enough codes when I worked at MHP. I liked helping people out when they needed it; that's one reason why I became a nurse. I had no problem in situations where it was clear that the person who coded had the potential for a quality life and would want to be saved. But they often didn't. I didn't like the idea of resuscitating someone who didn't want to be brought back and then would spend weeks, months, years, suffering, or in a vegetative state, connected to a respirator and being fed through a tube. I wouldn't want that. But children were young; they had potential; they were a different story. Or were they? I wondered.

"As I told you in our interview," said Cathy, "We usually transfer kids over to 'The Holy' before they go sour. This is a rehabilitation unit not a Critical Care Unit. Most of our kids are stable. Although lately, we've been getting a lot of kids who have really been labile. We have a little heart baby now, Angie, who's always blue. She has Tetralogy of Fallot."

"What is that?" I asked. "I remember reading about it in nursing school but I can't remember all the details."

"There are four defects," said Cathy, "VSD: ventricular septal defect, pulmonary artery stenosis, a problem with the aorta and I forget the other one. No matter. I'd know how to take care of her if I had to. It's pretty much the same for all heart babies. You'll learn. She's here to gain weight so she can go to surgery. She's a tough feeder, though."

Cathy patted me on the arm.

"Don't worry. Don't be afraid of these babies. You just have to pay attention. Look at them. Touch them. Be there for them. If you do that, you won't hurt them. Remember, too, that for some of these children, you couldn't possibly hurt them anymore than they've been hurt already. And I could tell in our interview that you're a secret softy under all those muscles."

I shook my head. I was having a lot of doubts.

"But these kids are really hurting. I don't know if I can do it."

"Maybe you won't like our kids, not everybody does."

"What do you mean?"

"They don't like kids with brakes; kids that vomit all the time, kids that stop breathing, kids that die."

"I didn't say I didn't like them. I just don't know if I can deal with all this pain. Maybe it's too much for me. I keep asking myself: What's the reason for this? What did they do to deserve this? They're innocent."

"Every day," said Cathy, her eyes filling with tears. "I ask myself those questions. Maybe a lot of these kids would have been better off if they'd never been born. But they were. And it's our job to make their lives as worthwhile as possible."

After a few moments, I nodded.

"We really need you on the unit," said Cathy. "Most of our kids have no father. They hardly ever see a man, except for some doctors and they're here and gone. There's Kevin. But he doesn't do patient care."

When Cathy told me about the other man on the unit, a play therapist, I told her I was happy he was here. I thought that if men took equal responsibility for the care of children, it would change the world radically. Men would look at themselves differently and children would see men differently. But I didn't like working with other men. One of the reasons why I became a nurse was to get away from men. I had problems relating to everything considered male: aggression, competition, sports, war. When I was in nursing school, there was only one other male in the program, out of 28, and I hung out with the females, teenagers for the most part, and I was in my 30s. I had cut out all of my male friends. I didn't like to think of myself as a man. I was a person.

"Isn't it nice to be needed?" said Cathy.

I stop rocking and look at Charles' face. He's asleep. I guess they don't need me anymore. I feel so sad. I can't believe that I'm really leaving Seaside House. I remember sitting in this rocking chair and reading Raheem stories. Raheem loved a good story. He was a great audience. He would listen so intently and get all excited and laugh. He came so far. After being in the hospital for over 3 years, all of his life, he walked out of here, with no trake and with a verbal ability appropriate for his age in sign language. The trake had damaged his vocal cords so he had problems speaking: he would twist up his face and growl when he tried to talk. I hope people, other kids, won't make fun of him but I know that they will and I feel for him. I remember what he was like when I first came here: a wild man. The first time I took care of him he scared me half to death.

I walked into the Baby Room and there was Raheem, dressed only in a diaper half open, his little penis showing, cruising around his crib, holding onto the rail like a drunken sailor trapped on a sinking ship. He had on a gargoyle face with tears like pearls and was coughing up golf balls of mucus from his trake. I could hear him wheezing from across the room. I ran over and grabbed a suction catheter. I cursed as I had trouble lowering the side rail. When I got it down, he crawled over and leaped into my arms as if I were his savior sent from heaven. Then he threw back his head and laughed like a con man after a sting. That was Raheem, always dramatic. He didn't just want his bottle when he was thirsty; he needed it like a man crawling in the desert needed an oasis. I can still see his hands shaking as I handed him his bottle. Every time I think about him, I get angry. He was a beautiful little boy; he didn't deserve what he got. I wonder how he's doing now. I'll have to ask Marianne when I see her in the morning.

I look at my watch: 0030. I gently lower Charles back into his crib, put two sheet rolls by his sides and wrap them against him with a baby blanket. These kind of kids like to be tightly wrapped; if they're not, they spaz out and wake up, crying. And I don't want to hear that. It's gotten to the point that I cannot stand to hear babies crying. Some of them, that's all they do is cry.

A screaming comes across the room. It's Reggie. I know what he wants; that's no mystery. All he wants is his bottle. He and his sister, Ronnie. When they first came here two months ago, they were skinny, dried up, garbage can kids with butts like raw hamburger; now, they're little piggies who'll eat until they explode.

"All right, I'm coming," I say, but first I go over and take a look at Jennifer, the little heart baby; she's sleeping peacefully in her oxygen tent. I look at my work sheet again. I have to give her meds at 0200 and feed her. I go over to the doorway and listen; no one's crying and I don't hear any monitors beeping. And Katie's out there.

I go back to Reggie's bedside and fill a baby bottle with SMA 20 and a few spoonfuls of rice cereal. As I lift him out of his crib, his eyes bug out of his head looking for his bottle. He clutches at it like a drunk grabbing for a taste of the hair. I sit in the rocker in the center of the room with him on my lap. I have seen so many of these kids since I have been here. Their only problem is that they are not getting enough to eat; they're starving, in the land of plenty. The problem is poverty; their parents are too poor or too out of it themselves to feed them properly. But Reggie's lucky, he was neglected for only a few months. When I first came here, I took care of a toddler, Francesca, who had been abused as well as neglected for over 2 years. She was found in an abandoned house in the barrio in North Philly. Her mother had disappeared, back to Puerto Rico; nobody knew where her father was. He was like most of the fathers of these children: out of the picture.

Francesca was in her crib, sleeping, curled up like a fetus. She had another fever, her third otitis since she came to Seaside House, so she was wearing only a diaper. She could've served as a model for a skeleton in an anatomy class. I wanted to let her sleep but it was after 6 in the evening and she hadn't eaten dinner. I had to get something into her, at least some fluids. She took only a few ounces of juice on day shift. I had to give her meds. I didn't want to have to put in an IV. I lowered the side rail slowly and called her name out softly. I shook her as gently as I could but she woke up screaming. I talked to her in a low voice until she stopped crying. Her eyes drained pus and tears and she wore a mucous mustache. I wiped her face with a cloth and she cried again. She didn't like anyone coming near her face with anything. I laid her down to change her diaper: another loose stool. Perhaps a side effect of the antibiotic. And malnutrition had damaged her immune system and ruined her digestive tract. The smell was sickening. I put on a pair of rubber gloves and took off her diaper. The acid from her gut had burned through her skin leaving a flaming flag across her butt. I cleaned her with a wet cloth and slathered her with butt paste. I put a cloth diaper inside her pamper and put it on her, then I took the diaper to the dirty utility room. I gagged several times as I put it in the bucket with all the other dirty diapers.

I went back to her and took her axillary temperature. It was normal. I looked at her nose; it was blocked with mucus. She had chronic sinusitis. I knew that she wouldn't want to drink with a stuffed up nose, so I laid her on her back and squirted saline drops up her nostrils. She fought me like a drowning woman fights her rescuer but she snorted out a long string of pearly white snot. I took a suction catheter and stuck it up her nose and got out so much mucus that I was afraid that I was sucking out her brain tissue. It took her about 5 minutes to calm down after that but she was able to breathe easier. I put a tee shirt on her, gave her a bottle of apple juice and put her in a highchair. Then I went into the medicine room for her Amoxicillin. When I got back to her, I sat in front of her and did the desensitizing technique recommended by the Speech Therapist.

Francesca was orally defensive. She had had so many NG tubes put down her nose and so many foul-tasting medicines put in her mouth that whenever anyone tried to go anywhere near her face, she would put down her head and throw hands like a boxer in a corner. I talked to her in my softest, sweetest voice and slowly put my index finger on her chin. She pushed it away. I put it back on her cheek and stroked it. She let me do that. I moved my finger slowly to her mouth and stroked her lips lightly. Her face softened and brightened and she tilted her head and gave me a wistful look. She had beautiful brown eyes. I showed her the syringe and said 'Medicine. I have to give you medicine. It'll make you feel better.' I put my hand on her chin and squirted the medicine in her mouth 1 cc at a time. It took a few minutes but she got most of it. Before trying to feed her, I stroked her face again, then I put my finger into her mashed potatoes and put some in her mouth. She spit some of it out but she ate a little, too. I gave her some more with my finger. I mixed some ground meat with the potatoes and she ate a little of that. I tried using a spoon but she gagged when I put it in her mouth. I gave her some fruit cocktail, piece by piece. But that was all she would eat that time. After a few weeks, she did better. She had put on some weight by the time she got into foster care. Last I heard, she was doing okay. But God knows what she'll be like when she grows up.

I wonder what Reggie will be like when he's older. All of these kids, what are we saving them for? I look down at his face as he finishes his bottle. What kind of life is he going to have?

One of the doctors, the first-year resident on call, walks into the room, stares at me, laughs, and says, "What's wrong with this picture?"

I look up at him for a moment and don't answer. I guess it must be a strange sight for him to see a white man with long hair and a full beard wearing a green scrub suit, feeding a black baby in a rocking chair. I take the nipple from Reggie's mouth, bend him over against my hand and pat him on the back. He burps loudly. I give him the nipple again. When I look up, the doctor is gone. I hear him talking to Katie in the Toddlers Room. A few minutes later, Katie comes into the Baby Room.

"That was Dr Bristol. He's going to try to get some sleep. He was just checking to see if everyone was okay."

"Are they?" I ask her.

Katie nods and shrugs. Her large lips turn down at the corners. I know she's worried about Billie, the kid with the brain tumor. His level of consciousness is decreasing by the day; he's only responding to deep pain now. Katie is just a kid herself, 20 years old and looks even younger, just out of nursing school, a rookie, so sweet, with her long red hair tied up in a bun and her big green eyes. She looks like a model in a uniform magazine, tall and slender, always wearing whites. She's never seen anyone die in her life. But she's got a good heart. She's smart and capable, much more than I was when I was her age. I'd trust her with my life.

By this time, Ronnie is crying and breast stroking in her bed like a frantic swimmer struggling up a white strand. Katie prepares a bottle, picks Ronnie up and gives it to her. She sits across from me in another rocking chair and we chat for a few minutes about the kids like two mothers in a nursery.

"You're such a father figure," she says to me. "Do you have any of your own children?"

I close my eyes and rock for a few moments, deciding how I want to answer that question this time.

"No," I let it slip out. "None that I know of."

She laughs.

"At least, you're honest."

She doesn't know what I mean. Lately, I was wondering if I had any kids wandering around Southeast Asia. A few months ago, I opened the Inquirer Magazine and right there on the cover was a picture of a blond-haired, blue-eyed kid who looked just like me as a boy, who was living on the streets of Ho Chi Mihn City. I threw the magazine across the room, it upset me so much. Even though, if the truth be told, I never had sex in Vietnam. But I did in Thailand so it could have happened there. I see that boy's face again. It's as sharp as an axe blade. His eyes as hard as hand grenades. He eats from garbage cans. He sleeps in doorways. He sells his body for a few dong. I feel sick to my stomach. I feel so irresponsible. I feel my face get hot. But I know that there's nothing I can do about it now. I can't remember any names. I wouldn't be able to find them even if I did. I have to believe that nothing like that happened. Or I'll go crazy. I never gave it a thought. When I was with the prostitutes, I didn't use birth control. I could only presume that they did. But maybe they didn't. Maybe one of them didn't. I don't know.

Katie laughs again.

"You're blushing. Don't be embarrassed. I know the facts of life. I have a boyfriend."

She might know about sex but she doesn't know the facts of life. She thinks she lives in the best country in the world, a free country, a democracy. Wouldn't live anywhere else, I heard her say. She's like most people her age. She doesn't know much about history, about the Vietnam War, about what we did to the Vietnamese. She doesn't know about political reality. I decide to open her eyes a little.

"It's not what you think. I'm not embarrassed about being sexual. I was thinking about something that's been upsetting me."

I tell her about the children that we left behind in Vietnam.

"There are thousands of them. Their fathers are Americans. Most of those guys don't even know that they have children there. Don't care, either. Nobody wants those kids. Their faces remind the Vietnamese of their oppressors, of the people who destroyed their country. They're outcasts. They don't belong anywhere. Like these kids here.'"

I see her look at me with new eyes. I know she wants to ask me if any of them are mine but she's afraid.

"You know, sometimes, I think that I came here to work to make up for the kids I helped to kill in Vietnam or almost killed. Do my penance. We killed a lot of kids in Vietnam. Nobody wants to hear that. But it's true. We burned them with napalm. Blew them into pieces with machine guns and artillery. Starved them. Like these kids here are starving. The war isn't over. It's here."

Katie starts to say something but then stops. She's naive, innocent. She thinks Ronnie Raygun is a nice old fella. She thinks Henry Kissinger is a smart man. She's a true believer. She thinks it's right to fight communism in Central America. She's like I was when I was her age. We come from the same kind of neighborhood, the same heritage; we're both Irish-American working class except I'm from East Falls and she's from South Philly. I don't want her to make the same mistake I made. If the United States invades Nicaragua, or anywhere else, she'd be one of the first to go. Like most nurses, she'd feel an obligation to the wounded. I want to do what I can to stop her from going.

Her lips twist up into a painful smile as she says, "I can believe that children got killed in Vietnam. It was war. But I don't believe it was done on purpose. The way you talk makes me think you must be warped by hatred or something."

I close my eyes and bow my head. She's right. It's true. I do let my hatred take me to extremes sometimes. Some crazy guys did some horrible things but it wasn't the policy of the US military to kill civilians. They weren't that bad.

Katie touches my arm.

"You were fighting for your country."

I shake my head.

"We fought for Big Business, for the Government, for the people in power, to keep just a few people rich. We didn't do it for the people of this country. The government, the establishment, they're not the country. They don't care about us, the working people, the little people. The Vietnam War isn't over. Now, it's in Nicaragua, El Salvador, Guatemala, the Philippines, Palestine, Ireland. Let's not forget Ireland. It's the same thing over there."

I wait for her to say something but she doesn't. She looks at Ronnie and talks to her instead. Too much reality can be a dangerous drug. But I don't have much time. I have to leave her with at least a piece of the truth.

"One of the biggest lies that we are told is that this is a country that cares about children. I shouldn't just say country, a world. It's the same everywhere. Look at these kids: Ronnie and Reggie; they were starving out there. That shouldn't be. There's enough food in the world to feed everybody. Poverty isn't hereditary or genetic or inevitable or a mystery. They're this way because of the economic policies of the big corporations and the government. In every country."

With that, Katie looks up and stares at me.

"Not everywhere," she says. "There are places where people care about children."

"JIMMIE! JIMME!"

I hear Andrew screaming my name. I get up from the rocking chair and quickly put Reggie back in his crib. I run out of the baby room, past the nursing station and into the Big Kids' room.

"Okay, man. I'm here. What's the matter."

Andrew is writhing on his bed, screaming and crying.

"It hurts. It hurts. My knees."

"Okay. Okay." I say as I go over to his bed. "I'll take you off it for a little while."

I unhook him from the traction and loosen the splints on his legs. Andrew has JRA (Juvenile Rheumatoid Arthritis). This is his second admission since I've been here. He's 8 years old and he has kneecaps as big as grapefruits. When he came in this time, his legs had contracted up to his chest, so he's in traction to straighten them out. When I touch his legs, he screams.

"I'm sorry, man," I say. "You got your last dose of Indocin at 10. I can't give you any now."

"Hot pack," he says in between sobs.

"Sure, man," I say. "I'll get you a hot pack. You're my buddy, man."

I go over to the sink and soak a couple towels in hot water. I put a chux around them to keep his sheets dry and wrap them around his knees.

"Hey Andrew. Remember that time, the last time you were here, when I took you downstairs and let you ride around McDonald's on your tricycle?"

"Yeah, man," says Andrew, in his Mister Kool voice. "I left you in the dust."

I smile. He's feeling better now. He's a good kid.

"You sure did. We had a good time that night, didn't we? You were going so fast, you were just a blur going by, whirling up a lot of dust."

Andrew laughs.

"Can we do that again? When I'm feeling better?"

I stop smiling and look down at the floor. I haven't told him that this is my last night here, that I won't be back again. I hate saying goodbye.

"Well, if it's not me, it'll be someone else. You can go with one of the ladies. I know you're a ladies' man, Andrew. I don't blame you. I'm a ladies' man, myself."

"Yeah," he says. "I like the ladies, especially the babe that's working with you tonight. Where is she?"

Andrew sits up and calls out the door in his Super Fly voice, "Hey baby, Hey honey. Come in here and give me a kiss."

I laugh. He's too much for 8 years old. So many of these chronic kids are precocious. Sometimes, they seem like little adults.

"Hey Andrew," I say. "Chill out. You'll be waking everybody up in the room. If you wake Jack up, I'll jack you up."

His bony hands shoot out from the sleeves of his hospital gown.

"I'll jack you up," he says in his Mister Tough Guy voice.

I give him a hug.

"Goodnight, bro'. Take care of yourself. Go to sleep. I'll put the traction back on when you're out."

Andrew nods and pulls the cover over his face.

I stand at the foot of the bed and look around the room. Everyone else is asleep. Jack, the Rooster Man, the kid with Spina Bifida, I don't have to wake him up until 6 o'clock when he has to do his cath. And Michael, the asthmatic, I don't have to wake him up at all. He's stable. He hasn't wheezed in days. As I walk out of the room, I have tears in my eyes. I'm going to miss these kids.

I walk over to the Nurses' Station. Katie is sitting at the carousel checking charts. She looks up and smiles.

"I heard him calling me. That little bugger."

"Yeah," I say. "He's something. The poor kid. He's always in pain. His knees look like they're about to burst. I can't take this place no more. I'm glad I'm leaving."

I sit down and bury my face in my arms. I feel like crying but I don't. I don't cry much anymore. When I was a kid, I never cried. I was too tough. Then I got into it for a while, when all the feelings came back, after I stopped drinking. But now, I don't cry much, once in a while. I've seen too much. I raise my head and look at Katie.

"Hey, Katie, I want you to know that I didn't do it. I didn't kill any kids myself. I didn't kill anybody. But we did, as a collective, as a group, and we have to take responsibility for that."

Katie looks at me with soft eyes.

"I know you didn't. You're not that kind of person. I know."

I smile and nod my head.

"I appreciate that. I'm not that kind of person, now. But I was. I was no different from the ones who did. But I changed."

Katie smiles.

"How'd you do that?"

I look at my work sheet. I have time for a break. A cup of coffee.

"I'll have to make a long story short," I say. "We don't have a lot of time. It's already past midnight. But I'll tell you what happened to me in Ireland, at Ranchhouse and in the circle of stones and how I came to be a pediatrics nurse if you want to hear it."

Katie nods and smiles.

"You were in Ireland? Well, your name's O'Rourke, so I know you're Irish. I'm told it's a beautiful country. I'd love to go there some day. My father's family, the Neary's live in Cork. When were you there?"

I look at my watch. There are 7 hours left until morning. And we have a lot of work to do, a lot of ground to cover. It's a long way from Ranchhouse to Seaside House.

"Once upon a time. Every story should begin with once upon a time," I say and recite the story of the swallow to her.

0100

We stand by Andrea's bed and watch her thrash around in it like a tired swimmer struggling for shore. I reach down and turn her on her back; as I do, she bends forward at the waist, her eyes bulging from their sockets like someone watching a horror movie, her tiny fists clenched with cortical thumbs and her arms flexed as if she were frozen to the wheel of a sunken ship. Gently, I push her back in the bed and tell her it's okay in a quiet voice. But it's not okay and she knows it. She cries and cries, a high pitched squeal of pain that breaks my heart. I look at her picture by the bedside. She was a beautiful little girl, with curly blonde hair and blue eyes. She was a normal child. Now she looks awful. I wonder how her parents can stand to look at her like this. Both come in every night. I feel for her father. He doesn't know what to do. He holds her once in a while and talks to her, but mostly, he just stands around, looking at the floor. Her mother carries her around for hours at a time. It's the only time Andrea stops crying. Brain damaged children are always like that. When I first came here, I asked one of the doctors why that was so. 'They don't have much to laugh about,' he told me. Which is true. But they sure have enough to cry about.

I have taken care of a lot of brain damaged children over the last 3 years. Some stand out in my mind more than others. When I first came here, there was a boy named Tony who had a big box-shaped head that was scarred like a baseball. His father had stuck a toy down his throat to keep him from crying but it had only worked for a little while; when the paramedics took it out, Tony started crying again and didn't stop for months, until he finally died. Then right after that, we had a little girl, Tamika, whose father had stuck a roll of toilet paper down her throat for the same reason, with the same result, except that she is still alive, the last I heard. She's probably crying somewhere right now. Not all kids with brain damage are a result of abuse; some are damaged because of accidents or as a sequela to spinal meningitis but they all have one thing in common: they cry all the time. Now I know why they cry. They cry because they're in pain from muscle spasms and because they are so lonely and so afraid, trapped inside their broken bodies, that all they want is for someone to hold them. They used to give these kids Valium, but not much anymore. It helped; they weren't as spastic. But many doctors are afraid they'll become addicted. I don't know what difference that would make. Being addicted to Valium is the least of their problems.

I help Katie take the splints off Andrea's arms and legs. We examine her for red spots, pressure points. She needs to wear the splints to keep her limbs in alignment; otherwise, she'd curl up like a fetus, her body trying to be reborn. She has a small, red spot on her arm so I massage it to bring back the circulation. Her arms and hands are puffy and blue with bruises from blood sticks and blown IVs. She's wet so we change her diaper and her gown. She's always sweating. I wipe her off with a cloth and Katie does her mouth care, her lips are chapped, with flaps of white skin, her breath smells of snot and curdled milk. When we finish, Katie picks Andrea up and sits in the rocker with her.

"Why don't you do some of your therapeutic touch on her," Katie asks me as she cuddles Andrea against her chest.

"I don't know," I say. "Maybe I'm having a hard time believing in it."

Katie shakes her head.

"But it worked with Neil. He stopped seizing after you did it on him."

"Yeah." I say. "I guess. But maybe it wasn't what I did. Or maybe it was the meds finally kicking in. That's what they think. And he was different. He hadn't drowned. He had some potential."

Andrea is a 2 year old who got out her kitchen door while her mother was breastfeeding her new baby and fell on her face in the wading pool in her backyard. By the time her mother got to her, a few minutes later, Andrea was blue. Now she is in a coma. Hypoxic encephalopathy is her diagnosis. She looks like she must have the day she came out of the water: terrified, her eyes bulging, her mouth moving in a silent scream. Her shaven hair stands in tiny bristles on her bumpy head. She often wakes up thrashing around as she must have in the pool that day.

"Are you telling me that she's not going to live?" Katie asks me. "I don't believe that."

"She'll live, probably," I say. "Maybe for a long time. But she's not going to have much of a life. She doesn't eat by mouth. She's not tracking. She barely has a gag. She's so brain-damaged. Look at her nystagmus."

We watch her eyes as her irises dart from side to side and float around like fish trapped in a bowl.

Katie looks at me and pleads.

"Can't you try again? It took a while for it to work with Neil."

I shrug.

"This is my last night here. When can I do it? I can't come back and do it again. The administration doesn't want me here anymore anyway because of what I said about Raheem and what happened with Richie Rich."

Katie stares at me. She knows that I'm burned out. I'm out of control. I've lost my place. I've forgotten that I'm just a nurse. I actually think that I know something.

A few weeks ago, one of the residents wanted daily weights on Richie, one of my primaries, a child that had been here for a year and I refused to do it. We had been through that before and it had been decided that we were not going to worry about his weight. If we tried to force him to eat or if we put down an NG tube, he only vomited more. He vomited three to four times a day as it was because of his trake. When he ate, he would aspirate a little and he would start coughing and then he would vomit. He was going to be a skinny kid, that's all there was to it. He was very difficult to feed; he didn't know what food was. He didn't know what the world was. He had been born with no eyes and half ears. He couldn't see, he couldn't hear, and he couldn't breathe without a trake because his airway was deformed. He had bad lungs and a little brain and only someone like Marianne could love him; his mother tried but she was only a girl herself. He was only alive because of modern technology. In every other country and at any other time in history he would have been long dead. And dying was not the worst thing that could happen to him. I say that as one who took care of him day after day. I fed him. I changed his diapers. I cleaned up his vomit. I rocked him to sleep. I even hugged him and kissed him. But I didn't love him as Marianne did. She had visions of him being another

Helen Keller. I saw him living on the streets of strange cities, uncared for and uncaring. I cared about him because he was a human child, despite his deformities but I felt that he wasn't meant to live. It seemed to me that the humane thing to do with a child like that is to give him only as much as he wants to eat and to make his life as comfortable as possible, but that if he stops breathing, he should be allowed to die. Not everyone agreed that he should be a no code but we had decided that we would only give him as much food as he would eat. We had stopped doing daily weights months before. There was no point to it. But then a new doctor came in on rotation and decided to change the plan. We were going to watch his weight and if he lost any, we were going to put down an NG tube. I didn't want to do it so I refused. If the doctor wants it done, I told them, then he'll have to do it himself. I was reprimanded and Richie was reassigned to another nurse. A couple of days later, they put down an NG tube; he vomited more, aspirated more, developed pneumonia and was transferred to the ICU. But what do I know? I'm only a nurse.

I feel my face get red.

"They think that I have an authority problem but that's not true, if the authority is legitimate. But the way it's set up, any doctor just out of medical school, no matter how little they know about the day-to-day reality in the hospital can tell any nurse what to do, no matter how much that nurse knows. I was told by the Head Nurse that if I can't accept the fact that nurses are subservient to doctors then I should get out of nursing."

I see Katie's eyes flash.

"Nurses aren't servants to doctors," she says. "I hate that."

I smile. I like her anger.

"That's right," I say. "I hope you don't forget it. Nursing has a different approach than medicine. They do a medical diagnosis and prescribe medicines and treatments. We do a nursing diagnosis and give the meds and do the care. We're more involved in the actual care of the patients than doctors are."

"Hands-on," says Katie. "That's the term my nursing instructor used. When you told me about therapeutic touch, I said to myself, that's just nursing. That's what nurses have always done. Why should you need a doctor's order to do that?"

I smile.

"You're right. We shouldn't need an order to touch patients. It's a matter of control. Doctors want to control nurses."

And control is domination, I think. Patty Byrnes is everywhere, I have to tell her that. But how?

"How can they control us?" says Katie. "There are no doctors here now, as usual. It's only us nurses. So why not try it again. It can't hurt."

I remember Neil as I look down at Andrea. Neil was a 4-year-old who came to Seaside House in Petit Mal Status Epilepticus. He had been seizing constantly for a couple months. He couldn't eat. He couldn't talk or walk. All he did was lay in bed and stare and twitch. The doctors had tried every combination of seizure meds in the book; they even put him on a ketogenic diet for a while. But nothing worked. He came here as a last resort. I was assigned to be his primary nurse. I talked with his mother one day about therapeutic touch. I had been wanting to use it for a long time but I had been too afraid. It was too weird. But his mom was an open-minded person. She was willing to try anything.

"Tell me more about it," she said. "What are you going to do?"

"I'm just going to touch him," I said. "Put my hands on his chest. On his heart chakra."

I noticed her looking at me strangely so I reassured her.

"I want you to be there with me," I told her. "I want him and you to feel safe. Chakra means an opening, a place where energy is transferred."

I showed her my palms.

"They're chakras. Notice how they're sunken like bowls. There's another one between the breasts. I'm going to transfer my energy, my life force, my health, into Neil."

"It sounds like the laying on of hands," said the mother.

I nodded. It was the same principle.

"I've always believed in God," the mother said. "And being touched can't hurt anyone. What do we have to lose? They're telling me that all I can expect is maybe a little improvement, maybe he'll be able to eat enough so they won't have to put in a gastrostomy. Maybe not. Maybe he'll walk again and talk, maybe not. Let's go for it."

She picked Neil up from his bed and followed me into the playroom. I had arranged with Kevin, the play therapist, to have use of the room when it was not being used by the other kids. I closed the door and put up a Do Not Disturb sign on it. I pulled down the shades so we could have privacy. I didn't want the doctors to know what I was doing. I didn't think they would approve. A friend of mine, Danny Stein, had tried doing it over at 'The Holy' and they had refused to give him permission even though they saw it work. Danny had used guided imagery on a child with hypertension and had lowered his blood pressure without using medications. But they didn't think it was good nursing practice; they considered it a form of magic, not science. And the medical profession distrusted any therapy that was done by human beings, not by technology or medications. It threatened their power.

I put a tape of Kay Gardner's **Moon Circles** in my cassette recorder and turned it on. As soon as I heard her flute fill the air, I sat on the mat with Neil and his mother.

I had to center myself. Concentrate. I had to make sure that my motives were selfless. That I had Neil's health as my priority, not that it would make me look good if he improved. I had to empty my mind of thoughts and voices, so the energy could flow freely. That was the hardest part. That was why I needed quiet, privacy.

I put my legs beneath me in a lax lotus and closed my eyes. I concentrated on my breathing and imagined myself back in the circle of stones. I felt the hands of Madeleine burning into my chest. She had told me that they would always be there whenever I needed them. I needed them now and they were there. I took slow, deep breaths for a few minutes until I felt myself relax and go into a trance. Then I opened my eyes and looked at Neil. I saw only him. I wished him well. Slowly, I raised my hands and held one a few inches from his chest and the other a few inches from his back. I moved both hands slowly back and forth, feeling for his energy field, until I felt it between my hands like a warm rubber ball. I inched my hands towards him carefully, as if I were about to touch a raw wound. I felt my hands burn into his back and chest and I poured all of my energy into him until I felt him go limp. I laid him on his back on the mat. He was sound asleep.

His mother looked at me and smiled.

"When he comes home, will you come up to our house and put him to sleep at night?"

I laughed.

"I'll teach you how to do it, so you can do it yourself."

I did another session with Neil a few days later with the same result. I showed his mother what I was doing and I gave her a book on therapeutic touch for her to read: **Healing Hands** and she said that she would do it at home. Neil showed a little improvement over the next week; he started eating more and talking but he still wasn't walking when he got discharged. I went to nights so I didn't see Neil again and I didn't talk to his mother; she called a couple times when I wasn't there and sent me a message that Neil was doing better. Then a few weeks ago, I heard that he was in to see his doctor and that he was running around and chattering like a child on Christmas morning. After he had his EEG done, his doctor said that it looked like he had a brain transplant done, his EEG had improved that much. Something happened.

"Let's do it now," Katie says. "We have some time. We can take her into the Playroom and you can do it there."

I was having a lot of doubts. I've tried doing it a few times since Neil and nothing happened. Maybe it was the meds, or maybe he was healed by something else or someone else. But who? Sometimes, I feel embarrassed for believing in these things. It's so hard to maintain. Nothing has changed. War still goes on. Children suffer. The rich get richer. The poor get poorer. I need a sign. As I look down at Andrea's face, her eyes focus on mine, lock for a few moments, then roll away. I take a deep breath. She's in there, I know it now.

I nod several times. Why not? What can it hurt? I'm not doing anything wrong. I'm just practicing nursing. Maybe I haven't been concentrating enough. Maybe it is just magic or maybe there's some mystery about it that I don't know, maybe it doesn't work but if everyone were to experience it and practice it on each other, there would be less violence in the world today. After doing it, the thought of hitting someone or hurting them is sickening.

Katie smiles and gets out of the rocking chair. I stroke Andrea's face as she goes by on Katie's shoulder. I look in her eyes as I follow them out of the room. We stop at the Nurses' Station and listen for the sounds of children crying and monitors beeping. But all is quiet. I go with them into the dark playroom. I turn on a low light and roll down a mat for us to sit on. Katie sits Andrea between us in a beanbag. I try to center myself but just as I feel myself go into a trance a monitor alarms in the Toddlers' Room. Katie jumps up and goes to check it out. I come back to reality. Maybe it's Billie. I hope he doesn't code tonight. I'm not up for it. The thought of being in another code makes me sick to my stomach.

I remember the last kid with a brain tumor who coded on us. Wayne was his name. The whole code was a mess. Everything went wrong. We even brought him back for a while. He was like Billie. His tumor kept coming back even though they had tried every kind of treatment. It was a classic case of denial. Everyone denied that he was dying: his parents, the doctors. Wayne was becoming more unresponsive by the minute, his blood pressure was dropping every time we took it and his respirations were going down but yet, they wanted to continue his tube feedings. Meanwhile, he was a full code. I hate it when it's like that. None of the nurses wanted to code him. The boy had suffered enough. But we had to legally. As the shift went on, he kept going down so we shut off the feeding anyway and called the resident. When he got there, I brought him into the room. As I walked towards Wayne, I didn't see him breathing and I said so. Well, he was still breathing but so slowly that it looked like he wasn't. The resident panicked and ran over to the bed and started pushing it towards the door trying to get Wayne into the Treatment Room instead of bringing the Crash Cart into his room. It was a bad decision. We had problems getting the bed out of the room and through the door. By the time we got him into the Treatment Room he had stopped breathing so the resident began CPR. He gave him the kiss of life and Wayne vomited into his mouth. While the resident was spitting it out Wayne vomited again and aspirated. By that time, there were at least twenty people in the room, everybody getting in each other's way, trying to get an IV started, getting the meds and doing CPR. Total chaos. This went on for about ten minutes until one of the Oncologists came in and stopped the code. They had decided that he was a DNR, but they hadn't had the time to tell anyone. By that time, Wayne was breathing again and had a regular heart beat. They transferred him up to ICU and he lived for a few more days, suffering, until he finally died.

Andrea starts to cry so I bring her over onto my lap while we wait for Katie. I figure that she would call me if there was a problem but still I worry. I don't want to be here when Billie dies. I'm glad that Katie is his nurse. The first thing his parents will want to know is: who was the nurse who was taking care of him. They're nice people but they haven't accepted the fact that he's dying. They still think he will become a normal little boy again. But he will never again be that little boy. How that must hurt. It hurts me when I think about it and I hardly know him. I get angry when I think about these things. I know that sickness and death are a reality but I am also convinced that a lot of these diseases could be avoided, if we lived in a humane society, one that cared about human needs instead of profit. But we are a long way from that. My anger subsides as I feel the child's warm body against me. I have to convert my anger into compassion. I lean back against the bean bag, close my eyes and try to relax.

Finally, Katie comes back into the Playroom and says that she's sorry she took so long but Billie's apnea light was lit and she had taken his vital signs and had watched him for a few minutes. His respiratory rate was 15, but his breathing continued to be irregular and slow at times; that probably was why the monitor had alarmed. His pulse was 80 and slightly irregular; he was probably throwing some PVCs. His BP was 125/65. No real change.

I take a few deep breaths. I can't worry about Billie now. Andrea deserves the best I can give her. She is a human being, a little person who is hurting. She is me. She is the child within us all. I decide to skip the heart chakra and go directly to the brain. There is a danger in that, I know. The energy could cause a convulsion, maybe even lead to her death, if that's where she's headed. That's what the energy does: it takes you in the direction you are going. But I don't think that Andrea is ready to die. Her eyes tell me different. I give her back to Katie and take a few deep breaths. This time, I am successful. I am at center. Katie places Andrea between us and holds her upright. Slowly, I place my hands on her head as if I were handling a delicate egg. I pour my energy into her until I feel her head grow warm as if it were about to hatch a chick. I look at Andrea's face; she's asleep. Katie smiles and says that I am amazing. It's not me, I tell her. I'm only an agent, a disciple.

I carry Andrea back to her crib, lay her in it and cover her with a baby blanket. She looks so peaceful when she's asleep. She looks almost normal again.

I check on the other kids while I'm there. I go over and stand at the foot of Billie's bed and watch him breathe; he's breathing irregularly, fast and shallow, then slow and deep, but he's been doing that. I feel my anxiety level go back up. I take a few deep breaths to calm myself. I would be afraid to send him some energy; he might use it to grow wings and fly off to heaven. I know that's what he needs to do but I hope that he doesn't go tonight, not on my watch.

The other kids in the room, Peewee, and his girlfriend Michelle, sleep soundly on their bellies by the door. I used to think that all children with Cerebral Palsy were mentally retarded, but they're not, although some of them are. These two aren't. They're smart little kids. Their problem is lack of muscle control in their legs. CP is caused by a variety of factors but it usually occurs because of cerebral anoxia; their brain is deprived of oxygen for some reason. From what I have seen, it seems that a lot of CP comes from poor prenatal care, prematurity and the fundamental disrespect that some doctors have for the birthing process itself. I have seen babies so damaged just from being born that they looked like they had been squeezed out through a wringer instead of a birth canal.

I remember the first baby I took care of with CP. His name was Deon. He was a typical case. His mother was 16, a poor girl from Mantua. She had no prenatal care. She didn't know she was pregnant until she was 6 months. Her usual breakfast consisted of potato chips and diet soda; she ate most of her meals at McDonald's. When her water broke, she went to the hospital where they put her on a Pitocin drip and pulled the baby out by his head with forceps. He had Apgars of 1 and 2. He was intubated and put on a respirator for a few months until he was finally weaned. By the time he got to us, he was a nervous wreck. He writhed and twitched in his bed like a junkie going cold turkey. He would cry whenever anyone touched him. It was easy to see why. He had been tortured all his life. Every day since he was born, he had needles stuck into his arms and hands and tubes shoved down his nose and throat. He had the air sucked out of his lungs with catheters over and over again. I can still see his face. He looked like a raisin with eyes. When I picked him up, he arched his back so badly that I could have used him as a bow to shoot squirrels. I straightened him out and tried to put the nipple in his mouth but he wouldn't take it.

'You have to bundle him,' Marianne told me. 'That's the only way these kind of kids eat. And you have to give him chin and cheek support.'

She showed me how to wrap him up in a baby blanket real tight so that his hips were flexed into a feeding position. He had a poor suck because his mouth muscles were weak so she showed me how to position the bottle so I could hold his mouth closed around it with my fingers. Marianne was my mentor. She took me under her wing when I first came here and taught me how to be a pediatrics nurse. I didn't even know how to change a diaper when I first came here. Some people are great intellectually; others are great athletically; Marianne is great emotionally. She had worked at Seaside House for years. She loved these kids. She never got angry at them. She was a great baby feeder. She could get any kid to eat. I could see why. If I saw that big beautiful face and those eyes smiling at me, I'd do whatever she wanted too.

'Move the nipple in and out,' she told me. 'And burp him more frequently, after every half ounce. Crying babies gulp down a lot of air so they have more gas.'

At first, I felt nervous feeding him. He would suck for a few minutes, then he would spit out the nipple, twist his head to one side and raise one arm as if he were about to fence someone. Then he would stand on my lap. Forget the image of a Gerber baby quietly feeding, cuddled up in your arms.

'He's having a muscle spasm,' Marianne told me. 'Rock his hips for a minute until he calms down.

I did what she said and it helped, and after a while, I felt more comfortable taking care of babies with CP but they are always diffi-cult. It's not easy to take care of a baby who cries all the time and who won't eat. The sound of a baby crying irritates me, makes me angry. I noticed that when I first came here.

I told Marianne about it.

'You're a man,' she said to me. 'Men get angry at crying babies. It's because they don't know them. They've lost their paternal instinct. All you have to do is find out why they're crying and do what needs to be done. Then they'll stop crying. Babies cry for only a few reasons: because they're hungry, because they have gas and need to be burped, because they need their diaper changed or because they're lonely and want some attention. If you do all of these things and they still cry, then call the doctor. They might have an ear infection or something.'

'But what if they won't eat?' I asked her. 'It gets on my nerves. All you want them to do is eat but they act like you're trying to poison them.' Maybe they're like little Oskar in **The Tin Drum.** They don't want to grow up in such a hostile world. I don't blame them. I don't want to live in it, either. I want to change it.

'Don't make mealtime a battleground,' she told me. 'Make eating a pleasant experience for him. Stroke his face with your fingers while he sucks. While you're feeding him, talk to him in sort of high-pitched, sing-song type of voice. Like this: hello honey, you little sweetie you. I know it's hard for you to do that. It's not macho. But babies respond better to that kind of voice, not a deep, loud voice. That startles them.'

It wasn't easy for me at first. I used to feel embarrassed talking to babies that way. But I got the hang of it. I noticed that I felt more comfortable being that way when there were no other men around. But lately, it hasn't mattered much to me. I remember when I first came here, I didn't like being around other men. They were too messed up. But over the last 3 years, I've met some men who are actually decent human beings. My friend, Danny Stein, is a good guy and so is rv, one of my old roommates. Kevin, the play therapist, is good with the kids. Maybe I'm feeling more comfortable with my own masculinity. I'm more secure in my new identity. I've come to realize that it is not masculinity that is the cause of the problems in the world today, although it is true that men do most of the killing and maiming and exploiting. But that has nothing to do with being a man. It is the belief in the right to dominate that causes the problem, whether it's men over women, women over men or white over black or rich over poor or people over nature. It is the inability to see that we are all connected.

I stand over the sleeping children like a gentle genie waiting for a wish. They are so cute. Peewee named himself that. 'I'm little,' he said, 'a peewee.' He wears a big pair of horn rimmed glasses on his tiny face that make him look like a child prodigy. Michelle is always giving him kisses. 'I like his face' she said. She looks like a poster child for the March of Dimes. Which she was. Her mother showed me her picture last week. She was standing in her braces, on crutches, in the middle of a football field, her long brown hair hanging down to her shoulders, a helmet on her head, a big smile on her face.

Last week, when I was on days, Michelle wheeled over to Peewee's bed and asked if he could come out of his cradle and play with her. Cradle. I laughed when she said that. She's funny but she also has a temper. When I put her in her braces the other day, she screamed and popped me on the nose. I had to put her on restriction for that. She couldn't go into the playroom and she had to stay in her bed, with the curtain around her, with no toys, for 15 minutes. That made her very unhappy. She kept calling me in her tiny voice every 2 minutes and asking me if she could come out. Every time I said no, she cried. But when her time was up, she said that she wouldn't hit anybody anymore. She's cute when she's asleep. I don't want to wake her up. Like a thief in the night, I tiptoe over to her bed to see if she's wet. I poke my fingers in her diaper like a pickpocket lifting a wallet. It's dry. Then I check to see if her leg extenders are still on properly; they are.

I go back to the Nurses' Station. Katie is not there. I hear her suctioning, Willie, the other BPD kid, in the baby room. I notice that my coffee is cold. I forgot about it when we went in to check on Andrea. I go into the kitchen and pour myself another cup from the pot. I look at my work sheet. It's time to heat Jennifer's feeding. I take her formula from the refrigerator, pour 60 ccs into a bottle and put it into a pot of water on the stove. I put a low light under it. I don't want it to get too hot. I remember to turn the pot handle towards the back. Marianne taught me that. It's a good habit to get into, she told me, so a small child can't reach up and pull it down on himself. I check Jennifer's formula with my finger tip; it's warm enough. I turn off the heat and leave it in the water until I'm ready for it. I'm going to miss Marianne. I'm going to miss all the nurses. They taught me a lot. I love nurses. They're what I'm going to miss the most when I don't work in the hospital anymore. As I sip my coffee, I think about what I'm going to do when I leave here. I don't have another job yet. I have this vague idea of going out into the community. That was my original intention when I was in nursing school: to be a community health nurse. But where is my community? The only community I've had since I came home from Vietnam has been in the hospital with the nurses and the children. And I'm leaving that. I feel bad about it. But what can I do? It's time for me to move on. I can't stay here anymore.

I just moved back with my mom into my old neighborhood, East Falls. I had been living over in Germantown with two women, Meredith Allen and Debbie Gessner. We were just roommates. Nothing went on between us. Some people found that hard to believe but it's true. They don't realize that I'm looking for someone to love not for uncommitted sex. I had enough of that. I know what people think about men who live with their mothers. They can think what they want. Mom was having a hard time. She has arthritis. She doesn't have much money. She just retired after working 17 years as a duplicating machine operator in the basement of Fidelity Bank. She didn't work when my brother and I were in school so she only has a little pension and social security and no savings to speak of. She stayed home to be there for us when we needed her. She's getting old. She needs me now. She's always been there for me. She's my mom and I love her. If it was my dad, I'd do the same thing. We have an obligation to our parents to look after them when they're old.

But I'm not sure if I fit in the Falls anymore. After I came home from the army, my name was dirt. Guys gagged as they spit out my name. I had turned against the war, against war itself and that made me a traitor in their eyes; worse, a worm and no man. They thought that I exaggerated my experience in Vietnam, made it worse than it was. One man's pain is another man's scorn. I know I became a whiner. I felt sorry for myself and people despised me for it. I can't blame them. I know now why I was that way. I hated myself. I had not lived up to my own expectations. I wanted to be a hero and I became a sad sack instead, a Beetle Bailey. But what happened in Ireland changed everything. After what I did there, I've gotten back my self respect. Maybe I can live in the Falls again. I'm a new man now.

I go back out to the Nurses' Station where I see Katie sitting by the carousel updating her nursing care plans. I have to smile. She's so dedicated. She reminds me of myself when I first came here. I would do whatever the hospital wanted. I'd do doubles. I'd work overtime. I'd take any patient assignment, no matter how bad. But no more. I don't do any favors for the hospital. They don't do me any favors. We are not friends. It's a business. That shouldn't be, I know. Hospitals should not be run as a business. We need a national health care system in this country. Health care is not an industry; it is a human right. If nurses would refuse to work so much overtime and refuse to take patient assignments that are unsafe, the hospitals would be forced to take action. I know what people think: but what about the patients? They'll be the ones to suffer. But they're suffering now. It can't get any worse than it is. I wonder if Katie will be like I am now in a few years. Maybe, I think, she cares. She has a good heart, that makes her a true revolutionary; she just doesn't know it yet.

Katie smiles.

"I wanted to ask you something. Did you learn how to do that in the circle of stones?

I nod. After I recited the story of the swallow to her, I told her where I had composed it.

"Madeleine did it on me," I say. "That was the first I knew about it. She healed me that way. Then about a year ago, I went with my friend Joanne Ruth to a circle in Vermont called the **Art of the Possible** by Dawna Markova and I learned more about it there."

Katie looks at me for a moment.

"Who is Madeleine?"

I smile. How can I tell her about Madeleine? I haven't seen her for 11 years, since 1973. 1 wrote to her a few times but she never answered. We had our time together. It's hard for me to believe that she's a real person, anymore. Time has made her into a myth in my mind.

"She was a midwife. If she had been born a few hundred years ago, she would have been burned at the stake as a witch."

Katie laughs again.

"A witch? She wasn't?"

I laugh.

"Yeah, she was, I guess. You could call her that. She was a healer, a nurse. She had special abilities."

Katie smiles.

"Were you in love with her?"

I look down at the floor.

"I don't know. I thought I was."

Katie smiles.

"How many times have you been in love?"

I start to laugh but then stop. I don't say anything for a few minutes, thinking. In love? Or in fatuation? Or in sex? When I was a boy, I remember thinking I was in love: with Annette Funicello on the Micky Mouse show, with Marilynn Monroe in **Some like it Hot**, with women in underwear in the Sears and Roebucks Catalog. I would look at those pictures and fantasize.

I dated quite a few girls in high school. I used to look at their pictures in the Hallahan year book and then ask my friend Mildred Noll to get me their phone numbers. But usually I only went out with them once or twice. I never went steady with anyone. Then in college, I made it with a lot of girls down the shore. A gang of us would rent out a house down the shore for the summer: in Avalon and Margate. That was in the 60s, during the Sexual Revolution. It was easy to make it with girls down the shore. I lost my virginity in Avalon the summer of my junior year. But I never got involved with anyone. I didn't want to. I remember telling a girl that I had too many things I wanted to do. I was going to go into the service, travel, have adventures. I didn't want to be tied down.

Then when I was in the Army I started going to prostitutes. Those experiences changed me. I had trouble relating to women after that. I felt guilty about it, dirty, like I was some kind of creep. I remember when it hit me how wrong it was. I was in Bangkok on R&R and I was with this beautiful Thai girl, a girl was all she was, maybe 16 years old and she told me how she had been taken from her family in the country and forced to come to Bangkok to work in a brothel. She was part of the slave trade. It was no lie, I knew that, no sob story, but the truth. I could see it in her eyes. After that, I couldn't do it anymore. That was the last time I ever went to a prostitute. I know some guys thought of those nights in Bangkok as the best time of their lives. Not me. I was never more unhappy than I was then. Part of the reason was because of that girl but I sensed that there was more to it than that but I wasn't sure what it was.

"It's hard to say. Once, maybe." I say to Katie. "What's love?"

She gives me a pitying look.

"Love is a choice not a feeling," she says. "Feelings are important and you have to be attracted to one another but that usually doesn't last. But the choice does. It's giving yourself to another: to make their life better if you can, to be there for them when they need you, to make sacrifices."

I feel my face get hot.

Not a feeling? If that's the case, I think, then I guess I've never been in love. It's always been physical attraction to me: good looks, nice body, someone interesting, a fun person to be with. I thought that I loved Maggie but maybe I didn't.

I shrug.

"If that's what love is. Then I guess I've never been in love."

I look at my watch. It's 0145. I don't want to think about these things. It only makes me feel anxious and inadequate. By that definition, I've never loved a woman in my life. But one thing's for sure, I've loved these children. Maybe someday, I'll be capable of loving a woman.

"I have a lot of things to do right now." I say as I stand. "I have to give Charles his meds and I have to give Jennifer hers and feed her."

Katie nods.

"Okay. I have some things to do, too. I'll talk to you later."

I nod and walk quickly into the treatment room. I go over to the med cart and look through the kardexes until I find Jennifer's. She gets her Digoxin and her Lasix and her KCL at 2. I look for a TB syringe to draw up her Dige but there are none in the cup. I walk around behind the washer and dryer to the stock area where I have to climb over boxes of diapers for the syringes. I grab as many of them as I can carry. As I stock the med cart with them, I think about how many we use once and then throw away. We waste so much here, not only the syringes, but the suction catheters and the NG tubes and the diapers. We live in a throwaway society. So many of these children are throwaways. Waste has become a metaphor for life. All life is waste.

Where do these diseases come from, I wonder, as I pour Jennifer's meds. Why does she have a heart defect? No one seems to know. There was a running joke in nursing school. Whenever the instructor would ask 'what is the etiology of this disease,' we would answer automatically: unknown. Despite all the advances in medicine, the cause of most sicknesses remains a mystery. I shake my head as I draw up the Dige in a syringe, pour the other meds into a plastic cup and go out of the treatment room. I ask myself, what's it all about? Why is there suffering? What's the purpose of it?

0200

I turn on the bedside light and peek into the oxygen tent at Jennifer. I see her sleeping quietly in a cloud of mist, surrounded by rolled up baby blankets and covered with a towel. Her heart monitor beeps the QRS complex across the screen in normal sinus rhythm. I see an occasional PVC, but her heart rate reads at 120 and her respirations at 30. I put the probe of the oxygen analyzer into the tent. It's still at 24%. I unzip the flap and put my head into the mist. I take a deep breath of the oxygen to wake myself up.

I look at Jennifer. Something is wrong. Her face is so pale that for a moment I think she is dead but then I see her dreaming, her eyeballs rolling under her blue lids, following the scene.

As I watch her tiny nostrils flaring, I realize what it is. She has nothing on her face. I lift the towel off her; it's wet from the mist. Then I see the tape and the NG tube lying beside her shoulder. She pulled it out, again. I curse under my breath. I retrieve the NG tube and ease my head from the tent. I look at the tube. It's clean. They just put a new one in on evenings, they told me at report. It's already measured. There's a piece of tape to mark the spot. Maybe I can put it back in without waking her up, I think, as I lubricate the tube with a little KY jelly. I tear off some tape for her face and paste it on the side rail. I look for and find her pacifier by the bedside. Marianne taught me this trick. I put my head back in the tent and put the pacifier in Jennifer's mouth. As soon as she sucks on it, I put the tip of the NG tube into her nose and push it quickly down the back of her throat into her stomach. I laugh. I did it. She sucked it right down. She didn't even gag. I tape the tube onto her cheek and check it for placement. I draw back on the syringe and get a cc of curdled formula. Just to be sure, I listen with my stethoscope on her stomach as I push the formula back through the tube. I hear it swoosh. It's in place. As I recap the NG tube, Jennifer wakes up and smiles around her pacifier at me. If she knew what I just did to her, she wouldn't be smiling; she'd be crying.

"I tricked you this time," I tease her, "I put that tube down and you didn't even know it."

I kiss her on her tiny forehead. She's cute in a funny looking kind of way. She has this tiny body beneath a head that is almost bald and is as big in the back as a being's from another planet. I look at her lips. They're pale, almost pink. That's about as good as they get. I unbutton her sleeper and take it off. It's a little damp from the mist. I look at her chest. She's retracting a little bit but that's her baseline. I can count her ribs; she's so thin. She's 6 months old and weighs less than 3 kgs, about 5 pounds. I take my stethoscope and listen to her heart. Her murmur is so loud that I'm not sure at first if I'm listening to her heart beat or to her respirations. Then I hear the lower-pitched sounds of her breathing. Her signs are little higher than the monitor reads, but now she's awake.

Her lungs are clear. I feel her torso and her head; she's cool to the touch so I don't take her temp. I check her diaper, hoping that she wet but she's dry. I put a new sleeper on her and ease back out of the tent. I pick up the syringes with the Dige and the Lasix. I'll give her the KCL after her feeding so it won't irritate her stomach.

Jennifer has a VSD (Ventricular Septal Defect). She has a hole between the right and left ventricles of her heart. The hole reduces her heart's ability to pump properly so blood backs up in her right ventricle, causing it to enlarge and putting her into heart failure. That's why she needs the meds. Digoxin slows down her heart and helps it beat more efficiently. She's here to gain weight so she can have surgery, the bigger she is the better chance she has to survive. But it's not easy to do. She doesn't have the strength to eat enough by mouth to keep herself alive. She tires easily. After a few sucks, she's done. That's why she needs the NG tube. If we give her too much formula, too much fluid, her heart can't handle it and blood backs up into her lungs. That's why they call it congestive heart failure. We have to measure her output to make sure that she's urinating enough. She put out enough on days and evenings though, so I'm not worried. And I'm giving her Lasix now. Lasix could get urine from a stone. I shoot the medicines down her NG tube then I flush it with a cc of water.

I pick Jennifer up and bring her out of the tent. I sit in the rocker with her. She loves being held. I know she's not supposed to stay out for long but she needs some affection. She can't stay in the tent all the time. It's like being in a wet prison. It's a strange environment to live in, I think. What a life: short and painful. The surgery is only palliative; it won't last forever. I think of Angie, the little heart baby with Tetralogy of Fallot that I took care of when I first came here. She died last year. I remember the night I coded her.

I was working nights. I was here only about 2 months. It was real busy, a full house. I was working by myself. I was the only RN for 15 kids. There were 2 Child Care Workers working with me, they were nursing students from Penn. We were running around like crazy people all night. Kids were vomiting. A kid's trake came out and I had to put it back in. Luckily, he was okay. I had a couple

IV's, a child with BPD was on an Aminophylline drip, another was on antibiotics. I was in charge. I had all the meds to give. I couldn't stop even to go to the bathroom. Then about 4 o'clock, things quieted down a little so I decided to take my break. I was sitting out at the Nurses' Station. I had just finished eating my dinner. That's a tough time for me. I get so tired around then. I was having trouble keeping my eyes open.

It was the last watch of the night, the time of attack in war.

All of a sudden, I heard Cathy, one of the CCWs, shouting my name, telling me to come right now. I could tell from the sound of her voice that it was serious. I ran into the baby room and there was Cathy standing by the crib, holding her hands to her face, crying like a mourning mother. Angie was laying on her back, totally limp, her head turned to one side and her little tongue sticking out of her mouth.

'I was feeding her NG,' Cathy told me between sobs, 'And I was talking to her and she was smiling, then all of a sudden, she coughed and stopped breathing.'

I took one look at Angie's purple face, picked her up and ran her into the Treatment Room. I shouted for Cathy to call the code. I put Angie on the table and went through the ABC's in my mind: Airway, Breathing, Circulation. Airway. I had a hunch. I grabbed the suction from the wall and stuck the catheter up her nose and down her throat. She coughed and I sucked up some white stuff out of her throat.

'Please, God, help us. Come on, honey,' I begged her. 'Breathe. You can do it.'

I suctioned her again and Angie coughed up some more white stuff. Then she cried like a little kitten. I was never so happy to hear a baby cry in my life. I was right. It was her formula. She had refluxed. That was the problem. It wasn't her heart; it was her airway. I looked at her face; it was pinking up. I reached over for the wall oxygen, turned it on and gave her 100%. Then I picked her up and hugged and kissed her like she was a friend come back from the dead. I sat down on the examination table; my legs were shaking and I felt a little nauseous. Finally, the resident on call came into the room, wiping the sleep from his eyes. Cathy hadn't called the code.

She called him stat, instead. But I didn't care. Angie was breathing again; that was the most important thing. The resident asked me what happened, so I told him.

'It sounds like a Tet spell,' he told me, very seriously, as if he had seen hundreds of them himself, which I knew he hadn't. There weren't that many kids with Tetralogy of Fallot and he was only a first-year resident.

'It wasn't.' I told him again what happened. 'She refluxed. The formula was blocking up her throat. I suctioned it out. I saw the formula in the catheter. She started breathing again after I did it.

The resident shook his head.

'It was a Tet spell. I'm sure of it.'

I couldn't believe it. He wasn't even there. It makes me angry when people do that. It's no wonder nurses get angry at doctors and at hospitals. Apparently, I had enough skill and knowledge to be the only nurse for 15 sick children, but when I told people what happened, they didn't believe me. 'Are you sure she wasn't breathing' they asked me that morning at report. As if I couldn't tell when someone wasn't breathing.

"You better not code on me," I whisper to Jennifer. I had enough of that. She lifts one side of her lip; that's her smile, and coos at me. I stroke her face and smile back at her. I hold her against my chest and rock her. I remember the last kid who coded on me, a few weeks ago.

I was working day shift for a change. I got assigned to a patient who had just come in the day before. His name was Eugene. He was a 12 year old with Muscular Dystrophy. All they told me in report was that he was a nice kid who was in for PT, that he had a lot of congestion in his chest but that he was afebrile. When I looked at his kardex, I saw that he was on no meds. He sat in a chair, his own from home and he could pretty much feed himself. I just had to set him up. I had a light assignment that day. The census was low; he was the only patient I had. I was supposed to spend the day upgrading nursing care plans and working on a pamphlet for parents about how to take care of a child with BPD. It looked like an easy day. I went in and woke Eugene up. He was a nice kid, polite and cooperative. I took his temp. It was normal. I watched him breathe, his respirations were elevated, in the 30s. I listened to his lungs. He had coarse rhonchi in all his lung fields. He coughed when I had him take deep breaths, which weren't very deep. He wasn't able to, with his chest; it looked like a B52 bomb crater: it was sunken that much. I asked him how he felt and he said that he was okay but that he was having some trouble breathing. I noticed that he was having a problem getting the mucus up when he coughed; it would get caught down in his throat. But his color was okay. I raised the head of the bed and put a washbasin in front of him on a bed table. I helped him take off his hospital gown. His arms and legs were as bony and brittle as a bird's and they were so bent and twisted that he looked like a yogi frozen in a posture. I helped him wash his hands and face and under his arms then I put down the head of the bed and rolled him on his side. I wiped him down as best as I could, making a mental note to put him in the tub the next day. His butt was a bony fan covered with red and puckered skin. I cleaned off the stool stain from the night before and lathered him with Balmex. I struggled his pants onto him then helped him into a dinosaur tee shirt. I lifted him out of bed and put him in his chair. His torso was so crooked that I had difficulty getting him seated properly. I had to prop pillows and towel rolls around his hips and sides and buckle him into his chair or he would have looked like the Leaning Tower of Pisa.

By the time I was finished, I was in a sweat. I wondered how his parents managed him at home. He was a lot of work and they didn't have much help. It's a shame. When I first came here, they used to admit patients for respite care so their parents could get a break. But now, the insurance companies won't pay for it. As I looked at him, I thought, this kid needs to be in a nursing home or a hospice. He can't live much longer like this. Then the doctors came into the room on rounds and asked how he was doing. I told them what I knew. The resident listened to Eugene's lungs and agreed with my assessment. They talked about giving him a treatment before breakfast to bring up the mucus. They decided to order respiratory to give him a Mucomyst treatment. It seemed like a good idea to me so I paged respiratory and she came in a few minutes. I left the room while she did his treatment and went out to the Nurses' Station to start work on the pamphlet. When I went back to Eugene's room, the respiratory therapist was holding an emesis basin in front of him. It was filled with mucus. She looked worried.

'He just keeps bringing it up', she said to me. 'I don't know where it's all coming from. That Mucomyst must have loosened up stuff that he's had down there for years. I'm going to call the doctor.'

'I'll stay with him,' I said, looking down at Eugene.

I watched Eugene as he coughed and coughed like a heavy smoker in the morning. Then he stopped and gasped a few times as if he were choking on a fish bone. I looked at his lips: they were turning blue. His head jerked up and back as if he had just been punched in the jaw and he thrashed in the chair like a convict getting the juice. I felt the adrenaline rush to my brain and everything slowed down. After what seemed like hours, I got him out of the chair and into bed. As I lowered his head onto the pillow, I looked right into his face and I saw him die. The life went from his face like light leaving a burnt bulb. But I called the code anyway. I had to do it. He had no code status. One of the nurses rushed in with the crash cart and we suctioned him and got an airway into his mouth. By the time the code team arrived, he was breathing again. But his color was poor and his respirations were shallow and erratic. It was obvious that unless he was intubated and put on a respirator, he would stop breathing again soon. With his chest, CPR was impossible; his sternum would crack with the compressions. The doctors called Eugene's attending physician who told them to do nothing until Eugene's mother got there. His mother lived 2 hours away and would be there as soon as she could. We stood around and watched Eugene breathe. He was dead. I had seen him die but he was still alive, somehow. He kept breathing until his mother came in and hugged him. Then he died. It was amazing. He had been waiting for his mom. I was very upset by his death. I didn't know why at first. I'd seen other kids die. I knew that it was time that he left that broken body behind and went back to God. Death was a reality. It was his time. If we hadn't given him the Mucomyst, he would have died of pneumonia. But when I thought about it some more, I realized that I was upset because I felt that I had let him down. I didn't comfort him while he waited for his mom. I had stood around like a mourner at a funeral. I could have at least held his hand. But I did nothing. That was when I realized how burned out I was. I had to do something different. I had to get out of the hospital.

I look down at Jennifer's face. She's getting a little blue around the lips. She's had enough TLC. It's time I started her feeding. I put her back in her tent on her belly. She cries as soon as she realizes where she is, so I pat her on the back until she stops. I pour the feeding into a 60 cc syringe and hook it up to her NG tube. As the feeding goes in, I stand beside the crib and pat her on her back through the open flap of her tent.

Katie comes into the room and asks if there is anything she can do for me.

I turn towards her and smile.

"No, thanks. I already gave Charles his meds."

That's one good thing about NG tubes. He had a slew of meds: Theophylline, Aldactone, Diuril, KCL. He would never take them all by mouth. They tasted terrible so I just dumped them down the tube. He didn't even wake up.

"I'll be finished here in a few minutes. I don't like to leave her alone when the feeding's running in."

I look back inside the tent and see that Jennifer has fallen asleep. I tell Katie about the time when Angie coded.

Katie shakes her head. She has never been in a code.

"That must have made you feel good," she says when I finish.

I shrug. She died later, anyway. But I guess it was worth it. She got to go home for a little while. She had people who cared about her and gave her some affection: her family, the nurses. But she suffered so much. She went through open heart surgery twice and all the pain that goes with that. She spent months in the ICU. She was intubated and put on a respirator for weeks at a time, getting suctioned, every hour or two, around the clock. How frightening that must be, to have the air sucked out of your lungs like that. Her care cost hundreds of thousands of dollars. Then her graft blew and she died, anyway.

"I don't know," I say. "I know a nurse who works in cardiac

surgery over at 'The Holy' and she's quitting. She can't take it any more. She was telling me how they get these kids in with really bad anomalies: Transposition of the Great Vessels, Tetralogy of Fallot and other ones even worse. They come here from all over the world. They think this is 'The Holy', after all. And they do surgery on them even though they know it's not going to keep them alive for long. Their parents don't know any better. All those kids do is suffer. They're experiments. You know the philosophy at 'The Holy': life at any cost. I know I'm not supposed to say this but the surgeons are making a lot of money on them."

Katie shakes her head.

"I don't know what to think about all this stuff," she says. "Nursing isn't what I thought it was going to be. I always wanted to be a nurse ever since I was a little girl. I just wanted to work with kids. I like kids. But all this, I don't know. I know what you're saying. But what can I do about it? And what should they do with kids with heart problems? Let them die, because they're just going to die later, anyway?"

I sigh and shrug.

"I don't know. I wish I knew the answer. There's got to be one somewhere. I think that we need a change in consciousness. We got to change the way we look at ourselves, at other human beings, at the world. We have to see that everything is connected, that everything is in relation to everything else. We need to get more involved politically."

Katie shakes her head.

"No. I don't want to get involved in politics. I don't understand it. And what does politics have to do with kids with heart defects, anyway?"

I smile.

"I know. But politics doesn't mean elections and conventions, the Democrats and the Republicans. That's what I used to think. Who wants to go around dealing with politicians. They're all phonies. They're like flags. They blow with the wind. The system is a joke. We need a whole new system, with different parties and a new constitution. I saw a magazine article the other day called **The Politics of Cancer** and it really opened my eyes. Like you said: what does politics have to do with cancer? With heart defects? Then when I read it, I realized what it meant. It was about how people get cancer because of chemicals that are dumped in the water by the big corporations or sprayed on the food we eat and in the air we breathe. And how the government allows it to happen. That in reality the government is big business. I've been thinking about where these kids get their defects. I'll bet that's where a lot of them come from. It'd be better if we could prevent these things from happening: by telling people about these kids and getting together in our neighborhoods and pressuring the corporations and the government to change their ways. That's what politics is, getting involved, participating, not voting once in a while."

Katie shakes her head.

"No matter what you say, our form of government is the best in the world."

I shrug. I wish I could believe that. I used to. What has happened to me? I've gotten so far away from who I used to be that I don't even recognize myself.

"And how am I going to do what you say. When you work full-time, you don't have the energy to do much else. I'm so tired when I go home at night. I just want to relax and watch TV or go out once in a while and have a good time."

I nod.

"I know. It's hard. That's why we need a four day, 32 hour week. 40 hours is too much. We need that extra day off to replenish our energy. We'd work better. We wouldn't get sick as much. It's always amazed me that doctors and nurses, people who should know better, don't take better care of themselves. But how can they? They're working all the time. When can they find the time to exercise and relax and cook the right food? We need more time off. I bet that if hospitals offered a 32 hour week with 40 hour pay and full-time benefits, that would end the nursing shortage. In fact, if everyone did it, there'd be more jobs for everyone. That would give us time to do stuff. But of course, they don't want that. We might have time to read, to think, to organize. And that's dangerous. We might find out what's going on in the world."

I notice that the feeding is almost finished. I pick up the potassium and go back inside the tent. I squirt the med into the formula at the bottom of the syringe, then I push it slowly into her with a plunger. Then I flush her NG tube with water, cover Jennifer with a dry towel and zip up the flap. When I finish, Katie is still standing behind me, watching me work.

"Are you involved in politics?" she asks me.

I shrug. I remember what Madeleine told me to do in the circle of stones.

"Not as much as I should be. I used to think that I was being political just by being a nurse, by being a man taking care of children. I thought that I could change things that way. I thought that if men took care of children the way women do, it would change the world radically I still think that but how is it going to happen? There are a few men doing it but not enough. Now I know that I have to do more."

Katie tilts her head.

"How would men taking care of children change the world?"

I look at my watch. It's 0230. I go over to the sink and wash my hands.

"We can talk about it. I'm caught up," I tell her. "I'm going to heat up my food. Take my dinner break. How about you?"

Katie nods.

"I'm not going to eat. I never eat when I work nights. But I'll have a cup of tea with you."

We go into the kitchen where I heat up my spaghetti and meatballs in a saucepan, while Katie boils some water in a kettle. We are so close that I can smell her scent. I find myself taking peeks at her body when she isn't looking. She's so lovely. I feel like putting my arms around her and kissing her and telling her that I love her. Marry me. Have children with me. But I know it would never work. It could never happen in reality. She is too young for me. We would run out of things to talk about after a while. I know that it is not her that I love but her youth. I miss my youth, the lost years. For a moment, I wish that I was 20 years old again. But then I remember what life was like then and I am glad that it is now. I wouldn't want to go through that again. I have to accept my age, as hard as that is. She is young enough to be my daughter. I should treat her like one.

We go out to the Nurses' Station and sit by the carousel.

I eat my dinner for a few minutes, organizing my thoughts.

"The problem is that we, or at least the vast majority of us, were brought up by one person, a female, the mother, right? Not many fathers actually take care of their children: feed them, bathe them, dress them. Some help out, change a diaper now and then, make supper, but it's usually the mom who does the care on a daily basis."

Katie nods.

"I know my dad did help out but it was my mother who was there all the time."

"Especially when you're a baby," I say. "So that your earliest memories are of a female, a woman. She's the one who comes when you cry, when you're hungry. Think about what a powerful figure she must be to a small child. She brings food and love. Or she doesn't. Maybe she's a bad mother. Or maybe she comes but not as fast as you want her to. As you know, a child wants everything now, not later. And no one can be there all the time. So even if you're a good mother, there's going to be resentment. Look at what happens with toddlers when they try to climb up on a chair and you take them off. They get mad at you even though you're doing what's best."

"But they're just little things," says Katie.

"Not to a child. They add up. The problem is that the resentment is directed at one person. Everything is blamed on the mother. It's her fault if anything goes wrong with the child. The mother and therefore women become the universal scapegoat."

"So if men take care of children, what would happen?"

I smile.

"Then they could blame everything on us, too. No. The way it is now, men are like mythological characters to kids. No, seriously. The son in search of the father is one of the major themes in literature. That's because the father isn't there. If the father was there, if he actually took care of children from the beginning, did everything that a mother does, then children would see men differently. They would have to come to terms with both sexes, not blame everything on one. And it would be good for men. When you think about it, the way it is now, most men hardly ever have any contact with other living beings all day. They deal with paper and tools and other materials. I know myself, it's helped me. When I'm really feeling bad, I come in here and pick up a little baby and hold her and rock her and I feel better. A baby can be a comfort."

Katie beams.

"I think it's a great idea. How did you come up with that?"

I smile.

"It came to me after what happened in Ireland, in the circle of stones. That's the message of the story of the swallow."

Katie shakes her head.

"You lost me. Run it past me again."

I recite the story of the swallow to her again.

"It's how I became whole. Let me put it this way. We come from both sexes, right? That's obvious. But we're brought up to be just one sex, to be all man or all woman. That warps us. To be healthy, we need to be both sexes. I guess you could say that I found the woman within me."

Katie stares at me.

"Are you telling me that you're gay? Please don't tell me you're gay."

I laugh.

"No, I'm not gay. I've never been erotically attracted to men."

Katie exhales.

"Thank God. I don't have anything against them but they're very confused people. They don't know the difference between the digestive tract and the reproductive system. I'm sorry. It's just not natural. It's also a moral disorder. Our pastor said once that homosexuality is acted out heresy. It denies that God has a purpose and a plan in creation. Yuck. It's so dirty: all that bacteria. Pardon me for saying this but one man's penis doesn't belong in another man's rectum. And the lesbians. Don't get me started on them. Them and their dildos. They don't want a man, only part of one. Talk about dehumanizing."

I find her amusing. She's so politically incorrect. If the gays heard her talking they'd go into hysterics.

"I know what you're saying but that's not what I was talking about. I meant that I came in touch with the female within me. It's called the anima, in psychological terms, I think."

Katie laughs.

"Do you wish you were a woman? You could have a sex change operation."

I laugh and laugh.

"No, then I'd have to become a lesbian. How weird would that be."

Katie shook her head.

"It's so sad. People who have those operations can't believe in God. You can't change how God made you. These people have themselves mutilated and get these fake sexual organs and go around thinking they're someone they're not. And they think we've got a problem if we don't approve of what they do. So don't tell me I have a male inside of me."

I laugh.

"Jung says you do: the animus. I'd bet any modern psychologist would say so too: animus, in the sense of hostility."

Katie shakes her head.

"It's not hostility. It's the truth. What you're saying sounds like psychobabble to me."

I shrug. Maybe it is.

"I'm not expressing myself properly. I haven't worked it out yet. I was trying to say that I found the child within, in the circle of stones."

"How did you do that?"

I describe what happened as best as I can.

Katie laughs.

"This is so weird, what you're telling me. I understand, I guess. Do you mean like Jesus said, 'You must become like a little child to enter the kingdom of God'"

I shrug.

"I guess. I hadn't thought of it like that."

Katie stares at me for a few moments.

"Do you think you'll ever have children of your own someday?"

I shrug and sigh as I think of the children I almost had. Children that I'll never get to know now. In a way, it's good that I didn't have any children. They might have wanted to imitate me. Do what I did. No way. I wouldn't want them to take the chances I took, to face what I faced. I'd be afraid to let them out of my sight.

I'd be too protective.

"I don't know. It's one of the contradictions of my life. It's still a possibility in my mind but it doesn't look like it's going to happen. It's getting late. I'm 38 now."

Katie shakes her head again.

"But my father was over 40 when I was born. He was a better father to me than he was to my younger brothers and sisters. I think that men who have children when they're older make better fathers. They're more mature."

"Yeah," I say. "You're right. I'd be a much better father now then I would have been when I was in my 20s. I wasn't capable of being a father then. My 20s were a waste. I went into the army when I was 22 and by the time I got my act together I was 30. At the time when most people were settling down and having a family, I was wandering around Europe, having adventures."

Katie smiles.

"There's still time. From the way you are with the kids, you're so affectionate with them, you're so kind and gentle. There's no doubt in my mind that you would be a good husband."

I take a deep breath. It's one of the frustrations of my life. Why haven't I gotten married? I thought that after what happened in Ireland, I would meet the woman of my dreams and get married, but I haven't. I thought I had met her when I met Maggie. But she didn't want me. I could have married Hanna. We went to nursing school together. She loved me. But I didn't want her. She was beautiful. But she was a born-again Christian and I couldn't deal with that. She wanted me to be a good Christian man: to read the Bible with her, to go to church on Sunday, to sing in the choir. She told me that I was secretly a Christian. That I was just being stubborn, stiff necked. She didn't know how wrong she was. She thought she knew me but she didn't.

"Yeah," I say. "I guess. Maybe now I'm finally over Maggie. She threw me off for a long time. I held back on other relationships because of her."

"Is she the woman you were in love with?" Katie asks.

I nod.

"It's a long time ago, now: 9 years. 1975. Two years after I came back from Ireland. I only knew her a little while, a few months. But I loved her. I thought I did anyway. I would have done anything for her, including staying out of her life, if that's what she wanted. Which she did."

Katie's eyes opened wide.

"A few months? And you've carried the torch for her for years?"

I shrug.

"Not anymore. I've over her now. When I met her, I was like a bionic man with the pieces put together with bubblegum and barbed wire. I had come through a bad time in my life, a long bad time. When we met, it seemed as if the nightmare was over. She was the first woman who really took an interest in me. She listened to every thing I said. She was so beautiful. It was almost as if she had me under a spell."

"What do you mean by that? Was she a witch, too?"

I laugh.

"No, not that I know of, anyway. I don't know how to explain it. I guess I mistook interest for love. I told her about what had happened to me in Ireland and she was very interested. She liked my stories, she told me. She encouraged me to write. But then she started to hear what I was saying to her and it freaked her out. That's easy to understand, I guess. I scare people sometimes. I don't mean to. I guess there's this aura of violence around me because of the places I've been and the things I've experienced in my life. I'm no angel. I was no lamb among wolves. I was a wolf, too. I know she told her friends about me. I'm sure that they were telling her to stay away from me. I don't blame them for it. I can imagine how I must have seemed to them: a crazy Vietnam veteran with a drinking problem who had been involved with the IRA."

'The IRA?" says Katie, her eyes wide-open.

Finally, she's heard me. I'd mentioned the IRA before to her but I guess she hadn't been paying attention or thought I was making it up. I think people hear about a tenth of what they say to each other.

"Yeah," I say. "That's who I met in Ballinskelligs, at a farm called Ranchhouse. A man named Patty Byrnes. He was a gun runner and a drug smuggler. He had been in jail and had broken out.

A bad dude."

I hear a monitor beeping in the baby room. I listen to it for a few moments, hoping that it will stop, but it doesn't. I get up to check it out.

Katie fidgets in her seat like a hostage looking for a way out.

"Don't worry," I say as I walk past her towards the baby room. "There's nothing to be afraid of. I didn't do anything wrong."

As I stare at her profile, I wonder if she believes me. I wonder sometimes if people think I'm lying when I tell them about what I did in Vietnam and in Ireland. For all they know, it could be a fiction I've created as a cover for my crimes. I could have been slitting throats and running guns.

It is Charles. His tachycardia button is beeping. By the time I get to him, he's having a fit. His face is wet with tears and his trake is bubbling up secretions like white oil from a well. I have to suction him several times before he sounds clear. I pick him up and hold him against my chest.

"I know man," I whisper, "I'm hurting too." I smell bm but when I take his diaper off, all there is a skid mark. But his belly feels as hard as a coconut. I take a look at his chart. He hasn't had a stool in two days. I put a thermometer up his rectum to see if I can stimulate him but it doesn't work. He only passes gas a few times and squeezes out a little mucus. He is constipated from the iron. He needs the iron because he's anemic but it binds him up. If he doesn't have a stool after he eats I'll give him a suppository. I am in no mood to clean up bm but I don't want to see him get impacted. While I have his diaper off, I notice that his stump sock has bunched down against his knee. When I pull it off, he jerks his stump up and down and around like a garden hose out of control and urinates through the back railing of the crib. I have to laugh at the sight. Then I imagine him years from now, sitting on the sidewalk downtown, jerking that stump up and down and waving a tin cup, and I stop laughing.

There are other reasons I haven't gotten married and had a family. It's not all because of Maggie. I can't make her the scapegoat. I can't put it on her. It's not that hard to get married and have kids. Anyone can do that. Prisoners on death row get married. But

I'm afraid to get married. I'm afraid to bring children into this world. It isn't a safe place for them. Children need that to grow, to live. Everyone needs it. But there is no safe place.

As I rewrap Charles' stump, I think about another reason. I'm afraid that I would have a disabled child. I'm willing to take care of them at Seaside House but I wouldn't want one of my own. Years ago, after I first came home from Vietnam, I got a woman pregnant. Or so she said. It could have been her husband's. She said that they weren't sleeping together but who knows? After her miscarriage, she told me that it was just as well because it had been a monster baby. She might have been saying that just to hurt me. I didn't know about Agent Orange then, but later when I did, my first thought was: that has nothing to do with me. Then I remembered Long Binh, the big base camp where I had been stationed. I don't remember seeing a blade of grass or a tree on the whole base. All I can remember is dust and mud, while all around it was jungle. It had never occurred to me how it had gotten that way until I heard about Agent Orange. It is probably just a false fear, though. A friend of mine, Packy, was definitely exposed to Agent Orange and he has two normal kids. But there's another reason why I don't want to be married and have children, I think, as I pick Charles up and carry him through the baby room. I have to find out what really happened in Ireland and who that woman was.

0300

I pace up and down in front of the Nurses' Station holding Charles against my chest. He's not crying now but he's restless. He frowns and grimaces as he sucks furiously on his pacifier. He raises his knees against me again and again as if he were trying to scale a mountain with a rope. He has a hard climb ahead of him, I think, as I put my hand under his little butt and give him a boost. He's hungry but he doesn't know it. He really doesn't know what food is. Children like him that don't eat by mouth after they're born but get fed by tube instead don't make the connection between food and hunger. They want something but they don't know what it is. They don't understand why we are always putting that that stuff in their mouth.

Charles is a typical BPD kid. Small and skinny and irritable. He is almost 8 months old and he weighs about 12 pounds. He only gets 100 ccs every 4 hours, a little cup of food. But if we give him any more than that, he starts having problems. He's got Cor Pulmonale - an enlarged right heart - from his BPD. He goes into CHF so he gets diuretics like Jennifer does, but his heart problem stems from his lungs, not from a heart defect. He's has a big heart but a small head, a small brain. He's going to be delayed, like so many of these kids are. As I look at him, I see the faces of other children that I walked up and down this unit over the last 3 years. His face is so familiar now: the ebony skin, the tiny nose with an NG tube in it and tape across the cheek, the dark eyes, the Mohawk haircut. I have seen him a hundred times. Sometimes, I think that there are no healthy children, only sick ones and that the whole world is sick and needs a nurse.

I am so tired.

I go over and sit across from Katie once again. I hold Charles by the shoulders and try to stand him on my knee, but his one leg buckles and his stump wiggles and he rocks back and forth and sways from side to side like a drunk walking the line.

"That's a shame about his leg," says Katie.

I study her face. I figure that she wants to hear about the IRA but is afraid to ask. It's safer to talk about the kids. That's how I should do it anyway, I think; that's what it's all about.

I shake my head. Charles lost his leg to a blown IV, in an ER. He had come in respiratory distress, so they had put a line in his foot. Obviously, no one had looked at it for hours because it came out of the vein and infiltrated the tissue, cutting off the circulation to his leg. The staffing must have been bad that night, as usual.

"That poor nurse must feel terrible," I say. "I know I would. I've made my share of mistakes but I've never made one that really hurt anybody. I've been lucky. It's so easy to do."

Katie shakes her head.

"I know. It's scary. When you think about it, there are only 2 of us here for 12 kids, sick kids."

I nod.

"You'd better get used to it. It's not bad here compared to other hospitals. When I worked nights at MHP, I had the whole floor. 30 some patients. On evenings, I had a whole side. I remember one time I was working 3-11 and I had 14 IVs. There were a few Aminophylline and Heparin drips, a few more with double and triple antibiotics. I needed roller skates to get around. I had all the other meds to give too, and there were plenty of them. I had to do all the dressing changes, all the family teaching and write all the notes. I hardly ever got to eat dinner or go to the bathroom. It's too much for one person to do but 2 RNs for 40 patients is considered to be adequate staffing by the hospitals. But if I make a mistake, it's my fault. And plenty of things go wrong, believe me."

Katie shudders.

"No thanks. I don't want to ever work med-surg."

"I know," I say. "If people only knew what happens on those floors. I heard about and saw so many things you wouldn't believe: IVs running dry; blood running in too fast, meds given to the wrong people, the wrong dosage.

I remember one day, I was doing meds for the floor. That's a lot of fun. The meds on day shift are incredible. There are dozens of them. You have to do all the IV meds. There are usually 4 or 5 patients who to get insulin at the same time. It's easy to mix them up. There's usually a lot of Dige to give out. It's brutal. It's easy to make a mistake. This one day, when I went to give this woman her Dige I noticed that the wrong dose was in the drawer. She was supposed to get .125 mgs but they sent up .25 mgs instead. I called pharmacy and they said that their order read .25. I checked the chart and the order read .125 and so did the kardex. Pharmacy had made a mistake somehow and had been sending up .25 mgs. I called the doctor right away and he told me to get a blood level stat. The woman had been sick to her stomach for a couple days and had been acting bizarre. They hadn't known what was wrong with her. Well, she was dige toxic. Three different nurses had double-dosed her for a week."

"What happened?" asks Katie.

"She died," I tell her. "They transferred her to the ICU and she went into complete heart block, coded and died."

Katie puts her hands in front of her mouth.

"Couldn't they put in a pacemaker?"

I shrug.

"I don't know what happened. Maybe they did but it was too late."

"How did those nurses feel about that? Did they get fired?"

I shake my head.

"They denied it, of course. But the evidence was there. Nothing happened. I don't think the family ever found out. But that's what happens when nurses are stressed out. No one should have to give out all those meds. But if you make a mistake, they don't want to hear that you were tired, that you forgot, that you had too much to do. It's not the hospital's fault for staffing like that. It's not society's fault. It's not the government's for allowing it to happen. It's the nurse's fault. If we lived in a just society, a humane society, hospitals would be forced by law to provide safe staffing and decent care or be held for liable criminal negligence. That's what they're trying to do in Nicaragua: the Sandinistas. They believe that health care is a human right, that everyone is entitled to it. And it's free. That's what they're trying to stop in Nicaragua. That's what the Contras attack: health clinics, day care centers, food cooperatives, anything that promises a better life. And the Contras do what the United States tells them to do."

Katie stares at me.

"Are you a Communist or something?"

I laugh.

"No. I'm not a Communist. There are some things I like about Communism: its rejection of greed as a motivating factor for people, that no one should be allowed to get filthy rich, that the community and human needs come first. But there's no sense of spirituality, no moral code to live by. Liberation theology makes more sense to me."

"What do you mean by that?" asks Katie. "I've heard of it. The Church doesn't approve of it, does it?"

"The Pope doesn't," I say. "And most of the Church hierarchy. They don't care about the poor. It's just a front. Look at how they live: in luxury. Liberation Theology is popular in Central and South America where so many people are poor. To me, it's just a return to what Christianity should be about: helping poor people have better lives. Justice. Peace on Earth. Why should a few people have so much and so many have so little? People aren't poor because God wants them to be that way. And there's nothing noble about suffering. You can see how these kids suffer here. They don't have to be this way."

Katie shakes her head.

"You have such a distorted view of the Church. I don't think you know the Church at all. I think you hate what you think the Church is, not what it actually is."

I shrug. Maybe she's right. I don't know. I don't care. As far as I'm concerned the Church is obsolete and irrelevant.

I look at Charles' face. He has the intense concentrated look of a sprinter coming down the stretch, his nostrils flaring, his throat tugging, his chest heaving. I lay him across my lap like he's a wayward child getting a spanking and listen to his lungs. They sound like a bowl of Rice Crispies: snap, crackle and pop. I cup my hands and pound on his back like a drummer beating on bongos. He closes his eyes to the music and goes back to sleep. It always amazes me that kids actually enjoy chest PT. I couldn't sleep with someone pounding on my back but they do. I look at the clock on the wall. I know what his problem is: He's hungry and full at the same time. That makes him upset so he wheezes. He'll be an asthmatic like Michael if he grows up. I look at his trake. It's only bubbling a little now, but one of these days, it'll plug, the way he acts.

When I finish his chest PT, I listen to his lungs; they're almost clear. A little coarse. He breathes easier now. But he's still restless. He cries and arches as if he were about to dive backward into a pool.

Katie clears her throat.

"So what were you saying about the IRA? Were you really involved with them? They don't believe in liberation theology, do they?"

I smile and shake my head as I think about how I'm going to tell her about Ballinskelligs and Ranchhouse and what happened there. From what she has told me, she has led a sheltered life. Her father is a private contractor; her mother, a housewife. She has three brothers and three sisters, all older than she is. She went to Catholic grade school, then high school at Maria Goretti; from there, she went to nursing school at Saint Agnes. She still lives at home. She has never been out of the country. The farthest she's been from home was to Washington D. C. on a high school field trip. People like Patty Byrnes and Mick Casey would seem like characters from a movie to her.

"Yeah, I was. And no, they don't believe in Liberation Theology. Do you really want to hear about it?"

Katie smiles.

"Yeah. I never knew anyone who's known those kind of people before."

I laugh.

"There are people just like them everywhere. They're no different than anyone else. I met them at an IRA safe house when I was in Ballinskilligs. It was there that all those things happened in the circle of stones, that I was telling you about."

I watch her take that in.

"What," she says slowly, "do you mean by a safe house?"

I laugh.

"A hideout," I say. Before I tell her about what happened there, I try to make sure that I express myself properly. I have gotten in trouble over this before with people.

"I support what the IRA is trying to do in Northern Ireland. The IRA are the Irish Viet Cong and the British are us. The British aren't over there protecting anybody. They're the problem. The first step for peace over there is for the British to get out of Ireland. It's an 800 year war of imperialism. There's no question that the Catholics there are oppressed. They're treated as badly as the black people in South Africa are. I agreed with the IRA's politics but I had problem with their methods, with some of their decisions. I can understand why they fight. I can understand their frustration and their anger and their hatred. I've felt the same way myself."

I tell her what happened between Patty and me. I don't bring it up again about how I found the strength to face him: by becoming like a little girl and a mother. I don't understand it myself. I just know that's what it was.

When I finish, Katie shows me her arm.

"I got goose pimples from what you said."

I nod my head a few times.

"I know. It was scary. It's a good thing that Madeleine was there."

Katie shakes her head.

"What were you doing there?"

I take a deep breath. It is always so difficult to explain the turmoil I was in at that time. How can I put it in words she'll understand?

"They were bad times," I tell her. "I had this idea that I would find there what I needed. And I did. I was sick. Hurt. Sickness often sends you in a direction that you wouldn't go otherwise. I hadn't thought about traveling to Europe or going to Ireland. Getting knifed changed that."

Katie leans towards me.

"You got knifed?"

I'm surprised that she doesn't know about it. I thought that it was common knowledge on the unit, part of the background on me.

"I got knifed in the back, twice, by two junkies, over in Germantown. I was living over there at the time."

Her eyes widen and a look of pain comes across her face. She reaches out and touches me on the arm.

"How horrible. What happened?"

I don't know why I brought it up. I don't want to talk about the knifing. I've told that story so many times and I've thought about it so much that I'm sick of it. But I find myself telling her about it anyway. I can't help myself. It's like a compulsion. It was the most traumatic experience of my life, but in a certain sense, it made me a better person.

"I'll tell you about it. But first let me say that some good came out of it. It made me realize that I had to live now, today, not tomorrow. I knew, knew, that I could die at any moment. That recognition made me appreciate life, how fragile it is, how vulnerable we are."

I pinch up the skin on my arm.

"Think about it. This is all that keeps our life blood inside. It's not armor. A knife goes through it easily. And it hurts. It made me identify with people who are victims, who have had violence done to them. I think it's one reason I can relate so well to these kids. I too have experienced violence and I don't like it. I think that to have another person kill you is the worst way to die."

Katie interrupts me.

"Why is that? Why is it worse than any other way?"

I sigh.

"There's something especially horrible and disgusting about another person doing that to you. If I had died that night, that would have been my last memory in life: another person killing me."

I shake my head.

"It happened in December, a few days before Christmas. That was a great Christmas present. 1971. It was about nine o'clock at night. I was walking down the street where I lived, Walnut Lane...

I stop for a moment as it hits me: Walnut Lane. That's the same street where I had that car accident as a young boy. Strange. That place has bad karma or something for me.

I continue.

"When I saw these two guys across the street. They were sitting on the steps of a church. One of the guys looked over and saw me. Then he got up and ran across the street towards me. It happened so fast. I was vulnerable at the time. I was trying so hard to get my life together. I was home from Vietnam. I thought I was safe. I wasn't ready for it. Anyway, he asked me for a quarter so I gave him one. Then he asked me for a dollar. I should have said, 'that's enough. I don't have anymore.' But instead I put my hand in my pocket and pulled out some bills. While I was doing that, he grabbed me around the neck and put a knife to my throat. 'Give me all your money,' he said. 'We've been smoking skag all day and we want some more.'

I stop talking and take a deep breath. It doesn't bother me as much as it did to talk about it but it still upsets me. I can feel the fear go through my body again as it did that night.

"I remember thinking, this is it. I'm going to die right here, right now, not later, now. By this time, his buddy, a real little guy, smaller than me, was yelling at me, telling me to empty my pockets. I took my money and threw it into the air, hoping, I guess, that they would go after the money and let me loose. I didn't know what I was doing, really. I was in a panic. But it only made them mad. The little guy picked up my money, 18 bucks was all I had, and punched me in the face. Then they dragged me over behind a hedge and pushed me down to the ground. I heard the little guy shout, 'stab the honky.' I put my arms around my head and curled into a ball. Out of the corner of my eye, I saw the guy raise the knife over his head and stab me with it, twice, in the back, just below the shoulder blade. I saw him and I felt it thump into my back. On some level, I knew what was happening but on another level, I didn't. After he did it, they ran down the street. As soon as they did, I got up and ran the other way, towards my apartment. I remember turning around and looking at the spot where it happened and I swear I saw myself laying there, dead, as if I were my ghost."

Katie moans and grimaces.

"How awful. What did you do?"

"I knew a guy who lived downstairs from me. We worked at the Employment Office together. I was working as an employment counselor for the state at the time. I rang his bell and he let me into his apartment."

I laugh.

"He was there with a friend. Those poor guys. He asked me what was the matter. I told him that I had been mugged. 'They must have kicked me in the back.' I said to him. I knew that I had been knifed. I guess I just couldn't believe it. I took off my jacket. I had been wearing a navy pea coat. It probably saved my life because it was so thick. When these two guys looked at my back, they started shouting, 'Oh my God! Oh my God! Look at the blood.' I remember putting my hand back there and coming away with blood on my fingers. But I still didn't believe it. I went into the bathroom and took off my shirt and looked at my wounds in the mirror. The blood was just oozing out of my back. It was like I had to see it to believe it. Then they took me to the hospital and they patched up in the Emergency Room. The doctor told me how lucky I was: the knife hit only muscle. Lucky? I guess."

I snort.

"While I was on the table, the cops came in. The hospital had called them. There were two of them, one white and one black.

They asked me what happened and I told them. The black cop didn't believe me."

"Were the guys who knifed you black?" Katie asks me.

I nod.

"Yeah. But that doesn't matter. I'm not stupid. I hated those two punks. I used to fantasize about killing them but I'm not going to blame all black people for what two guys did. But they were black and I said so. Well, the black cop, says he thinks that maybe the truth was I had been in a fight and that I hadn't been mugged. I told him again what happened. But he kept insinuating that I was lying. I mean, I wasn't in a very good mood by that time. I was hurting. It hadn't hurt when it happened but by then it did. So I got mad. I showed him my hands and shouted at him, 'Look at them, there are no marks on them. I wasn't fighting.' I let loose some thunder words on him. So he got mad and started yelling at me, telling me that if I didn't watch my mouth, I'd get locked up. I couldn't believe it. I get knifed and I'm going to be the one who goes to jail. He says to me that if it was true what I said, then why didn't I call the police right away. 'I was shook up,' I said, 'I just wanted to get to the hospital. And you want to know why I didn't call the police? Just look at the way you're treating me.'"

The memory of that angers me so much that I have to stop talking. It made me feel like I was a character in a novel by Kafka.

"So what happened?" Katie asks after a few moments.

I shake my head.

"Nothing. They finally decided that I was telling the truth and took me down to the 39th District over on Hunting Park Avenue and had me look through some mug shots. But I couldn't remember what they looked like. It was dark. It happened so fast. And my back was hurting so bad, I just wanted to get out of there and go home. They never caught the guys, of course."

"You didn't stay in the hospital?" Katie asks.

I shake my head.

"No. I didn't want to stay there. I was afraid that maybe those two guys would find me and finish the job. That's happened before. I've read about it in the paper. I just wanted to be someplace safe. I went home to my parents and stayed there for a while. It took me a couple weeks before I could go back to my apartment and go past the scene of the crime. But I made myself do it. A couple of weeks later, I came out of Smoky Joe's bar up near Penn when this guy comes up behind me and asks for money. When I heard that, I snapped out. I jumped around into an attack crouch and shouted at him, 'Come on! Come on! I'm gonna kill ya! ' He backed off and ran down the street sideways pleading with me not to hurt him. He was probably just a harmless panhandler. Thank God, he didn't come after me, if he had, I would have beaten him to death. That's when I knew I had to get out of the country."

I look over at Katie who's staring at the floor.

"Katie, please don't be afraid of me. I was like a wounded animal who'll claw you if you come too close. I'm not in to hurting people. That was a long time ago. I'm a different person now."

Katie looks at me with tears in her eyes.

"I'm not afraid of you. I'd have acted the same way if it had been me."

Charles is crying and wiggling in my hands like a fish out of water. I look at the clock on the wall. It's 0330. I should try to feed him now.

"So, anyway," I say, "I wound up in Ireland, in Ballinskelligs. I had this crazy idea that I would be safe there. It made me realize that there is no safe place."

I take Charles back to his crib and put him in it. I decide not to even try to feed him by mouth. He won't take it, I can see that. He's got himself into a frenzy. I'll give it to him NG. I measure his formula in a baby bottle and pour it into his syringe. Then I check the tube for placement. I connect his feeding to the NG tube and run it slowly into him. He continues to arch and cry so I pat him on the back. He raises his knees to his stomach and grunts. I hear a squirting sound then I smell stool. Charles quiets down after a minute; he stops frowning and grimacing and almost smiles. As soon as the feeding finishes, I put a chux under Charles and turn him on his back. I take off his diaper and look at the stool. I breathe through my mouth so I won't gag. As I wipe his backside, Charles smiles. All he needed was a good bm. I put another diaper on him, bundle him back up and put him on his belly. He's content now.

Katie comes out of the treatment room with meds for Willie. I stand across the crib from her and watch her give Willie his Theophylline through his gastrostomy tube. This kid is worse off than Charles. He has both his legs but only half a gut. He has a trake, a gastrostomy, and a colostomy: a triple whammy. He had NEC (Necrotizing Enterocolitis) right after he was born. He got that because he was a tiny preemie who had severe BPD. The theory being that if the heart and brains are not getting enough oxygen, the body shuts down the flow of blood to the gut in favor of the more vital organs. If it goes on too long, the gut becomes necrotic. Since the food can't be absorbed there, he has a colostomy to bypass the dead area.

I watch Katie as she undresses Willie. She curses when she sees that his colostomy bag has come off. There's diarrhea all over him. The stench in the room in nauseating. I help her clean him up and put on a new colostomy bag. Willie cries the whole time we do it and has to be suctioned several times. As I look at his miserable face, I feel a flash of hatred for him. He's so pathetic. I feel like plugging up his airway and sending him to his death, putting him out of his misery. But I know I can't do that. I've felt this way before. At first, I thought that I was going crazy, that I was a sadistic person, a monster. But now I understand where it comes from. The sight of such suffering angers me so much at times that I just want to see it end. I think that's why nurses sometimes do crazy things like taking people off of respirators and letting them die. But I'm not crazy. It's not my place to decide when someone is to die. I'm not going to do anything that would cause me to lose my license, my ability to make a living. And I'm not going to jail for anybody.

"This poor kid," I say. "Do you think he has enough tubes? He has a tube to breathe and a tube to eat. Maybe we can put one in his head and drain out his brains while we're at it."

We laugh.

"If people saw us now," says Katie, "they'd be horrified. But we have to laugh, sometimes. It breaks the tension."

"Yeah," I say as Katie hooks up the feeding to the gastrostomy tube. "We have to. We see some terrible things here."

After we're done, we sit in the rocking chairs while Willie

gets fed.

"That kid is so messed up," I say. "He would have been better off if he had never been born."

Katie shrugs.

"Well, he was. So we have to make his life as good as possible."

"Yeah," I say. "Do you think maybe he should have been aborted?"

"No!" says Katie. "How can you say that? What do you mean? If a child's not going to be normal, he shouldn't be allowed to live?"

I thought she would feel that way. Not many Catholics approve of abortions. They can't. They believe that life comes from God.

"No, I'm not saying that. I'm just saying that, sometimes, abortion is necessary. It seems to me that this kid would have been better off if he had been aborted."

"I don't agree," say Katie, angry now. "Abortion is murder. I don't understand you. You spend your life resuscitating children, bringing them back to life and taking care of them. And you think it's okay to kill them in the womb? You took a Maternal and Child Development course in nursing school, didn't you? Are you trying to tell me that an embryo or a fetus isn't human life? If it isn't, what is it? A fish?"

She has a point. I wonder at myself sometimes. I feel like a walking contradiction. Do I really believe in what I say? Or is it someone else speaking? Am I really the person I think I am? If not, who am I?

"You should at least be honest," says Katie. "And admit that what you're doing is supporting the taking of human life, an innocent human life: murder."

"Not everybody thinks that," I say, thinking about Marie and her abortion. We barely knew each other. It was my fault she got pregnant. All she really wanted was affection, to cuddle and kiss but I had to have sex. She didn't want sex. She didn't want a child. What a disaster that relationship was. I shudder as I remember the way we fought after it. One night in a drunken rage, I hit her a couple of times. She said that she didn't want a baby of mine because I wasn't even a person. I was an ogre. That hurt me as much as that knife did. So what did I do? I proved that she was right and acted like a monster. Didn't really hurt her. But that's no consolation. She forgave me later but I still feel guilty about it. How do you get rid of guilt? I wish I knew. Any woman who found out I did that would want no part of me and justifiably so. I told Maggie about it and that was the end of that relationship. She believed as most women do that when a man hits a woman he'll do it again. Not true in my case. But who would trust me?

"I had a baby of mine aborted once. Twice, maybe." I tell her. "One miscarriage and one abortion. As you know, a woman's body will spontaneously abort a child. Is a miscarriage murder, too?"

Katie stares at me for a few moments. She doesn't want to open up that can of worms. But I do.

"That's the problem with calling abortion murder and making it illegal again. Should women have to go to court whenever they have a miscarriage and prove that it wasn't an abortion? Think about that. Or if they did have an abortion should they go on trial for murder?"

"No." says Katie. "Only the abortionists. Like it used to be. The women would not be punished."

"Oh, no?" I say. "They would if the Church had its way. The Church hates sex. It hates women. It has power over people. It has great influence."

Katie shakes her head. She doesn't want to hear that.

"You're wrong. The Church doesn't hate women. The Blessed Mother is a woman and she's the greatest saint. Many women are saints. One of my great aunts was a nun and she was the principal of a school, long before any woman in the world was. The Church doesn't hate sex, either. It made marriage a sacrament. That's why we take vows. Sex is sacred. Have you forgotten your catechism?"

I don't know what to say about that. My catechism? She can't be serious. The Baltimore Catechism: that children's book. Who made me? God made me. What nonsense. My parents made me.

"How did you feel about it?" she asks me. "Having your child aborted?"

I shrug and shake my head.

"I was upset. I felt irresponsible. Marie had the abortion before I even knew she was pregnant. I really don't know what I would have done if she had told me beforehand. Maybe I would have wanted her not to do it. But it wasn't my decision. It was hers. It was her body. It was a painful experience: for her, especially. She felt awful about it. She cried. She suffered over it. It's not that she was a cold-hearted person. She felt that she had to do it. Neither one of us was capable of being a parent at the time, at least I wasn't. I had no idea of how to bring up a child, what to teach him about what was right or wrong. I really don't know what's right or what's wrong about so many things. It was an accident. We weren't planning on having children. But unfortunately, neither one of us knew much about birth control. That's how a lot of kids are born: by people who are not in control of their sexuality, who have no idea really about what sex is or how to do it right, how to treat each other."

It sure had an effect on me. I didn't want to go through that guilt again. I couldn't bear the thought of being responsible for another dead child. I stopped having sex for years because of it. I don't know if that makes me impotent or not. But I didn't want sex. Not without love.

"That may be true what you say about sex," says Katie. "But I still believe that abortion is wrong."

"It's not good for women," I admit. "To their uterus. In an better world where women were in control of their bodies, it might not be as necessary. Or if we lived in a world that cared about women and children. I can't tell someone else what to do. It's their choice, not mine."

Katie shakes her head as if she were refusing to let what I'm saying into her brain.

"I couldn't do it," she says. "I could not choose to kill my baby. On Pro-life Sunday, our pastor told us that Christians cannot choose abortion because of the Incarnation. Jesus was a person before he was conceived, the second person of the Blessed Trinity. Because of that event, we become persons the moment we are conceived. A person is a being capable of knowing and loving and choosing. Capable. Even if not at a particular time like some of these children here: the babies and Andrea and Billie. Once a person always a person. We're persons from conception into eternity. The word person, or persona, used to mean an actor's mask but it came to mean the union of the human and divine in Jesus. Now, it also means the union of the human and divine in each of us. God became man so that man can become God."

I don't know what to make of what she said. An actor's mask? Man becoming God? Where did she get that?

"Maybe it's wrong to base abortion on individual choice," I concede. "It sounds so selfish and I can relate to what you said about us being persons. But what about him? Look at him. He's so messed up. What kind of life is he going to have?"

Katie smiles, a little.

"I know what you're saying. I know you mean well. He has a terrible life but you never know what's going to happen. One of my brothers cried all the time when he was a baby. My parents thought he was going to have so many problems. They took him to one doctor after another. They couldn't find anything wrong with him. Once he became a toddler, he was all right. There's nothing wrong with him now, other than being a pest. No matter what you say, I can't agree with abortion. Life begins at conception."

"That's because you were brought up a Catholic," I say. "Not everybody thinks that way. Some people believe that life begins at birth or at 6 months when the fetus is viable. Can't you have an open mind to other people's beliefs? Abortion should be a minor issue, just one small part of family health care. But they make it into this big deal."

Katie stares at me for a few moments with a look of disgust on her face as if I were a child molester shrugging off his crime.

"A minor issue?" She whispers. "Killing a baby is a minor issue? Wrong is wrong. It' s not a matter of belief. It isn't a philosophical issue, part of an abstract argument. It's a life and death issue."

I view her as a fanatic and continue with my point. She's thinking with her emotions not with her mind.

"The Church wants to divert attention away from the larger issues like why are so many children being born so sick and so small and why are so many women having children that they can't take care of and don't want? If kids aren't wanted, they're often mistreated."

I'm referring to Raheem and she knows it. After he was discharged, no one saw him or heard anything about him for months.

His mother didn't bring him in for follow up care and could not be reached by phone. She told us when she took him home that she wanted to cut the ties between us and him. She was his mother, she said, not the nurses, and he had to learn that. Which made sense, to some extent. But it was unfair to him to cut him off from us so completely. We had brought him up. We were worried about him. He was better when he left here but he still had special needs. He had bad lungs. He had problems talking and chewing. He had tracheomalacia. He had a piece of his rib bone in his throat. When they took out his trake, his trachea collapsed and closed off his airway, so they had to insert in a piece of bone from his rib to keep it open, before they could take the trake out. He was still vomiting a lot when he left, not as much as he used to, but a couple times a day. He had been through so much. He was very sensitive. He had more scars on his body than a combat veteran. His mom thought that he was a wimp. She didn't know how brave he was, how much he had gone through. She hadn't wanted him. She never bonded with him. She didn't even know him. The whole time he was in the hospital, she visited him maybe 6 or 7 times, in over 3 years. Raheem didn't know who she was when she came into visit. He didn't cry when she left. It makes me sick to think about what happened to him.

One day, Kevin, the play therapist, saw him going into a special school in North Philly. He told me about it and we went over to see him. He recognized us right away and was glad to see us. He jumped right up into my arms. He was thin when he left us but he had lost weight since then. He looked like a child from Biafra. He had forgotten most of his signs and his voice was still only a growl. His teachers told us that he had just started there a few days before. His mother dropped him off in the morning and picked him up in the evening. They said that since he'd been there, all he'd wanted to do was eat. When I examined him, I noticed that he had little sores all over his body that looked like cigarette burns. Both of us felt like taking him back to Seaside House with us but we knew we couldn't do that. When we got back to Seaside House, we told Marianne, his primary nurse and the social worker about what we saw and they contacted the Welfare Department. We heard nothing for over a week. Then we learned that Raheem had been admitted to 'The

Holy'. His mother had taken him in because she said he had been having trouble breathing. When they asked her how long that had been going on, she said 'for a couple days.' She had brought him to the ER the day before, but when she saw how crowded it was, she had taken him back home. When they examined him in the ER, they found that he had a piece of food stuck in his throat. They also saw the scars on his body and how thin he was, so they admitted him. He was placed in the custody of the Welfare Department. When we found out that he was in 'The Holy,' we asked that he be sent back here. But Seaside House refused to take him back. They didn't want to have to deal with his mom. I got in trouble over that. I was so mad. I thought it was a disgrace and said so. That was another reason why I have to leave here.

Katie shakes her head.

"She's crazy: Raheem's mom."

"Yeah," I say. "She was wrong to do what she did but I'm not going to put all the blame on her. I am not going to dump on the most maligned people in our society, black women on welfare; they have enough people dumping on them already. How about the father? No one even mentions him. They don't even know where he is. Raheem's mom is as much a victim as Raheem is. She is one of life's lost people. She is overwhelmed by her life. She couldn't take care of Raheem. She should have never had him. The fault is in the way we live, in the system."

"Do you think he should have been aborted?" Katie asks me.

I sigh.

"I don't know. He's a person now. All I'm saying is, that if we're not going to give all of the children that are conceived good prenatal care and make sure that they get enough food to eat and a nice house to live in after they're born, then maybe they should be aborted."

"That's absurd," says Katie.

"I know," I say, after a few moments. "I'm just frustrated. But the way it is now, we do a lousy job. If these kids got enough therapy, enough follow up care, they could develop. But it's not that way. We spend millions of dollars to keep these kids alive. Then when they survive, they're on their own. Well, almost. There are some services but they're only a band aid and under Ronnie Raygun, it's getting smaller and smaller. He doesn't care about the family or health care. None of the people in power do. All they care about is money. They don't care about these kids. Nobody does, except us."

Katie turns and faces me.

"Can I ask you something?"

I nod.

"I hope you don't take this the wrong way," she says, "But why do you still live here, in this country, if you hate it so much?"

I wipe my face with my hand.

"I don't hate the country. I don't even hate the people in power. They're too pathetic. No, let me take that back. I do hate them. They know what they're doing. They know they're hurting people and they do it anyway. They don't care. It's a failure to evolve. Sure, they're smart; there's nothing wrong with their brains. It's their feelings, their emotions that are stunted. They can't see other people in themselves. I hate the system. I hate the belief that profit is more important than people. And this is where I grew up, where my family has lived for generations. Why should I leave because of them? I'd live in Ireland if I could, but I can't, not now, anyway. We're in the belly of the beast here. This is where the change has to come if we're to live in a better world."

"What about Russia?" says Katie. "Doesn't Russia cause a lot of problems? You can't blame everything on the United States. It seems to me that everybody has the same problems."

I shake my head.

"Yeah, in a certain sense, that's true. But it's in the United States where the lie is most deeply rooted."

"What lie?"

"The lie that our way of life is the best way, the only way, that people can't be happy unless they have a lot of money and a lot of things: TVs, VCRs, a big house, big cars...."

Before I can finish my list, we hear the alarm going off in the Toddlers' Room and it doesn't stop, so we jump from our chairs and run in there, fearing the worst.

0400

We stand by Billie's bed and watch him seize. It's a awful sight. His head is twisted to one side and straining upward like a baby bird's coming out of a shell. His face is twitching and grimacing with pain. His shoulder is jerking up and down as if he's trying to pull his hand from a trap. His eyes dart in his head like a paranoid's looking for an ambush and foam flows from his mouth; like the wet beard of an old man, it covers his face and drips down his chin.

Katie looks at me.

"What should we do?"

I go over and put my hand on Billie's chest and lift his head off his knees. I put my other hand on his back and hold him that way for a few moments as if I'm sending him some energy but I'm not. This is absurd, I think, the suffering has to stop sometime.

"There's nothing more we can do. The bed's padded so he can't hurt himself. We'll have to let it run its course. If it keeps up, we'll call the doctor."

"But he's almost blue," says Katie, her voice shaking. She reaches up for the oral airway over his bed.

"Don't bother," I say. "You won't be able to get it in. His teeth are clenched. Can't you hear them grinding?"

It is over in less than a minute. We take his vital signs. He's breathing like a runner after a marathon, but his heart's only a little tachy and his blood pressure is 110/60. I start to feel a little anxious. I flash a light at his pupils. The left one responds slightly but the right remains fixed and dilated. This is nothing new. Katie wipes his face with a wet cloth. I record the data on his seizure flow sheet. It's the third one he's had today. I think about calling the doctor, but I know that he's not going to do anything now. They just increased his seizure meds: his Tegretol and his Phenobarb. There's nothing more they can do. He's had his brain tumor, a glioma, resected twice; he's had all the chemo and radiation that is possible. They even tried an experimental drug from France. But nothing has worked. The tumor came back.

I look at his face and then at the picture by his bedside. He had a nice, thin face, long brown hair and the soft eyes of a sensitive kid.

Now he is almost bald from the chemo and has a burn on his head from radiation. His face is bloated, his eyes puffy and his cheeks fiery red from the steroids. If the disease doesn't kill you, the cure will. Years from now, I hope, those therapies will be considered as primitive as bloodletting is today.

"What do you think?" asks Katie. "His blood pressure at 2 o'clock was 100/70. His pulse pressure is widening."

"It might be," I say. "Take his vital signs again in 15 minutes."

"Okay, Charge Nurse," she says, then whispers, "I'm glad that's over. I was afraid he was going to code."

I shake my head.

"Nah," I say. "I wasn't."

But I'm worried just the same. He doesn't look good. With his poor color and his bloated face, he looks like a body just dragged out of the water.

I ask her if his Broviac is patent. Billie has a central line. He's had so many IV's put in over the last couple years that he has no surface veins left, so they had to put one into his subclavian vein, a deep one that goes directly into the heart.

Katie nods.

"I just flushed it at 2."

"Okay," I say. "You have a line in. You'll just have to watch him. If you called the doctor that's what he would tell you to do."

"Why don't you do some of that therapeutic touch on him," she asks me as we turn him on his other side and put pillows behind his back and between his legs. I put a towel next to his face to catch the drool.

I know she wants me to heal him. Who does she think I am? Jesus Christ? I can't heal this kid. He's as good as dead. But I could end his suffering. For a moment, I am tempted. If I really tried, I could send him enough energy to kill him. It wouldn't be that hard. I have the power, I know it. All I'd have to do is to channel all the anger and hate I have inside of me and send it to him and it would kill him. Is that what I want to do? Then I remember what that woman said to me in Ballinskelligs. I don't want to be responsible for anyone's death. I don't want his last memory of life being another person killing him.

I shake my head.

"Why not?"

I stroke his forehead with my fingers and look into his eyes. He doesn't seem to be aware that I'm even there. I wish I knew what he was thinking if he was thinking at all, at this point. Maybe he's like Eugene. Maybe he wants to die in his mother's arms or maybe he'd just like to get it over with and be out of his misery. I would if I were him. But I'm not him.

"Death is a reality", I say. "It's his time. Let nature take it's course. Death is natural."

"But how about Andrea," says Katie. "It didn't hurt her. She's still sleeping. She looks so peaceful."

I shrug.

"She's different. She's going the other way from Billie."

We go back out to the Nurses' Station and sit down.

I am so tired.

It's the last watch of the night.

Katie gives me a resentful look.

"There's something cold and hard about you," she says. 'Death doesn't seem to bother you."

I don't say anything for a few moments. She's right. There is a part of me that is cold and hard.

"It's a defense mechanism," I say to her. "I've seen a lot of people die over the years."

I tell her about my father.

"He died of cancer 10 years ago this month from a brain tumor that had metastasized all through his body. He suffered so much! We brought him home to die. I helped my mom take care of him and so did my brother, Richie. But mom did most of his care. She took a leave of absence from her job at the bank to take care of him. She used to be up all night with him. I remember one night, I woke up and saw her in her white nightgown. In the darkness, she looked like an angel of light."

"Was this before you became a nurse?"

"Yeah," I say. "It was in 1974. He died a few months after I came back from Ireland. I came home in time to make peace with him, to show I forgave him for what he did."

"Forgive him for what?"

"For bringing me up believing in war and in this country. For not believing me when I told him what was going on in Vietnam. And I asked him to forgive me for leaving him when he was sick to go to Ireland."

"Did his sickness have anything to do with your becoming a nurse?"

I lean back in the chair and think for a moment. There were a lot of reasons why I became a nurse, but it started when that woman came to me again and told me that was what she wanted me to do. So I did.

"Maybe. But when my father died I didn't know what I was doing. I was just trying to hold on at that point. It was a tough time. When I came home from Ireland, I was broke. Penniless, literally. I only owned two pair of pants and they had grape stains all over them."

"Grape stains? From what?"

I have to smile.

"The vendange. After I left that farm in Ireland that I was telling you about, I had to go to Luxembourg to get my flight back here. I was going to go to London but I changed my mind and went to France instead and picked grapes for a few weeks."

Katie laughs.

"Picked grapes? You're kidding me."

I shake my head.

"No, I'm not. When I went to France, I didn't have much money. I didn't even have a map. When I got on the ferry at Rosslare to go to La Havre, I had no idea how I was going to get to the vineyards. It was like landing in New York and trying to get to Chicago. I couldn't speak French. I took it in high school, but I didn't learn much."

I muse at the memory. I knew I would be all right. After what had happened in Ireland, I had the sense that I was protected. I had done what that woman wanted me to do and she was looking after me.

"How did you get there?" asked Katie.

I laugh.

"I was walking around the ferry, when I noticed a young guy

wearing an US Army jungle fatigue shirt with a Big Red One patch on his shoulder. So I went over to him and asked if he had been in Vietnam. He said no. Here, he was an Irish kid, maybe 19 years old. He had bought the shirt in a shop in Dublin. Apparently, they sold them there. I don't know where they got them. I asked him where he was going. He said 'to France to pick grapes'. I asked him if he spoke French. He did, enough, anyway. So I joined up with him and we went together. We got the train at La Havre and went to Paris for a few days."

I laugh.

"His name was Martin. We went one night to the Pigalle in Paris, the red light district. He wanted me to go with him to a house of ill repute. I talked him out of it. It's not a good thing for a young man to do, I told him."

"It's not good for women, either," says Katie.

I nod my head.

"For sure. So anyway, they had these employment centers there and we got sent to a farm near Lyon. We picked Beaujolais wine grapes. It was hard work and I wouldn't want to do it all the time but it was a great experience."

I smile as I remember those days.

"I slept in a barn with a dozen people. Men and women slept in the same place. We had an outhouse for a bathroom and we washed ourselves with cold water from a bucket. We worked from dawn to dusk every day except Sunday. For the first time in my life, I felt that I was doing real work - God's work - working in the vineyards. I saw a lot of beautiful sunrises and sunsets. We ate well. We had bread and cheese and chocolate and coffee for breakfast. We worked until noon, cutting the grapes from the vines with a small knife. I got a lot of cuts on my fingers doing that. They gave us a huge lunch of meat and salad and bread and cheese and wine: all the fresh wine you could drink. It was the best wine I had ever tasted. We worked all afternoon until the sun went down, then ate a huge supper with more wine. After that, the only thing to do was sleep. It was good for me, though. The food and the hard work made me strong."

Katie smiles.

"It sounds like fun."

I laugh.

"Yeah. In a way. But by the time I got home, I had no clothes. I had no shoes. No money. I was literally down to my last dollar when I got back to Philly. I came home in a pair of worn-out sandals. I had to wear a pair of my dead uncle's shoes to my father's funeral."

Katie shakes her head.

"What did you do?"

I shrug.

"I finally got a job with the Welfare Department as a case worker. They were the only ones that would give me a job. It was either go on welfare or work for the Welfare Department. I did that for a couple of years, until I couldn't take it no more. After that I had a couple different jobs before I finally started nursing school. I worked for a while as a security guard. I even worked as a laborer in a cemetery, cutting grass and shoveling dirt onto dead people. The same job one of my great-grandfathers did after he came over from Ireland."

Katie smiles, then looks at her watch.

"I hate to break up this conversation but I have to take his vital signs again."

I sit at the Nurses' Station and think about those days. I felt that I was surrounded by death. I had one foot in the grave myself. But I pulled it out. With the help of that woman.

Katie stands in the doorway of the Toddlers' Room.

"His blood pressure is 120/50 and his heart rate is 70."

"He's been down that low before," I say. 'Take it again in another 15 minutes. If it drops anymore, we'll call the doc."

Katie sits down again.

"I hope he's all right. I wouldn't want to code him. He's suffered so much."

I nod.

"What would be the point? All we would be doing would be prolonging the dying process."

"We have to. though," says Katie. "He's a full code."

I sigh.

"Yeah. We could always do a slow code. I did that once."

"What do you mean?" asks Katie.

I shrug.

"We stand by his bedside for a few minutes, deciding whether he's still breathing or not, then we talk about it for a few more minutes, whether we should call the doctor and have him decide, since he's the authority around here and we're only nurses; what do we know? Then we could walk slowly out and call the code. When we draw up the bicarb and the epi, we take our time, so we don't make a mistake with the dosage. Maybe by that time he'll be dead."

Katie stares at me.

"Did you actually do that?"

I nod.

"Yeah. An old woman with cancer. It had metastasized all over her body. She used to just writhe in bed with pain. Every time I gave her a needle, she screamed for ten minutes, until the drug took effect. It broke my heart. One day, I went in and I saw that she had stopped breathing. I called the code but I did it slow enough to let her die."

"How could you do that? How could you take that kind of responsibility? Weren't you playing God?"

I shake my head.

"No. The hospital was playing God, the doctors. The only thing that was keeping her alive was the IV and the medications. She would have died long before. All I did was let nature take its course. She was long dead, already, Katie. I just let her stay that way."

Katie shakes her head.

"I couldn't do that. If Billie codes tonight, I'm not doing no slow code."

I shrug.

"All right. I'll help you until the code team comes, then you can work with them and I'll watch the rest of the unit."

Katie nods.

"But he's not going to code."

I feel nauseated. Maybe he won't, but then again, maybe he will. I look at the clock: less than 4 hours to go.

As we sit there, I think about all that I would like to tell her but I can see that she doesn't want to talk now. She's worried and afraid. She doesn't know much about death.

A monitor beeps in the Toddlers' Room and Katie jumps up to see if it's Billie's. I think about following her but I don't. I stay where I am and bite my nails instead. I hope it's not him. I hate this. I wouldn't care if he were a no code. I don't mind taking care of dying people, dying children, if it's accepted that they're dying. But it's this kind of situation that I can't stand. I close my eyes. I hear Katie talking to Billie so I know he's not dead yet. But it won't be long. I can see the dead in the darkness like a fog with faces.

0500

I pace up and down in front of the Nurses' Station. I'm really starting to get worried. Billie's blood pressure is 125/45 and his heart rate is down to 60. He's going. I know it. I didn't think it would happen this fast. Now we're waiting for the doctor to come and see him. I don't know what he can do, though. I know what's happening. Billie is herniating his brain stem; the tumor is pushing his brain down into his neck, cutting off his vital centers. It's just a matter of time until his heart stops. Katie is staying in there with him, while I watch the rest of the unit.

Right now, everything is okay, because everyone is asleep and no one needs anything, but there's going to be a lot to do at 6 o'clock. There are several feedings and meds to give out. If we only had another nurse, we'd be all right. That's the problem with skeleton staffing. It's okay if nothing happens, but if something does, then it's a crisis. I could call Marianne and ask her to come in early but I don't want to do that unless I have to. She does it too often as it is.

I see the resident, Dr. Bristol, go into the Toddlers' Room, so I walk over and stand in the doorway.

"What's his blood pressure now," he asks Katie, as he looks at the Vital Signs sheet.

"130/40," she says. "His heart rate is 52 and his respiratory rate is 12."

"Billie," the doctor shouts as he pinches the boy's neck. But he gets no response. Then he checks his pupils with a flashlight.

"Hook up an IV to the Broviac," he says to Katie. "D5 for now. Run it slow: 10 cc's an hour. I'll see if I can get him transferred to the ICU."

He nods to me as he passes me in the doorway.

I go with Katie into the Treatment Room and help her set up the IV. I prime the tubing while she sets up the pump. While we do that, Dr. Bristol comes into the room.

He is short, about the same size as I am, but his hair is black and curly and he talks with a Southern accent. He has to be in his late 20s but he looks like a high school kid to me. I wonder where he's from. I look at his eyes; he's wide awake. I don't know how. He had worked all day and I know he hasn't had much sleep. Doctors usually don't. Maybe he takes speed, I think, but then am annoyed by the thought. I'm being petty. He probably didn't mean anything by his remark to me earlier in the shift. I never worked with him before but I heard the nurses say that he is a good doctor. Nurses don't say that about many doctors so he must be okay. Overall, the doctors here are good, though, at what they do. But they're handicapped by the nature of their profession and by the way the hospital system is set up.

The medical profession is so macho. I would never want to be a doctor. They work too many hours, have too many things to do, and yet they never seem to be around. They usually only spend maybe a few hours a week on the unit. I think that it would be better if doctors worked 8-hour shifts like nurses do. There should be a doctor on the unit at all times. That way, they could get to know the kids and the nurses and see what really goes on. They write orders for meds and treatments with no conception of the staffing. It's easy to write orders, but if there are not enough nurses to carry them out, then the orders are useless. If they were here more often, maybe things would change. But then again, who would want them around all the time, with their superior ways.

"There are no beds in the ICU," he says. "Everyone is too sick to bump. And Oncology has a full house. I guess that we'll just have to manage him down here."

"How are you going to do that?" I ask him.

He gives me a look like a professor annoyed with a rebellious student, then he grins.

"With drugs," he says. "We can keep people alive for a long time with drugs. We only have to hold on for a few hours, then his attending can come in and take over."

"I don't know if he's going to make it that long," I say. "He's a full code."

"I know," says the Resident. "I don't agree with it but it's not my decision to make."

"Yeah," I say. "Those decisions are always made by people who aren't here when it happens."

The resident nods.

"They're at home sleeping in their beds, while we do the dirty work."

I feel a little bit better. He's someone I can work with.

"Take his vital signs every fifteen minutes," he says. "I'll be here for a while. I'm going to call the second year resident. Maybe he'll call the attending. Maybe they'll make him a no code."

I smile. Maybe we'll get help from the tooth faery, too.

Katie and I push the IV pole and the pump into the Toddlers' Room. I look at Billie and notice that he is breathing slowly and very irregularly. I take his blood pressure while Katie gets the IV ready. It's 140/30 and his heart rate is 48. I tell Katie what his signs are.

"What drugs will he use?" asks Katie as we walk to the other side of the room to talk.

I shrug.

"Mannitol, I guess, to try and control his blood pressure, and Atropine, maybe, to raise his heart rate. I don't know. That's ICU stuff. We shouldn't be doing these things down here. No matter what they do, it's not going to make a difference. It's like trying to do the impossible, I'm afraid. You know what's happening, don't you?"

Katie nods.

"The tumor is increasing his intracranial pressure."

"Right," I say. "Like they told us in nursing school, there's only so much room in the head. Something's got to go, either the brain or the tumor. It's going to be the brain. They're not going to operate again. That's why he should be a no code."

"Why isn't he?" asks Katie.

I shrug.

"A lot of people can't come to terms with death, especially doctors. They believe in life at any cost. It's hard for a lot of them to admit that they can't control everything. They think that if people die, then they've failed, somehow, especially if they're kids."

Katie shakes her head.

"It is a shame. To die so young. He's only 9 years old."

"Yeah," I say. "But I don't think that death is necessarily a bad thing. It's part of the process of life. Energy cannot be created or destroyed; it can only be transformed. That's what we are: energy fields. It's the transition that I worry about, how you die. Maybe it wouldn't be so bad if you died in your own bed, surrounded by people who cared about you, or in a hospice, a quiet, peaceful place where you had medications for pain, maybe a little THC to mellow you out and nice music, Mozart, maybe, or Kitaro. But to die in a hospital, in an ICU, with a crowd of strangers standing over you and someone banging on your chest and sticking a tube down your throat. That's no good."

"What can I expect to happen?" asks Katie.

I sigh.

"It won't be anything dramatic. He'll probably just stop breathing. They had a kid here a couple of years ago that they just let die. He had no face. He had a big hole where his nose should have been. He had a tiny brain; he was an anencephalic. He just kept breathing slower and slower until he finally stopped. His mother and his nurse took turns holding him. He died in his mother's arms. He wasn't in any pain. He just died."

Katie cries as she looks over at Billie.

"I don't know what to do," she says as she wipes her eyes.

I stroke her back.

"Just do the best you can," I say. "That's all you can do. Just remember that no matter what happens, you believe that you're doing the right thing. Who can say what's right and what's wrong here? You know what to do in a code. Remember your ABCs: Airway, Breathing, Circulation. Get an airway in. There's one over on the bedside. Breathe for him. Bag him. Then someone, the doctor, will do compressions. One breath for every 5 compressions. Then the code team will be here. They usually give bicarb or epi first, then calcium. Try to keep track of the time. It's hard. You go into a time warp in a code. Everything slows down."

"You'll help me won't you?"

I look at Billie. I don't want to participate in this but I can't let her down, either.

"If you need me. Only if you really need me, but you won't. You can do it. You stay here with him. I'll take your other patients."

"It's too much," she says. "Why don't you call Marianne and ask her to come in a little early. She's done it plenty of times before."

I think for a moment. It would be nice to have her around here.

"Maybe I will," I say as I walk out of the room.

The resident is hanging up the phone as I get back to the Nurses' Station.

"The attending says he's a full code. We're going to try to get him in the Unit in the morning. I called the parents and told them that there's been a turn for the worse. They're on their way. I'm going to start him on mannitol. I'm writing the order now."

"Is that going to do anything?" I ask. "Isn't that more for edema?"

The resident shrugs.

"We have to do something. Make it look good."

As I look at the order he's writing, I hear Katie shouting in the Toddlers' Room.

"Help! I need some help in here!"

The resident gets up and runs into the room and I follow after him. The monitor is alarming and Katie is putting an airway into Billie's mouth. I can see right away that he is no longer breathing. His face is blue and his body is totally limp. The resident runs over and starts doing compressions.

I walk back out to the Nurses' Station and sit down at the desk. I don't want to do this. It's wrong. But what can I do? If I don't do it, I'll get in trouble, but if I do, Billie is going to suffer needlessly. Only for a little while, though, I think. He's already suffered so much. What does a little more matter? I have to think of myself. My fingers tremble as I punch out the numbers and my voice shakes as I call the code. I go into the Treatment Room for the Crash Cart. I roll it into the room, lift the board off and start to push it under Billie. As I do that, the code team comes running into the room. One of them helps me with the board, while another opens the crash cart and pulls out the syringes containing the bicarb and the epi; two more hook up the EKG machine and put on the leads.

I stand back and watch the scene. Katie is bagging Billie. As she does, he blows up like a plastic punching bag. I don't want to see anymore. I creep out of the room like a thief leaving the scene of a crime. I go out to the Nurses' Station and call Marianne. Her husband answers the phone.

"John," I say, "This is Jim, from Seaside House. I'm sorry to wake you so early. Is Marianne there?"

"She already left," he says, his voice hoarse. "What's the matter?"

"We're having a little problem here. One of the kids is going bad and we need some help."

"Is it Billie? She said last night that she was going to go in early today. She had a premonition that there was going to be a problem with him."

"Marianne is amazing," I say. "Good. Talk to you later."

After I hang up, I look at the report sheet and the kardexes. I make a list of things that have to be done at 6 o'clock. As I'm doing that, I hear someone wheezing. I look over and see Michael standing in the doorway of the Big Kids' room.

"Michael," I call to him. "Are you okay?"

He nods and shakes his head. He stares up at the ceiling as if watching a spaceship coming in for a landing. I walk over to him. He stands stiff as a sleepwalker, his eyes clouded with dreams. I gently shake him awake and tell him to take deep breaths. I listen to his lungs. I can't tell where the wheeze is coming from. I place my stethoscope on his neck and follow the sound. It fades as I move down his chest. His color's good and he's only a little tachypneic. He's moving air well. He's not due for his Slo-Bid until 8. He has a PRN puffer, though. I can give him that if I have to. But he's all right. He's wheezing because he wants to so he makes the sound with his throat. He probably heard the code, heard all of the commotion. Tension is in the air and these kids are very sensitive to it.

"You feel okay?" I ask him.

He both nods and shakes his head.

I smile.

"Yes or no?"

He continues to nod and to shake his head.

"Do you want something to drink?" I ask him. "Some juice?"

He just nods this time.

"I'll get you some," I say as I lead him back to his bed. "Sit down. Take it easy, my man. You're okay."

I go into the kitchen and get him a cup of juice. It seems that we're getting more and more asthmatics these days. I didn't realize until I came here how serious asthma is. Michael had over 25 ER visits last year and was hospitalized 6 times. He even had to be intubated and put on a respirator once. Kids die from asthma. It should be taken more seriously. More studies should be done to find out why so many children have the disease. But just like everything else, if we look too closely at it, we might just have to change the way we live to cure it Asthma is an obstructive disease of the lungs. People breathe in something from the air, or they eat something they're allergic to and their airways narrow in response to it. Wheezing is the sound of air whistling through the narrow opening. Sometimes, it's pollen from plants and dust and animal hairs, but I think that more and more of it is coming from chemicals from factories and cars. And a lot of it comes from anxiety. When people get anxious about something they may wheeze. It's easy to understand. There's enough to be anxious about. Most asthmatics come from broken homes or families under great stress and right now the nuclear family is splitting under the pressure like an atom bomb exploding in the desert. It had to happen. It's too much pressure for two people. A man and a woman alone should not be solely responsible for the care of children. It should be a community responsibility. That's why we need day care centers and preschools and community health centers. But that's not going to happen. Not in this system. In a dog-eat-dog world, who cares about the puppies?

I take the juice to Michael. He's still sitting on the bed just as I left him, like an orphan waiting for adoption. I put my arm around him as he drinks his juice. I look at him with affection. When I first saw him, I thought he was about 8 years old. When I heard he was in high school, I couldn't believe it. He's small and thin with a birdcage chest and chicken-like limbs. On those hard city streets, he's a victim waiting for an executioner. All he has to protect him is his mother, and who's going to protect her? When he finishes his juice, I stand and tell him to go back to sleep.

He looks at me with big eyes and asks me what's going on in Billie's room.

"He's sick," I tell him. "The doctors are with him now."

"Is he going to die?"

I look at him for a moment, deciding what to say. I try to take the easy way out. I give him the textbook answer.

"Everybody dies sometime. That's a reality of life."

"I know," says Michael. "But is Billie dying right now?"

I sigh. I don't want to lie to him. Children need to hear the truth.

"Yeah, I think so. It's hard to tell exactly when someone is going to die. But it'll be soon."

Michael wrinkles up his face and tears come to his eyes.

"What happens when you die? Is Billie going to heaven?"

I try to smile but my eyes fill with tears. I see no point in believing that death is the end, that life ends in the grave. It doesn't make me feel good to think that and everywhere I look I see rebirth.

"Nobody knows for sure what happens or where you go when you die. Different people believe different things but nobody knows for sure. Nobody has ever come back to tell us. Whatever happens, I don't think it's bad. Nothing to be afraid of. We just go back to where we came from. What do you think, Michael?"

"Jesus came back from the dead and he said that there's a heaven. That's where my father is and my little brother who died. We'll all be together again, there, where kids don't get sick, where nobody has asthma."

I pat him on the shoulder.

"Don't worry about Billie. He'll be all right."

Michael nods and closes his eyes.

I back slowly away from him and stand in the center of the room. The other boys are still asleep. I go out the door and through the Nurses' Station to take a look at the code. They are intubating Billie now. Katie is right in the middle of it. I watch her as she hooks up the ambu bag and squeezes it. One of the doctors is doing chest compressions. I look at the small EKG screen. It looks like ventricular fibrillation to me. I wonder if they're going to shock him, defibrillate him. I hope not. I notice that Peewee and Michelle are awake. They sit and watch the code and cry. I go between their beds and try to hush them but they pay no attention to me. They can tell that something sad is happening. I could pull the curtains around them but that would only frighten them. I decide to take them out of the room. I go over to Peewee and ask him if he wants a piggyback ride.

He stops crying and nods his head.

I sit on the edge of the bed and he puts his arms around my neck. As I stand up, Michelle asks me if she can have one too.

"I'll be back in a minute," I tell her and run out of the room like a fireman bringing out a survivor. As I do, the unit door opens and Marianne comes in. She laughs when she sees me.

"Giving piggyback rides so early in the morning, Uncle Jimmy?"

I shake my head and nod towards the room.

"What's going on?" she asks me. She stops laughing and looks in the window at the code.

"I'll tell you in a minute. I'm taking the little ones into the play-room."

I run Peewee in there and put him in a beanbag.

"You stay here," I tell him.

Marianne brings Michelle in on piggyback and puts her in another beanbag.

"Aren't you guys lucky," Marianne says, "You get to sleep in the playroom. You have plenty of company in here. Look at all the dolls and the toys."

She gives them each a couple stuffed animals to cuddle while I go out and get some blankets from the cart. We cover them and tuck them into the beanbags as best as we can. When they seem settled in, we go back out to the Nurses' Station and I tell Marianne what happened.

"Oh, God," she says. "Poor Billie. And poor Katie. Is she in there?"

I nod.

"She's doing fine. But Billie isn't."

"I knew this was going to happen," says Marianne. "I knew

when I left here yesterday. I don't know why they always put things off. They knew he was going down."

"Denial," I say. "They figure that if they deny it, it won't happen. How many times have you seen that?"

"I know," she says, sadly. "We have to open up that Center soon."

I nod. That's one of our mutual fantasies. Every once in a while, we talk about opening up a place run by nurses, a children's center. It would be a great place. Each family would have a private room with a whirlpool and a steam room. Everyone would sleep on futons or water beds. There would be a stereo system in each room and a refrigerator and a stove so they could cook their own food if they wanted. On the grounds there would be all kinds of animals: horses and dogs and cats and rabbits and chickens. There would be an aquarium with all kinds of fish and there would be gardens and fields where we would grow our own food. The meals would be mostly gourmet vegetarian but with meat for the diehards. We would practice therapeutic touch and guided imagery and hypnosis and we would use herbs and roots instead of pharmaceuticals. Maybe some day that'll happen, but for now we would settle for a room of our own. Just a room where we could try that stuff. A quiet, peaceful place with mats and tables and music. My friend Danny Stein has a proposal and a plan for a way to do it but no one'll fund it. I can understand why. People are afraid of change. It's all so strange. There are times when I feel embarrassed for believing in it myself. It helped me. It can help others, especially those whom modern medicine has failed.

"Do they need any help?" she asks.

"There are enough people in there already," I say. "There's a lot to do at 6. You can take Katie's other kids. Andrea and Willie and Ronnie. They need to be fed. They all have meds. Peewee is okay until breakfast."

"I'd better go see," says Marianne. "Poor Katie. Maybe she could use some help."

I watch her run over to Billie's room, then I go in and take another look at Peewee and Michelle. They're sitting in their bean-bags, leaning and listening like two sentries on guard duty.

"Why are all the doctors in our room," asks Peewee.

"They're taking care of Billie," I say. "He's real sick."

"I want my mommy," says Michelle.

"I know," I say. "Your mommy'll be in soon. It's real early in the morning. You need to go back to sleep, both of you."

"Can you stay here with us?" asks Peewee.

"I wish I could," I say. "But I have to take care of the babies. Don't worry. I'll be right out there. I'll come back in a little while. You don't have to be afraid. I'm here. Marianne is here. Okay?"

I look at them but neither one says anything They know that everything is not okay.

When I get back to the Nurses' Station, Marianne comes out of Billie's room.

"That poor kid," she says. "They're not having much success. He has a heart beat but he's not breathing on his own."

"How's Katie holding up?" I ask.

Marianne's eyes shine.

"Good. She's doing the chest compressions now. She looks like a real vet in there."

I close my eyes and take a deep breath. She's seeing death for the first time.

"Did you take the bloods to the lab?" Marianne asks.

"Oh, no," I say. "I forgot. I meant to do it, but we got talking."

"Uncle Jimmy," she says. "Were you up on your hobbyhorse again? Saving the world? Poor Katie."

I laugh.

"Yeah, you know me. I'm wired. After all, it is my last night here."

Marianne comes over and hugs me, then holds me at arms length.

"I'll talk to you before you go but I want you to know that no matter what anyone says, I think you're wonderful."

I laugh.

"So are you," I say.

"I'd better take those bloods over," she says. "Before we forget them again."

I feel sad as I watch her go out the door. We had our time together.

COCK-A-DOODLE-DOO! COCK-A-DOODLE-DOO!
I look into the Big Kids' room. It must be dawn. The Rooster
Man is awake.

0600

Jack, the Rooster Man, is lying on his back with his legs spread
and his arms above his head like a sunbather on the beach. I put on
a pair of rubber gloves and insert the catheter. I put the end of it into
a urinal and watch the urine flow through. It's as thick as cream of
wheat and it smells bad so I know he still has an infection. I have
already given him his Bactrim. He took that with no problem but
refused to do his own cath. He's behaving like the adolescent that
he is. I shouldn't be doing this for him. That's why he's here: to
learn his care. But I don't have the time to argue. I have too much to
do. I asked him several times to do it himself but all he would do
was laugh and shout, COCK-A-DOODLE-DO at the ceiling over
and over again and he wouldn't stop no matter what I said. When I
first heard him doing that I thought it was funny but it's getting old.
I felt myself getting angry. He would wake up the other kids when I
wanted them to stay asleep. I had a vision of myself stuffing a sock
in his mouth and tying his hands to the bed but brushed that quickly
out of my mind.

Instead, I pointed my finger at him and said, "Okay, I'll do it
this time but you lose time in the playroom."

He stopped shouting and puckered up his lips.

"I don't care," he said, "I don't like going in there anyway.
None of the other kids like me. Nobody likes me."

As I sat there and watched him cry, I thought about what it must
be like to have Spina Bifida: to be born with part of my spinal cord
outside of my body, to be a paraplegic, with no control over my
bowels and bladder. Spina Bifida kids have such difficult lives. It's
not too bad when they're babies and toddlers; all children are incon-
tinent then. It's when they're older that it becomes a real problem
especially for adolescents like Jack. Kids can be so cruel. I can hear
them saying, 'ugh, he smells.' And I can see people looking at his

hump and shriveled legs and slinking away from him; I have seen people do it in the hospital. I have to admit that when I first saw a kid with Spina Bifida, I felt repulsed, myself. But as I talked to the child, I realized that there was a person in there, just another kid, born that way. It wasn't his fault. He should be seen for what he is: a boy like anyone else, with a special problem. He should be able to have a life as full as anyone else's. No one is more discriminated against than a person with a "handicap." It is arrogant of us "normal people" to look down on them when we're handicapped ourselves, by our inability to feel.

"I like you, man," I said. "But I like you better when you do your own care."

"What for?" he said. "I'm sick of doing those caths."

I can understand that. If I had to do it four times a day for as long as he's had to, I'd be sick of it, too. It seems like such a bizarre thing to do. The first time I did it I felt nauseated. There's something repulsive about having a tube stuck up there. It seems like an attack on your sexuality. But it has to be done. If the bladder is not fully emptied, the urine becomes stagnant, a breeding ground for bugs.

"You have to do them," I said. "That's all there is to it."

"No, I don't," he said. "My mom'll do them."

"You can't always be dependent on your mom," I told him. "She can't be there all the time. The more you can do for yourself the better. And you don't want to be sick all the time. If you don't do it, you'll just get more infections."

"So what?" he said. "They can just give me Bactrim for it."

"No, Jack," I said. "If you get too many infections, you'll ruin your kidneys. You can't live without your kidneys. Well, actually you can, but you'd have to go on dialysis and you don't want to do that."

"I don't care," he said. "I don't want to live. I want to die."

I wasn't sure what to say to that so I said nothing. In a way, I can't blame him. I wouldn't want his life. But I'm not him. I decided to go ahead and do the cath myself.

My back hurts from bending over him, so I sit on the edge of the bed and try to find some words to say to him. He needs a psychiatrist, I think, as I press down on his bladder to speed up the process and to help it empty completely. But what he needs more than that is a new spinal cord. I wish I could heal him. I wish I could put my hands on him and reconnect his spinal cord, but that seems beyond my power. But maybe it isn't. Who knows what we could do if we really tried or if scientists devoted as much time and energy for research to healing as to building new kinds of bombs and ways of killing people, maybe we could heal spinal cord injuries, even Spina Bifida.

"Hey, Jack, listen," I say. "I know you have a hard life. I know it's not easy to keep on going. I feel the same way myself, sometimes, and I don't have Spina Bifida. But you have to have hope, man. Who knows what could happen in the future? Maybe we'll find a way to cure Spina Bifida."

Jack shakes head.

I feel my face flush. That was a mistake. I shouldn't have said that. It sounds too far-fetched.

"You have to make the best of what you have," I say. "You're not stupid. You have a brain. You could study and make something of yourself. Get a good job."

"I don't want a job," he says. "I want a girl friend."

"Yeah," I say. "So do I. I can't find a girl friend either."

Jack laughs.

"No wonder. Who would want you? You're so weird."

I laugh.

The cath is finished. I pinch the catheter and slowly pull it out.

I hold the urinal up to the light. It is over half full."

Look at all that urine," I say. "What were you doing? Drinking beer last night?"

He laughs.

"No, I wasn't drinking beer. You were drinking beer. You're crazy."

I laugh.

"Yeah, you're right. But no more than anybody else."

Poor Jack, I think. Who will ever love him? He will never have normal sex. There are other pleasures in life besides sex though. There are plenty of people who live happy and fulfilled lives who aren't sexually active. And who knows? I remember seeing a guy on the street one day who had little flaps for arms and he had a girlfriend. He rolls on one side so I can put a new diaper under him. As he does that, I check his back for breakdown; he has a small bedsore on his sacrum, right on top of his hump. I take the bandage off it and check it for drainage but there's none. It's not a bad bedsore. When I started nursing school, I thought bedsores were little red spots. Then I saw one. It was so large that I could put my arm inside. It ran all the way up the woman's back. This one is the size of a dime. I clean it with peroxide and water and put some Bacitracin on it with a Q-tip. Then I cover it with a piece of Teflex and tape it to his skin. I tuck a diaper under his butt, then have him roll toward me. He lifts up a little so I can get it on right.

"Go back to sleep," I say to him as I put out his bedside light. "Breakfast'll be up in a couple hours."

"Hey, Jim," he says. "Do you really like me?"

I smile.

"Yeah. Do you think I'd come in here and do all this if I didn't like you? But you make me work too hard. I'd like you even more if you learned how to take care of yourself."

Jack laughs.

"I like making you work hard."

I stop smiling.

"I'm not kidding you, man. Everybody will like you more if you learn to do for yourself."

Jack pulls the cover over his head.

I stand there for a moment wishing that he would pay attention to what I'm saying. Maybe he will someday.

I go back out to the Nurses' Station. The code is still going on. As I stand there, the unit door opens and a man and a woman come in: Billie's mother and father. I saw them a couple times but I never talked to them. I had never been assigned to Billie.

"How is Billie?" his mother asks me as she looks anxiously towards his room.

I try to think of their nationality; they look like immigrants from some European country. I can't place her accent. Then I remember. They're Portuguese. Seaside House is like the United Nations. People from all over the world come here. A couple of months ago, we had a kid from Cambodia who also had a brain tumor but he was in remission. What a life he had. He survived the war and the refugee camps only to come here and develop a brain tumor.

"They're working with him, now," I say.

"Which nurse is taking care of him," Billie's father asks.

"Katie" I say. "She's in there with him. She's the one in whites."

"Can we go in?" she asks.

I look around for Marianne. I see her through the window of the Baby Room. She's suctioning Willie. I take a deep breath. It's always difficult to know the right thing to say in these situations.

"Are you sure you want to, right now?"

Billie's mom is crying and nodding her head.

"I want to be with him. If he's going to die, I want to be with him when he does."

"I don't know if they'll let you in right now, hon," says the father. "They're busy working on him. You'd only get in the way."

"I'm his mother," she wails. "How can I be in the way? My boy is dying. I don't want him to die alone."

I look around and see Marianne behind me. She has tears in her eyes and I'm almost crying myself. His mother is right. I'd want to be in there if my son were dying. She should be with him but a code is a terrible thing to see.

Marianne goes over and puts her arms around the mother.

"Let me go talk to the doctor," says Marianne. "I'll find out what his status is."

The mother nods and Marianne goes into Billie's room.

The parents huddle together and look anxiously into the room. They look so forlorn. I want to go over and put my arms around them and comfort them. I try to imagine how they feel. I don't know if I'd want a strange man coming over and hugging me at this time so I hold back. Maybe I'd be intruding on their grief. I decide to let Marianne handle this so I go into the Baby Room to do my feedings.

All of the babies are crying and all of the monitors are alarming. It drives me crazy. I scurry around the room like a mad medic checking on the wounded. Everyone is still breathing. Their tachycardia buttons are beeping; they're all upset. I put pacifiers in Ronnie's and Reggie's mouths, then I go to Jennifer and check her diaper. She's soaked; the Lasix finally kicked in. I weigh her diaper on the scale and record the amount on her I&O sheet. 150 ccs. A good output. As soon as I finish changing her, I run into the kitchen and heat up her formula by running hot water over the bottle. It's a little cold but what can I do?

As I run past the Nurses' Station, I see Billie's parents going into his room. I hook Jennifer up to her feeding as quickly as I can. Luckily, she has gone back to sleep.

When that's done, I wash my hands. Then I go over and suction Charles and change his diaper. He's had another stool. I wash my hands again. I've washed my hands so many times tonight that they're starting to bleed. I rub some cream on them and stand in the center of the room. Willie has stopped crying but he's restless. It's just a matter of time until he starts again. I see that Marianne has already hooked him up to his feeding. He's probably having gas. These kids are so hard to evaluate. They have so many things wrong with them that it's hard to know what it is that's bothering them, whether it's their lungs or their brain or what.

I am reminded of last summer when we had an epidemic of RSV, a respiratory virus. Two kids died and a couple others got severely sick. I probably helped to spread it around. I washed my hands between kids as best as I could, but I'm sure that I didn't once in a while. It's not easy to feed 3 or 4 babies at the same time, Especially when they have trakes. But that is what I had to do. I did 9 feedings one night. I had to stand in the center of the room and run from one baby to the next as each coughed and cried. I suctioned them and tried to comfort them but I was only one person. Unfortunately, I have not yet learned how to bi- or tri-locate. That's something I'll have to work on. Infection Control, of course, blamed the nurses. We weren't washing our hands enough, they said. Which was unjust. All of our hands were cracked and dry from washing them so much. It wasn't the hospital's fault that the staffing was so poor that one person would have to take care of that many kids at the same time. Of course not. It was my fault that I couldn't do the job. I probably wasn't managing my time properly.

I decide to feed Reggie first; he's crying the hardest and the loudest. Ronnie will have to wait. Unfortunately for her, she's got a quiet cry. The loudmouths get the attention first. I pick Reggie up and give him his bottle. I walk around the room, holding and feeding him. Willie's crying again by this time, so I go over and pat him on the back, holding the bottom of Reggie's bottle with my chin as I do so.

As I'm doing that, Marianne comes running into the room.

"Are you all right?" she asks me. "I'm sorry I haven't been in here but I got busy with Billie's parents. They've decided to stop the code."

I take a deep breath.

"Who did?"

"The parents," says Marianne. "His mom would not stay out of the room. As soon as she saw Billie, she told them to stop. You know what it's like. I mean, it was a good code, in the sense that they were doing it right. But you know how awful it looks."

I nod. I wouldn't want to see someone I loved looking like that: blue and bloated, with a tube stuck down his throat and someone pushing on his chest.

"Is he dead?"

Marianne shakes her head.

"Not yet. He still has a heartbeat. But it won't be long. His parents are with him now. His mother is holding him in her arms. It reminds me of the Pieta."

I feel sad but I'm glad for Billie's sake that it's over. He has suffered enough.

"How's Katie?" I ask.

"Holding up," says Marianne. "She's with the parents. She's upset but she's all right."

Marianne picks up Ronnie and gives her a bottle.

We sit in rockers in the center of the room and feed the babies.

I ask her how Raheem is doing.

"Reemie Roo Roo is doing good," she says. "I called his foster mom last night. He's back in school and he's putting on weight. He's lucky. He got into a good foster home."

"I feel like we failed him," I say. "We didn't take care of him as good as we should have. We shouldn't have let them discharge him the way they did."

Marianne shakes her head.

"There wasn't anything we could have done about it. We did the best we could. You and Kevin looked after him. You guys went on your own time to see him. How many people would do that? You cared. You told me how he was. I told the Welfare Department. We got him into foster care. He's safe now."

"Yeah," I say. "Maybe I expect too much".

Sometimes, I think I want to be like Holden Caulfield, the catcher in the rye. I want to protect them all. But that's impossible.

"Uncle Jimmy," says Marianne. "Are you really leaving us?"

I nod.

"I wish I wasn't. I wish there was some way I could stay here but there isn't. I'm going to miss Seaside House."

"We're going to miss you, too," she says. "Especially the kids, they're going to miss you the most. You were their daddy."

I feel myself choke up and tears come into my eyes. I don't trust my voice so I don't say anything. I hold Reggie against my chest and close my eyes and rock.

I am so tired.

I could go to sleep right here in this chair but I can't do that. I have work to do. I have to get ready for report. Day shift will be coming in soon. I look at my watch. It's 0630. I stand and walk over to the window. It will soon be light. The snow has stopped. It looks like only a few inches have fallen.

I decide to go for a run as soon as I get home. I'll run up the Wissahickon. The woods will be beautiful in the snow. I want to appreciate life for as long as I have it. Sometimes, I think it's a miracle that we live through each day in this world. There are so many ways to die. I think about how it must feel to be dying right at this minute. I shudder as I remember how I felt when that guy had his knife to my throat. But that's not dying, naturally; that's being killed and there's a difference. Dying is the ultimate adventure, the big step into the unknown.

"The roads aren't bad," says Marianne. "Just be careful driving home. Oh, that's right. You don't drive anymore. I forgot."

"Yeah, I'll take the train at 30th Street," I say.

I quit driving a couple of months ago. I got sick of it. I don't like cars. They're destroying the environment; they're too expensive and they're the epitome of selfishness. I don't mind taking public transportation. I can sit back and daydream or read the paper or a book. I get a lot of reading done on the train. And it gives me time to think. I'll have a lot to think about this morning.

I put Reggie back in his crib and go check on Jennifer. Her feeding is finished and she is still asleep. I fill out her I&O sheet and copy the numbers onto my work sheet, then I do the same for the other kids. I go out to the Nurses' Station and look into the Toddlers' Room. The code team has left. The room looks like a hurricane hit it: 4x4s, syringes and EKG paper litter the floor near Billie's bed. The drawers of the crash cart are open and overflowing like the bureau of a sloppy child. The curtain has been drawn around Billie. The forms of people move behind it like actors after a play.

As I stand there, I look over at Andrea. She's awake and lying quietly in her bed. I walk past her and pick up her clipboard. Her eyes follow me. I stop and look at her for a moment. As I do, Marianne comes in to do her feeding.

"How's my little sweetheart?" whispers Marianne.

I smile.

"Good," I say. "Watch this."

I walk in front of Andrea again and her eyes follow me across the room.

Marianne folds her hands in front of her as if she were praying.

"Oh, my God. She's tracking."

Marianne runs over and picks Andrea up and holds her in her arms and hugs her.

"It's a miracle," she says.

As we stand there and marvel at Andrea, a loud cry comes from behind the curtain and we know that Billie is dead.

I motion Marianne out of the room and she follows me out to the Nurses' Station. She doesn't know whether to laugh or cry so she does both.

I tell her what we did.

"Uncle Jimmy," she says. "You have special talents."

"No, I don't," I say. "It wasn't me. Anyone can do it. Don't tell anyone what I told you. I don't want anyone else to know."

"Why not?" Marianne asks me. "This should be made known."

I shake my head.

"Uh,uh. Not now. I don't want any people to know. It's not time for that yet. The time will come."

Marianne shrugs.

"Okay, Uncle Jimmy. But we need that center soon."

I nod.

"I'll do what I can."

I go quickly into the Treatment Room and check the med kardexes to make sure that I have given out all of my meds. I have. Then I go around and check on the kids one more time before report. I want to make sure everyone is okay. I don't want any more kids dying tonight.

0700

I sit in the Nurses' Station feeling like a prisoner at interrogation. Nurses stand around drinking coffee and firing questions like detectives in the Roundhouse: "When did it happen?" "How did it happen?" "What did you do?" I raise my hands in surrender. It's always this way after a code. Death is dramatic, a break in the routine. Everyone wants to hear about it. It gives them something to talk about. Some of them are just glad that they missed it, while others are convinced that mistakes were made that wouldn't have happened if they had been there.

"Wait until everyone gets here," I say. "I just want to go through it once. And I can't give you all the details. Katie'll do that as soon as she is ready."

I finish my nurses' notes, then go over my work sheet, making sure that I have all the information I need to give a good report. The numbers and words blur in front of me so I take off my glasses and rub my eyes so I can see.

"Who am I talking to?" I ask, yawning. "Who's in charge today?"

"I am," says Carol. "Aren't you lucky? You get to give me report on your last day."

I laugh.

Carol is well-known as a difficult person to give report to. She has reduced some nurses to tears with her questions. She has even driven some nurses out of the hospital. They have quit working here because of her. She's built more like a wrestler than a nurse and has the gruff voice of a truck driver. But we get along okay. I look around me. Everyone is here now.

"Okay," I say. "I'll start with Billie, since he's the one you want to hear about. On evenings, he was the same as he was on days. He was only responding to deep pain. He had one seizure for them. His usual: myoclonic, arm jerking, eyes rolling, but his vital signs were stable."

Carol interrupts me.

"Did they call the doctor?"

I nod.

"Yeah. He came to see him but he just said to watch him. He had the same kind of seizure for us about 4 o'clock, I think."

"Did you call him about that?"

I shake my head.

Carol opens her eyes wide and raises her eyebrows at me like a judge questioning a criminal.

"You didn't call him?"

"It wouldn't have made any difference," I say. "He wouldn't have done anything. We called him later when Billie's vital signs changed."

I tell them what they were.

"It seems like he went down the tubes fast," says Carol. "Did anything happen?"

I feel my face get hot as I remember holding him by his heart chakra.

"It wasn't that fast. Nothing happened."

"You should have called him," she says, a look of disgust on her face.

I take a deep breath. No matter what you do as a nurse, it's never enough. I'm glad I'm leaving. Who needs this crap, anyway?

I remember the day I decided to leave MHP. I came in one day at 3 o'clock after being there the night before until 2 a.m.. It was the time I had 14 IVs. I didn't sit down once. I ate my dinner at 1 o'clock in the morning while I wrote my notes. I had to change most of the IV bottles, some of them more than once. I got out all of my meds on time; all of the treatments got done; all of the orders got taken off; nobody died; everyone was taken care of and as soon as I walked in the door the next day, the Head Nurse takes me over to the IV board and criticizes me because I forgot to sign out one of the IV bottles: One. Not one word of praise for all that I did right, just criticism for the one thing I forgot. That's when I decided I had to find another job. But it's the same everywhere. I feel like getting out of nursing completely. It's a shame. There's nothing wrong with being a nurse and wanting to take care of people when they're sick. But nursing is such a thankless occupation.

"What could he have done?" I ask Carol.

"CYA," she stage-whispers.

"It's covered," I say, my voice rising. "The doctor was here. The code was called. They did everything they could. The other kids got taken care of. What more do you want?"

"Take it easy," says Carol. "No one's accusing you of anything."

"Hey, everybody," says Marianne as she walks in front of the Nurses' Station holding Andrea in her arms. "Look at this little sweetheart. She's tracking."

Everyone looks at Andrea as Marianne passes a tiny doll in front of her face. They squeal and shout for joy as they see her eyes follow it.

"Will wonders never cease," says Carol. "When did that happen?"

I shrug.

"She was the same as she had been on evenings. I noticed that she was tracking this morning."

"I guess something in her brain just clicked," says Carol.

Marianne and I exchange looks.

"I guess," I say, smiling. "She just decided that it was time to wake up."

I wait a few minutes for everyone to calm down, then I go on with report.

"Peewee, a 4-year-old with CP, is fine. He's sleeping in a bean-bag in the playroom. I took him and Michelle out during the code. They were getting upset. His appetite was fair on evenings. No bms, none for 2 days. He might need a suppository. His MAFOs are still on. There's no sign of breakdown."

I look at his kardex.

"He's for PT at 9 o'clock and OT at 10, whoever is his nurse. Michelle, a 3 1/2-year-old CP kid, who is also asleep in the playroom, is okay, too. She had a poor appetite at dinner but she ate a good snack. She had a bm and wet a few times. Her leg extenders are on as ordered. She's for OT at 9 and PT at 10. I already gave you report on the other two kids in the room."

"Wait a minute," says Carol. "You forgot a few things. Andrea's splints? When are they due back on? And how is her gastrostomy site? And what was her output on evenings?"

I give her that information.

"Then in the Big Kids' room, there is Andrew, an 8 year old with JRA. On evenings, he had one of his patented bms, about 20 little balls rolled into a one big ball. I don't know how he does it. He must take it out and paste them together himself."

Everyone laughs.

"Other than that, he's okay. He woke up once last night, complaining of pain. I took him out of traction for a while and gave him a hot pack. After he fell asleep, I put the traction back on and he's kept it on. He's for PT at 11.

Then we have Jack, the Rooster Man, a 14-year-old with Spina Bifida. He's still refusing to do his own caths. He gave them a hard time on 3 to 11. He finally did it but he did a sloppy job. I wound up doing the cath at 6. I didn't have time to argue with him. He needs a psych consult, that boy."

"Cock-a-doodle-do," says Carol. "Is he still doing that? It's a riot. I told my husband about it. The first time I heard it , I almost wet myself laughing."

When she stops laughing she says," He had a psych consult the last time he was here. It didn't help."

I shrug. What can they do for him, anyway?

"Then there is Michael, a 14-year-old with asthma. No wheezing on evenings. His peak flows were good, in the 300s. Behavior good. For me, he slept until about 0530. The code must have woken him up. He was wheezing but it was an upper airway wheeze. I gave him some juice and he went back to sleep."

"Did you tell the doc about that?" Carol asks.

"No," I say. "I wasn't going to go and interrupt the code to tell him that. I took care of it myself. He's all right. Damn."

I take another deep breath. I wish report was over and I was home in my bed. It's taking so long. But at least, there are only 12 kids. I remember giving report after working nights at MHP. It would take an hour. Sometimes close to 2 hours.

"Then in the Baby Room we have Captain Ahab. He's all right. His stump sock was on when I last checked. He had two good bms on my time. His lungs sound coarse, clearing with percussion. His vital signs are stable. His secretions are thin and white. He vomited once for 3-11 and once for me. Poor p.o. on both shifts; got most of it NG."

"He needs a fundo," says Carol. "And a gastrostomy. Who's his Primary Nurse? Lisa. She'll have to get on them about that."

I nod. It's funny when I think about it. I'll probably never find out what happens with these kids. I'll probably come down and visit once in a while, at first, then I'll probably stop. That's the way it is when you leave a job.

"Then there's poor Willie. A sad case. He's all right, for Willie. His gastrostomy bag came off once for them and once for us. His lungs sound coarse, clearing. Tolerated his feedings. He's been crying a lot. I'm not sure why. Gas?"

"How's his neck?" asks Carol "Did you change his strings?"

"No," I say. "We were going to change them before his 6 o'clock feeding but in all the turmoil, we forgot."

"How was his neck on evenings?"

I look at my work sheet.

"Raw. Broken down."

"That's probably why he's crying. I'd cry too, if I had a neck like he has. It must be really broken down now. You should have changed them earlier."

I sigh.

"How about Charles? Did you change his strings?"

I shake my head.

"His neck is all right. We don't usually change them on nights. There were only two of us here. What do you want?"

"Okay, okay," says Carol. "But you should have done Willie's."

"I know," I say. "But we didn't."

I feel like crying. I know I'll go home and ruminate about that for hours and feel guilty. I do that every time I make a mistake or forget something, no matter how little it is.

"Did his mother come into visit?" asks Carol.

I shake my head.

"The only parent here on evenings was Andrea's."

"She's always here," says Carol. "It's funny how some parents never come and some never leave."

Carol starts to tell a story about one of the parents but I interrupt her.

"Carol. I want to finish report. I'm tired. I want to go home. Then there's Reggie and Ronnie They're fine. Eating like pigs. You don't need their I&Os, do you?"

Carol shakes her head.

"Then last but not least, there's Jennifer, a 6-month-old with a VSD. She's on 24% O2. Her color's good, for her, her usual. She vomited once on evenings. She lost both her NG tube and about 30ccs of formula both of which they replaced. She pulled out her NG tube once for me."

"That little bugger," says Carol. "Did you put a sock on her hand?"

I shake my head.

"That doesn't stop her. She pulls it out anyway. Her vital signs are stable. Good output, no bms."

I go over my work sheet again.

"I guess that's about it. Any questions?"

Carol shakes her head.

"I think you've covered it. Well, how does it feel? Your last report at Seaside House?"

I shrug.

"I guess it hasn't sunk in yet."

"I have to hand it to you. You lasted here longer than any other man ever did."

I shrug as I stand It's a long time for anyone. Most nurses only stay here for a year or two at the most. It's too depressing. Speaking of depressing, I decide to go and see if Katie needs any help with post-mortem care.

As I go into Billie's room, I remember the first time I handled a dead body. It was when I was in nursing school. I was assigned to a patient who had come in with an enlarged lymph gland in his neck. He was a young guy, around my age at the time, 30 or so. When I went into his room, he was pacing around the room, smoking a cigarette. He was waiting for the orderly to take him down to X-ray to have a chest film done. I talked with him for a little while and took his vital signs. He was tachycardic. His heart rate was over 120. I noticed that it had been that high before, so I figured that he was just nervous. After the orderly came for him, I went downstairs to the cafeteria for a coffee break. When I got back up to the floor, I noticed that something was going on. I saw some doctors running and other patients were standing around talking in excited voices, then I saw a trail of blood in front of the Nurses' Station. I followed it into my patient's room. There was a big crowd in front of his door. My nursing instructor called me over to him, then took me off to the side and told me that my patient had coded. I couldn't believe it. After returning from X-ray, he had come out to the Nurses' Station holding his hand to his mouth. He told the nurse that he had coughed up some blood; then all of a sudden, blood started gushing out of his mouth like a fountain. The nurse had quickly escorted him to his room and called the code. But it was futile. He had exsanguinated.

They found out later when they autopsied him that a tumor in his lungs had eaten through an artery in his chest. There was no way they could've stopped the bleeding in time. When I went in the room to do his post-mortem care, it looked like the scene of a slaughter. There was blood all over the walls, all over the floor and all over him. I cleaned him up as best as I could, bagged him and tagged him, and sent him down to the morgue. I remember talking about it with the other students in post-conference that day. They were more upset about it than I was. They cried. I didn't. I thought it was a shame but I didn't even know the man. People die everyday, I said to them. They thought I was cold. But I was the one who did his post-mortem care. No one helped me.

I push back Billie's curtain and ask Katie if she needs any help.

Katie stops washing Billie's hand and nods. I can see that she has been crying.

"Are you okay?" I ask her.

"Yeah," she says. "I'm so glad that it's over."

I go over and put my arms around her and I can feel her body shaking as I hold her.

"If you ever go into the military, you'll see a lot more people die."

She pulls away from me and looks right at me, her eyes full of tears.

"I don't like the idea of being in a war, seeing people killed and wounded. But I'm a nurse. It's my vocation. If my country calls, I'll go. No matter how much it hurts. No matter what you say."

I can only nod my head. I have to admire her. I think of how sensible and balanced she is: unlike me.

We are silent for a few moments as we look at Billie's dead body.

"I feel awful. I think I broke his ribs when I did the chest compressions."

"I did that once," I say. "That doesn't mean you did it wrong. Even when you do it right, you can do that. It's a sickening sound, isn't it?"

Oh, God," says Katie. "What did we put him through that for? It was like he was being punished."

"Punished,' I say, "For what? What did he do?"

Katie shrugs.

"It just doesn't seem like we were meant to die. It causes so much pain. His poor parents. I felt so bad for them. You're right. We need a pediatrics hospice. No one should have to die like that. But he's with God now. He has to be. He was only a child and he suffered so much."

I look at Billie and take a deep breath. It's always a shock seeing a dead body. I pucker up my lips to keep from crying. I'll do my crying alone. I wonder where he is now. I look around the room as if I could see him floating around, watching us and listening to what we say about him.

"What's it like where you are?" I whisper, then I say to Katie, "Don't you wish the dead could speak?"

Katie gives me a look that says I knew you were weird but I didn't know you were that weird.

"Uh,uh. That would freak me out."

I nod.

"Yeah, I guess it would. But I have a lot of questions I'd like to ask him. It's so strange, isn't it? Death. I wonder why it's set up like it is: a mystery. I can't believe that we go through life and learn so much and experience so much and then it's over and everything you learned is wasted. And how can someone who is so important in your life, like my father was, just disappear? It's so hard to understand."

"Maybe we're not meant to understand it," says Katie. "Maybe it's a test of our faith, that we just have to learn to accept that death is not the end. Like Jesus said in the Gospel last week: there are many rooms in heaven, in our Father's House. Your father's in one of them and Billie's in another now. Waiting for the resurrection."

I shrug my shoulders.

"Well, maybe you're right. I hope so. I guess that's enough philosophy, theology for now. We'd better get him ready to go downstairs."

I take the dressing off his Broviac and slowly pull it out of his chest. As I do, a little blood oozes out so I put a 4&4 over it. Then I take the EKG leads off his chest while Katie pulls the airway out of his mouth. We clean his body with soap and water, then cover him with a sheet. I tie a tag on his toes to identify him.

"Is there anything else I can do for you?" I ask her.

Katie shakes her head.

"You've done more than enough. Thank you very much."

I shrug.

"What did I do?"

"You've shared your life with me," she says. "I appreciate what you were trying to do. You taught me a lot. You should write a book about what happened in Ireland and about what happened here."

I smile.

"Maybe I will."

"This has been some night," she says. "I'm going to miss you."

I feel myself choke up.

"I'm going to miss you, too," I croak. "Take care of yourself, okay. Hey, by the way, before I forget, Andrea's tracking."

"What?" says Katie "For real?"

I nod.

"For real. I don't know what it means. How much she's going to get back. But it's a beginning."

Katie smiles through her tears.

"It's our secret. And Marianne knows. But don't tell anyone else, okay?"

Katie shakes her head.

"Why not? You should be proud of what you did."

I shrug.

"I prefer it that way. And anyway, it wasn't me. I can't take the credit for it."

"Okay," she says. "If you say so. You're not going to disappear now, are you? You'll come back and visit us, won't you?"

I can only nod. I give her another hug then turn around and head for the door. I have to get out of here before I start to cry.

I stand by the door for a few moments and look back on the unit. I feel tears come into my eyes as I realize that I'm really leaving Seaside House. These kids taught me so much about myself. I will remember them for as long as I live. As I open the unit door, Marianne runs over.

"Trying to sneak out, Uncle Jim?"

I try to smile but my lips quiver.

"Yeah. I don't like saying goodbye."

Despite myself, I start to cry.

Marianne puts her arms around me and hugs me and I cry on her shoulder for a few moments.

"We'll see you again."

I pull away from her and wipe the tears from my face.

"Maybe I won't leave," I say. "Maybe they'll let me stay."

"No," says Marianne. "You've made your decision. We're going to miss you around here but it's best that you leave now. You'll find another job. That's one thing good about nursing. You can always find a job. There's home care. There's Children's Heart Hospital. There are a lot of kids out there who need a nurse, especially one like you."

"Yeah," I say. "You're right. I'm not sure what I'm going to do but I'm going to stay in pediatrics. You know, I love these kids."

"I know you do," she says. "And they love you, too. Take care of yourself, Uncle Jim."

"You too," I say. "And hey, thanks for everything."

I open the door and head for home.

4.

No Hocus Pocus

C asey stood across the street and stared at the church: Saint
Bridget's, a large Gothic structure with a steeple reaching to
the sky like thin fingers of hands held in prayer. It was solidly built,
with thick wooden doors and large gray stone blocks quarried from
Plush Hill, a section of the Falls. He thought about all the work that
had gone into building that church. It had thousands of those stone
blocks, each of them weighing twenty pounds or more and many of
them had to have been lifted up onto a scaffold. It tired him out, just
thinking about it. It must have cost a fortune. The Catholic people
of East Falls hadn't had much money but somehow they had found
a way to do it.

Last year, he had researched his family tree and he found out
that his family, the Caseys, had been one of the original families of
Saint Bridget's. They had helped build the original church on
Stanton Street in the 1850s and this church in the 1920s.They had
come to Philadelphia from Counties Derry and Donegal in Northern
Ireland during the Famine and had found jobs laboring in the mills
of East Falls and Manayunk, making textiles.

He remembered his Aunt Marg saying that without the
Catholic Church the Irish people would have been lost in America.
He could hear her voice and he remembered her pounding her fist

on the kitchen table, 'It was the Church that kept them together. The Irish should never have forgotten that. But we did. It's a disgrace that we forget how much we owe the Church. Now, we're forgetting about God, Himself. We're driving Him out of our schools and out of our homes. We think we don't need Him, but we do.' He remembered feeling embarrassed and ashamed of her, thinking that she was a nut, a religious fanatic. She was always dressed in black and going to funerals.

Then behind him, he heard the sound of the train pulling into the East Falls Station and he remembered his Aunt Marg taking him on his first train ride to the Reading Terminal and on his first bus ride up the Roosevelt Boulevard. When he came from Ireland in 1973, she let him stay up on her third floor until he got a job with the Welfare Department. What a place to sleep! The room was filled with old furniture and old clothes and yellowed newspapers and magazines dating back to the 1940's. There were boxes stacked to the ceiling and chairs piled on top of tables and several broken down chests of drawers jammed in between the remnants of old beds. There were several mirrors hanging on the walls and others on the floor propped up, some were broken and some were whole so that he could see his reflection broken in bits and pieces throughout the room. His aunt hadn't been up to that floor in years because she couldn't climb the steps so the room hadn't been cleaned since the last time she was up there. When he opened the windows for the first time so much dust blew around that he felt like he was in a sand storm in the desert. It took him a couple hours to make a pathway from the doorway to the bed so he could sleep in it. But it was a place to stay and after living at Ranchhouse for three months, it seemed like a luxury suite. At least there were no fleas. By the time he left there to get his own place, he had cleaned and painted the whole third floor, all except for one room. His Aunt Marg also paid his health insurance for a year until he was covered by the state. She was always doing good things for people. He remembered her sitting on the front steps making rosaries for the missions. She used to take her vacation each year to help with the clothing drive for the Saint Vincent de Paul Society and on holidays she always had people over for dinner who had nowhere else to go. Years ago, she took in a poor man, Chris Ganster, who had nowhere to live and he stayed with her until he died. She ignored the scandal it caused because she knew that they were doing nothing immoral. He had no doubt in his mind that his Aunt Marg was a perpetual virgin. Maybe she wasn't a fanatic after all but a good Christian like the rest of his family.

Last year, when he decided to research his family tree, he had hoped that he would find that they had been Irish rebels but he discovered that they all had been baptized, married and buried in the Church. No radicals as he had hoped, all church people. So many of his family had been brought up in Saint Bridget's: his great-grandparents, his grandparents, his aunts and uncles, his cousins. Both his parents had received the sacraments and had gone to school there, the same as he had done. It had been his parish for the first twenty-one years of his life. But those times seemed like another world to him, now, a world that was dead and gone and him along with it.

The last time he was in Saint Bridget's was at his father's funeral, eighteen years ago last month, January 1974, only a few months after he had returned from Ireland. He could see himself and his family climbing those same slate steps to the front door of the church, his father's casket wrapped in an American flag. That was the last time he had gone to Communion. His mother had insisted that he go to Confession and Communion for his father. His little mom.

There he was, twenty-seven years old. He had been to Vietnam, had survived being murdered, had been face to face with big-time bad guys, had traveled around Europe by himself: sleeping on the street, on park benches and on the beach. He was no wimp. No one told him what to do, but when his mother told him to go to confession, he went. He lowered his head and laughed at himself. But this time, his mother had not pressured him at all. When he told her he was going to church today, she didn't say a thing but that was because she was too choked up to talk.

The church bells were ringing and people were hurrying up the steps for Mass. It was time. Suddenly, he felt paralyzed and sick to his stomach. He took a few deep breaths, trying to calm himself down. He couldn't do it. He couldn't go back to the Church.

He heard the voices again, sneering and shrieking like scream-ing-meemies but they went as quiet as a church mouse when he saw his family going up the steps: his great-grandparents, his grandparents, his father, his aunts and uncles, his cousins, an endless stream of people, smiling and waving to him, calling for him to join them. Come home. 'Why not,' he said to himself, remembering what he had decided to do. He would go to church, maybe even go to Communion, make an appearance, talk to people, reassure them. He was one of them. He was okay now. He wasn't lost anymore. He was home.

He crossed the street and joined the crowd of people who were walking up the path in front of the rectory. He went in the side door as he always had done as a kid. Just inside was a holy water font. He almost dipped his fingers in it, then drew his hand back. A superstitious ritual, he thought. He was beyond that. He went and sat in one of the back pews, near the door, figuring that if he had to flee for some reason, he could just slip away without being noticed. He was surprised to see that the church was crowded. He had expected it to be half-empty. He had heard that attendance was down; that people were leaving the Church in droves but that didn't look like the case, at least not today. But it was the last mass, proba-bly the earlier ones were less crowded.

As he waited for Mass to begin, he looked around the church. There were the same pews, the same stained glass windows, the same Stations of the Cross, the same floor that he had walked on as a little boy. Then all of a sudden, he saw that little boy, dressed in a white suit and a blue tie, his hands folded, his first Holy Communion, the May procession, the church filled with flowers and everyone singing to the Blessed Mother.

Casey almost broke down and cried. He had tears in his eyes and he felt such pain, such a sense of loss. What had happened to that little boy? Suddenly, he felt so dirty. He looked at himself. Though he was clean on the outside, he was dirty within. The contrast between the innocent little boy he had been and the sinful man he had become broke his heart. He felt so sorry, so sad. He kept his head down so that no one could see the tears in his eyes.

When he looked up, they were singing the Gloria. The Mass

seemed so different from what he remembered. He knew that the Mass had changed, that it was in English with the priest facing the people, but he had been out of the Church so long that his main memory of the Mass was when it was in Latin.

A woman went up to the pulpit and began to read. He didn't know women were able to do that. That's good, he thought. Maybe the Church has really changed.

It was a reading from the Old Testament about David. Like most people, he knew the story of David and Goliath and had always thought of David as a warrior-king but he didn't remember this story: of how David had the opportunity to kill Saul but had refused. He knew that Jesus was called the Son of David but for the first time, he could see a correlation between the two. Then a man got up and sang a psalm. As he listened to the refrain: "The Lord is kind and merciful," and the psalm itself which was about forgiveness and kindness and how the Lord redeems us from destruction, he felt tears come to his eyes again. Then the woman got up again and read a letter from Paul. It was about how Adam was the first man, a man of the earth, and how Jesus was another Adam, a man from heaven. First came the natural man and then the spiritual man, Jesus. Finally, according to Paul, we will come to be like Jesus.

Jesus was a spiritual man and Adam wasn't? thought Casey. What did that mean? Adam didn't have a soul, a spirit? What was a natural man? It was the Saint Paul that he remembered: confusing and puzzling.

They stood for the Gospel and the priest processed over to the pulpit accompanied by two altar boys with candles.

It was the familiar reading about Jesus telling us to love our enemies and to turn the other cheek. 'To do the impossible, in other words,' thought Casey. 'Maybe God could do those things but how could we? We're human, not God.'

After the Gospel, the priest began his homily.

"In the name of the Father and of the Son and of the Holy Spirit. This Gospel is, of course, a collection of the most difficult sayings of Jesus. Ones that we all have the most difficulty in putting into practice. We tend to look at them as unrealistic, as impossible to do. How can anyone love his enemy? Or when slapped, turn his other cheek and offer that cheek to be slapped as well. Who could do that? A wimp? A coward? A fool? Or the sons and daughters of the Most High? In the first reading, from the Book of Samuel, we hear the story of how David spared the life of his enemy, Saul. Now we know from the rest of the Book of Samuel, that David was certainly not a wimp, or a coward, or a fool. He was a great warrior. He killed his tens of thousands. He slew the giant, Goliath, with a slingshot. He went on to be a great king, the greatest king Israel ever had. During his reign, Israel became wealthy, a powerful nation, one that other nations respected and did not try to attack while he was in command. He brought peace to Israel. And yet, he spared the life of his enemy, Saul, a man who had hunted him down and had tried to kill him many times. Why would David not kill Saul? Because he would not harm the Lord's anointed. What does this mean, the Lord's anointed? In the Old Testament, the prophets and the priests and the kings of Israel were anointed with oil and were thus made sacred. That meant they belonged to God and were not to be harmed. In the New Testament, this process of anointing was extended to all. In our baptism, we are anointed. All of us become kings, prophets and priests. Kings, in the sense that we are in control of ourselves, prophets, that we proclaim Jesus Christ by our words and life, and priests, when we offer sacrifices by the holiness of our lives. I'll bet that not many of you ever thought of yourselves as kings, prophets and priests. We are sacred. We are not to be harmed. In the second reading, from the first letter of Paul to the Corinthians, we hear about Adam being a natural man and Jesus being a spiritual man, a man from heaven. A natural man is one who has body and soul but does not have the spirit, the Holy Spirit. Without Jesus, without His baptism, the anointing of his Spirit, we are natural men and women. In other words, we live like men and women of the world and then we do not live out our baptismal promises, which unfortunately many of us do not. We do not love our enemies. We hate them. We do not turn the other cheek when someone slaps us. We hit back. As Saint Paul tells us: 'Just as we resemble the man from earth, so shall we bear the likeness of the man from heaven.' How do we do this? How do we become transformed from being natural men and women to become sons and daughters of God? People who are capable of loving our enemies and turning the other cheek? By living out our baptismal promises when we reject Satan and all his works: sin and death and violence. As Jesus did."

The priest turned and pointed to the crucifix which hung above the altar.

"I doubt that any of us would say that Jesus was a coward, a wimp or a fool. He faced Satan and all the powers of evil and death and he defeated them by dying on the Cross. As we say in the Mass: 'Dying you destroyed our death, rising you restored our life. Lord Jesus come in glory.' Jesus took the sin of the world, death and violence, and transformed it into a saving act: our redemption. Rather than commit sin and violence, He took it upon Himself. He died for us and restored our life."

The priest stopped talking for a moment as he scanned the congregation. Casey had the feeling that he was looking right at him.

"They taught us in the seminary that the homily is meant to inspire, to reflect upon the words of Sacred Scripture, not to teach, that teaching should be reserved for the classroom or for study groups but I am afraid that there are many of you out there who have not been properly educated in the teachings of the Church, especially those of you who grew up since the 1970's; in many ways, I'm sorry to say, we have failed you. And there may be others of you who have been away from the Church and have forgotten what you were taught or no longer take it seriously. You may not have been to Mass in a long time or you may be only coming when it suits you. You may be involved in an adulterous relationship or having sex outside of marriage. Maybe you have participated in an abortion or are practicing artificial birth control. You may stealing from your employer or cheating someone of their just due. Your hearts and minds may be filled with anger and hatred toward others and heaven forbid, you may have done violence to someone. If you are doing any of these things, it would behoove you to go to Sacramental Confession before you come to Holy Communion. I say this for your own good. These are sacred things and are not to be taken lightly. Saint Paul tells us in the same letter to the

Corinthians that we just heard read that, 'Whoever eats the bread or drinks the cup of the Lord unworthily will have to answer for the body and blood of the Lord.' And he goes on to say, 'you eat and drink judgment on yourself and that is why many among you are ill and infirm and a considerable number are dying.' Whew! I don't know about you but they are frightening words to me. Answer for the body and blood of the Lord! In other words, if you receive holy Communion unworthily, you will be declared guilty of the death of Jesus and it will effect you in this life as well as in the next.

That being said, in a few minutes, we will be re-presenting on the altar the same sacrifice of Calvary. Not doing it again. Christ died only once. He does not die at each Mass. He lives forever and it is the risen and glorified Christ who comes to us. Without leaving heaven. He comes in sacrament. 'The sacramental world is a new world created by God, entirely different form the world of nature and even from the world of spirits.' It is not magic. No hocus pocus. No absurdities. It is not as if Jesus is trapped inside of a piece of bread, imprisoned inside of tabernacles. It is not as if He is flying down from heaven and zooming around to all the altars all over the world at the same time. No. Although He is present at every Mass everywhere, everyday and has been since the Last Supper, in the consecrated bread and wine. How does it happen? It is, of course, a mystery but we can come to some understanding of it.

Listen carefully to what I am going to say to you.

What are called the accidents of the bread and wine, the external appearances, remain on the altar during the sacrifice of the Mass, even after the consecration. But there is an inward element of reality in the bread and wine which the sacramental consecration changes into the Body and Blood of Jesus Christ. We call it Transubstantiation. It is the changing of the substance of bread and wine into the body and blood of Jesus Christ. How is this done? By the power of the Holy Spirit and by the words of Jesus at the Last Supper, which was a foreshadowing of Calvary, our gifts of bread and wine are transformed into the Body and Blood of Jesus Christ.

With all due respect to our separated brethren: This can only be done by bishops and priests of the Catholic Church. The Catholic Church follows the lead of Our Lord. He was the first priest of the

Church and all priests are his sacramental image. He chose only men to be apostles and they were the first ordained priests. By the laying on of hands by the apostles to their successors, the bishops and down through the centuries to their successors and to all ordained priests, this ability, this gift is handed down. At Mass, the priest re-presents Jesus Christ Himself. That is why only a man can become a priest.

When we eat of His Body and Blood, Jesus will come into us and we will become like Him, sons and daughters of God. When we eat natural food, we transform that food into us. When we eat spiritual food - the bread of life and the cup of eternal salvation - we are transformed into Him. In the order of grace not of nature. By becoming Him, we will be able to do as He did: to love our enemies and to turn the other cheek, to resist Satan and sin.

But ah, some of you may ask: How about those who are not Catholics. How do they become like Jesus? The Holy Father, Pope John Paul II, reminds us in his first encyclical , **The Redeemer of Man,** what the Second Vatican Council taught: that by his Incarnation, Jesus, in a certain way, united himself with each person, so that everyone has him within us, some more than others. Are the Presbyterians or the Lutherans up the street part of the Church? How about those in those storefront churches that we hear shouting out for the Lord Jesus? Is Jesus present there? Of course. The Second Vatican Council teaches that all of those who believe in Christ and have been properly baptized are put in a certain, although imperfect, communion with the Catholic Church. As are all people, even non-Christians who seek God with a sincere heart and moved by grace, try in their actions to do his will as they know it through the dictates of their conscience. But any one, Catholics or otherwise, who does not persevere in charity, in love, will not be saved. The question then arises: If we do not love our enemies and do not turn the other cheek, does that mean that we can't be saved? For after all, how many people do love their enemies and turn the other cheek? The Psalmist gives us an answer: 'The Lord is kind and merciful. He pardons all your iniquities.' And as Jesus Himself says in the Gospel: 'He, God Himself, is good to the ungrateful and the wicked.' Some of you may ask: What does it mean to love our enemies? For some, it may mean simply that we wish them no harm. For others, do them no harm. For all of us: to pray for them. Some of you may ask: What does it mean to turn the other cheek? For some, it means letting insults go, or if possible, walking away from a violent situation and not participating in it, which can only be done with the grace of God. For others, it may mean martyrdom, following Jesus right up onto the Cross, and imitating him by allowing themselves to be killed rather than to kill.

How many of us are saved? Only God knows for sure. What we can say, however, is that God has predestined all of us to be saved. It is we ourselves who choose not to be saved, not to be with God. How can this be? You may ask. Who would not want to be with God?

A priest friend of mine who worked for many years in a prison ministry told me that there are people in prison who want to be there. They like being in prison. They like hurting people and committing crimes. They like it. Our saints tell us that is what makes a person evil: he likes sin. So just as there are people who like prison, there are people who choose to be in Hell and away from God. Let us pray today that we are not among them.

May God bless you."

Casey heard every word of the sermon. He had never heard the consecration explained like that before but most of it went right over his head. He wished that he had a copy of it so he could read it over again. And it seemed like the priest had been talking directly to him about going to Confession before receiving Communion. As he thought of what he had been about to do, he felt sick. What had he been thinking of? He should have known better than that.

As they recited the Creed, he felt like he was listening to a long-forgotten story from his childhood. But as he listened, he realized that he had never really understood it. He knew that the Church believed that God the Father was the creator of the universe and that God became man in Jesus but he had never thought of Jesus as being the creator as well. Yet that's what it said in the Creed itself: "through him all things were made." If that were true, then every-thing the Church teaches is also true. If Jesus created the universe in all its vastness and complexities, he could do anything: cure the sick, raise the dead, walk on water, change bread and wine into his body and blood.

Casey could hear them praying for the Church, the Pope and the Bishop but he didn't respond with them. He was too stunned to speak. Then they prayed for those who had lost their faith. When Casey heard that, he thought, 'all these years, people have been praying for me and I didn't know it.' As they prayed for the sick and for the homebound and for the dead, Casey responded in a tiny voice: "We pray to the Lord."

Casey sat down and closed his eyes. He felt a deep sense of gratitude for all the people in the Church who had remained faithful, who had not abandoned ship as he had done.

When he looked up, he saw the priest raise a large, white piece of bread and say, "Take this, all of you, and eat it: This is my body which will be given up for you." He realized that it was the Consecration. Then the chalice and the words: 'Take this, all of you, and drink from it: This is the cup of my blood, the blood of the new and everlasting covenant. It will be shed for you and for all so that sins may be forgiven. Do this in memory of me."

The priest was speaking the words of Jesus, the creator of the universe.

Casey felt like crying again. He had been so wrong about so many things. He could feel the woman next to him staring at him. He covered his eyes with his hand. He felt like he was in another world. He could feel them standing up and praying the Our Father and exchanging the sign of peace but he just knelt there, overcome with thoughts and feelings and memories. Then he heard the priest say, 'This is Jesus, the Lamb of God who takes away the sins of the world. Happy are those who are called to his supper." He looked up and saw that piece of bread, so big and white and shining and innocent and suddenly, he believed. It wasn't a piece of bread, anymore. It was Jesus Christ, Himself.

As he heard them pray, "Lord, I am not worthy that you should come under my roof, but only say the word and my soul shall be healed," he knew he could not go to Communion, not until he went to confession. He was too dirty, too sinful. He stood up and let the people in his pew out and then went back in and knelt down. He would call Father Joe tonight and ask if he could go to Confession as soon as possible.

When Mass was over, he went up to the front of the church and looked at the sanctuary. It was different from what he remembered. There was now an altar where he used to kneel behind the priest during the consecration. But there was no tabernacle on the altar, no altar rails. No one knelt to receive Holy Communion anymore: He noticed all that. He walked over to the side altar, the one with the statue of the Sacred Heart of Jesus bulging from his tunic.

He could hear the voice of Father Kavanaugh reading his first assignment: '6:30, side altar, William Casey.' He remembered that when his mother woke him at 6:00 a.m. that day he had told her, 'It's too early. I quit. I'm not going.' 'Oh, yes you are,' she had said as she dragged him out of bed and stood over him as he dressed, then handed him his pressed white surplice on an iron hanger and his collar in a round hard candy tin and pulled him by the ear, literally, all the way to church in the dark. He wondered how old he was then? Fifth grade, ten years old. 1956. Thirty-six years ago.

He looked up at the statue of the Sacred Heart of Jesus and saw a golden tabernacle with Sanctus on the front. As he stood there, he saw a woman come out of the sacristy, genuflect, open the tabernacle and put a small golden object inside; then she genuflected and closed the door. He didn't know what to make of that. When he was an altar boy, no one but the priest was allowed to do that.

'There sure have been a lot of changes,' he thought as he went out the back door. 'It seems like another church and yet, the same.' He looked at the holy water font for a moment, then dipped his fingers in the water and blessed himself. He peeked into the sacristy. It looked the same as it did when he was a boy. He saw himself, dressed in a black cassock and white surplice, helping the priest vest for Mass.

Feeling nostalgic, he decided to take a walk around the grounds. He went around the back of the rectory, climbed the steps and stood at the back of the new school. The new school! It was almost fifty years old. When he had started there in 1952, it was only a few years old. It looked the same, only dirtier and more run-down. He wished that he had made a lot of money on his books; if he had, he would donate it to Saint Bridget's to have it cleaned up and repaired. He walked up the ramp past the old school where he had spent the first three years before moving next door to the new school. As he stood outside the fence that surrounded the playground, he saw an image of himself running across the yard and he remembered a short story he had written: **The Lie.** He had written it as a funny story, a satire, really, but now, he would recall it with new eyes.

It was during Lent. You know how the Catholic Church is. They have you doing these silly things during Lent: not eating candy or ice cream, no meat on Friday, of course, and if you did, it was a mortal sin. You could go to hell for that. Oh, no! Not there! Just because you ate meat on Friday? Crazy stuff! And then there was the Stations of the Cross. We had to do that every Friday in Lent. I hated the Stations of the Cross.

Let me tell you what that is, if you don't know. All around the church, they have these pictures of the trial of Jesus Christ and scenes of his journey to Calvary and then his crucifixion and death. The priest would go around before these pictures and pray in front of each one of them; there were about twelve or thirteen of them. The pastor, Father Cartin, used to say the prayers in such a slow, droning voice that he would put you to sleep if you weren't kneeling. The way he said them reminded me of the way my Uncle John talked when he was drunk. We had to kneel the whole time; it was like torture. I never could understand what it had to do with me. It was something that happened long before I was born, to someone I didn't know, someone who the Romans or the Jews had put to death but apparently, not only them but we did as well. Somehow, in some way, all people since the beginning of time to the end were involved. In fact, before I was even born, someone died for sins I had yet to commit. Huh? What was that about? Absurd. What's more, this man who was put to death for my sins was God. Sure! If he was God, why did he let them kill him? And how could God die? And who was Jesus Christ to me? I didn't get it. All I knew was I hated going to the Stations.

I must have been in the fourth grade, because the first three grades didn't have to go; they were too young, I guess. Since I was the smallest boy in the class, I had to lead the rest of the school in procession down to the church. It was a great honor, the nuns told me. Hah! We lined up on Stanton Street and then walked across the schoolyard to the big wooden door that opened to stairs that led down to the church. The door had this iron ring that you had to pull to open it. I remember Sister had to help me with it, I was so little. That was embarrassing. Then I had to hold the door open as the rest of the school went past me down the stairs, some of them smirking and snickering at me when Sister wasn't looking.

Then when everyone had gone down, I looked around and I realized that I was alone. I heard this voice in my head: 'Take off. Go home. You can go in the back yard and play with your army men. They won't find out. No one will miss you.' It was my chance. So I closed the door and ran back across the playground to Stanton Street. But as I got close to Skiddo Street and freedom, who came out the front door but Mother Superior.

'Where are you going, young man?' she asked me.

Without even hesitating, I told her a lie.

'Sister said I could go home,' I said, rubbing my belly. 'I have a stomach ache.'

Then she asked me if I wanted some medicine. She could take me to the nurse's office.

'Sister already gave me some,' I said. It amazed me how easily the lies came to me. I didn't even have to think about them; they just came out.

'Then you run along home,' she said.

So I did. And I told my mom the same lie. But then I wasn't allowed to go out and play and I had to stay in the house. I got caught, of course. The nuns counted everyone and noticed I was missing. They didn't miss much. My mom was so mad at me that I had to stay in after school for a week because of it, after detention. I got detention for a week from Sister: double punishment. But, at least, I got out of the Stations of the Cross. I didn't have to spend the afternoon kneeling and listening to tales of torture and death. Children shouldn't be forced to listen to such things. They should be learning about life not death.

It was a warm day for February. Though he was only wearing a sport coat and slacks, he was sweating. Casey stood for a few minutes remembering the story. After what he had just experienced at Mass, he felt embarrassed by it. He was glad no one had published it. He had written it to ridicule the Church but now he read it in a new light. From the beginning, he had rejected the Cross. That was why he had become so bitter. He had expected life to be a party and it had become a trial instead. The Church was right to begin with the Cross. They wanted to prepare us for what was to come. If you start off thinking that life is just a party, eventually you will find yourself on the Cross and you'll be like the bad thief cursing God. If you begin with the Cross, you may first find sorrow and pain but in the end, you will be like the Good Thief, with Jesus in paradise.

That might have been my first sin, my original sin, he realized. I don't think I ever confessed it. So that was how it began. The first thread of the tangled web his life was to become. He remembered reading somewhere that the first sin was a lie: that we should be the ones to decide what was right and what was wrong, not God and that if we do this we shall not die, but he had lied and he had decided what was right and what was wrong and he had died.

For years, he had blamed his education for the problems he was having. He remembered bad mouthing the school, telling people that they had been brainwashed, and force-fed religious myths and told lies about sex, that the nuns had abused them by slapping their hands and faces, that their minds had been twisted by fears of eternal punishment. But he was the one who lied, who distorted the past. To tell the truth: for the most part, his memories of Saint Bridget's were good.

He hadn't realized how fortunate he was. The school was safe. Some kids had been troublemakers, certainly, but none were dangerous. Yes, the really bad kids were thrown out, as they should have been. As the nuns used to say, you can't let a few bad apples spoil all the whole bushel. No one would even have thought of bringing a gun to class. He could walk back and forth to school and go home for lunch. His mom would have been there or if she wasn't for some reason, he could have lunch at his Aunt Ann's or his Aunt Jean's or at his grand mom's. Sure, the nuns were strict and had their faults, as we all do; but most of them were good to him: Sister James Anise, Sister Rose Olivia, Sister Theresa Concilii: he remembered them fondly. They had taught him the basics: reading, writing and arithmetic and the fundamentals of the faith. The fact that he hadn't lived it was it his own fault. He felt sick to his stomach. Why had he betrayed them, the school and the Church? To blame them for his own failures, his own sins, that s why, he realized now.

He looked up Stanton Street and imagined he could see swarms of children running and playing games during recess: hopscotch and kick-the-can, red-rover come-over, and tag, you're it. Across the street, there used to be a crowd milling around Mudge's buying candy: green leaves and nonpareils and Hershey bars with almonds. Mudge's wasn't there anymore: It had been converted into an apartment but the school was there, doing its work, with the Sisters of Saint Joseph no longer wearing their long black habits and white cardboard bibs, now in normal dress, but still teaching the children the Catholic faith. Thank God for them.

As he walked up Stanton to Skiddo Street, he saw an image of himself wrapping up his safety belt and running up the street, abandoning his little charges to go and watch the Yankees play the Dodgers in the World Series. He was no catcher in the rye then. 'They'll be all right,' he had heard a voice say. 'You don't have to watch them. You don't have to protect them. No one will hurt them.' He was drummed off the Safeties for that dereliction of duty. Another thread in the web. It started way back then, his rebellion, before he was even aware, really aware, of what he was doing. Now, he knew. It wasn't growing up in the Falls. It wasn't going to Catholic schools. It wasn't his parents or his family. It wasn't the Army. It wasn't being knifed. It wasn't Vietnam that had caused his problems. It was sin, his own sin.

He crossed over the bridge that went over the railroad tracks and stood on the corner of Cresson and Calumet Street. His grand mom and grand pop had lived on this street halfway up the block. The house was still there, and so were they, he realized, but in another world, with all who had gone before them. He remembered stopping there after his first day at school. His grand parents had been so proud of him. What would they think of him now? What would all of his family think of him if they knew how he had turned out? Ashamed? Embarrassed? Disgusted? He couldn't blame them if they did. That's how he thought about himself.

He walked up Calumet to the gates of RavenHill. He saw an image of himself, walking away in anger, carrying his white surplice and hard candy tin. He remembered another story he had written, or tried to write, that is. **I will not serve**, he had called it. The story was about his refusal to serve Mass that day at RavenHill which was then a private girl's school, run by the Sisters of the Assumption, now, part of Textile College. The altar boys at Saint Bridget's served Mass there with the priest at 6:30 a.m.. Traditionally, only the new altar boys served the Mass. No one liked doing it because it was so early. He had done his turn when he was in the fifth and sixth grade and thought that he was finished with it when he went to the seventh grade but a new priest, Father Fee, came in and changed the sched-ule. He said that everyone had to do it. It was only fair. Casey remembered being furious with the priest for doing that and he rebelled when he got the assignment. In real life, he had gotten up to do it. He had to. His mom made him. But when he arrived at the gates of the school, he turned around and went home the long way, so his mom wouldn't catch on. That day, he was called in to see the priest and was kicked off the altar boys. His mom was furious but he refused to repent and apologize. 'It wasn't fair,' he had told her. 'I served my time up there.' But as he wrote the story, he wanted to change it, to make it more dramatic. He saw his rebellion as a sign of maturity, not the disobedient selfishness that it was. Like Stephen Dedalus, he was echoing Satan. He was going to have the boy stand up during the confiteor and say, 'No mea culpa. I am not sorry. I will not serve,' and walk off the altar, out of the chapel. But he couldn't remember enough of the details to make it credible, so it was left unfinished. It would stay unwritten now.

As he turned the corner off of Calumet Street and walked up Warden Drive, he heard voices in his mind, 'Don't sweat it. You were just a kid, doing kid things. Besides, that priest was wrong. Fair is fair. You were right to rebel.'

But then in his mind's eye, he saw that big white host being raised and in its reflection he saw the truth. It was another thread in the web. Ten years later, that web was as thick as cotton candy and he was like an insect waiting for the spider.

As he looked up the hills of the grounds surrounding RavenHill, 'The Nuts,' they called it. He saw an image of himself, drunk, arm in arm with a woman he had met in Quinnies' Bar, a married woman, the mother of a young child. He saw the two of them stagger up into the woods, lie down in the grass and make love. They were the nuts, alright. Her husband was at home, shotgun in hand, waiting to shoot. Only the cry of his child stopped him from shooting them, they found out later.

The thought struck him hard. 'Make love! What a farce! They didn't love each other.' See it for what it truly was: they had committed adultery. They had broken a commandment of God. He had never seen it as that before. He was just home from Vietnam, only a few weeks after R&R in Bangkok. To him, she was just another whore and it was just another score. He had fallen that far. His buddies had clapped when he left the bar with her and he had raised his arms above his head: touchdown. As he saw that image of himself, he hated what he saw.

He closed his eyes. He saw himself as a little boy sledding down those same hills, the whole world white and full of wonder. He knew he could never be that little boy again but he yearned to be as white as that snow, if that were possible. He remembered the words of Father Joe. 'Anything is possible with God.' He had to get to confession. His life depended on it.

5.

The Imposter

Casey paced up and down the train tracks. He looked at his watch: 3:30. The train was late. He couldn't wait. He thought of his alternatives: he could walk back up to Henry Avenue and get the 32 bus or he could walk down to Ridge Avenue and catch the 61. Both of them could take hours. Or he could run down along the river and arrive at Saint John's all sweaty and smelly. He wasn't dressed to run. He had on his Sunday go-to-meeting clothes: sport coat and slacks and winged tip shoes. He had dusted them off the other day. He smiled at the picture. He could imagine people looking at him like he was a white-collar criminal on the run. Who is that guy? Some madman?

He had to get downtown to confession, right now. Since Sunday, he had been going back over his life, examining his conscience. He had so much to confess. The guilt he felt was weighing him down so much that if it got any heavier, he would be crawling on his belly like a reptile. He had worked evenings at Children's Rehab over the weekend and yesterday so he hadn't had the time to go to confession before this. Where was Father Gal when he needed him? He had called the Shrine several times but they told him Father Joe was sick and was not taking calls. For the life of him, he couldn't remember the name of the priest who was reading his books. He had called the rectory at Saint Bridget's but the pastor was at a meeting at Saint Charles Seminary. Just as well. He'd feel better being anonymous, a voice in the dark, a face behind a screen. His mom told him that they heard confessions at Saint John the Evangelist in center city every afternoon so he had decided to go down there. Tomorrow was Ash Wednesday. He really wanted to go to confession for Lent and start with a clean page. He had spent the last two days thinking about what he was going to say. How could he remember all the sins he had committed over the last eighteen years? And that doesn't include the sins he hadn't confessed before that, like those he remembered Sunday. Did he have to confess them, too? He hadn't gone to confession that often, even when he was a kid. He had never liked going to confession. It became a numbers game: 'I cursed ten times, I disobeyed my parents three times, I lied twice, I masturbated, no, I don't think I ever confessed that. I didn't even know what it was when I first did it and when I did realize what it was, I was too ashamed to confess it.'

When he got older, he decided that whenever he couldn't get any sex, he would masturbate. It was better than nothing. He knew that psychologists said that there was nothing wrong with giving yourself some pleasure so that's what he had done, until a few months ago when he had finally stopped. He remembered the last time he had done it. Afterwards, he had felt so alone, so isolated. He saw himself floating in a dark smoky prison, trying to give himself pleasure, but failing; no women were there, and no matter how hard he tried, nothing happened. Then in desperation, he cried out for help, for that woman, whoever she was, to come again and rescue him, as she had done in Ireland and so many times before. Then suddenly, she was there, in the background, somewhere, telling him that if he stopped, now, love would come to him and he would no longer be alone. He did what she said and he had not masturbated since that night. But where was love?

What else had he never confessed? Getting drunk. He didn't remember ever telling that in confession. He couldn't count the times he had been drunk in his life. Hundreds of times, he guessed, from the time he was sixteen until he finally stopped, when he was pushing thirty, in 1975.

He walked to the back fence of the train station, crossing over the open space where the ticket office and waiting room had been. The East Falls train station. He remembered the times he hung out there instead of going to Mass. How old was he then? 16? He had stopped going to Mass in high school. Why? Across the station road, he saw the spiked-iron fence that they used to crawl under to get to the caves. That was where he had gotten drunk for the first time. He wrote a short story set there called **The Cave boys**. He wasn't sure why he wrote it. It also told of one of one of the most shameful things he had ever done. Perhaps that's why the details were so embedded in his memory that he could recall them verbatim.

It was the first time I had ever gotten drunk. My dad had let me have a beer a few times when we were at a family gathering but I had never drunk more than one. That was enough, my father would say. I didn't argue with him. I saw how silly my Uncle John and other people got when they drank too much and I didn't want to be like them.

But, for some reason, when I was sixteen, I started hanging out with Lurch and Quell'heure and a few other guys and went out drinking with them. They liked going down the caves to drink, they told me, because they didn't have to worry about anybody jumping them down there. If the cops tried to come after them, they could run back further in the caves and hide out. That's what they were: caves. They used to be storage rooms for Hohenadel's brewery but they were real caves, not man made. There were two of them: the big cave and the little cave. It was a spooky place like something in a horror movie. It was dark and dirty with rats and bats and snakes and all kinds of bugs inside and it smelled like dead things and every kind of filth.

We were standing in a circle in the back of the big cave, drinking from a case of Black Label beer that Phil the Bum had gotten for us. I remember being nervous and uneasy. It was a new experience for me.

I heard Lurch laugh.

"I can't believe that Dangme's here, drinking with us. I thought he was a holy roller."

The others laughed and agreed with him.

"The altar boy. The honor student," said Quell'heure. "Can you believe it? What happened, Dangme? What brings you down here to the underworld?"

I shrugged.

"I don't know. I guess I just got tired of being good all the time. I wanted to have some fun."

"Well, here," said Packy, handing me another beer. "Have some more fun."

I really didn't want another beer. I already had three bottles and it tasted rotten but I took it, anyway. It was as if someone else was in control and I had to do what he wanted me to do. My other self, I called him. I took a swig and felt like vomiting. It was warm and bitter but I forced myself to finish it. When I was done, I felt woozy. When I turned to take a leak, I staggered and almost fell. Everything was spinning around and around. It was as if the whole world had turned upside down.

I heard the others laughing and shouting.

"Look at him! He's drunk! Dangme's drunk. Dangme's drunk. Dangme's drunk"

With that, we heard a voice from Arnold Street.

"Keep it quiet up there or we'll call the cops."

Lurch cursed out the cave, chug-a-lugged from his bottle then threw it against the wall. The sound of breaking glass echoed through the caves.

The cops! I felt a moment of panic. I couldn't get arrested. What would my parents think? I started scrambling into the back of the cave but Lurch grabbed a hold of me. He was laughing.

"Don't worry, my man. They won't call the cops on us. They know better. Let's go down the Lower End and see what Kelly and Doyle and those guys are doing down there. They're always out looking for trouble."

He bear hugged me and dragged me to the hole of the cave and dumped me out like a wrestler throwing his man over the ropes.

I hated him doing that and I felt humiliated, but I wasn't about to fight Lurch. I knew that he had been in a lot of fights and he never lost, never. He was taller than I was and he knew how to fight. I was only in one fight in my life and that was when I was a little boy. Beside, I was too drunk to fight. I could barely stand up at that point.

I followed after the others and we staggered through the weeds to the iron fence. Lurch was punching the leaves of the trees and shouting, "Just 'cause I'm drunk, don't mean I can't fight. 'Cause I can."

We ducked through the hole under the fence and straggled down the Station Road like a drunken platoon on patrol.

As we passed by Saint Bridget's, I hoped that Father Cartin couldn't see me. What would he think? What would my parents think? I felt like a bum. I was no good. I was a bad kid.

Just then, we passed this black guy who was standing by the five-and-ten cent store. He was waiting for the 52 trolley, I guess.

When I got next to him, I let loose a racial slur.

I regretted it as soon as I said it. I didn't even know that I was going to say it. It just slipped out.

The guy snapped out. He came right up in my face.

He started shouting, "What did you call me? What did you call me?"

I didn't know what to say. I felt like apologizing but my tongue was tied. I just backed away. When Lurch saw what was happening, he came over and got between us. Then the other guys got into it. The next thing I knew, Magill's bar across the street emptied out and the guy was surrounded by a crowd of angry white people who thought he was the one causing trouble. Meanwhile, I slipped away and staggered up Indian Queen Lane. I hid up in the alley next to the Baptist church and watched the whole thing. Finally, the cops came and broke it up and put the guy on the bus. I didn't go down the Lower End that night. I went home instead and puked my guts out.

Casey felt sick to his stomach and weak in his knees as he saw that image of himself, being drunk and stupid. It was wrong what he did to that man. That poor guy. After Mass on Sunday, he began reading the first Gospel. Now he knew what Jesus meant when he said, 'whoever says, you fool! will be liable to the fire of hell.' Fool had to be a weak translation. It was whenever you made someone less than a person. He had to tell that in confession. To say what he said to that man was a sin. He put the man through a terrible ordeal and he almost got the man beat up or killed. Thank God, it didn't happen. He hadn't been brought up to be a racist. His parents didn't hate black people and they didn't teach him that in school. It was a sin to hate people because of the color of their skin.

He never would have said that if he hadn't been drunk. He paced up and down the tracks, thinking of all the trouble alcohol had caused him and his family. When he started coming home drunk, his parents got so upset about it. They couldn't understand what had happened to him. All of a sudden, his grades in school had slipped. He stopped being an honor student. He got arrested a couple of times for possession of alcohol. He had gotten into fights. He drove drunk. He was lucky he hadn't wound up in jail.

He knew the standard explanations of why people became alcoholics: It was genetic; it was hereditary; it was environmental; it was a disease. But none of them had ever satisfied him. His grandfather had been an alcoholic but his father wasn't. He drank but he wasn't a drunkard and his mother hardly drank at all. A lot of people drank in the neighborhood but not everyone did. So why he had started drinking was a mystery to him. Now they were calling it a disease but it didn't seem like a disease to him, not in his case, anyway. Other diseases like infections and cancers came to you but you had to go to alcohol. If you didn't drink it, there'd be no problem.

He had tried to stop drinking many times over the years. He would go on the wagon. He would take vow upon vow to stop, and he would for a while, but then his other self would appear and he would fall off the wagon and roll in the mud again. But after that horrible night when he had hit Marie, he knew that he had to stop drinking for good. He had thought he had been healed in Ireland but obviously he hadn't been. He had gotten worse. How did that happen? Where did he go wrong? He walked up the Forbidden Path and down along the river, trying to talk with that woman but there was no answer. He knew that he had fallen out of favor with her and rightfully so. He begged for forgiveness and pleaded with her to tell him what to do. Finally, after hours of walking, he could hear her voice but only faintly. Then the answer came: he had failed in his mission. What mission? He was to tell the story of what had happened in Ireland. But what had happened? He would find out as he wrote the story. So he made telling that story the purpose of his life and he had stopped drinking. The big test came when he went back to Ireland in 1975 to get what he needed to write the book. He stayed there for 3 weeks in the winter and not a drop taken. Mick couldn't believe it. 'You're a new mahn,' he said. Not really, not yet. Since then, he had written draft after draft and he still didn't know what his mission was. He remembered reading a prayer of the fictional writer of the story of another monomaniac: that he hoped that God would keep him from ever finishing anything because he wanted the search to continue until obliteration. Not Casey. He wanted to finish his story and be recreated. Even though he would say that he no longer had a drinking problem, that he was not an alcoholic, he had the sense that his other self was alive and lurking in the darkness like an impostor waiting to take over.

Just then the train pulled into the station and he ran over to catch it. As he got on the train, he remembered the times he had taken it with his father. They rode it to the station at Allegheny Avenue and then walked down 22nd Street to Connie Mack Stadium at 21st and Lehigh to see the Phillies play baseball. He loved going to the games with his dad. He saw himself, just a little guy, wearing a red Phillies cap and carrying his baseball glove, running along beside his father. He tried to fit that picture into the image of himself just a few years later, drunk and acting stupid but they didn't match up. He had become someone he wasn't.

How had it happened? How had he lost who he was? He had no excuse. For the most part, he had a good childhood. His parents were always there. They loved him. He had gone to Catholic schools where they taught him the difference between right and wrong, and yet, he had done wrong, over and over again. Why? Since Sunday, he was beginning to see how it happened. It was a gradual process. One sin led to another and to another: more threads in the web, wrapping around him like a strait jacket, paralyzing him.

There was that word again: paralyzed. He sat upright in his seat, remembering that car accident again. There was something about it that was key.

He was driving down Walnut Lane, getting ready to turn onto Henry Avenue. He had the green light. He saw another car coming towards him, on the other side of Henry Avenue on Walnut Lane. He knew he had to put on the brakes and let the other car continue but for some reason, he couldn't do it. It was as if he were paralyzed. He just let his car smash into the other one. The next thing he knew, he was standing in the street with blood running down his face. Then what? He tried to remember what happened after that but a darkness fell over his eyes, blinding him.

He bent over and made a tiny sign of the cross. He prayed: 'Jesus, have pity on me. Open my eyes so I can see.'

He felt a peacefulness come over him and it all came back to him.

He is in the Emergency Room at Roxborough Memorial, with blood all over his face. His vision is still impaired. People look like trees walking. He sees his mother and father come in.

He hears his mother say, 'Oh God, Bud, his eye. Look at the blood. I hope he hasn't hurt his eye.'

I point to my eyebrow and say, 'It's not my eye.'

'Thank God' says my mother.

Then she turns to my father and says, 'Oh Bud, your car. You worked so hard for that car and waited so long to get it and now it's wrecked.'

My father shrugs.

'It's not that important. He's okay. That's what matters.'

I think, 'My mother doesn't love me.'

Casey leaned forward in his seat as if he's watching a tragedy unfold before him.

'Why did I think that? It doesn't make sense. Her first concern was for me. I had never doubted that my mother loved me. That's why I didn't cry on the first day of school. There was nothing to cry about. I knew she would be waiting for me at home.'

He heard a voice.

'She didn't hug you or wipe the blood from your face.'

He answered.

'Yeah, sure. I wouldn't have let her. I was a boy, a little man. We don't let moms hug us. That would make us little girls.'

He heard the voice again.

'She cared more about the car than about you.'

He answered.

'Yeah, sure. All my mom ever cared about was her family. She never stopped loving me, even when I was bad. Neither did my father. He never criticized or blamed me for the accident. I was too young to drive was his explanation. I ignored his response and focused on my mother and what she said and for some reason came to the conclusion that she didn't love me. Why?'

Casey leaned back and reflected on what he had remembered.

'I don't know. It doesn't make sense. All I know is that I started drinking after that. Why? Open your eyes and see.'

He saw himself talking with Bogie a few days after the accident.

'The car's totaled. We can't go up to the golf course anymore. I don't know what to do now at night.'

Bogie shrugs.

'You could always hang out with Lurch and Quell'heure and those guys and go drinking with them down the caves.'

He hears a voice.

'That's it. Go out and get drunk. And skip going to Mass. You know that'll hurt your mom. You know what she thinks about that. That's it. Your mom doesn't love you. And neither does God. Go out and get drunk. And instead of going to Mass, go and hang out up at the train station with Packy and the other guys.'

He consents. As he does he feels an emptiness deep inside of him.

Casey sat straight up in his seat as sober as a judge. He had repressed that incident for all these years.

'So that was how it started,' he thought. 'That's why I started drinking and getting into trouble. It was as if there was someone inside of me, speaking to me: my other self, the impostor. Who is he? I don't know but whoever he is, he's a liar.'

Casey sat back in his seat and took a deep breath. He remembered what Father Joe had said to him the other day.

'He is a liar and the father of lies. Satan. Is that who I'm dealing with here? Is he behind it all? Is he my other self? Is he the impostor?'

His set his face towards the church.

As the train pulled into Market Street East, he rehearsed in his mind what he was going to say to the priest in confession.

6.

The Sacred Bleeding

Father Michael McDonald walked up the ramp to Saint Catherine's Infirmary. He was on his way to see Father Joe Gallagher. Father Joe had just returned from Germantown Hospital where he had been hospitalized for the last few days with an infection in his heel. He had gone to see him yesterday in the hospital and had anointed him with the holy oil of the Sacrament of the Sick. Father Joe was in no danger of dying, but nonetheless, he was a sick man. Hopefully, he wouldn't lose his foot.

Father Joe was in Room 101, the first room past the refectory. Breakfast was just getting over and Father Mike saw a few of the priests finishing their breakfast. Father Hurley, Father Flaherty and Father Henry were sitting at one of the tables talking. He heard Father Flaherty protesting in his loud voice about the suppression of the Old Latin Mass and then proclaiming its comeback. He was from the Old School. Father Hurley was agreeing with him but Father Henry seemed bored by the conversation. For Father Mike the Mass was the Mass whether it was in English or Latin. As long as we had the Word of God and the Body and Blood of Jesus Christ, we had all that we needed.

Father Mike stopped for a moment at the statue of Saint Catherine Laboure, dressed in a blue gown and white headdress, the

Daughter of Charity to whom the Miraculous Medal was manifested by the Blessed Virgin in Paris in 1830.

'What was it like,' he thought, 'To actually see the Blessed Mother and to touch her? Saint Catherine was the only visionary to actually touch a heavenly person. What a privilege.'

A couple of months ago, he had reread Father Joe Dirvin's book on the life of Saint Catherine: a great story. Some people called it the beginning of the Marian Age but they forgot about Our Lady of La Vang. The Blessed Mother came to La Vang in 1798. She appeared to a group of Vietnamese Catholics who were being persecuted by one of their kings. He had talked to Father John Kennedy the other day about her. Gippo had been in Vietnam in January, giving a retreat for the Vietnamese Daughters of Charity. There had been thousands of pilgrims at the Cathedral at La Vang. The Church was still alive in Vietnam. According to Gippo, there is also a Shrine in a cave at Nui Ba Dinh or the Black Virgin Mountain honoring a Lady Buddha who is also called the Lady of Consolation, which is another name for the Blessed Mother, and the Catholic pilgrims share the Shrine with the Buddhists. The Buddhists know in their hearts that there is a special woman who intercedes for them; they just haven't recognized her yet. They will someday.

Father Mike stood for a few moments in front of the statue of Saint Catherine and said a few prayers. A couple of people he met over at the novena on Monday asked him to pray for them. He had remembered them this morning when he said Mass and he prayed for them again now. He went over to the bulletin board next to Room 101. He looked at the prayer list and saw Father Joe's name on it. He took out his pen and wrote in another name: Bill Casey. For conversion, he wrote after the name. He reminded himself that he wanted to read Casey's other book **The Circle of Stones** today; after reading **The Story of a Swallow** he had more trust in the author. Later this afternoon, he was going down to Saint John's with Father Brandenburger to hear confessions. The Vincentians helped parishes throughout the city with their Lenten penitential services, in addition to their usual assignments. They went down there once a week to help the Franciscans. Tomorrow was Ash Wednesday and there would be much to do during Lent.

The door to room 101 was closed so Father Mike knocked softly before entering.

He heard the voice of Father Joe: "Enter, ye who dare."

Father Charles laughed as he went into the room. He saw Father Joe sitting in a recliner, his bandaged foot propped on a pillow.

"Welcome home," said Father Mike."

"It's good to be home," said Father Joe. "We're really fortunate to have this infirmary. It beats being in a hospital any day."

Father Mike agreed.

"I remember visiting Father Phil Dion in this very room. As you probably know, he was one of our priests who helped build this place back in the seventies. A great man and a good priest."

Father Joe nodded.

"Speaking of a great man and a good priest, I just had a visit from Father Charlie O'Connor. He was regaling me with stories of his days in China: He and Father Mottey hiding from the Communists in the jungle. Scary stuff. Then being kicked out of China at gunpoint and put on a Japanese freighter of all things, a rusty one at that, and then the long voyage around the Cape."

Father Mike nodded his head.

'Then who did I see but Black Bob Crawford, himself," continued Father Joe. "I didn't get the chance to talk with him. I just saw him go by when I was in the refectory for breakfast."

Father Mike shook one hand as if it were on fire.

"Ah, yes, he comes back to the Motherhouse every year for a checkup. He's exposed to a lot of exotic diseases in the Philippines. He looks great: like a native with that tan."

They talked about Father Bob Crawford for a few minutes. He had gone back to Southeast Asia after the end of the Vietnam War to help the boat people. He was a legend in his own time: a real hero. His story was well known in the Vincentian Community. He was the missionary par excellence. He was in Vietnam from 1954 until 1975. He ran an orphanage in Saigon for handicapped children and he stayed there until the end, when the Communists were on the outskirts of the city and then he got all the children in the orphanage out of the country, over a hundred of them. Somehow, through a friend, he found a plane that would fly them to the US. It was not easy to do such a thing in Saigon in 1975 but he got it done: a miracle. Then when they had landed in California, the customs officials were not going to let them in: They had no visas, they needed medical care, they had nowhere to go. But Father Bob got them in, somehow, and found an orphanage in Arizona that would take them; and he stayed with them until all of them, over a hundred handicapped orphans, were placed in private homes.

Father Mike told him about what Casey had written about the children of Vietnam.

"Obviously, he didn't know about Father Crawford and he wasn't aware of **Operation Babylift**, an operation that was one of the greatest rescue mission of the century; hundreds of Vietnamese-American orphans were flown out of South Vietnam to the United States. At a great risk. If you remember, the first plane out of Tan San Nhut crashed and exploded killing over a hundred people including many of the children."

Father Joe shook his head.

"How awful. I remember reading about it in our bulletin. Father Crawford makes me proud to be a Vincentian.."

Father Mike nodded.

"I know what you mean. But at least you were a missionary. I was safe within the halls of Saint John's."

"I don't know about that," said Father Joe. "I'm sure it wasn't easy being there, during the 60s, especially."

Father Mike sighed.

"Yes, those were the days: the 60s. Like the 60s of the first century: times of trial and persecution. When I was ordained in 1950, we were under such tight control by the Church. The rules were clear. We knew what to do. Then we were like redcoats all in a line, picked off one by one by the Vatican Council. Well, not the Council, but those interpreters of the Council. Those with an agenda of their own. The Spirit of Vatican II, they called it. The smoke of Satan in the sanctuary."

Father Joe shook his head.

"I have to admit I got caught up in all the changes myself. It embarrasses me to say this but I remember throwing out my rosary beads when I was down in Panama in the 70s. Medieval nonsense, I called it. Mary-worship. Superstition. 'Don't rattle on like the pagans,' I used to say. But then I saw the love that the Panamanians, the simple country people, had for Mary. La Madre de Dios, they called her. They made me ashamed of myself. An old woman said to me once: 'God tells us to honor our father and mother. She is the mother of Jesus, the Mother of God. We need to honor her. As Jesus did.' That did it. I went out and bought another rosary and have been saying it every day since then."

Father Mike smiled. He had never lost his devotion to the Blessed Mother. He'd been saying the rosary every day since he was a little boy.

"Speaking of the Blessed Mother," said Father Joe. "Have you had the chance to read Casey's books yet?"

Father Mike shrugged and nodded.

"I read one of them: **The Story of a Swallow.**"

Father Joe smiled.

"Is it any good?'

Father Mike turned one hand over as if he were opening a door and then back as if he were closing it again.

"It's not bad. I have to admit, I was surprised. I was just going to skim over it but as I started to read it I got caught up in it. Those poor children gasping for breath, holding onto life by the skin of their teeth. It's a gripping story, painful to read at times. I could do without the scatological details although you could say that's part of the reality of a hospital. The writing is a little choppy and disjointed at times, probably because of being revised frequently. There are frequent time shifts that can be confusing and he uses many medical terms which were unfamiliar to me. It probably could use a glossary. Overall, though, it rings true. But it can't stand on its own. It doesn't work as a separate book. It would have to be read as part of a larger narrative. I still don't know why it's called **The Story of a Swallow**. There are elements of truth in it - of goodness. But then there are parts which are false: wrong. The young nurse, Katie, that he works with has more sense than he has. He should listen to her. Casey's character Jim O'Rourke reminds me of **Lord Jim** in Conrad's book. If you remember the story: He was a mate on a ship that was transporting pilgrims to Mecca when it looked as if the ship was going to sink. He had always wanted to be a hero but when the opportunity presented itself, he abandoned ship instead and left the pilgrim to their fate. Well, the ship didn't sink and he felt guilty about what he did and he spent years of his life trying to expiate his guilt. Casey's character also wanted to be a hero but failed to be one, in his mind, anyway. Obviously though, Casey's character lived and didn't die as Conrad's character did. However, whatever happened in Ireland didn't expiate his guilt. It couldn't really. Only Sacramental Confession can do that. I have to take issue with him on some of the other statements he made. You told me that he wanted me to tell him where he went wrong in his books. Well."

He made a motion of unrolling a scroll.

"I have a laundry list this long. I'll mention them to him if and when I talk to him."

Then he laughed.

"Like Fulton Sheen said, 'For all the people who claim to hate the Church, how many of them really know it?'"

"Casey should know it," said Father Joe. "He's an educated Catholic. But, unfortunately, they're often the worst."

"'Corruptio optimi, pessimi'" said Father Mike. "The corruption of the best is the worst. When you fall from grace in the Catholic Church, you fall hard. Let's hope he can reverse the fall and be raised up to full stature."

Father Mike sat back in his chair and looked at the ceiling, musing.

"Casey's problem is that he's a romantic and like all romantics, when he sees imperfection and sinfulness, he becomes disillusioned, bitter. He wants to change the world which of course he can't. No one can. He's a utopian as all socialists are. They foolishly believe that we can have heaven on earth. But all we can do is to preserve whatever is good and overcome whatever is bad and guard against all the destructive forces that from time to time erupt out of the bowels of hell. But to his credit, Casey cares about the poor and the sick. And God bless him for the work he does. But because poverty and sickness still exist, that means no one cares, except him, of course, certainly not the Church."

Father Joe shook his head.

"Certainly, we don't do enough. And the Church is full of sinful people. But world-wide, the Catholic Church does far more for the poor and the sick than any other organization. It was the Church that founded the first hospitals and orphanages. Look at our own Saint Vincent de Paul's Society. We've been providing families with clothes and food and furniture for hundreds of years."

Father Mike agreed.

"But as Fulton Sheen also said when he heard someone berating the Church: 'What's your sin?' I think our man Casey got lost in the funhouse as a boy, in sexual fantasies, the house of mirrors. Masturbation leads to narcissism and a loss of contact with reality. No wonder he's had problems with women; they weren't real people to him, only objects for his own self-satisfaction. But he can't see that, so he blames the Church. 'The Church hates sex,' he said."

Father Joe shook his head.

"I'm not surprised. In many ways though, it's our fault. We haven't gotten out the message properly. When's the last time we gave homilies on sex and marriage? We've allowed ourselves to be intimidated. Fortunately, the Pope isn't intimidated. I just read a wonderful book entitled **Covenant of Love**. It's about The Holy Father's teaching on sexuality. The Pope says an amazing thing: that marital sexual love is an act of worship; when it is a true giving of the self, a communion, it is an icon, an image, of the Trinity."

Father Mike nodded.

"Absolutely. That's what happens in all the sacraments. When a husband and wife make love, they experience God. While it is true that we have not gotten out the true teaching of the Church on sex, it may be God Himself who is silencing us on it. I believe it was Saint Gregory the Great who said, 'that frequently, the preacher's tongue is bound because of the people's sins. They are unworthy to hear the truth.'"

Father Joe nodded.

"Didn't Saint Paul said something along that line also, that God handed them over to impurity for the degradation of their bodies?"

"Yes. Exactly," said Father Mike. "Their sins are their own punishment. We see it today: all the broken families, all the people on drugs, the violence in the schools, in the streets, the crime. All the result of our sinfulness: promiscuity, adultery and their after-math: abortion. A child is made in the image and likeness of God. When we kill a child, not only are we killing a person, we are, in effect, killing Christ."

Father Joe sighed.

"I guess it goes without saying that Casey is pro-abortion."

Father Mike shrugged.

"He appears to be. But I get the impression that he doesn't really believe what he says. Apparently, he had a child of his own aborted. He doesn't want to truly face what he did, so he rationalizes: they didn't know enough about birth control; they had no other choice; they weren't ready for a child; it's her body; they would have been bad parents; the world is a terrible place. The usual demonic litany. Anything but face the reality: they sacrificed their own child on the altar of selfishness, irresponsibility and ignorance."

"Speaking of child sacrifice," said Father Joe, "is anything in there about sorcery? There were rumors going around that Casey had some strange ideas and had done some weird things in the hospital."

Father Mike shook his head.

"No, I wouldn't call it sorcery. Strange stuff, though. He does this ritual called therapeutic touch. Has to do with sending energy through what are referred to as 'chakras', openings in the body or something. He says he learned how to do it in Ireland, in the circle of stones. Apparently, he healed a couple of children doing it."

"Do you buy it?" asked Father Joe.

Father Mike held his hands as if he were praying.

"I'm still skeptical about the circle of stones, but yes, I do believe that they really happened, that he's writing from experience. He isn't always able to do it and he knows his limitations. And he doesn't take credit for it. When he does it, it seems like he's praying although he's too confused to know how to pray properly. When I read it I couldn't help but think of the passage of Saint Paul in Romans: 'We do not know how to pray as we ought, but the Spirit itself intercedes with inexpressible groanings.' Although I don't know if I would call it a miracle as one of his characters does, although you never know. As the character Kent in **King Lear** says, 'Nothing almost see miracles but misery,' and that place was full of misery."

Father Joe shifted his bottom and moved his foot. He grimaced and grunted.

"Maybe he can heal my foot."

Father Mike smiled.

"Maybe. But Casey wouldn't take credit for it. He's only a disciple, he said at one point."

"A disciple of whom?"

Father Mike shrugged.

"We know it can't be the triple goddess of Ireland. She doesn't exist. In some ways, Casey reminds me of Flannery O'Connor, though she is the more accomplished writer by far. He doesn't use the grotesque as she did. The children he describes aren't grotesque. They're sick and they've been badly damaged. And God bless those nurses for taking care of them. They're living the Gospel. O'Connor's characters keep trying to deny Christ, but they can't. The same with Casey's character, O'Rourke. But without Christ, life doesn't make sense."

Father Joe agreed.

'The composer, Rachmaninoff, once said, after he wrote his Second Symphony, that if one note were missing, just one note, the symphony would fall apart. You could say that Christ is the keynote of the symphony of life."

Father Mike smiled.

"Yes. Amazing. One note. It goes to show you how structured true art is. And life itself."

He stopped for a moment. He had been trying to make a point about Casey's book.

"Oh, yes. Casey also imitates O'Connor in another way. I don't know whether it's as conscious in his case as it was in O'Connor's, but I could see, when I read his book, the sacred, the supernatural, bleeding into the story: a drop here, a drop there."

"In what way?" asked Father Joe.

"Words would suddenly appear," explained Father Mike. "Penance. Heaven. The laying-on of hands. God."

"How about the Blessed Mother? Does she come into it?"

Father Mike hesitated.

"Not that I can see. Although a couple of times he uses the

phrase 'that woman'. He says he did what 'that woman' wanted him to do in Ireland and he doesn't seem to be referring to Madeleine, a woman that he met there. Maybe I'll know more when I read his first book."

With that, Helen, the head nurse came into the room.

"Excuse me," she said. "But I have to change the dressing on Father's foot."

She wagged her finger at Father Joe.

"If he had only come over here when he first started having problems, this wouldn't have happened. You priests never learn. You have to take care of yourselves. We need you. There are not enough of you now."

The two priests looked at each other and smiled. They had listened to Helen's lectures more than once. She meant well. They knew that she truly cared about them.

Father Mike excused himself and slipped out the door before Helen could question him about his medications. A couple of his prescriptions had run out and he hadn't renewed them. He would bring them over before he left for Saint John's.

When Helen was finished changing Father Joe's dressing, Bridie, his aide, came in and made his bed and then Shelly, from the kitchen, came in and filled his water pitcher. Being in the infirmary was like living in a fish bowl. He had people looking at him all day long. Like most priests, Father Joe was a very private person and he wasn't used to being around so many women. He appreciated their attention but he couldn't wait to get back to his own room in the seminary.

When he was finally alone, he closed his eyes and tried to sleep. He was so tired. He hadn't gotten a good night s sleep in the two nights he had been in the hospital. Nurses had been in and out of the room taking his vital signs and checking the IV. They had done finger-sticks every few hours for his blood sugar: It was high, his blood pressure was high, and he was down in the dumps. His room-mate had been on a heart monitor and its alarm kept going off. The man had the TV on all day and all night: talk shows and sit coms, commercial after commercial. Maddening. He had been unable to read or think. He had felt like he was losing his mind. What a trial that had been. Thank God he was in the Infirmary, now.

With that thought, he picked up his breviary and went to the Office of Readings. How providential it was that the Church was reading the Book of Job this week. How often that seemed to happen: That the liturgy matched the particular need that he had at the time. As he read Job cursing the day he was born and how he had no peace and no rest, Father Joe could empathize. He prayed for all the sick people around the world that they would not lose heart and that, like Job, they would be restored to health and prosperity. He prayed for Bill Casey that he would find his way back to Our Father's House. As he prayed, he felt his spirit lift and he was at peace.

After leaving Father Joe, Father Mike took a walk around the garden that was in the center of the square made by the seminary, the old novitiate and the infirmary. The old novitiate was now an archives for the Eastern Province; the seminary, now a home for priests like him: independent living they called it.

He walked over by the fish pond. He remembered helping to dig that pond years ago when he was in the novitiate. How different it was, then, in those years, after the war. They were in that building all day long: studying and praying, wearing their cassocks. On Sunday afternoons, they went for long walks together; all of them wearing Panama hats in the summer. Germantown was a vibrant neighborhood then, with large houses with lawns and shade trees and a variety of shops and stores and restaurants. The people respected priests and the Church in those days. Of course, there had been a lot of Catholics in the neighborhood then. Immaculate down the street had been a large parish with thousands of parishioners. Now they were numbered in the hundreds. It was all part of the Paschal mystery. Just as Jesus, their head, had suffered, died and was buried and then rose again, so had the Church. After the French Revolution, the newspapers were proclaiming the death of the Church, only to see it rise again a few years later, stronger than ever. Ever ancient, ever new. During the 1960s, it had happened again: The Church had suffered and died. Now it was rising again.

'Just as this garden will rise again,' thought Father Mike.

It was a beautiful garden, especially in the spring and summer. There were a variety of trees: a large oak and a small one, a cluster of white birch, a couple linden trees, some holly trees and bushes, a

Chinese dogwood, a ginkgo, a Korean boxwood and a few big leaf magnolias. Since this was a shrine to the Blessed Mother, in the summer there were plenty of rosebushes and marigolds, petunias and impatiens.

It wasn't spring yet, so nothing was in bloom, but it wouldn't be long. All that was dead would be coming back to life: The beauty of God's creation.

'God so loved the world that He sent His only Son to redeem us.'

That line from John never ceased to amaze him. 'God so loved the world.' Christianity has often been called other-worldly: a false accusation. The Church has always taught that we can come to a knowledge of God through His creation and through our reason. God comes to us in the sacraments: in water and oil, bread and wine. God has power over the whole realm of being.

Using our reason, we can see the complexity and design in the universe and come to a realization that it was created for a purpose. Every symphony has a composer. Every book has an author. This is the basis for all the truths of the faith. If you believe that there is someone powerful enough to create this vast and complex universe, then everything else is easy to believe. Jesus Christ is the key piece. Without Him, life is a puzzle, a mystery, impossible to solve. As the Council put it: 'Only in the mystery of the Word Incarnate does the mystery of man truly become clear.'

As Father Mike strolled around the garden, he was reminded of the first garden, of Adam and Eve: Paradise. Everything in it was very good. But through Satan sin entered the world. What happened to Adam and Eve happens to all of us. It is the story of every man and woman. And so it happened: the Fall. We fell out of the garden and into the briar patch: of sickness, suffering and death. Like Br'er Rabbit we may have been 'bred and bawn in the briar patch,' but it's not our home and we can't get out as easily as Br'er Rabbit did. We needed someone help us out. We needed a savior and God sent us one: His Son, Jesus Christ, true God and true man. Christ as 'the new man' shows us what the human person truly is. It is only by 'putting on Jesus Christ' that we become our true selves.

With that thought, Father Mike made the sign of the cross and left the garden. He went into the seminary side of Saint Vincent's.

As he walked down the hall, he heard the sounds of men working. Some were tearing up the carpets and putting down new ones while others were painting the walls and ceilings. One housekeeper was wiping the pictures of Jesus and Mary and the angels and the saints until they shone; another was cleaning the windows and letting in some fresh air. It was as if they were preparing the House for the homecoming of a long-lost son. He took the elevator up to his cell. It wasn't much but it was home. It was small space with a bed, a recliner and a desk. He had several cases filled with books. He turned on his stereo and put on a tape of Bach's **Saint Matthew's Passion** conducted by John Eliot Gardiner then he sat down at his desk and began reading **The Circle of Stones**. He wanted to finish it before he went down to Saint John's to hear confessions.

7.

The Circle of Stones

"For he comes the human child, to the waters and the wild,
with a faery, hand in hand, from a world more full of weeping
than he can understand."

William Butler Yeats, The Stolen Child.

Ballinskelligs.
As James read the name of the village on the signpost, he
flashed on the Skelligs Rock: a stone shaft with a halo of crimson
clouds rising from the sea. A sacred place, according to Mick.
James wanted to take the boat out there this time. Maybe there, he
would find what he was looking for and do what he had to do to be
healed. But first he had to talk with Mick again. Mick would show
him the way.

Any minute now, he would be at Ranchhouse. Through the
trees, he saw the glass roof of the backroom. Several dogs barked as
he turned onto the path that led to the front door of the farm.

He entered Ranchhouse and stood in the doorway, shouting
Mick's name, until a short man with long blonde hair appeared out
of the darkness of the kitchen and greeted him in German.

Startled, James asked if Mick Casey was at home.

"Up the pub," said the blonde man after several moments.

James stared at the man, not sure of what to say. James wanted to ask him who he was but decided not to. The man could be anyone: a gunman on holiday, a poet on sabbatical, or a student on vacation. Through the backroom window, James saw another man and a woman playing guitars in the garden by the haystack. Or he could be another lost child.

Abruptly, the blonde man turned and disappeared into the backroom.

James slipped out of his backpack and propped it in a corner.

He decided to go up to the pub and talk with Mick himself. He was the man James had come to see.

James hesitated outside the door for a moment, deciding whether to walk down to the beach and go up the pub that way or take the road he had just left. He decided to visit the beach later. As tired as he was, he did a little skip up the road. He saw a donkey behind a hedgerow and a few cows chewing the bright green grass of a field. Black birds flew through the fog that was floating around the mountains that were guarding the bay. He took a deep breath. Excited, he picked up the pace. He was back in Ballinskelligs and he was going to meet Mick again. Suddenly, he felt thirsty. He wanted a drink. He stopped walking and looked out over the sea. He could not drink, he reminded himself. He had to stay sober. He had to be aware and in control or he would fail in his mission.

Several minutes later, James passed the shop and post office and entered the pub. He saw Mick standing by the bar, drinking a pint of stout. Mick pushed back his straw hat, squinting through the smoke curling around his face.

"Well, well, welcome to the barroom floor. James O'Rourke, is it? Of course, I remember you. You were with me last summer, for a week or two. 'Farewell to Philadelphia. It's a place you'll ne'er see more.'"

Mick laughed as he slapped James on the back.

"My God, mahn. I was just thinking of you. Must have been a case of? What do they call it?!"

James laughed.

"Mental telepathy."

"So tell me, mahn. How have you been since you left here? No more astral trips, I hope."

James shook his head. He felt embarrassed about that. He would never take acid again.

"Surviving, that's about it."

"That's all we do here. 'Life, a weary puzzle past finding out by mahn.' That's what we were just discussing."

Mick waved his hand at his audience: several men hunched over their pints along the mahogany bar, a solitary old man seated in shadows by the cold fireplace, and the bartender, a sullen man who questioned James about a drink.

James felt his resolve weaken. If he didn't drink, Mick would be suspicious of him and wouldn't talk to him. But he had to be careful. He would have just one pint.

"Sure. Why not? It is almost evening. A pint of Guinness for Michael and myself and whatever they're drinking."

The local men protested meekly but quickly submitted.

Mick introduced James to the men.

"You may have met him last summer. James is interested in our way of life, our history and our politics. He's one of our exiles. Isn't that right, James?"

James nodded.

"Tell me more, mahn. When did you arrive in the magical, mystical country of Ireland, the land of the faery folk, the leprechaun and the banshee?"

"Got into Dun Laoghaire three days ago."

Hand in hand with a faery, he mused. He quickly sketched his journey to Ireland, not mentioning the three females who had escorted him. He didn't want to tell Mick about them. Mick wouldn't understand. Maybe he could talk with Deirdre about them, if she still lived at Ranchhouse. He asked Mick about her.

Mick grimaced as he waved the question away.

"She left a month ago. She's in Dublin now. Did you stay there at all?"

"Only for a night. I talked to Christy at the Dollymount. You know him. A tall, skinny guy. One of the crowd I came with last year. He told me not to come here. That you were too upset about something."

Mick lit another cigarette.

"Now, what could that be? Know him? That idjit, I know him well. He stayed with me for four months last summer. Ate away half of me spuds. Drew the dole for drink. And me, without a tuppence to me name. Mooning over Madeleine. She wouldn't have him so he went on a drunk. If he gets wind that she's here now, there'll be no holding Christy in Dublin."

"Who's Madeleine?"

"Madeleine Chadwick, the midwife. She comes from an old village family, the Murphy's. She's staying in her grandmother's house up on the mountain. Her grandmother died a few years ago. Madeleine lives in London, now. Her mother married and moved to England, years ago. Married an Englishman. Good mahn, though. Madeleine's been coming here every summer on holiday since she was a little girl. You just missed her last year. A lovely lass about your age, James. Smart. She recognized Christy for the fool he is. And I'm happy to hear that you ignored his advice and came down anyway."

James smiled.

"I was happy to hear that you were still alive."

Mick grimaced and waved one hand, the other cupped to his hip.

"Ah, mahn. I'd be better off out of it. I won't live much longer. Getting old. Damn tobacco."

Mick coughed into his crusty handkerchief.

"Me throat's almost gone now."

James felt like laughing. He felt the same way as Mick did. But he felt dead already. It was the end of the world. Apocalypse now.

"After I left Dublin, I hitched down the coast. Took the road from Wicklow. What a desperate road that is. There wasn't much out there. I felt like I was lost in the wasteland, the only man left alive."

Narrow roads wound around cliffs beneath which the sea arched and foamed over rocky beaches. Feeling like a piece of trash washed upon the shore, he had walked through deserted farmland and ruined houses that offered no food or sanctuary but only served to remind him of where he had come from and why he was there.

James finished his pint. He felt his tension ease. That was his limit, he reminded himself.

"The first day, I had to walk twenty miles. Nobody would pick me up. I don't know why."

Mick laughed.

"I hate to be the one to tell you this, mahn but you do look a little rough. Like a mahn on the run."

James tried to see himself as others did. His hair curled up around his collar and he needed a shave badly. The customs inspector in England had taken one look at his fatigue shirt, dungarees and combat boots and insisted on seeing his return ticket to America. He told Mick about it.

"You didn't tell him you were coming here, did you, mahn?"

James shook his head.

"I didn't tell him anything. I told him I was a tourist."

"Good mahn. You have to be careful. The British know about Ranchhouse." said Mick. "Let me buy you a pint."

James started to protest but he had to laugh as he watched Mick fumble through the trouser pockets of his dusty black suit and bring forth a crumpled pound note the size of a small coin, hold it to the light for inspection, then smooth it out and place it on the bar.

"Don't worry," said Mick to the bartender. "It's good. I just saw it made."

James laughed. He felt like celebrating his return. He needed to lighten up and have a good time. Then maybe later, he would be able to talk about his dilemma. Mick would straighten him out.

James gulped down half the pint.

"Can we sit down? I'm tired. I had to walk all the way from Cahirciveen, carrying that pack. With no food. I haven't eaten since yesterday."

As he followed James to the table in the corner, Mick yanked a dark object from James' back pocket and shouted, "What's this, Yank?"

"You know," said James. "It's a cap."

James flushed as he remembered trying it on in front of a car window in Killarney and being laughed at by a woman pedaling her bicycle.

Mick grinned.

"Why aren't you wearing it? Instead of carrying it, stuffed in your back pocket?"

James shrugged. Usually, he didn't wear a hat. It seemed like part of a uniform and he hated uniforms.

Mick shouted to his audience.

"Cad a gloamed air?"

An old man twisted a rheumy eye from over his pint and blurted, "Fir i hata."

Mick laughed.

"Fir i hata, you don't know how to wear it."

Mick tugged the tweed cap down over James' eyes and pushed back its visor.

"Wear it like that. Like a local boy down from the mountain."

They sat beneath a photograph of the first transatlantic cable station that had been housed in County Kerry many years before.

"Talk to me, mahn. Why are you here?"

James lit a cigarette and drank from his pint.

"Ever since I left here, I wanted to come back. It's beautiful here. I don't want to live in America anymore. I felt like I was going crazy over there. I don't know what to do with my life. What kind of work to do. Any job you do is connected to the system in some way and I don't want anything to do with that system. They sent me to Vietnam to get killed and then treated me like trash when I came back."

"Like I told you last year, mahn: you are welcome here. Stay as long as you like. Why go back? 'Farewell to Philadelphia. It's a place you'll ne'er see more.' Legend has it that it'll be the third generation who will return and restore Ireland to its former glory. You're third generation Irish-American, aren't you?"

James shrugged.

"That's another reason why I came back. I don't know much about Irish history, about my roots. I don't even know why my ancestors left Ireland. Their story's lost. I guess it was because of the Famine. I was hoping you'd be able to teach me about it."

"Famine," Mick scoffed. "You mean starvation, don't you? The blight only affected one crop: the potato. There were ten ships a day leaving Waterford City loaded with livestock: cows, pigs, poultry, you name it, mahn. To feed the British while the Irish starved. That's right. The same British that we're at war with now, in Northern Ireland."

After a moment, Mick calmed down.

"Sure, I'll teach you, mahn. In many ways, our history is a sad one. We've been dominated by the British Empire for eight hundred years. But we'll continue the fight until the day the bloody British are gone. We will never give up. Life is hard here,mahn. Make no mistake about it. The land is beautiful to look at, but God help the mahn who has to work it for a living. The young people pull out of Southwest Kerry every day. They are not willing to work so hard for such little reward. Life in the fishing boats taxes the will of any mahn. They work sixteen hours a day, six days a week, all year round, in the lashing rain, on high seas. Boats sink. Men drown. It's no way of life for the faint of heart."

As James listened to Mick talk, he longed for that kind of life. He sought connection with the living environment, away from the artificiality of city life. He felt the need for community, a place where he belonged. He needed something to believe in, a cause worth fighting for. But he didn't know anything about farming or fishing. Maybe Mick would help him learn.

"Who's here now?" asked James. "I met a hippie-looking guy at Ranchhouse. With long blonde hair."

"That was Dieter," said Mick. "A good mahn. An East German. Served in their army for four years."

"Why's he here?" asked James.

"He's like you, mahn. Doesn't fit in civilian life. Feels restless and rootless."

"Who's the other guy? The one with the long red hair?"

"And the dirty feet?" Mick laughed. "That's Milton. A follower of the Guru, of the Divine Light. He's another idjit . Always too busy praying, meditating, he calls it, to help wash the dishes or sweep the floor. And he's always too busy licking his plate to pay for his food. And his feet? The smell from them would run you off to a field."

Amused, James asked who the woman was.

"Billie. A German girl from Hamburg. She's a student at the

university there. She's interested in our politics here. They're the only ones with me at this time. But any day now, the Provos will be here: Patty Byrnes and the boys. You didn't meet him last year, did you? A Belfast mahn."

James wondered if that were true. The year before, Mick had talked about the Provos and about how he belonged to the IRA. When he did, Mick would lower his voice to a whisper and look conspiratorial. But James hadn't seen any Provos and he found it hard to believe that Mick was an IRA man. And Patty Byrnes was probably just another barroom revolutionary.

"None of lads from Dublin down?"

Mick waved his hand in disgust. As cinders from his constant cigarette floated towards his pint, he covered it quickly with one hand.

"Oh no. That's all I need. Ashes in the Guinness. Make you sick, mahn. I have none of them with me, not now at any rate. Those idjits. Must have been fifteen down over Easter. They tore the place apart. Never washed a dish or swept the floor. Up all the night, drinking the jungle juice and smoking dope. Without dope, there's no hope. That's what they believe in, mahn. They had their dole mailed here. When they drank up all their money and we ran out of toilet paper, they used a towel. All head cases. I was happy to see them go."

Puzzled, James asked, "Why do you let them stay, Mick?"

Mick spit shreds of tobacco from his tongue.

"Ah mahn. It's not their fault. It's the fault of the five-headed monster: the parents, the church, the state and society. With them standing over you, telling you what to do. They're brainwashed. It's the life that they live up in Dublin that does it to them. The fast life, where money, power and fame's the name of the game. It drives them mad. Their parents have complained about me. Me, Michael Casey. But tell me: What am I to do? Their children come to me. Their fathers sell insurance. Dublin is full of insurance men. Now, you tell me: What kind of mahn sells insurance? So, the young people come here. To drink. To live in the past. They're bloody well lost. 'Ah, another mahn lost on the long highway.' You see? Everyone who comes here is crazy."

Mick rose to his feet and moaned.

"We're at war, mahn. Our way of life is at war, with the insurance men, the industrialists and the foreign invaders who want a United States of Europe and a Common Market. The people of Ballinskelligs can't eat the fish they catch. It all goes to the Continent. And up in the North of Ireland, in the six counties, we're at war with the British Empire, with imperialism and international capitalism. Be damned. All day in the saloon. It's getting worse. I've been trying to go to the meeting of the waters for the last hour. Couldn't find the time to do even that."

Mick bent sideways at the hip, stretched and limped towards the toilet. He stopped by the door and stared at James.

"'Where have all the young men gone? Gone to graveyards everyone.' Isn't that right, James?"

James stared into his pint and nodded.

Those who weren't dead, should be, thought James. He should have died in Vietnam, not the ones who did. He had not been a good soldier and yet, he had lived, while others, far better men than he, had died. And how had he survived that knifing in Philadelphia? Again, he had been careless and unaware, and again, he had been spared. Why? Luck, that's all, Packy, one of his buddies, a former grunt had told him. It wasn't his time to die.

He waited in the fading light for Mick to return. Through the window, he heard the low lapping of waves upon the shore.

The old man sitting in the far corner, his face an ash gray in the darkness, raised his glass of stout in salute, strangled an inarticulate cry, baring toothless gums, lowered the glass to the table, then carefully reddened his pipe.

James looked at the old man and saw Mick in a few years. And himself. He had to stop drinking before it was too late.

A stray chicken scratched the iron grate of the fireplace. The old man stood, muttering threats and protests against the British. The strange ambience of the pub created a sense of unreality. Time had run down here. The clock on the wall had stopped at midnight. Or noon.

"Who's the old guy over there?" James asked as Mick sat at the table.

Mick laughed.

"That's Old Dan. Dan lives only in the past. And with me up at Ranchhouse. The poor mahn has no home of his own. He sleeps up in the second chalet. I have another old mahn with me as well, Kelly, who sleeps upstairs. There's a case of opposites for you: Old Dan drinks all morning to the evening, whereas Kelly drinks all evening to the morning. When they pass back and forth on their way to the pub, they don't speak to each other for Dan's throat's too lubricated to talk and Kelly's throat's not lubricated enough."

James laughed along with Mick.

"They probably don't see each other either, 'cause one's too drunk and the other's too anxious."

"Two men that live in the same place, but never see each other, nor speak to each other. If they're not ghosts, who is?"

"I am," said James.

"Have to get this down," said Mick, gulping the rest of his pint. "To bring the spirit up. Let's have some more spirits ourselves. Another jar, mahn. Drink up. For there is no tomorrow. Tomorrow has been abolished, by royal decree."

Mick's words hit him like a punch to the gut and it was if he had the wind knocked out of him. He might as well get drunk. He banged his jar on the table. He wanted another one right away. He shouted for service and banged the jar again.

The bartender, John, stooped under the half door of the grocery store in front. He wiped his hands on his apron and frowned.

"Please, my dear sir, glasses are dear."

John glared over his granny glasses at Mick and said that it was half-seven in the evening, the time civilized people ate dinner.

"Half-seven? No dinner again this evening. A hard life it is."

A shadow wavered in the dim light by the door and croaked a sound.

"What's that, Dan? Mick cupped a hand to one ear. "Ah, good evening to you too."

As Dan staggered out the door, Mick whispered, "A shadow of a gunman."

"What do you mean by that?" asked James.

Mick motioned James closer and whispered, his tattered crown cocked over one eye, "Old Dan's a gangster. A real hard case. One of the original IRA gunmen."

"Really? Him too?"

James didn't know if he should take this seriously or not. He admired Mick's ability to play the part so well, but sometimes, he didn't know how to take the man. The previous year, James had felt that Mick was sending him some kind of message: that behind all the innuendo and hyperbole, behind the poetry and the history and the pathos, something more was being said.

Mick nodded.

"After the Civil War, Dan went over to America, to Chicago, during the twenties. He was with a Chicago gang and even spent some time in prison there, I believe. A hard case. One of the original IRA gunmen who fought against the Black and Tans. Or, so he says. He receives a pension from his days with the IRA. Keeps him drunk."

"Who were the Black and Tans?"

"The Black and Tans threw me from my cradle. Yes, they did, mahn. They came to the house drunk. Only my poor mother was present, God rest her soul, holding her broom. My father was off working the fields. They shot up the walls of the house, terrifying my mother. Then, one of them, a fiend if there ever was one, with a savage sweep of his arm, flung me from my cradle to the floor. They leaped to their cars and roared away. My father came running, shaking his pitchfork."

Mick cursed the Black and Tans and sent them howling into the bowels of hell for all eternity. He drained half his pint before continuing.

"They were English convicts recruited from prison to police the unruly Irish during the War of Independence. They raped and murdered. Ah mahn, they love the bloodbath: the imperialists, the capitalists, be they English or be they American, don't they?"

Mick jabbed his cigarette in the air, his green eyes gleaming with hatred.

"You know what I mean, don't you, James? You were in Vietnam. You saw what they did." James shook his head.

"You're right. They love the bloodbath. But I didn't see it. I hid in the rear."

Mick leaned back in his chair, his eyebrows lifting in surprise.

"You did? But I thought there was no such thing as a rear in Vietnam. In a guerrilla war? You said that last year."

James shook his head.

"No. There was a rear. In the big base camps. There was no safe place, I said that. That's true. But there was a big difference between being there and being out in the bush. I avoided combat."

"How did you manage that, mahn?"

James shrugged.

"I was lucky."

James looked around to see if the pints were ready. They were. He needed a drink. His hands were shaking and he felt weak. It upset him to talk about these things. He was afraid of what Mick would think about him. He paid for the pints with a traveler's check. He thumbed through his billfold. He only had a few hundred dollars left. When that ran out, he would have to do something. But what? He didn't want to think about it. As John cashed his check, James went into the toilet to relieve himself.

As he carried the round to the table, he thought of how he was going to answer Mick. He had to tell the truth. Time was running out.

"What happened was," he said as he sat at the table. "After basic at Fort Bragg, North Carolina, I was trained for combat, in the artillery, at Fort Sill, Oklahoma, to fire howitzers. To be a cannon-cocker. But after I was there a week, I had to go home on emergency leave. My brother, Richie, got sick, real sick. He got better when I got there but I stayed home for a few weeks, anyway. So when I got back to Sill, they put me in another training brigade. The first brigade I was with all went to Vietnam, as artillerymen. When my brigade was finished training, we went to Europe. I was supposed to go to a field artillery unit in Germany, but when I got there, to Frankfurt, they sent me to Italy. Vicenza. Not far from Venice. I was supposed to do OJT, on-the-job training, with nuclear missiles. But when I got to headquarters, the clerk saw that I had some education, so he asked me if I could type. Type? Me? I can type fifty words a minute, I told him. So they made me a clerk. In an Intelligence Unit. In a missile brigade. I couldn't type five words a minute. I just wanted to get out of the field. But they didn't send me back, for some reason. I don't know why. I was incompetent as a clerk. I never could figure it out."

"So how did you get to Vietnam from there?" asked Mick.

James grimaced.

"I volunteered."

"Why did you do that, mahn. It must have been good duty in Italy."

James shrugged.

"It was okay. But I was, I don't know, in bad shape. There was something wrong with me. I don't know what. I was drinking too much. I felt guilty for being there. I should have been in Vietnam. So I volunteered for a few reasons. What triggered it was my brother going into the army. I went back to the states on leave to try to talk him out of it but he wouldn't listen. I couldn't believe that the army was going to take him. He still wasn't healthy enough, I thought. But I guess they needed bodies that bad. I even tried to slap some sense into him but that didn't do any good. I was afraid that if he made it through basic training they'd send him to Vietnam. I figured he'd never make it. He'd die over there. So, since two brothers don't have to serve in a combat zone at the same time, if one would be the sole surviving son, I decided to go. I was a clerk then. I figured I'd have a better chance of making it than he would. So I volunteered. And I made it, somehow."

"What happened with him, mahn?"

"He got discharged after a couple months. Incompatibility. He couldn't get through basic. He shouldn't have been in there. The army isn't for everyone. He just kept going AWOL until they discharged him. He wised up fast. I tried to get out of going to Vietnam but it was too late. I had to go."

"That's too bad, mahn. But it took a lot of courage to do that. And you must have cared about your brother very much."

James shrugged.

"Yeah, I do. He was my little brother. And I felt like I owed him one. He kept me from going there as an artilleryman. But I don't want to give you the impression that I did it because I'm a nice guy, because in a lot of ways I'm not. I also wanted to go because I had friends over there. Packy and Mad Dog Daily were there. You remember him. We came here together last year."

Mick nodded.

"Ah, yes. A redheaded Irishman. Did a lot of shouting and arguing. A good mahn, though."

James agreed.

" And a good friend, too. I felt that I had to be with him and Packy. We grew up together. And I guess I just had to see for myself what it was like, if we were right to be there or not. And I was so screwed up at the time that I didn't care if I lived or died."

"Where were you stationed?" asked Mick.

"In Long Binh, a big base camp near Saigon. I was assigned as a clerk to an Intelligence Unit in a Headquarters Company, First Signal Brigade. I had a few different jobs. I drove a jeep and a truck. I pulled bunker guard out on the perimeter. That was the worst duty I had. It was scary out there but nothing like being out in the bush. We were out there with machine guns, and hand grenades and M-16's, with orders to kill anyone who tried to come through the wire. There was always the danger of sappers attacking. Every once in awhile, they'd fire in a rocket and blow up a building, but nothing major ever happened while I was there: no attacks. But we didn't know nothing was going to happen. I got there a year after Tet. By that time, most of the VC were dead."

As he said that, James laughed. He wondered why he was laughing. What was so funny about people being dead?

"The rest of the time I spent processing SIRs: Serious Incident Reports. They were crimes committed by US military personnel: murder, rapes, robberies, accidents. We had stacks and stacks of them, so many that the Lieutenant burned hundreds of them to get rid of them before inspection. And then in '70, we started to get more and more reports of fraggings..."

"I've heard of them." said Mick. "We've had other veterans pass through here and they've talked about it. Soldiers killing their officers with hand grenades."

James nodded.

"There were quite a few reported cases. Reported. God knows how many were never reported. That was all Top-Secret. I had a Top-Secret Security Clearance. The army didn't want the American people to know about those things, that the army was falling apart. By 1970-71, they didn't have an army. That was one of the reasons why they finally pulled out. I didn't have it bad over there but it really wasn't the same as being stateside, like the grunts said. The dangers were different, like getting hooked on heroin or going to the Long Binh Jail, the LBJ Ranch, for flipping out on somebody. The lifers were constantly on our backs. You gotta remember I had a combat MOS hanging over me. They could have sent me back to the artillery but for some reason, they didn't. Thank God. This sergeant I had: Costello. I hated him. He was always threatening to send me to Nui Ba Dinh, the Black Virgin Mountain, to get my sorry self killed, he said whenever I did or said something he didn't like and I did plenty of that, believe me. I was always ridiculing or cursing out the army. The Black Virgin Mountain was one of the most dangerous places in Vietnam. It was up near the border with Cambodia. We had a signal battalion up on the top of the mountain where we monitored all the VC communications in the area. The VC and NVA lived in these caves underneath our base camp and they were always trying to destroy it. Thank God, I didn't get sent up there."

Suddenly, James remembered that he and a couple of other guys had threatened Costello.

"We told him that if he didn't stop harassing us, he'd hear a rock on his roof. A rock was a warning; the next sound would be a hand grenade. Costello thought we were serious and he reported us to the CO, but we just laughed it off. Sarge was paranoid, we said. We were only joking. I guess. I hated him but I wouldn't have killed him. He never actually did anything to me but yell at me and curse me out. But thank God, he didn't hurt me because I don't know what I would have done if he had. I had a terrible temper then."

"I'm sure it was no picnic," said Mick. "But I've been told that the combat in Vietnam was some of the worst in history."

"It was, Mick. A lot of guys got wasted over there. I'm glad I missed it. Although there are times when I feel guilty about it."

"I don't blame you for staying out of it. You did what you had to do to survive. And you saw that the war was wrong, that it was a war of aggression and that you wanted no part of it."

James nodded and took a deep breath. He was glad that Mick felt that way and didn't think that he was a coward.

"Actually, I didn't understand what the war was about while I was there, the history, the politics: that came later. I only had a vague feeling that something was wrong. I guess I just couldn't see how we were helping those people when we were killing so many of them. It hit me one day: how were we defending America ten thousand miles away from home. And when I saw the people, they were so poor. How could they be a threat to us? It didn't make sense."

"But you never killed anyone yourself then, mahn?"

James hadn't killed anyone but he felt like he did. And he felt guilty for being alive, for not even being wounded.

"No. I never fired a shot. But I remember one night, right after I came home from Vietnam. I went with a buddy of mine, Packy, to see another guy from our neighborhood, Eddie, who had both legs shot off above the knee. Packy had come through it, some real heavy combat, with only a minor shoulder wound. Now, me and Packy hadn't seen Eddie since it happened. It was a shock to see him like that, cut in half, almost. As soon as Eddie saw Packy, he waved him over close, like he was going to tell him a secret, but instead, he punched him in the mouth. 'That's for coming home whole,' he said. Packy wasn't going to take that, even from Eddie, no legs or not, so he punched him back, sending him rolling across the room. I can still see his stumps wiggling in the air. It was such a sad sight that I sat down and cried. Both of them stopped fighting and came over to ask me why I was crying. 'Because I didn't even get wounded,' I told them. How weird is that?"

Mick reached over and stroked James on the head.

"Not that weird, mahn. To be wounded in battle is a sign of distinction. And you wanted to share in their suffering. Well, well, who do we have here?"

James turned towards the door and saw the youths from Ranchhouse enter and walk towards them.

Mick asked them where they'd been.

Milton grunted and shrugged his shoulders to Dieter who said, "We were having tea."

"Tea?" said Mick. "And you couldn't bring me any? Some bread and cheese, perhaps. You knew that I was trapped up here with no food. And you, Milton, are you wearing your shoes? No, I didn't think so. Come closer, Billie. Sit between me and my friend,

James O'Rourke, from Philadelphia."

Billie sat next to Mick and scolded him for staying so long in the pub. The two men sat at an adjacent table and argued, in whispers, in German, with their heated faces close together for a moment, then separating as they reached into their hip pockets for tobacco and rolled cigarettes, continuing their argument with mutterings and ejaculations. The pub lit up and began to fill, with tourists from the village youth hostel, some in gay native costume, others dressed for mountain climbing, and the local men in their serge suits and tweed caps. The smoky pub was alive with light and movement and there was the sharp smell of stout and whiskey in the air. The tourists chattered in their native tongues, their conversation broken with English words and phrases. The Irishmen gathered in the far corner by the hearth and played blackjack, banging the cards on the table.

James began to get drunk. As the others talked, James drank, feeling left out. As Billie squeezed against him, talking with Mick, James felt aroused by her beauty. She didn't look German with her long black hair and blue eyes.

He lurched up from the table and cruised through the crowd, looking for a woman. He eyed the few women who were left in the pub, and made a pathetic attempt to talk with one of them, but she ignored him. Feeling rejected, he staggered into the toilet, relieved himself and then went and looked in the mirror over the sink. He took off his glasses and put his face close to the glass. His face was flushed a bright red and his eyes bugged out of his head. He looked like a madman. He got angry at himself for getting drunk again. He splashed his face with water, and then went out and stood in the doorway and breathed in the cool night air.

As he turned to go back with the others, the lights went out and the pub was plunged into darkness. He felt a moment of panic.

Then he heard someone call out.

"Time! Ladies and Gents. Time!"

He heard Mick shout.

"Let there be light! We've had eight hundred years of darkness! Let there be light!"

Then the lights came back on. It was last call.

James felt sobered up a little so he went back and sat next to

Billie. He racked his brain, trying to think of something to say to her. Just be normal, he told himself. When Mick went to the men's room, he had his chance.

"What part of Germany are you from?"

"Hamburg, " said Billie. "Have you heard of it?"

She lifted her long beige skirt and scratched her slender legs, which were covered with small insect bites.

"Yeah," said James. "My father went through there in 1945, when he was in the army. He said it was one big pile of rubble, then."

Billie frowned.

"It's all built up now. There are few traces of the war left. Except for the American soldiers, who are still there, occupying my country. We want the troops out, my party does."

James nodded. He used to think that the American troops were there to protect the Germans from the Communists, but now he knew how absurd that was. They weren't there to fight the Russians in a conventional war. If a war did break out, neither side would let themselves lose. Instead they would resort to the use of nuclear weapons. When he was in Italy, he had seen the war plans. There were no plans to fight conventionally. No matter what happened, Germany, all of Europe, would be destroyed, the whole world would be destroyed.

"They are in Germany to protect the capitalist system," said Billie. "Not from the Soviet Union but from the German people, once the most powerful proletariat in the world. The American government has built up once again the cartels in Germany, the industrialists, the corporate capitalists, that the Nazis used. They have taken over from the Nazis. Amerika is the Fourth Reich."

James grimaced. As much as he hated to admit it, what she said was true. Ever since he came home from Vietnam, he had been re-reading history and was beginning to see America with new eyes. The US had troops all over the world. It was no different from any other empire. Vietnam was no aberration, no mistake. It was just another example of America's domination of a native people, the same way it began. Despite himself, he felt tears come into his eyes. He had believed in America. He mourned for his dead self.

"What's the matter, mahn?"

James looked up to see Mick standing over him. He shook his head and took a deep breath.

"Talking with Billie. Something she said. That we were the new Nazis. She's right. We were like the Nazis in Vietnam. I grew up hating Nazis. Then I became one."

"Go easy on yourself, mahn. You did nothing criminal, did you?" James shook his head.

"So what is all this nonsense about being a Nazi?"

"Without people like me, they couldn't have done it. I was a good German. I made my choice: life or death. I choose death and I got it. Maybe I didn't kill anybody, but I would have, so I'm just as guilty as the ones who did. The army's smart like that. They only have a few guys do all the killing. That leaves everybody else off the hook."

"You should not feel guilty," said Billie. "You were brainwashed. Just like my father and many of the men in the Wehrmacht. They had to join the Nazis, just as you had to go into the army. Blame the capitalists and the politicians and the military leaders. They are the guilty ones, not you."

James shook his head.

"I'm sorry, Mick. I'm sorry. Please, forgive me. I've heard that argument before. But you can't be always be putting the blame on somebody else."

"I can't help but wonder, mahn, how you came to feel like this."

James grimaced.

"I don't know, Mick. My Catholic upbringing, I guess. None of the other vets I know feel this way. Guilt will cripple you, they say. But shouldn't you feel guilty if you've done something wrong? And what we did to the Vietnamese was wrong. It's wrong to kill people like that. I hope the two creeps who knifed me that night feel bad about it, but they probably don't. It wasn't their fault, they'd say. It was the system that made them that way."

"Knifed you? What are you talking about, mahn?"

"A couple of years ago, about a year after I came home from Vietnam, I got knifed in the back by two junkies. Took my money. 18 bucks. Left me for dead in the street. Freaked me out. Still have nightmares about it."

Mick stroked him on the head.

"You're a survivor, mahn."

Billie put her arm around him and hugged him.

"You know what it is to be a victim."

James grimaced.

"I hated being a victim, having somebody try to kill me like that. I was trying to change, be nonviolent, peaceful. Like Christ. I didn't even fight them. And look what it got me."

"Every mahn has the right to defend himself. And so does a country. It's wrong to kill people, but sometimes, you have to do it."

James cried.

"I don't know. It's a terrible thing to have done to you. I know. I feel like I'm dead."

"Sure you're dead. Dead drunk. C'mon, mahn. It's time you rolled off to bunk."

Mick raised James to his feet, put his arm around him and led him into the warm summer night.

The early morning sun shined through the cobwebbed window of the chalet, rested lightly on James' eyelids, and awakened him. He tasted the thick crust of foam that lined his mouth and felt nauseated. A sharp bite sent him rolling from his bed. He cursed and scratched his legs which were covered with red bite marks. He saw tiny black insects leaping in the filthy sheets that covered the cot. Fleas. He was no better than a dog. He had sunk that low. As he stood up, he stumbled and almost fell. He had slept with his boots on and his feet were so numb that he had trouble standing. Blurred images of the previous night flashed through his mind. He saw himself drunk and crying, talking nonsense and feeling sorry for himself. He felt disgusted. He remembered staggering back and forth across the road to Ranchhouse, falling in ditches. He looked at his hands. They were filthy. His vision blurred, then focused on his backpack propped in a corner. He wondered how it got there. Mick must have put it there. He flashed on Mick with a raised rifle.

'C'mon, Dan. Get up.'

James awoke in confusion. He stared over the wooden partition of his cubicle and saw Mick with a raised rifle in the center of the room

Dan whimpered. 'Get up? What for, Mick?'

'To meet your maker, mahn.'

'What?'

He heard Dan plead in his whiskey voice. 'Please don't shoot me, Mick. Please, Mick.'

'Why not?' Mick growled. 'Aren't you ready to die?'

'No, Mykill,' trembled Dan.

James didn't know what was going on. He couldn't believe what was happening.

'Mick! What are you doing? What's going on?'

Mick spun towards him and lowered the weapon.

'Ah, you're awake, James?'

Mick walked across the room and explained in a stage whisper.

'Last night, Dan went down on his knees and begged me to shoot him. Put him out of his misery. So, now...

He winked at James.

'I've come to do it.'

Mick stomped back to Dan and shouted.

'Which is it?'

Mick raised the rifle.

'Life or death?'

'Life, whispered Dan.

'Louder, mahn.'

'Life! shouted Dan. 'For God's sake, let me live.'

Mick recoiled in mock surprise and lowered the rifle.

'What changed your mind?'

Dan was silent.

'Nothing happened. But yet, you want to live. For what? To stay drunk?'

'Yes, Mick, said Dan.

'All right then, Dan. Return to the unquiet grave.'

Mick shut off the light, paused by the door and shouted, 'Are you rolling out, James? It'll soon be dawn. Soldiers and farmers rise before dawn, mahn.'

'I ain't a soldier anymore, Mick,' James grumbled. 'And I sure as hell ain't a farmer, either."

Mick cackled his maniacal laugh.

'Once a soldier, always a soldier. Didn't you know that, mahn? Like I told you: it's the river of no return.'

Mick slammed the door and was gone.

James wondered whether it had happened or whether he had dreamt it. Moaning and holding his head, he looked behind him at Dan's rumpled bed. On the table, beside an ashtray piled high with burnt matches, lay an empty whiskey bottle. He staggered over and poked his head into the bathroom. It was littered with wet and soiled newspapers and glossy photographs of naked women. The stench was overpowering. He retched a few times as he quickly washed his hands and face in the dirty washbasin, next to which was a wire wastebasket overflowing with filthy tissue paper. Holding his breath, he urinated into the blocked-up toilet, then back stepped quickly outside. He ran, bent over and threw open the chalet door like a man who had been buried alive and stepped out into the wet grass. He stood there with his head thrown back taking deep gulps of the fresh sea air. He did that for a few minutes until the sickness subsided a little.. He saw two playful pups wrestling in the weed grown vegetable garden. He stared into the sky fringed with fleecy clouds that served as a backdrop for the bay, whitened by a shimmer of sun rays.

He walked along the garden past the first chalet, noticing the stacks of empty stout bottles by the window. Three dogs swarmed him. He chased them away with a rush and stomp of his foot.

He entered Ranchhouse.

"Good morning, mahn."

Mick sat at the end of a long table that was cluttered with greasy pots and pans and dishes and covered by a stained tablecloth, in the center of which wobbled a purple vase full of dead flowers.

Dressed in dirty khaki pants, a stained muscle tee and a cowboy hat, Mick was reading the morning paper and drinking tea. Flies buzzed around the room, which reeked of rotting vegetables and dead fish.

"Bolloxed drunk you were last night, mahn."

James grimaced.

"I know it. My whole body hurts."

Mick poured James a cup of tea.

"Try a cup of this. It's good for what ails ya."

James saw the leaves settle onto the bottom and wondered what they said. He asked Mick if he could have something to eat. He would replace the food later.

"Sure, mahn. Break the fast. You need to eat. An army mahn has to keep up his strength."

As James boiled some eggs and made toast, Mick read the news aloud. A bank had been robbed in County Tyrone, by three men wearing the black hoods of the IRA.

"That was probably Patty Byrnes and the boys."

"Is that how they get their money?" James asked as he sat at the table to eat.

"Some of it," said Mick. "What better way to get money, than to take it from the capitalists? They stole it from us. We also get money from the Irish in America. I got a twenty-dollar bill in the post today from New York City."

James thought about what Mick said. He had never seen a bank robbery as a political act before.

"The Irish in America have always supported us. They send us money for guns. That's what we need in Ireland. It's the only way to fight the Brits. Remember: Power comes from the barrel of a gun."

"Is is possible, Mick? Can the IRA defeat the British militarily?"

"Why not, mahn? Didn't the Vietnamese defeat the powerful American Army?"

James grimaced.

"Yeah. They did. But they took some terrible losses. Millions of Vietnamese died. But what about the Protestants? Won't they still be there when the British leave? Aren't there a lot more of them in Northern Ireland than Catholics? Won't there be a blood bath?"

Mick put down his cup and lit another cigarette.

"It's a blood bath now. They are slowly bleeding us to death. But with the British Army gone, the battle will be between Irishmen. And maybe one of these days, the Protestants will see that they have more in common with the Catholics than they do with the British. Divide and conquer has always been the policy of the British Empire. Both the Catholics and the Protestants are mostly from the working class. The war in Northern Ireland is a class war not a religious one. But we have to kick the British Army out of Belfast. That's the first step toward a united Ireland."

James remembered Mick telling him about the War of Independence the year before, but he had trouble keeping it straight in his mind. He hadn't grown up hearing about these things, so the names and the dates didn't stick.

"How did it get that way, Mick? I know you told me about it last year but I haven't gotten it down yet."

Mick grimaced.

"We were betrayed, mahn. By Michael Collins. He was our leader and he sold us out. In 1921, he signed a treaty with the British that left the country divided. He had to compromise, he said. Let them have the Six Counties. For now. We'll get them later. Well mahn, it's over fifty years later and the Six Counties are still part of the British Empire. You can't shake hands with the devil, mahn. And Michael Collins died because of it. He was murdered weeks later. After the treaty, we had a brutal civil war. Until 1922. It was brother against brother. Between those who opposed the treaty and those who supported it: the Free Staters. And they won, mahn. The British still have the Six Counties. And the war goes on."

"But how did it get that way, Mick? How come the Protestants are so powerful up there?"

"They came from England and Scotland and drove the Catholics out, mahn, and took their land. Hundreds of years ago. It's our land and our country. The only solution is for the British to get out of Ireland. Ireland un-free will never be at peace, mahn."

As James finished his breakfast, he felt a little better. What Mick said made sense. The problem was obvious and so was the solution. No ambiguities. They knew who the enemy was and what to do about it. James envied them. He looked fondly at Mick who sat quietly smoking and looking off into the distance as if he were looking into the future. Mick looked so strange in that cowboy hat. The year before, Mick had told him that a friend from Texas had sent it to him. Mick thought so highly of the ranchers from Texas that he named his farm as a tribute to them. He admired their toughness and resistance to change.

"It's hot, mahn. This heat wave has been blazing up Southwest Kerry for days. it's been in the 80's for a week."

James laughed.

"You think this is hot? Vietnam was hot. But it's hot in this room because of the glass roof. It's like a hothouse in here."

Mick gritted his teeth.

"It's been a hothouse here ever since the war broke out again up in the North in '69. Patty Byrnes first came here that year. The British and the Gardai were here many times looking for him. They were hairy times, mahn. I was tempted to take to the hills and leave Ranchhouse for good. This place that I built with my own two hands."

"You built this place?" asked James.

He had difficulty seeing Mick as a farmer and a builder of houses. He had never seen Mick do anything but drink and talk. Mick was a small man but muscular. He had good definition in his arms and neck and his stomach was still hard. Mick looked strong for a man of 50.

"I threw it up myself, with some help from the people of Ballinskelligs. Beyond that wall is the house where I was born. It now serves as a kennel for the dogs. Ah, I'm no better than a dog myself, mahn. Throw me a bone and I'm happy. I also built the three chalets. My mother and I did the tourist trade with them for a few years, until she died, God rest her soul, four years ago."

Mick wiped tears from his eyes.

"I ate no solid food for two years after she died. Lived on milk and Guinness. I still only eat an occasional egg and some spuds. No appetite."

James sympathized with Mick. If his mother died, he would be sad too. He missed his mother and knew that she worried about him. He was her first born son. She had prayed for him every day he was in Vietnam and was probably praying for him now. But what could he do? He had to find his own way in the world. He would write her a letter soon and tell her he was safe. He would make Ranchhouse seem like a working farm where he was learning how to grow food and take care of animals. A harmless lie.

James left Mick with his memories and went into the living

room. He stopped by the mantelpiece and read the plaque on the wall. It was a replica of the Easter Rebellion Proclamation of 1916. Mick had told him about it the year before, about how the men of the Irish Republican Brotherhood had seized the main post office in Dublin, and held it for a week against overwhelming odds, until they finally surrendered and were executed by the British. James felt stirred by the words, especially the ones about the contribution of the exiled children of America. He wanted to do something for Ireland. But what? He had no money to give.

He walked around the room, reading some of the quotations, slogans and poems that covered the walls. One of them was written in red lipstick with the letters diminishing and tailing off to scribble at the end: "The roads of excess lead to the palace of wisdom." William Blake.

James grimaced. He had followed the road of excess the night before and all he had gotten out of it was a hangover, no wisdom. Beneath Blake, a wiser man had written: "A sober Ireland would be a free Ireland."

He remembered writing a quote on the wall last year. He walked over to the corner by the window and looked for it. It was still there, in tiny letters: "Hell is the inability to love." Father Zossima. The Brothers Karamazov.

He wasn't sure why he had chosen that quote. He wasn't sure what it meant. Was he unable to love? If he were honest with himself, he would have to say that he had never loved anyone in his life, really loved anyone. There were times when he cared about others, of course. He was no monster. He had said that he loved people: his parents, his family, girls he had known. He knew the definitions: loving is wishing other people well, wanting what's best for them, giving of yourself, but actually doing it? No, he had never really loved anyone for any length of time. But is that hell? Hell was a place, wasn't it? Where you went after death? But he had to admit, he felt like hell, now.

His hangover made him feel scattered and restless. He paced around the room, trying to organize his thoughts. He had to stop drinking. He couldn't stand being hung over anymore.

He leafed through a pile of dated magazines and dusty books

that were stacked in a corner. Through the window, he watched a blackbird alight on the stone wall that bordered the main road and the macadam path that ran past the house to the strand.

He sat on the bitten bench stretched in front of the window and watched an ant worry a morsel of bread across the threadbare carpet that was littered with cigarette butts and bottle caps and that had, according to Mick, soaked up more stout than any man in Southwest Kerry. Empty whiskey and stout bottles covered the table in the center of the room. Along the far wall stood a flea-infested chair, next to which a sofa sagged.

He had to think. Some of what Mick said made him nervous. He didn't know much about Communists, but Mick talked like one. Class war was a Marxist term. James had read some of the statements made by Ho Chi Minh and Ho had used some of the same terminology that Mick did: imperialism, colonialism, international capitalism. He wondered where the others were. Plotting something, perhaps. They were probably Communists too. Billie talked like one and Dieter was from East Germany.

"What are you doing in there, mahn?"

Startled, James jumped to his feet.

"Nothing. Just reading the writing on the walls. How did that start?"

James stood in the shadows behind the doorway, trying to steady his nerves.

Mick answered in a sad voice.

"I have no one to blame but myself. If my poor mother saw that room. One night, at the end of a great debate, the usual debate about Republicanism, Communism, Capitalism, all the isms, I wrote, in desperation, that the only thing you have to do is die. Right over the doorway there. That started it."

"Don't you have to pay taxes here?" asked James. He knew that would set Mick off.

Mick snorted.

"Taxes? I have no income to pay taxes. Mahn does not live by bread alone but by his wits. I learned that long ago. No, mahn. I pay nothing to the state, our so called Republic, and I take nothing from them. I've been offered social services, otherwise referred to as the dole, several times, but I've run the bastards off. Told them we were diseased here. Foot-in-mouth disease."

James walked past Mick towards the kitchen, stopping to stare at a tattered world map that hung on the wall.

"I see by this map that Ireland's on the same longitude? latitude? as Newfoundland. No wonder the water is so cold. I'm going to take a walk along the beach. Gotta clear my head."

Mick approved.

"I have to get washed and dressed and run a blade across my face, maybe I'll slit my throat while I'm at it. Then, I'll go up to the pub, to the confessional box,"

"Confessional box?" echoed James.

"The phone booth," explained Mick. "I have to make a personal call to Dublin."

James started to laugh, but when he saw Mick's sad face, he stopped. He wondered if Mick could be calling Deirdre. He wanted to ask Mick about her, why she had left Ballinskelligs, but Mick wouldn't look at him, so he didn't. Instead, he muttered something about going to see the Skelligs Rock.

James walked into the kitchen and adjusted his eyes to the swarming darkness and his nose to the strong odor of dogs and turf. Sunlight flashed through the window and played gently on the features of Kelly, who slept in front of the fireplace, one thick hand over his eyes, the other hanging on the floor. Kelly was dressed in farmer fashion, in his worn serge suit and tweed cap. James remembered Kelly from the year before. They had talked for several hours one night in the pub. Kelly had spent over fifty years eking out a living on a small farm in Dungannon. But, as he got older, he could no longer work the long hours of a farmer, so he had been forced to sell his land and move in with his nephew, Mick. James remembered Kelly crying as he talked about how much he loved his farm. Kelly supported himself by helping the farmers bring in the hay and dig the potatoes. Most of the time, however, he spent in the pub, smoking his pipe and drinking his pint, talking only when spoken to.

James looked around the kitchen. A plate stamped with the likeness of John Kennedy hung on the green cupboard lined with dusty cups and saucers. Next to a picture of the Blessed Mother was the

Sacred Heart of Jesus bulging from his tunic; beneath it a lazy Scottie curled in a corner of a quilted settee. Over the mantle stretched a row of clocks, each stopped at a different time.

James paused by the front door and listened for a sound. The year before, Deirdre had told him that the room knew if you were afraid of it and would make a noise just to scare you. But he heard nothing. Deirdre was a strange woman. She looked like someone who had just gotten over a long illness. She liked to take long walks in the hills, and when she came back, she would sit in a corner with a blanket over her head, smiling to herself, not talking to anyone, then would suddenly say something strange. She cut onions with a knife held between her toes, because she didn't like to cry. But she was kind. She took care of the cats and dogs and she had nursed Kelly and Mick when they were sick. James wondered why she left. He had heard her say that she never wanted to leave Ballinskelligs and never wanted to go back to New York. She would understand how he felt.

James lifted the latch and stepped beneath the wooden archway twined with white rambling rose and laurel, and walked onto the path that wound down past the convent, the nuns' summer retreat, to the strand. A small stream purled down along the one side of the path to the beach where it struggled through the sand to the bay. A pair of pigeons cooed in the branches of a swaying spruce tree. Bumblebees and butterflies flitted through the yellow furze and blackberry bushes that lined the path.

He walked down and stood on the small wall that overlooked the beach and looked out over the bay and the ocean beyond, where years ago, according to Mick, the coffin ships could be seen sailing away to America, or more likely, to the bottom of the sea. His ancestors had passed that way long ago. He wished that there was some way that he could see the ships, see the faces of his people and ask them about their lives, but all he could do was imagine them.

He walked along the beach, past two children pailing in the surf and a few adults sunbathing on beach towels. Seagulls dipped across the waves, cawing. He took deep breaths of the sea air and tried to relax. What had he gotten himself into? It was no lie: Mick was crazy. What if Old Dan had said shoot? Would Mick have done it? James couldn't believe that he would have. The whole scene seemed like an act, designed for him. Maybe Mick was trying to tell him something. That he had to make his choice. Maybe what's his name really was coming: Patty Byrnes. And the Provos. James knew that they were the radicals: the violent ones. He felt the adrenaline rush. Supposing they wanted him to do something for them? He would have to make his choice. Which side was he on? But he dismissed the idea. Why would they be interested in him? He wasn't a combat vet. And they didn't recruit just anyone to join them.

Peals of laughter rang through the air, disturbing his thoughts, and for a moment, he thought that it was directed at him, but when he looked up, he saw that it was coming from a circle of women who squatted and swam in the water beneath the ruins of an ancient monastery.

Lightheaded, James staggered up the beach and sat in the cool sand beneath the grassy cliff that faced the sea. An image floated through his mind of a knight, in shining armor, carrying a silver sword, coming upon a small pond buried deep in the woods. He jumps from his mount, and slowly, his armor clanking, leads his stallion to water. Through a clearing in the underbrush, he spies a circle of wood nymphs, naked to the waist, their long hair floating behind them on the water.

Screams shattered his fantasy and he looked up to see the women scattering frenziedly towards the shore as if a shark had surfaced in their midst. He couldn't figure out who they were. As the women ran up the beach, they were laughing and giggling and calling each other sister, until they saw him watching them and they hushed and slowed to walk in single file before him, their heads bowed as if in prayer. Then it hit him: They were nuns, from the summer retreat. He had to laugh. He put his head between his legs, so they wouldn't hear him. Then he realized that he was missing his chance to see nuns in bathing suits, so he raised his eyes to watch them go by. They had bodies, after all. As he eyeballed their bodies, he felt like a secret judge in a strange beauty contest: Miss Nun of the Year. They had no sex, no life, none. He laughed. Why did women become nuns anyway?

To get away from men.'

He heard her words as clearly as when she had said them. He stopped chuckling and felt his face flush. He had asked her the same question three days ago on the train from Luxembourg. Rosemary was her name. She had come up to him in the train station and asked him in a Boston accent if they exchanged rand there. Rand? What was that? He could only stammer 'Uh, Uh, I don't know.' All he could see was her beautiful blue eyes that seemed to swallow him up. She curtsied and danced to the back of the money exchange line. When they were finished changing their money, he followed after her like a little bird after its mother and hopped on the train she took just to talk to her. She didn't seem surprised that he did so. She said that when she saw him, she had an intuition that they were fated to meet each other. After talking about fate and what it meant, he blurted out that he was on his way to Ireland to redeem himself for participating in the Vietnam War. When she asked how he was going to do that, he shrugged. She told him that she was a teacher on her way to Brussels to do some research on a book she was writing about goddess worship in Europe and Africa. She told him about the nuns she had known in Soweto and why they had become nuns: to get away from men.

'Why? What's wrong with men?' he responded.

He looked out the window as he heard the distant thunder of an impending storm. He saw a cow twist its fly-swarmed face to puzzle out the train as it howled through a black tunnel.

When they came out of the darkness, she looked at his fatigue shirt and said,' You were in the army? And you can ask that?'

He didn't know what to say. To the military, there was nothing lower than a woman. All of the insults were sexual in nature. If you didn't want to kill, you were a little girl, not a man.

'I know what you mean,' he said. 'We're sick. Sometimes, I hate men. I wish I could get away from them, too.'

'I don't hate men,' she said. 'I hate what they do and the way they treat women. But if you want to get away from men, why are you going to this farm to see this man, Mick?'

He shrugged.

"I never met anyone like him before. My mom thinks that I see him as taking the place of my father. Maybe she's right.'

'Is your father dead?'

James pursed his lips as he thought about his father.

'No. But he has cancer. I'm angry at him. I wanted to be like him: be a soldier, fight the bad guys, be a hero. But it didn't turn out that way. I'm all mixed up. I don't know what to believe in anymore. I went to Vietnam as a clean-cut, patriotic young man and I came home, hating the war, hating the military, hating the United States. My father doesn't understand what happened to me. But Mick does.'

'Is Mick a pacifist?'

James laughed.

'No. Mick supports the IRA. Used to belong to the IRA. I think maybe he still does. I don't know.'

She frowned.

'How did you meet Mick?'

James laughed.

'I just sort of stumbled onto him. Last summer, I was traveling around Europe with a friend of mine, Mad Dog Daily, another Vietnam veteran. I went to Europe because I just had to get out of America. I wanted to see the world before I died. The way I was going, I thought I wasn't going to live long. Anyway, we traveled around the Continent for about a month. We started off in Copenhagen, then we hitched down through Germany into Austria. Bavaria is so beautiful. Then we hitched, walked through the Alps into Italy. No one would pick us up. I can't blame them. We looked like two wild men. We went to Rome and Venice and Naples. It was a great trip but by that time, we were really getting on each other's nerves. We were both wishing that we had come with a woman instead of another man. We decided to go to England and Ireland, because at least there they spoke English and maybe we could meet some women. We took the train from Rome. It was so packed that we had to stand for 8 hours. We stayed in London for a few days, then decided to go to Ireland, since we're both of Irish descent. So anyway, while we were in Dublin, we met some Irish kids in a pub, the Dollymount, and we got to be friends with them. They told us about this place in County Kerry where they could stay for free and they asked us to come along. We figured, why not? So we went. I never met anybody like Mick before. He speaks with a thick Kerry brogue. I have to really listen to understand what he's saying. He talks a lot about Irish history and politics. And he's a poet. He's always reciting poetry.'

'A warrior-poet,' she said. 'Do you agree with him about the IRA? Do you still believe in war, in the use of violence?'

James sighed.

'I don't know. But I do know that, in reality, there are people out there who will hurt you, kill you, if you don't fight. And what else can people do when an army comes into their country and burns down their houses and kills their families?'

She nodded.

'I know. It's hard. It's like that in South Africa. The ANC started out as a peaceful organization but they were driven into violence by the white South Africans. It's so sad.'

James nodded.

'Sometimes, I think there's no hope for the world.'

She reached out and touched his hand.

'Don't think that way. There's hope. There's a new god coming and soon there'll be no more war. It will be impossible.'

James lifted his eyebrows.

'Really? A new god?'

He squirmed in his seat, thinking that she was a little crazy and hoping that she wouldn't start insisting that he get down on his knees and pray with her.

She smiled.

'It's not what you think. But I found god in Africa. The god within.'

James had heard of that before: the personal god.

'It was a gradual process. I considered myself an agnostic. But I started going to early morning prayers with the nuns and I noticed that they prayed more to the Blessed Virgin than they did to God the Father. And I watched their faces as they prayed to her. They had a glow about them. And I started to think that they were on to something, something that had been distorted, perhaps. I had always scoffed at the idea of the Blessed Virgin because it seemed to be a celebration of celibacy and that was something that I couldn't accept. But I began to see the Virgin in a new light. In the past, a virgin was a woman not possessed by a man, a free woman. It had nothing to do with sex. As I prayed to the Blessed Virgin, I came to realize that I was praying to myself, that god was within me and that god was a woman.'

James frowned. He had heard about women who believed as she did. It was too far out for him.

'I think it's dangerous to think that you have God inside yourself. That makes you God, doesn't it? And if you're God, you can do anything you want. We thought that we were God in Vietnam. We had the right to kill people.'

She shook her head.

'I'm talking about something different.'

'But what about men? Are you telling me that we have a female god within us?'

She stroked his arm.

'Yes. You just have to find the way to her.'

James looked at his arm where her hand had been. He could almost feel her warmth. But what did it mean? At Brussels, she got off the train, waved goodbye and walked away. She was the first of the three females who had escorted him to Ireland.

He walked up the road that ran behind the pub. He thought about going in to see Mick, but decided against it. He was afraid that if he did, he would start drinking again. He wanted to sweat the alcohol out of his blood.

He went up the road and passed the quiet youth hostel and the crowded butcher shop in whose window hung a leg of lamb and a shank of beef. He turned right at the empty schoolhouse and began the ascent up the mountain. As the climb steepened, he had to breathe harder and harder. After a few minutes, he stopped, took out his cigarettes and threw them into a ditch. He slowed his pace and breathed deeply through his nose until he got a second wind.

Around him, in the purple hills and valleys, he saw some isolated farmhouses but no people. Along the road, he passed a few derelict houses, their owners dead or gone to the cities. A goat bleated in a field hidden by high hedgerows. Large insects buzzed by his face.

When he got to a top of a rise, he sat on a crumbling stone wall by the side of the road. His head felt clearer already. He looked down into a valley and noticed a stream gleaming in the sun. Beside it, he saw a figure dressed in brown, squat, then jump up and run along the water and squat again, then duck walk several feet.

He wished that he had a pair of binoculars. He stood on the wall to get a better look. It was a woman. He could tell by the way she ran. But she didn't look like one of the village women. She wore pants and a large, floppy hat. He couldn't figure out what she was doing. He was mesmerized by her. He jumped from the wall and started towards her but then hesitated for a moment. There was no one around. She might become frightened when she saw him coming. But he knew that he wasn't going to do anything to her, so there'd be no harm done if he took a walk down.

He stomped through the knee-high grass of the field and slowly made his way down to the stream, making plenty of noise so she would hear him coming. As he came near to her, she stood and faced him.

"Hello there," he said and waved his hand.

She didn't answer, only stared at him with her hands on her hips.

He came to within several feet of her and stopped.

"Did I invite you over here?"

He was taken back a little by her tone.

"No, you didn't. I'm sorry if I disturbed you. I was just wondering what you were doing."

Her face softened, a smile twitching on her lips.

"Are you staying at the youth hostel?"

James smiled.

"No, I'm staying at Mick Casey's."

He stopped smiling as he saw her eyes go cold again and her face tighten around the jaws.

She turned abruptly away from him and walked quickly up the side of the field and disappeared over a rise in a hill. He wondered what that was about and who she was. Maybe she was Madeleine, the midwife. He thought that there weren't any midwives anymore. He had pictured them as old fat women with no teeth and sunken cheeks. But she was beautiful. She was tall and lean with curly red hair and big black eyes. She had been about to smile and talk with him until he mentioned that he stayed at Ranchhouse.

He walked slowly back up to the road and sat on the wall again. He sat there for about an hour, breathing in the sweet mountain air and listening to the wind as it whistled through the purple heather, and he heard the cows lowing in the dark green fields around him and he saw the village unfold beneath him in a vast panorama of land and sea and sky. He saw a tiny trawler anchored out in the bay and he could just barely make out the outline of the abbey where the monks had lived long ago.

'A mahn does not live by bread alone but by his wits.' Words of wisdom from Michael Casey.

James knew that he needed his wits about him now. Who was Mick? And what kind of place was Ranchhouse? Maybe it really was an IRA house. He jumped from the wall and paced back and forth, thinking about how Mick talked to him, how he always seemed to be hinting at something. Maybe Mick wanted him to join the IRA. James laughed. That was absurd. The IRA wouldn't want him. They didn't know anything about him. He was a nobody. And what could he do for them? Rob a bank? Blow up a building? Shoot somebody? James stopped laughing. But what if they did want him to join them? What would he do? He had a sudden impulse to sneak down to this chalet, pick up his pack and get out of there. But go where? He couldn't go home. He had to stay and do whatever he had to do. But this time, he would make the right choice, he vowed, and be on the right side.

A donkey cart carrying silver tins of milk rattled past and the farmer sitting sideways on it wished him good day with a gentle, downward twist of his bearded face.

James ran down after the cart and asked the man if he were going near Mick Casey's.

"That I am," said the man, in a thick Kerry brogue. "I'm going to the dairy near Cahirciveen. You're welcome to sit in the back."

James jumped onto the cart and sat as far away from the bouncing tins of milk as he could. He looked up into the hills above him, hoping to catch another sight of her, but he saw no one and he heard nothing but the rattle of the wheels and the clopping of the donkey's hoofs.

As James walked through Ranchhouse, he heard a distant guitar being tuned and he smelled stew cooking on the stove in the back-room. He found Mick pitching hay into the garden and spreading it between the rows of vegetables. Mick stopped working, took off his straw hat and wiped his face.

"Where have you been, mahn? There's work to be done."

"I was walking. I was going to see the Skelligs Rock but I didn't make it that far. I got about half-way up and I met a woman, up by that stream. Tall, maybe six foot. With curly red hair. And big black eyes."

Mick leaned on his pitchfork.

"That was Madeleine. Did she talk with you at all?"

James sat on a stool.

"No. I tried. But as soon as she found out that I stay here, she split. Why's that, Mick?"

Mick began pitching hay into the garden.

"Take a shovel, mahn, and dig some potatoes. A couple of baskets full."

James found a rusty shovel in the high grass by the garden. He had dug potatoes several times the year before, because he enjoyed the work and he liked the feel of the damp earth between his fingers. He pushed the shovel gently into the soil, then lifted it, and turned over several small potatoes. He brushed them off, then tossed them into a basket.

He looked up to see Mick watching him.

"You never answered my question, Mick."

Mick picked up a shovel and joined James in the potato patch.

"I've known Madeleine since she was a little girl. She was born here. Her mother came home from London for the birthing, to be with her mother, Mary Murphy, the midwife. Madeleine was a fiery one from the day she was born. A mind of her own, she has."

"She's a midwife, too."

"That's right," said Mick. "In London. She only comes here on holiday. Usually, her family comes as well, but they couldn't make it this year for some reason, so she's staying up there alone this summer."

"Is she married?"

Mick laughed.

"No, mahn. I don't think there's a mahn alive who could tame Madeleine. Christy tried last year but he got nowhere. She's had a boyfriend or two in London, I've heard, but I've never seen them. They say she lives in a commune in North London with a few women. I don't know. I don't talk much to Madeleine. She rarely comes to the pub and she won't stop here anymore."

"Why's that, Mick?"

Mick began digging potatoes and encouraged James to do the same.

"We'd better get to work. We'll be needing plenty of spuds, mahn, to feed the army when it comes."

"What army?"

"The Provos. They'll be coming tonight. I just talked to them on the phone. Patty Byrnes and his brother, Eamon. And God knows who else will be with them."

James began digging deeper and faster, unearthing scores of potatoes. He searched through the black dirt, sorting out the small potatoes from the large and throwing them into baskets. He straightened up and took a deep breath, calming himself.

"Who is Patty, Mick?"

Mick stopped working and faced James.

"I've watched you. You listen, mahn. You hear what I am saying to you. And I've heard you talk. I know a good mahn when I see one. When your country called, you answered. I admire that. You have courage, guts. We need men like that here."

James shook his head.

"But I was on the wrong side, Mick. The VC were right to fight against us. We were the only foreigners over there. We were wrong. We were the aggressors."

Mick nodded.

"I know it, mahn. Just like the British are here. And just as the Vietnamese defeated the Americans, we shall conquer the English. But you were a young mahn. You did not understand the politics. But you admitted your mistake and learned from it. I like that, mahn."

James smiled.

"I appreciate what you're saying, Mick. But you still haven't answered my question."

"What I'm trying to tell you, mahn, is that I trust you. Patty Byrnes is a Provo from Belfast. He's wanted by the British and by police all over the world. Patty's a hard mahn. He will be staying here for a few days, maybe more. The Gardai may come here looking for him. The local people know who he is but they are with us for the most part. There may be an informer amongst them but I doubt it. They would be too afraid of what Patty would do if he found them out. He's a good mahn with a revolver."

"Is he why Madeleine won't come here?"

"He's one reason. She had a run in with him several years ago. But she also doesn't agree with our politics. She's against guns and violence. And that's what Patty brings us: guns. What we need to fight the British Empire."

"Why's he coming here?"

"He needs to lay low for a while, before heading up north. And he wants to meet you."

James felt the adrenaline rush.

"Meet me? How does he know about me?"

"I told him about you, mahn, last year. That you were one of us. And I talked with him on the phone today and told him you had returned."

James thrust his shovel deep into the earth. He dug furiously for several minutes, his excitement driving him. He got down on his hands and knees and clawed through the soil like a madman digging up a grave. He was being given another chance. He pulled the potatoes from their roots and drew them to him like a happy gambler grabbing his stake.

While James and Mick rested from their labor, the others prepared dinner. Billie cooked a carrot stew made from mutton bones sent down from the convent, using the potatoes that Milton washed and peeled. Dieter went to the shop and bought brown bread and cheese. When dinner was ready, they cleared a place at the back room table and ate ravenously; all except Mick who would only eat a few small potatoes and drink the bottle of raw milk that a neighbor sent him every day. After dinner, Mick and James sat by the fireplace, while the others washed the dishes.

"Have you written to your father?" asked Mick. "To tell him that you are safe and well."

James shook his head and grimaced.

"Why not, mahn? He is your father."

"We're not on good terms, Mick. There's hard feelings between us."

"About what?"

James hesitated for a moment, thinking about how complicated it was. As a boy, he had been close to his father. They went to ball games together. They read the same books. They agreed about politics. Until he came home from Vietnam.

"The war, Mick. What else? I'm mad at him. And he can't understand what happened to me. I went into the army patriotic and came home against the war. He wouldn't listen to me: his son. I told him that we had been lied to, that we weren't there to help the Vietnamese and that they didn't want us there. But he wouldn't believe me. He believed them instead: the politicians, the military. He made his choice. He turned against me, his son."

James had to stop talking for a moment to hold back the tears.

"What does your father do for a living?"

James hesitated. His father wasn't working at all now. He was out on sick leave. But James didn't want to get into all of that with Mick. He felt guilty about it, being in Ireland while his father was dying. Before James left, his father had asked him not to go, or to go later, because he thought that he might be needing him. 'I have to go now, dad,' James had told him. 'I have to do this.'

James grimaced.

"He's a timekeeper at Budd's. They make automobile body parts for General Motors. He keeps track of how fast the men work. He's been there for 25 years. He's a member of the UAW, the United Auto Workers Union. His name is Walter, though everyone calls him Bud. Not after his company. When he was a little boy, his brother Ed called him my budder."

"City working class, you are, mahn. Just like Patty Byrnes. His father worked for a time in the shipyards of Belfast, before they got rid of him for being born Catholic. Now there's a mahn who can tell you about labor unions and the rights of the working mahn. Just like your father, I'm sure."

James shook his head, thinking about how strange it was that he had never seen himself as being part of the working class. He had never thought in terms of class. He knew that some people were richer than others but he had never thought about why.

"My father seems like he's more for the company than he is for the union. I don't know why. We weren't poor but we didn't have a lot either. We lived in an apartment all our lives. My parents still do. We didn't have a car until I was 16. My father's basically a good man. He always worked. He didn't run around. He wasn't out boozing it up all the time. But he's blind about America. It can do no wrong. He votes for the Republicans. We had a big fight last year when he voted for Nixon and I voted for McGovern. "

"He sounds like a good father to me, mahn but he is under the spell of the capitalists. In America, I am told, many men in the working class have been deceived into thinking that they are in league with big business, when in fact, they are being used by them. It is their children who fought and died in Vietnam, not the children of rich. Am I right, mahn?"

James nodded. He was angry with his father for not stopping him from going into the army. His father should have known better. He knew what war was. A son climbs the cross, while the father stands by, approving of the sacrifice. ''Must Christ die every day to save those with no imagination?" Someone had written that on the living room wall. He wasn't sure what that meant exactly.

"Sometimes, Mick, I think that fathers shouldn't send their sons off to war. Sacrifice them like that. Fathers should protect their sons, not send them off to die in some strange country. Was your father in the IRA?"

Mick lit another cigarette.

"Of course. My father was Captain Casey. He served in the Kerry militia during the War of Independence."

"So you followed in your father's footsteps, too?"

Mick stared into the empty fireplace for a few moments.

"For a while, I did. But I stepped out of them a few years ago. As you can see, mahn, I don't do much of anything anymore. When a mahn lets go of life as I have, it's difficult to begin again. But yes, I served in the army, in London, in the '50's. I was with an IRA cell over there. Our job was to get guns, get them anyway we could. Some of our men joined the British Army, so we had men inside."

"That takes a lot of guts," said James. "The VC did that too. A lot of ARVNs are VC. And we wonder why they won't fight, thinking that they're just cowards."

Mick grinned.

"That's an old IRA tactic. Destroy them from within. Ho Chi Minh studied our methods, I am told."

"Did you have much success? Getting guns?"

"Some. We stole some. We bought some. I remember one night, we were picking up a load of guns from a warehouse where we had an in, when a guard saw us loading up a truck and blew the whistle on us. We had to get away fast that night, mahn. Nothing like the sound of bullets going past your head to make your heart beat faster."

James heard two cars pull up outside and cut their motors. A moment later, the door banged open and a greyhound leaped into the room and ran over to Mick.

"Freedom. How are ya, boy, " said Mick as he rubbed the dog's head. "Where's your master?"

"Right here," shouted a short man with frizzy black hair who stood in the doorway. He burst into song. "We go to Michael Casey's and we go there for the craic. We go to Michael Casey's and we're always coming back." He raised a fist into the air. "Up the rebels."

"My God, mahn," shouted Mick as he jumped up and embraced the man. "Eamon. Good to see you. Where's Patty?"

"He's coming. He's outside talking with Maura."

The two men embraced again.

"I see you have a bottle of poteen," said Mick. "Where'd you get it?"

"In County Tyrone," said Eamon. He drank from the bottle, then handed it to Mick. "We just come from there."

James stood apart from the men as they talked. He wiped his hands on his pants.

A large man loomed in the doorway.

"Is this him?" the man asked Mick.

James walked towards Mick, who introduced him to Patty.

"Behold the mahn."

His head cocked to one side, Patty sidled towards James.

"Why are you here? That's what I want to know."

Instinctively, James came to attention, his face tightening around the jaws. Patty stood over him like a drill sergeant looking for dirt. James studied the sharp nose, crooked teeth and cold gray eyes of the man. That was what he had come there to face.

James shrugged, stepped back and sat casually at the table. Show no fear, that's the key, he thought. And keep cool. Don't talk too much.

Patty took a step towards James, then stopped, twisting his head from side to side and muttering to himself.

Mick came over and stood between James and Patty.

"James is a good mahn. He can be trusted. Take my word for it. Tell him, James, why you are here."

James stared up at Patty, his mind working furiously. He knew that he had to say the right thing.

"I liked it here last year: the country, the people, Mick. So I decided to come back. I had to get out of America and I didn't know where else to go."

Eamon stepped towards James and put out his hand.

"Good to meet ya. I remember Mick talking about ya last year but I never thought I'd meet ya. Mick thinks a lot of ya, he does."

Patty walked over to the fireplace and stared at James.

"I'm going to want to hear about Vietnam and what went on over there. I don't trust Casey's judgment anymore. He's nothing but a worthless drunk now."

Milton, Billie and Dieter walked into the room, smiling and nodding at everyone.

"Who are you?" demanded Patty as he swaggered towards the trio. "You look like hippies. Are you believers in this peace and love rubbish?"

"I believe in the Divine Light," said Milton, solemnly.

Patty roared with laughter, then slapped Milton on the back, almost knocking him across the room.

"The Divine Light! It's a bit of a joke. What is this idjit doing in our house. No wonder the house is a mess. I don't understand why you let these parasites stay here. I guess the two old men, Kelly and Old Dan, are still here. Who do you think you are, Casey? The father of the world?"

"Leave him alone," wheezed Eamon. "Don't kick the man when he's down. He's just being what the Irish are well-known for throughout the world: hospitable." He waved the bottle of poteen. "Let's have a drink. Then a bite to eat. We're hungry."

Patty continued staring at the three Germans.

"I want them out of here, tonight."

"How about the woman?" asked Eamon. "She's a looker."

Patty walked in circles around Billie who blushed and protested as Patty examined her body.

"Maybe the bird can stay," said Patty, grinning as he made a lewd comment about her.

"Cut it out, mahn," said Mick. "Leave her alone. She's one of us. She's a young communist from Hamburg."

Patty did the hanging on the corner rock.

"Oh yeah. I've seen her type before. A dilettante, having her fling, before she marries her dull middle-class husband and has her two brats and a nanny in her own little ranch house in the suburbs."

"No," cried Billie. "That is not true. I am not a dilettante. I am a committed revolutionary."

Patty whipped a revolver out from beneath his leather jacket and pointed it at Milton.

"Here, take this and blow this idjit's brains out with it."

Billie stared at the extended gun for a few moments then shook her head.

"Then get out of here," Patty snarled. "What good are ya? And take that religious idjit with you. Who's the other bloke? Do you believe in the Divine Light, too?"

Dieter shook his head.

"No, we are not traveling together. It is coincidence we come here at the same time."

"What part of Germany are you from?" asked Eamon.

"East Germany. Near Leipzig. I left there because I wanted to see the world and they would not let me."

"He swam out into the Baltic Sea every night for two weeks," said Mick. "In that cold water, in the dark, waiting for his chance. Shows you the kind of mahn he is.

"I was picked up by a Swedish ship," said Dieter. "That took me to Stockholm. I traveled the Continent for about one year, then I came to Ireland. Mick has been kind to let me stay."

"Are you a Communist?" asked Patty.

Dieter smiled, his blue eyes blinking in his pointed pink face.

"In theory, yes, but in practice, no. I was as a young man. I served four years in the army, as a common soldier. I was stationed in Berlin. I came to think one day that there was more to life than this. After my discharge, I wanted to travel, to live, but they would not let me, so I defected."

James didn't know what to make of it. He looked at Dieter's slender frame and couldn't imagine him serving in that hard German army and swimming out into that cold Baltic Sea. He watched Patty studying Dieter.

"Why should I believe you?" asked Patty.

Dieter shrugged.

"Because it's true."

Patty looked at Eamon and Mick.

"I don't like this. All these people here."

"James and Dieter seem all right to me," said Eamon. "Both were army men. Let them stay and send the others packing."

Mick agreed.

"I've watched Dieter for two weeks and I've talked with him. You know what I do: give a calf enough rope and he'll hang himself. But Dieter is a good mahn. And of course, James, there's no better mahn than him."

"All right," said Patty, as he holstered the pistol behind his back. "But those two have to go." He looked around to look for Milton and Billie but they had already disappeared through the back door.

Mick passed James the bottle of poteen.

"Drink it raw, mahn. It's Irish bootleg whiskey."

James took a drink, feeling the whiskey burn into his stomach. It sent tears to his eyes and he almost gagged.

"Where's Maura?" Mick asked Patty.

"She's outside," said Patty. "Taking a walk on the strand. She's on the rag. She'll be in later, when she smells the joint."

They filed out of the kitchen, went into the backroom and sat around the table.

Patty took a silver block and a knife from his pocket and placed them on the table. He unwrapped the block, took out a large piece of hashish and cut a piece of it off. He sprinkled it into a long cigarette that Eamon had rolled.

"I have some good dope here," said Patty, grinning. "Black Moroccan. I picked it up in Algeria last month."

Patty lit the joint, took a few hits from it, then passed it to Eamon.

"So tell me, James, did you have a bit of fun in the Nam? Wasting a lot of gooks?"

James looked over at Mick who was staring at the roof. What had he told Patty?

Patty curled his lip.

"How could you go there? Didn't you know what was going on?"

James stared at Patty. He didn't know what to say.

"Tell me, man. Why did you go to Vietnam? To protect the poor gooks from the evils of Communism?"

As James looked at Patty's mocking face, he felt his temper rise. He clenched his fists. He was sick of people judging him, condemning him, for believing what he was told.

"Yeah, that's what I thought. Communism was bad. That after the defeat of the Nazis, Communism was the new evil in the world. I was only a boy during the Korean War, but I remember seeing newsreels and movies about it. Pork Chop Hill. The Chosin Reservoir. They made me sick. I hated them: the Chinese and their human wave attacks. And Stalin and his concentration camps. They were trying to take over the world. They told us that the Communists from North Vietnam were trying to take over another country, South Vietnam. We had to stop them there, or else someday we'd be fighting them in California."

Patty whistled.

"Boy, were you brainwashed. Don't you know that it's the United States and their lackeys they're trying to take over the world?"

James took a drink of poteen.

"Yeah, I know that! Now!"

He cursed America and everything it stood for at the top of his voice.

"But I didn't then! I volunteered for the army! I volunteered for Vietnam! I put my life on the line for a lie! I hate America! I hate it!"

Patty pushed back his chair and stood with his arms away from his sides, his hands twitching

"So tell me, man, do you work for the CIA? There was a CIA man here a couple of years ago. Dressed like you are. Quoting Chairman Mao from his little red book. Putting down the US. Do you know what I told him when I found him out? And we have our ways, man, of finding out?"

James couldn't believe what he was hearing.

"What?"

"That he had 5 minutes to live."

He looked over at Mick but Mick wouldn't look at him.

"The CIA? You're kidding me, right? After what they did to us? They were the ones who got our soldiers hooked on heroin. They flew it down in Air America from the Golden Triangle. You know where that is, don't ya? It's a triangle of land in Laos, Cambodia and Thailand."

Patty nodded.

"And how do you know this? If you weren't one of them?"

James felt his legs shaking. He looked at Mick again.

"Hey, Mick. I don't know what this is all about. But I don't work for the CIA. Never did. I only know about this because I just read a book about it by, I can't remember the guys name, McCoy, I think. It was called **The Politics of Heroin in Southeast Asia**. Do you think that I'm one of them?"

Mick grinned.

"No, mahn. Patty is just testing you. We know that the CIA is hand in hand with the British. They have operatives in Ireland. Some are Vietnam veterans. But no, mahn. You're not that good of an actor. And besides, we've already checked you out."

Patty and Eamon laughed.

"Mick told me that you were trained for combat," said Patty.

"But that you managed to stay out of it. A smart man."

James took a deep breath. His legs were still shaking.

"Not smart. Just lucky."

"But you know how to handle weapons?"

James shrugged.

"Yeah. I guess you could say that. I fired just about every weapon they have: .50 caliber machine guns, M60s, grenade launchers, LAWS, M14s, M16s, howitzers. But it's been a few years. And I really didn't like doing it. I couldn't get into it."

Patty grinned.

"That's because you knew you were wrong. You would feel differently, if you were on the right side, righting against oppression. Like we are here. Think about it."

"Is anyone hungry?" shouted Mick. "I see that we have some spuds hammering away on the cooker. And there's some stew left. Now that Billie's gone, we'll have to find another cook."

Eamon said that he could eat some spuds, so Mick handed him some, steaming, inside the lid of a saucepan.

"As you can see, mahn." said Mick, as he ate a egg from inside an empty cigarette pack. "I'm not much of a host. I'm not used to serving people. My mother was too good to me."

Patty ate a bowl of stew, while the others sat around the table, smoking the joint and drinking the bottle of poteen.

James took a few hits from the joint. He had to do something to relax. His legs were still shaking. He had never smoked hash mixed with tobacco before. He didn't like it. It was too harsh. He'd rather smoke it in a pipe by itself.

"Tell me, man," Eamon asked. "Did you smoke much dope in Vietnam?"

James shrugged.

"Nah. Not really. I didn't get into it until I was short. I used to think it was bad for you. Something only hippies did. Thank God, I never got into heroin. Some guys in my company did but I didn't. I smoked my first joint on bunker guard, out on the perimeter. One of the guys asked me if I was nervous. Yeah, I was nervous. I was always nervous out there. 'Smoke this,' he said. 'It'll make you feel better.' He took a couple joints out of a cigarette pack, Park Lanes, they were called, they were already rolled, with filters, and he gave me two of them. I figured, why not? Everybody else was doing it. I smoked both of them, one after another. I found out later they were OJs, opium joints. I got so stoned that I rolled around on top of the bunker, laughing, for what seemed like hours. Everything seemed so absurd to me. What was I doing in Vietnam? But then it was like I wasn't really there anymore. I was this detached observer. Out in front of us, a few miles away I guess it was, there was a firefight. I could the tracer bullets coming down from the sky from a helicopter and in the distance, some jets were bombing what seemed to be a mountainside, the bombs were exploding high up. I felt I was in the presence of evil. It might have been the Black Virgin Mountain for all I know. Or it could have been in the Iron Triangle. That was a VC stronghold that was only about 15 miles away; I found that out later. It was like watching a fireworks demonstration but I could feel the ground shaking under us so I knew it was for real. For a moment, I felt some sympathy for those enemy soldiers who were underneath all that but just for a moment. I knew that they would kill me if they had a chance. That night, when the Officer of the Guard came around to check on us everybody was so stoned that nobody could get up. We weren't even looking the right way. Until, finally, at the last minute, one of the guys jumped up and challenged him but he gave the wrong password. He gave the one that the Officer was supposed to give. The Lieutenant was thrown by that for a minute. He didn't know what to say. Then he got hissed off. He started shouting and cursing. 'What was going on? Why wasn't our machine gun loaded? Where were our M16s?' They were down in the bunker. Then one of the guys, an ex-hippie from San Francisco, who was wearing wire-framed glasses, just looked at him and said, 'What difference does it make? We're not killing anybody, anyway. That's not our thing.'"

Everyone laughed.

"That Lieutenant didn't know what to do. He just looked at us like we were crazy. He said something after that, but I don't remember. I was too busy trying not to laugh. He never came back and he didn't report us. He must have known we were stoned. I guess he didn't care. Nobody cared about nothing over there. I guess that's why some guys liked it."

"It's no wonder you lost the war,' said Dieter, laughing. "I cannot imagine doing that in our army."

James grimaced.

"That's not why we lost the war. The serious soldiers didn't smoke on guard duty and I know we seemed like the three Stooges on laughing gas but the rest of the time I was on guard duty, I was stone-cold sober. Don't get me wrong. If any VC had tried to come through the wire, I would've shot them. I wouldn't let any of my buddies get killed if I could help it. But we lost the war because no one can win that kind of war: a war of aggression. No one can defeat a guerrilla army that has the support of its people."

"Up the rebels," shouted Eamon. "That was a good craic, Seamus. Now, we need some poetry. Recite us a poem, Michael."

Mick took up a poetic pose and recited in a deep voice.

"'I wander down through the glen today/ my heart was sad and sore./ Filled with sorrow and wracked with grief, for the days that will come no more./ Foolish I know to be mourning so, but I cannot check the tears/ that fall like rain when my thoughts again go back over all the years./ Over all the paths that the Gael have trod in their fight to a lowly state,/ and we the children of freeborn men on masters like slavelings wait./ Where all we do is an empty mock, degrading, mean and base./ We wince and cringe and lick the feet of a soulless and alien race.'/"

"We don't lick anybody's feet," shouted Patty, pounding on the table. "Stuff that sentimental, romantic rubbish. Come with me, Eamon."

The two men went out through the kitchen. Several minutes later, they returned, hurrying a bulging valise, out of which a rifle barrel gleamed. Quickly, they carried the bag into the living room and up the stairs.

Mick looked at James and cackled his maniacal laugh.

"Bang! Bang! It's the only language the Brit's understand."

"I see you haven't changed, Michael," said a woman who now stood in the doorway. She was a vision of the Irish female: freckled face, blue eyes and curly black hair. She sat wearily at the table across from Mick

"Maura, you startled me," said Mick. "Where have you been?"

"Taking a walk and thinking about Deirdre. She was smart for getting out of here when she did. I wish I could. I don't have the stomach for it anymore."

Mick laughed, then recited, "'A woman in a bitter world must do the best she can. Must bear the yoke, do the stroke and do the will of mahn.'"

"Michael!" said Maura. "Cut the bull. Robert Service. Are you still quoting him? It's no wonder Deirdre left you."

Mick sobbed.

"Stop it," said Maura. "If you had treated her better, she wouldn't have left you. She wanted to stay and bring up the child in Ballinskelligs. But you would have had to stop drinking so much. And you cannot do that, can you, Michael?"

Mick looked at his hands and didn't answer. He had tears in his eyes and a sad face.

"I'm sorry, Mick," said Maura. "I'm being a real witch, tonight. Is Deirdre still in Dublin?"

Mick nodded.

"Has she delivered yet?"

Mick shook his head.

James couldn't believe what he was hearing. Deirdre was pregnant? At his age, Mick was going to be a father for the first time?

"When she leaving?" asked Maura.

"As soon as she's up and around," said Mick, wiping away tears.

"So she's finally going home to New York," said Maura. "Like I always knew she would. That's what they all do. Going back to her rich parents. Think of it, Michael. Your son will be brought up by an American capitalist. He'll grow up a rich man's son."

Mick jumped up howling from the table and ran into the living room, with Maura following after him, apologizing.

James was stunned. He looked over at Dieter who seemed lost in a fantasy of his own. These people were too much for him. He needed to be alone. Feeling dizzy from the hash, he lurched from the room and went out into the garden. His head spinning, he sat on a stool and took deep breaths, trying to clear his head. Through the window, he saw Patty and Eamon enter the backroom, with their arms around Mick. James ran towards them, then stopped and ran up to his chalet. He would pack his bags and be on the road before they knew he was gone. But where would he go? He stopped outside the chalet door, his chest heaving. He paced up and down for a few minutes, thinking about how much money he had. If he had to start paying for a room, his money would run out in no time. Then what would he do? There was no money at home. Then he remembered that Patty was only going to stay for a few days. He would lay low until he knew what to do. He heard shouting and singing at Ranchhouse. He decided to walk along the beach and hide out there until it was late and he could sneak back to his chalet and get some sleep.

James stared at the weed grown white cross by the side of the road. It commemorated an IRA soldier, Tom Keating, who had been killed by the British in 1921. On that very spot a man had died. The thought chilled him and he shivered in the cool morning air. Mick had told him about it the year before. He wrapped his arms around himself, picturing the scene: a car roars by, a gun pokes through the window, a flash of light. Terrible pain.

No, no pain at first, only shock. He hadn't felt the pain until later. And then what? Darkness? Light? He had come so close to finding out. The knife went into his back, twice, without puncturing a lung, without cutting an artery, or severing his spinal cord. Death missed him by an inch, or less. He couldn't come any closer to death than that. Why hadn't he died then? He would have been out of his misery and there would be one less problem in the world, one less germ. He was a sick man in need of a doctor.

There was something wrong with him. He'd be better off dead. Like Tom Keating was. It was a beautiful place to die. He looked around him. It probably looked the same as it did in 1921. Beyond a green field, the bay foamed white in a wide horseshoe upon a rippled strand. Smoke curled from the chimneys of lopsided farmhouses in whose front yards chickens policed for food. Cows chewed their cuds alongside a trilling stream that ran under a stone bridge. It was a beautiful place to live. It was like being in another century, another age, peopled with poets and mid wives and revolutionaries. He wanted to stay in Ballinskelligs forever. But how could he do it? Eventually, his money would run out, and then what would he do? He had spent most of the night, walking up and down the beach, trying to think of a solution. There were no jobs in Ireland, not for him, no legal jobs. Maybe he could get a job as a bank robber. Or a bagman. Patty had plenty of guns. And drugs. He laughed at the idea. Then a feeling of dread came over him. Something terrible was going to happen. It was no joke, no romantic fantasy. It was the river of no return. There was no way out, no way back, but only forward into more lies, more pain, more death.

Like a vampire fleeing from a cross, James ran down the road. After a few minutes, he slowed to a trot and then to a walk. As he walked, he calmed down. He always felt better walking. He came to a crossroads where a group of smoking farmers stood between their donkey carts that were loaded with tins of milk and parked along the side of the road.

A tall man with a pock-marked face and a toothless grin called out, "La braeg. A fine day it is." The rest of the men smiled and tipped their hats to him.

James tipped his hat in return. He wished that he was one of them. The farmers had a hard life: up early in the morning, milking the cows, feeding the chickens, digging the potatoes, but a simple one. But what was the use of wishing? He was a city kid. He didn't know how to farm or how to grow anything. He knew nothing of the rhythms and cycles of life. He didn't know how to live himself. And how could he learn that? Who would teach him?

A rabbit darted from a hedge and hopped across the road, his white bottom blinking like a bulls-eye. It gave him an idea. They could breed rabbits. They could eat the meat and sell the feet. He laughed. Then they could buy a cow, somehow, and some chickens. He wondered how much they cost. And with plenty of potatoes and cabbage, they would have enough to eat. Mick had told him that anything would grow in Ballinskelligs. Mick could teach him how to farm. They could survive but that was about all. And if he didn't make it, he might as well die there as anywhere. He had nowhere else to go. He decided to talk with Mick about it when he got back to Ranchhouse.

He felt hungry. He walked past several small cottages until he came to a grocery store with a gasoline pump in front. He went into the store and bought a loaf of bread and a bottle of milk. He ate and drank while he walked. When he finished, he picked up the pace to a forced march, focusing his mind on his muscles and his breathing, pumping out his fears and frustrations. He was strong. He could make it. Nothing was going to happen to him. That knife had been an immunization shot, a protection from violent death.

After a few hours, he came into the outskirts of Cahiriscveen, Gaelic for the town beneath the mountains and above the sea, for that's where it was. He stood by the side of the road and stared down at the patchwork quilt of blue and green water that crashed white against the steep walls of the deep gorge far below. He craned his neck to see the Skelligs Rock in the distance but it was hidden in a fogbank.

He continued down the road and passed the infirmary and the dairy, and then went into the center of town with its two story brown and gray houses and brightly painted shops. He saw a butcher in his bloodstained apron hang a flank of mutton on a steel hook. On the corner of a side street, an old woman, wearing a black dress and bandanna, hawked fresh fish from a wicker basket. A Wimpy's snack bar appeared sandwiched between a small shop with fresh fruit upon display and a used furniture store.

He remembered Mick talking about Wimpy's.

'It frightens me, mahn. Seeing that sign hanging there with all the great Irish names: O'Neil, O'Connor, O'Brien...Wimpy's. It makes me want to cry.'

James laughed into his hand. Good old Mick. He was so funny. James felt a sudden urge to be back in the pub with Mick, drinking pints and telling stories. He almost turned in the direction of Ballinskelligs but then thought better of it. Patty would be there as well and he wanted to stay away from Patty for as long as he could. He passed by Casey's garage. In front of it, a greasy mechanic knelt, changing a flat tire.

James wondered if the man was Mick's brother, William.

'Owns a shop in town, mahn. He's all for business. A petty bourgeois is what he is. His family has enough to eat, a home to live in, a car to drive. And stuff the other mahn and his family. If they don't have enough, it's tough luck. It's dog eat dog. That's capitalism for you. Clever they are: the British and their ways. They've turned brother against brother. And for what? Money. Who needs money, mahn? The birds have no money and yet they eat.'

That was easy to say, thought James. But he was no bird. He needed money to live. He calculated in his mind how much money he had left: with half an airplane plane fare, maybe $300. What could he buy with that? A feeling of despair swept over him as his dream of the morning disappeared like a hashish hallucination. A pipe dream was all it was.

He wandered up and down the street, clenching his teeth to keep from crying out. What was he going to do? Where could he get more money? He went over and over in his mind what had happened the night before and what had been said. Maybe they did want him to join the IRA. Maybe they would give him some money for joining, an enlistment bonus.

He stopped walking. He grimaced and clenched his fists. He was oblivious to the people around him. He felt as if he had been punched in the chest. He took a few deep breaths. What was he thinking of? Join another army? When he got out of the army, he had sworn never to have anything to do with the military again. Like Yossarian in Catch 22, he had vowed never to have anything good to say about the army. And here he was, actually considering joining another army, a very different army to be sure, but still an army.

He walked into the open square in the center of town and in it was a large statue of a soldier with a rifle at port arms that stood in front of the library. He went over to it. It was a memorial to the men of the town who had died in their War of Independence from the British Empire. As he read the names on the block beneath the soldier, a mongrel dog trotted over, lifted a hind leg and relieved itself on its base.

He had sympathy for the statue. That's how they treated us when we got home. At least the Irishmen had died for a just cause. He thought of the men who had died in Vietnam. What had they died for? For nothing. For a lie: that we were there to help the Vietnamese. We weren't there to help them. We were there to kill them, to stop their revolution, to keep them under control: US control. It was a war of imperialism, the same kind of war that was going on in Northern Ireland.

He felt so tired. He didn't know what to do. He didn't want to get involved in another war. But he had to do something to make up for Vietnam. He wanted to sleep for days, blot it all out. He saw a bench in front of the library. He went over and stretched out on it. He covered his eyes with his cap and fell asleep.

A man stood over him, a hideous grin on his face, a bloody knife raised, ready to strike. He wanted to stand up and defend himself but he couldn't move. He waited for the knife like a penitent accepting punishment.

He woke up sweating, his heart beating wildly. When he realized where he was, he wiped his face with his hands and took deep breaths until he stopped shaking. He had that nightmare over and over again since he had gotten knifed. Only by getting drunk could he stop it.

He jumped to his feet and walked in the direction of Ballinskelligs. In the center of town, he hitched a ride with a pig farmer who took him as far as the neighboring village of Dungannon. He had to walk the rest of the way from there. It was early evening by the time he got to Ranchhouse. It was deserted.

A ribbon of clouds scudded across the sky and plumed over the purple mountains. A hunchbacked old woman, wrapped in a tattered black shawl and fingering rosary beads, hurried along the glistening road. As she passed by James, she peered at him through the fringes of her shawl and made the sign of the cross three times.

James walked down the path to the strand, passing the convent, a golden glimmer in the trees. He thought of the woman on the train from Luxembourg and wished that he could have stayed with her but he knew that would have been impossible. He wasn't capable of loving a woman and he wasn't worthy of a woman's love. He was too dirty. He looked out over the bay and saw a boat cutting water between two small islands and he remembered the second female, a teenaged girl who had come to him on the midnight ferry to Dover. He had wished for her to come to him and she had.

He walked up the wooden ramp of the ferry and entered its large central room. He sat in the first empty seat he saw and took off his boots like a weary soldier back from bivouac. In his haste to get next to the woman he met in Luxembourg, he had boarded the wrong train. That made him miss the afternoon ferry from Ostende and he had to take this one. He had walked for hours around the town and harbor thinking of her and the strange conversation they had about the new god that was coming, the female god. She had been the first woman he had been able to talk with in years without feeling guilty.

He tucked his feet beneath his legs to allow two young men and a woman to pass him to their seats. She sat next to him and the men sat opposite each other by the window. With their backpacks, sleeping bags and their long blonde hair, they looked and sounded like Scandinavian students on vacation. James looked over at the trio and saw the girl put her head on the shoulder of the boy beside her and take his hand in hers. The sight made him feel like a loser. He was so tired. He closed his eyes and drifted asleep.

A man stood over him, a hideous grin on his face, a bloody knife raised, ready to strike.

He jerked awake in a sweat and groaned. He turned and looked into the soft eyes of the girl beside him. They seemed to swallow him up. When he came back to himself, he felt dizzy. His face flushing, he bent down and put on his boots. What was going on here? He stumbled out onto the deck, lit a cigarette and leaned over the railing. He felt so lonely. What if Mick weren't there? What if Mick were dead? Where would he go then? How would he live? He watched movement flutter in the darkness, then gray to seagulls searching for food. He would be like them, eating people's garbage to survive. The thought frightened him. Living like that, who would love him? He would be out of the world of women forever. Feeling depressed, he went back inside, found his seat in the darkened room and fell asleep immediately.

He was awakened by kissing sounds and sighs. It was the couple next to him. The sounds of their passion awoke within him a deep yearning for a woman. He hadn't made love with a woman for several years, not since that night up The Nuts. He wished for a woman to come and comfort him. As tears welled up in his eyes, he felt a foot rub the top of his foot. He couldn't believe it. It was the foot of the girl beside him. He shifted his foot from beneath hers, but she replaced her foot on his, then toed his calf bare. He gripped the arms of his seat, his excitement rising. Then she put her head on his shoulder. He looked over at her friend who was sound asleep. He felt as if he were in a trance. In slow motion, her head slid down his arm onto his lap, her blonde hair hanging down onto the floor. What was she doing? What did she want? It couldn't be sex, not here, not now, with her boyfriend beside her. Then the thoughts came to him: maybe she sensed his loneliness and his pain and just wanted to comfort him. He was amazed. He had gotten what he had wished for. What did that mean? he asked himself. That there was someone out there, listening, watching, waiting? He hoped so. He stroked her hair for a few minutes, then he closed his eyes and fell asleep.

When he came back to himself, he looked out over the water in the direction of the abbey ruins where the nuns had swum the day before and he saw a brown figure squatting in the surf. It was Madeleine. He watched her scoop seaweed into a bag on her hip. This was his chance, he said to himself. He was attractive to women after all. He wouldn't have any problems making it with her. He swaggered up to where she had left her towel and hiking boots and sat beside them in the sand. After a few minutes, she stopped scooping and stood facing the bay, erect and steady as a soldier waiting a command. Then she turned and walked out of the water towards him. Her black eyes widened when she saw him, but she made no other sign of recognition. He stood and faced her.

"What are you going to do what that seaweed?" he asked her, smiling. "Eat it? I ate it once, wrapped around rice." In Vietnam, he thought but did not say.

She reached down, dried her feet, put on her socks and boots, threw the towel around her shoulder and walked up the beach.

He stood there, speechless for a moment. What had he done wrong? He walked up quickly beside her.

"Why won't you talk to me? Is it because I stay at Mick's? Hey look, just because I stay there, doesn't mean that I'm one of them."

She whirled and faced him.

" Get lost. Why should I talk with you? Who are you to me?"

She looked at the name tag on his fatigue shirt.

"O'Rourke. I've heard about you. You're the Yank that was here last summer, aren't you? Christy told me about you. What a great drinking man you are. He admires you for going to Vietnam. You're one of his heroes. You and that Patty Byrnes. And don't tell me you're not one of them. If you weren't, you wouldn't have come back. You wouldn't be here."

With that, she whirled away from him.

James stood and watched her for a moment, stunned by what she said. That wasn't the way it was supposed to happen. Christy admired him for going to Vietnam? He couldn't believe it. He had told Christy how much he hated the army. And he wanted to stop drinking. She had him wrong.

He ran up beside her.

"Wait a minute, please. I need to talk to you. I need help."

She turned and faced him, her black eyes tiny as pinheads.

"Oh, you need help, do you? Poor boy. And just what makes you think that I have any help to give you? That's all you men ever want. Help me. Give me. I want. I need. I. I. I."

James grimaced.

"It's not what you think. I don't know what Christy told you last year. But I'm against war. I hated the army. And I'm trying to stop drinking. But I can deal with that myself. What I need help with is finding out about Patty Byrnes: who he is."

Her eyes widened.

"What about him? He's come back, hasn't he?"

James nodded.

"I just met him last night. I didn't know about him before. When I was here last year, Mick talked a lot about the IRA, but I didn't meet any of them. I didn't come here to join the IRA."

Madeleine tilted her head to one side.

"Oh no? Why did you come here, then?"

James looked over the mountain towards the Skelligs Rock as if the answer was up there, somewhere.

When he turned back to her, the crash of the waves and the calls of the birds ceased and he heard nothing but the pounding of the blood in his ears and the sound of his own breathing and he saw nothing but her face which rose above him like a full moon. He felt as if a cocoon had enveloped them, providing a safe place where he could speak the truth.

"To find peace."

Madeleine snorted.

"Peace? At Ranchhouse?"

James grimaced.

"Not at Ranchhouse. Here, in Ballinskelligs, somewhere, somehow. After I left here last year, I was obsessed with coming back. I kept thinking that, somehow, I would find here what I was looking for and do what I had to do. Whatever that was, I didn't know. I don't feel like I belong anywhere, anymore. I thought maybe I could live here."

Madeleine smiled.

"In all that mess?"

James sighed. He knew how absurd it seemed.

"I know. But I thought that maybe I could help fix it up. Get it working as a farm again."

Madeleine shook her head.

"Good luck. Mick hasn't done much of anything but drink since his mother died a few years ago. It's a shame. Mick's basically a good man. He's been good to me in the past. But he's really gone down hill over the last few years. He's gotten worse ever since Patty Byrnes came down here a few years ago."

"How well do you know Patty? What's he like? Mick told me that you had some sort of run-in with him."

Madeleine stopped walking and turned and faced him, her eyes as hard as pebbles.

"Run-in? That's a funny way of putting it. Patty tried to rape me was what he did. But I screamed bloody murder and fought him off. Until Mick came up and put a stop to it."

Her eyes narrowed to daggers and she cursed every man who had ever lived, for all the crimes committed against women. James stood before her, his eyes downcast, and did not say a word. He had no defense. He was guilty. He knew that men hurt women every day. He was ashamed for his sex.

When Madeleine calmed down, she apologized.

James reached out to touch her but stopped his hand in midair, then returned it quickly to his side.

'There's no need to. I'm sorry. I didn't know. Mick told me that you disagreed with their politics. I thought that you had an argument or something."

Madeleine turned down her thick lips at the corners.

"Oh, I had arguments with them. But Mick's wrong. I don't disagree with their politics. I disagree with their methods, their tactics. I want the British Army out of Belfast. I want Ireland to be free and united. But it can't be done with guns. Or with men like Patty Byrnes."

"Why not?" James asked. "What's wrong with Patty?"

"It's not just Patty," said Madeleine, sighing. "It's most of the men in Ireland, in the world for that matter. They need to change their way of thinking, their way of perceiving reality, their way of relating to other people, especially women."

"Yeah, I know what you mean," said James. "But how do you do that?"

"There is a way," said Madeleine, her face tightening like a red mask over her cheekbones. "But they won't listen. They are afraid of surrender. But never mind that now."

James wondered what that was about. 'Surrender? Surrender what? To who?' Her face had changed so quickly. She looked almost menacing. For a moment, he felt afraid but dismissed the feeling as paranoia. What could she do to him?

They reached the road that ran behind the pub. He heard shouts and bits of songs coming from inside it.

"Patty is a dangerous man," said Madeleine. "You must be careful."

James smiled.

"I will. May I see you again? I'd like to talk with you about what's happening."

Madeleine shrugged.

"Perhaps. But I can't promise you. I'm very busy. I have work to do."

"Work? Mick told me you were here on holiday."

"I am," said Madeleine. "But while I'm here I do what I can for the people in the village. There's no medical person here and the nearest hospital is in Cahiriscveen. I'm a nurse, so I try to provide some service. I try to make myself useful."

She pointed to a bag on her hip.

"I've been collecting seaweed for my neighbor's garden. She's too old to do it herself."

"What were you doing the other day when I saw you down by the stream?"

"Gathering herbs and roots."

"Herbs and roots?"

He had a fleeting vision in his mind of three witches stirring a big pot in front of a fire. 'Double, double toil and trouble; Fire burn and cauldron bubble.' Where did that come from?

Madeleine smiled.

"For my practice in London. I distrust modern medicines. Many of them originally came from plants, you know. I like to use them in their natural state. They have less side effects that way."

"You have your own practice?"

Madeleine nodded.

"With a couple other midwives."

"That's interesting," said James. "I'd like to hear more about it."

"We'll see," said Madeleine, after a few moments. "But I really must be going now. Cheerio."

She turned and walked briskly up the road in the direction of the youth hostel. He hoped that she would turn around so he could see her face again but she continued walking in her purposeful way up the road. James decided to ask Mick exactly where she lived so he could go up there and accidentally run into her. He stood outside the pub for a few minutes. He didn't really feel like going in and facing all of them, but he didn't know what else to do. After a few minutes, he decided to go in for a while, but not to drink. He had to be careful, now.

He entered the crowded pub and joined the people from Ranchhouse who were in the usual corner.

"Where have you been, mahn?" Mick shouted. "I've been worried about you. Thought maybe you cleared out."

James laughed.

"Nah, I went for a hike, to town."

He gripped the rolls of fat on his hips.

"I have to get back in shape."

"That's a good idea, " said Patty. "A man should always be fit. I run the hills whenever I can. Maybe we can run together some morning. Where did you disappear to last night? We looked for you everywhere. I wanted to hear more about your experiences in the American army."

"I fell asleep on the beach," James lied. "I didn't wake up until this morning. I was tired for some reason."

Eamon laughed.

"You were stoned. The hash was too much for you."

James grinned.

"Yeah. And the poteen: No more of that stuff."

Everyone laughed.

"Have a bit of the hair," said Mick, waving a bottle.

James shook his head.

"Come on, man," said Patty, tilting back on his stool. "We're celebrating. The first time I came to Casey's was three years ago today. Right after I escaped from Crumlin Road Jail."

James couldn't believe that Patty would say that out loud. He looked around at the other people from Ranchhouse. Dieter nodded out in the far corner. Maura smoked furiously on her cigarette, looking at no one. Eamon shouted, "Up the rebels," as he punched his fist into the thick smoke over the table.

"That summer I became known as the ghost of Ballinskelligs."

Patty laughed as he unbuttoned his brown leather jacket and exposed his white woolen sweater. He lowered his voice.

"The locals still talk about it."

"They look for you every night," said Mick as he adjusted his cowboy hat and rolled down the sleeves of his khaki shirt. "For the Second Coming."

"**The Second Coming?**" echoed James. "Isn't that the title of a Yeats poem?"

"Yeats? That reactionary," Patty snapped. "Don't tell me you like that romantic rubbish he wrote?"

"Some of it," said James, surprised. "I thought that Yeats

supported the Irish revolution. I haven't read that much of him. I just remember that poem for some reason."

Patty sneered at James.

"Well, forget it. It doesn't apply here, certainly not between you and me. Let me get on with my story: one night, at closing time, I put on a white, well almost white, sheet of Casey's. And just as the old men were coming out the door of the pub, I ran past them, a-moaning real loud with the sheet over me head just a-floating in the breeze. Then I jumped over a hedge and hid in a field. I could see the old blokes just looking at each other and I could hear them saying, 'Did ya see that, mahn? What was it? Why is was a ghost if ever I'd seen one.'"

As he asked each question in a trembling voice, Patty darted his head in different directions like a big bird.

"Then I burst through the hedge and floated past them again. They ran down the road as fast as their legs could carry them. They still call me the ghost of Ballinskelligs."

Patty laughed until tears came to his eyes.

"Ah yes. But they were good days, though. Political people, revolutionaries, from all over Europe and the Middle East would come to Casey's and we would sit around the turf fire, smoking joints and talking about changing the world. And doing something about it, man. They were people with their heads together. But now? It's nothing but a hippie haven. Peace and love rubbish. That's all it is."

Patty noticed that James wasn't drinking anything.

"Hey, Seamus. Why aren't ya gargling tonight?"

James shrugged. He knew that he had to stay away from alcohol. It messed him up too much. He wanted to see what was going on. And he had to watch his money.

"C'mon, mahn." Patty insisted. "Have a gargle."

James shook his head.

"Not tonight."

Patty went over to James and put his arm around him. He whispered in James' ear, "What's the problem? A little low on money?"

James shrugged.

"Yeah. I just have to watch what I spend, that's all."

Patty whispered.

"How would you like to borrow a few thousand?"

James stood and pulled himself away from Patty.

"A few thousand what?"

Patty put his arm around James again and pulled him over to a corner away from the others.

"A few thousand pounds."

James didn't understand what Patty meant by borrow. Was Patty some sort of loan shark? What would be the interest? James pulled away and looked Patty in the eye. He didn't like what he saw. He didn't trust Patty.

"Nah, I don't think so," said James. "I'll be okay."

Patty stopped grinning.

"Think about it, man. It'll be easy money."

"Let's go to town," shouted Eamon, cursing the pub and its owner. "Someday, we'll own this place. We'll be the shortest landlords in history. We'll walk in one night with a bomb." He imitated the voice of the owner of the pub, John Maloney. "Time. Ladies and Gents. Time." He resumed his normal wheezing voice. "You've got five minutes to get out or be blasted out. Then we'll blow the place to pieces."

Everyone laughed.

Patty turned to Eamon and patted him on the back.

"Good idea. Let's go to town, then. We can see some people while we're there about that job."

"Coming Casey?" shouted Eamon. "We'll all go."

"No, mahn," said Mick. "I'd rather not be seen in town. Haven't been there for over a year."

"I know what you mean: your brother," said Patty. "Let's go, Maura." He lifted her beneath both arms.

"Leave off," said Maura, swinging free. "Don't pull on me like that. I'm coming. What else am I going to do?" she cried as she ran through the crowd.

"I don't know what's wrong with her," said Patty. "She's been this way ever since we pulled that job in County Tyrone. She's lost her nerve. But what else can you expect from a woman?" He followed Eamon towards the door, saying that they would be back at Casey's later for a sing-song.

After they were gone, Dieter asked Mick if Patty had really escaped from jail.

"That's right," said Mick. "Patty's a wanted mahn. A hard mahn."

"How did he do it?" asked James.

"He told me about it the first time he came down here. In 1970. Tommy Sheehan, a friend of mine from Dublin, also a Provo, told him about me, so he came down here to hide. He was arrested after some gun battle with British soldiers. I don't know all of the details. He cut his way through the bars, somehow. Then he hid near a wall, in a blind spot, I believe. Then, when the guard wasn't looking, he scaled it, somehow. It was in all the papers. One of the first men to escape from Crumlin Road Jail."

James was starting to feel really nervous. He wondered what he was doing with these people. He decided to have a drink, after all. He went up to the bar and brought back a round of pints.

"It was a hairy time," Mick continued. "The Gardai were here looking for him several times but he kept well concealed. He had to stay inside the third chalet for weeks at a time. Everyone in the village knew he was here. But it was kept a secret."

"Well, it's no secret now," said James. "I mean: the pub's full of people and he just shouts it out for all to hear."

"They all like that up North," said Mick, grinning. "Everyday, it seems you pick up a newspaper and right there on the front page, there's a picture of a wanted mahn at his brother's wedding in his home town. They feel no guilt for what they've done. And why should they? With all the repression up North?"

"I know that this sounds like a stupid question," said Dieter, who suddenly seemed more alert than he had been. "But we didn't study much Irish history in Germany."

"Out with it," said Mick. "There's no such thing as a stupid question. It's only stupid not to ask it."

"When did all the trouble start?"

"When did it start?" answered Mick. "800 years ago. When will it stop. That should be the question."

"I mean this time."

"In 1968" said Mick. "In Belfast, the Catholic people marched for their rights, to vote, for jobs, to be treated as human beings. It was a peaceful demonstration, mahn, and the police beat them with clubs and sticks."

"Was that when Patty got involved?" asked James. He remembered seeing that in the news. They had signs saying, **We shall overcome**, and pictures of Martin Luther King.

"That's right, mahn," said Mick. "He was there on Bloody Sunday when the British soldiers came down with clubs and armored cars and tanks and guns, mahn. They beat and killed the Irish people: men, women and children. We've had too many Bloody Sundays in Ireland. After that, the IRA rose up like the phoenix from the ashes to carry on the struggle, eight centuries of struggle. Men taking up arms to justify their existence. And what mahn wouldn't? Remember: it's not he who commits the crime, but he who causes the darkness who is the criminal."

James agreed with what Mick said. He could understand why a man like Patty would pick up the gun. What other choice did he have? It was easy for Madeleine to say that the British could not be defeated with guns. She didn't live in Belfast.

"When did the English first come here?" asked Dieter.

"It all started in 1154," said Mick. "When Pope Adrian IV, an Englishman, granted Ireland as an inheritance to the Norman King of England, Henry II."

"An inheritance?" said James. "Where did he get the right to do that?"

"Right?" Mick snorted. "Might is right. They did because they had the power to do it. And you've got to realize that there was no united Ireland as such at that time. There was only a loose federation of independent kingdoms, so it was difficult to oppose them. Disunity and factionalism has always been our problem. For the next several hundred years, the English would come into the towns and villages and burn the little thatched huts of the people. Like the American army in Vietnam, huh, James. The Irish people would flee to the forests and fight the English in the valleys and glens with axes, swords and pikes, mahn."

James stood and walked over to the bar. He wished that Mick

would stop saying things like that. He wondered why Mick kept doing it. All right, so he had gone to Vietnam. He couldn't change that fact. He had to learn to live with it, somehow. He had to redeem himself. But how? He wanted to ask Mick what Patty wanted, but he would have to wait until they were alone. He watched as Dieter finished his pint, shook Mick's hand and walked toward the bar.

"I'm going to Ranchhouse," Dieter told James. "And pack my bags. I will be leaving in the morning."

"You are?" James asked. "Why?"

Dieter grimaced.

"I do not like this Patty Byrnes and his friends. I have known many men like him in my country. He is an extremist. He sees only in black and white. He thinks he knows all the answers."

James shrugged. War was black and white. You were either on one side or the other.

"Where are you going?" asked James.

"To France. Bordeaux," said Dieter, smiling. "Soon, the vendanage will begin."

"Vendange?"

"The grapes, the wine-picking. Why don't you come with me?"

James thought for a moment. The idea of picking grapes for wine appealed to him and it was a way of making money."

"It's hard work, isn't it?"

"Yes, it is. But it's good work. You see the sun rise and set every day: magnificent. The grapes taste so good, especially in the morning when they are covered with dew. And at night? You sleep in a barn, it is true, but you sleep well, the sleep of the just. And the pay? Ten francs a day. But the food is delicious. In the morning, you eat the French bread, the long loaves, with honey and hot chocolate. And the other meals? Soup and salad and meat and cheese. And all the fresh wine you can drink. It is wonderful."

"It sounds good," said James. "But I don't know. I'd rather try to work here."

Dieter shook head.

"Forget it. Ireland is a dying country. Come with me. I did it last year. After Bordeaux, I went to Alsace-Lorraine and picked champagne grapes. Then, I followed the sun to Spain for the olives. In the spring, to Holland for the tulips. You should learn how to live: see all the colors. Forget about politics."

James listened to what Dieter said. He was tempted. But how long could he live like that. He wouldn't make much money. He would be rootless, wandering around the world like a man without a country. He would drink too much and eat too little. He shook his head.

"Goodbye, then," said Dieter as he walked towards the door. "I wish you luck. You're going to need it."

James looked over to the corner and saw Mick waving an empty jar. James ordered two pints, then went over and joined Mick.

"Mick. What does Patty want from me?"

Mick motioned James closer and whispered.

"He wants you to carry information to his contacts in Belfast. It's difficult getting information across the border. The roads are blocked. The phones are tapped. Any Irishman who crosses the border takes a chance of being arrested and questioned, maybe even tortured by the British. They're cruel and vicious, mahn. They keep you in a metal box for days, naked. And they like to put the hot end of a cigarette butt on a man's testicles. Patty thought that you, being an American, could cross the border unmolested and carry information concerning the guns, as to when, where and how they are to be delivered."

"Oh, man, Mick," said James, taking a deep breath. "Why me?"

"Because you've been tested, mahn. You have the nerve. You've been in tight spots before. You would know how to act. You would be a great help to us. You know we need guns up there. And Patty will pay you well for it. He has plenty of money from the hashish. He sells it all over Europe. Afterwards, you could come back here, if you wanted, or you may decide to stay up there."

James gulped down his pint.

"I don't know, Mick. I don't know if I'm cut out for that."

"Sure you are, mahn. There's no better man than you."

As James thought about it, he felt the adrenaline rush. He could do it. He saw himself coolly crossing across the border, posing as an Irish-American looking for his roots.

Mick nudged James and nodded towards an old man who stumbled into the pub and plunged through the crowd to the bar. He pawed his tangled beard with his hand and stood at a quivering attention like a drunken soldier at inspection. He stared at the bartender then slowly withdrew a red handkerchief from the pocket of his dusty black suit, snapped it out full length and honked his nose. After stuffing his handkerchief back into his pocket, leaving a lolling red tongue of it visible, he shouted for a jar, rooted through his pockets, turning each one inside out, until he found, examined, and clacked a fifty-pence piece on the bar. He swayed the pint to his lips, tilted back his head, plopping his hat onto the floor and exposing his shock of black hair. He gulped down the stout, slammed the frothy glass on the bar and shouted in a staccato voice for more drink.

"He looks like a Gypsy," said Mick. "A traveling mahn. All Irishmen have a trace of Gypsy in their blood."

The old man picked up his dusty hat from the floor and tilted it rakishly onto his head. He stood in front of Mick and James and took a bow.

James sat back, trying to remember where he'd seen that face before.

Mick glanced at the old man's clothes, then looked at the man's grinning face. Mick roared with laughter.

"It's Christy in disguise."

Christy danced a jig across the floor to the bar where he hooked a pint of stout with his cane and drank half of it. Rolling his eyes, he licked the froth from his whiskers. He belched, rubbed his belly, downed the remainder of the pint, then fell flat on his face.

"C'mon, Christy," said James. "We know you're acting."

Christy sat up, grinning. He yanked a pillow from under his coat and removed his beard.

"You'd better remove that hat," sputtered Mick. "It hasn't been worn in years. By now, the moths living inside it have probably devoured your hair."

Christy removed the hat, looked inside it severely, pantomimed trapping escaping moths with it, then beamed at them.

Mick and James roared with laughter.

Christy got up and sat at the table.

"I didn't know how I stood down here," Christy said to Mick. "Because of last year. So I thought that I'd better come in disguise."

Mick slapped Christy on the back.

"No hard feelings, mahn. I haven't laughed like that for years. You had us fooled. We thought you were a mad mahn from the mountains."

Christy and James shook hands.

"It's all right if I stay for a while, then? said Christy.

"Sure," said Mick. "There's a bunk in the third chalet that you can roll into. Patty Byrnes is back so there's no room in the main house."

"Patty Byrnes himself? Himself? And just in time."

Christy took a small ball of tinfoil from his pocket and unrolled it. "I'm running out of dope."

He rolled a long joint filled with tobacco and sprinkled with black hashish. He took a hit and passed it to James.

James refused it. He didn't think they should smoke joints in the pub. Someone might report them to the police.

"I met someone you know today," James said to Christy.

"Who?" asked Christy as he took another hit.

"Madeleine."

"That frigid witch," said Christy as smoke exploded from his mouth.

"Hey, man," said James. "What's your problem? She's a nice person."

"Ah, I get it," Christy sneered. "You're hot for her yourself. Let me tell you: you're wasting your time. She doesn't like men."

James started to say something but stopped. He stared at Christy for a moment, disliking him. They had some good times the year before but Christy had become more dissipated since then. When James had talked to him in Dublin, Christy had been shabbily dressed and had looked as though he hadn't bathed in weeks. James looked at Christy's black fingernails and yellow teeth. He had chosen his disguise well.

Christy then told Mick how the rest of the Dubliners were doing: none were working, Larkin was in the hospital with hepatitis from a dirty needle, Martin was in jail for robbery and a few were in Liverpool drawing the dole.

James had heard enough. He knew why they were the way they

were. They had lost hope. They were alienated. They had little chance for a decent life in Ireland. But they made him angry. Why didn't they try to do something about it, instead of wallowing in despair and self-pity. If he were one of them, he'd join the IRA. He stood and excused himself.

Mick asked James where he was going.

"Wait for us, mahn. We'll be going back in a few minutes, as soon as we get a few bottles to go. We'll go back to Ranchhouse and have a sing-song."

James shook his head.

"I'll join you later. I have some things to think about. You know what I mean."

Mick grinned.

"Good idea, mahn. I'll talk to you later, then."

James went through the crowd at the bar and walked out onto the road. He stared up into the darkness in the direction of the Skelligs Rock. Madeleine was up there, somewhere. He pictured her in a rocking chair before a fireplace reading a book about babies or nursing a sick child in some isolated farmhouse. He felt a deep longing inside himself for a wife and a family. But he sensed that was not to be his fate. He had another mission, other work to do. He walked past the silent henhouse, through the high grass of the cliff, then down the rocky trail to the strand. He heard the waves slapping against the shore and the cows lowing in a nearby field.

As he walked along the beach, he thought about what Patty wanted him to do. It was his chance to redeem himself. He would be on the right side this time. And he would make some money doing it. He could use the money to fix up Ranchhouse and make it a working farm again. But as he passed by the ruins of the old abbey, he thought of Madeleine once again and what she had told him. He had to find out more about Patty and the IRA before he made up his mind. In the direction of Ranchhouse, car lights lit up the darkness like a flare, then dimmed out. A dog howled in the distance. Freedom. The Proves had returned.

James looked out the window of his chalet at the rain blowing in gusts across the dark green fields, beyond, the bay was gray with mist. He had been awake since dawn. He had only slept a few hours; his mind was too active to sleep. He had been racking his brain, trying to remember everything he had ever heard about the IRA. It was confusing. There were two groups, the Proves and the Officials and they were also divided into factions. The Officials were the communists. They were against the armed struggle in the North because they believed that the revolution had to come from the South, somehow. The Provos believed that the only way was through guerrilla warfare. They were the ones responsible for the bombings in England. James had problems with that. It was one thing to use arms in self-defense against an army that was occupying your country. But to kill innocent people was something else. He didn't know how that could be justified. He also wanted to know what the Provos' political and economic program was. Were they communists or capitalists? Did they believe in the rule of the elite or the democratic rule of the masses? He wanted answers to these questions before he would make up his mind to help them or not.

James looked out the window again. The rain had diminished and out over the bay, he saw a bit of blue. He ducked his head beneath the window as he saw Christy stagger out of the third chalet and stumble down towards the main house. James pulled his sleeping bag over his face. He wanted to be left alone. But he knew that he couldn't hide all day; eventually, they would come looking for him again. There was no escape. He had to face them sooner or later. Later, he thought, as he drifted asleep.

A gunshot jerked him awake. Sweating and shaking, he sat up and looked out the window. Eamon was running from the first chalet, carrying a shotgun in his hand. He stopped beneath a tree, picked up a dead bird and waved it in the air.

James took some deep breaths. He felt like splitting. But he knew that he couldn't. He had nowhere to go. He was trapped. He pulled on his boots and went out into the light rain. He ran through the swaying garden to the backroom. He heard Patty Byrnes shouting in the living room.

"How can it be justified?"

James looked from behind the doorway and saw Patty standing over Christy who sat at the table with his head bowed.

"What are they doing there? Tell me that! What are British soldiers doing in Ireland?"

Patty stalked around the room, his arms flailing.

"Oh, you'll agree with me all right. Shake your head at the injustice. Sing songs up in the pub. But will you pick up a gun and go do something about it?" He cursed Christy as a worthless hippie, one of the dregs of society then asked him what he did.

Christy made a motion of smoking a joint.

"Smoke joint?" Patty screamed. "Who doesn't smoke joint? I'm asking you to tell me what it is you do. What do you contribute to life? Do you work? Do you write poetry? Do you talk? What do you do?"

Christy got up and ran out of the room.

Patty sighed at the ceiling, sat down at the table and rolled a joint, which he lit and passed to Eamon who sat next to him, plucking feathers from the pigeon.

Patty reminded James of his drill sergeant at Fort Bragg who had intimidated him in the same way with his power and his rage. Sergeant Cox. He hated that man. The only way James had made it through basic training was by fantasizing about killing him. But, of course, that was the program: make you hate him so much that you wanted to kill him or anyone he ordered you to.

Mick came down the stairs, followed by Maura who looked as if she had been crying.

Mick noticed James in the background.

"What happened to you last night, mahn?"

"Yeah," said Patty, standing. He swaggered over to James and put his arm around him. "You're an elusive bloke, you know that? We looked all over for you last night. Eamon and Christy combed the strand while I checked your chalet. Where were you?"

"Up on the cliff, listening to them call my name. I was lying in the grass, looking down at them."

"Hiding from us, were ya?" said Eamon as he disemboweled the pigeon and cut off its head with a knife. "Why's that?"

"I need to be alone a lot," said James. "Sometimes, I don't like talking or being around people."

"He's a lone wolf," said Mick. "A scout."

Patty breathed in James' ear, "Have you thought about that offer I made you last night?"

"Yeah," said James, shrugging off Patty's arm. "But I haven't made up my mind, yet. I want to be sure about what I'm doing. I'm no mercenary."

"Who said you were?" Eamon asked.

"You wouldn't be doing it for the money," said Mick. "But because you believe in our cause here. And I know you do, mahn."

"Go up to Belfast," said Patty. "And take a look around. See for yourself what's going on up there. See how our people live: the wretched holes they call home. They have no jobs, no future. And it's all because of British imperialism. We have armored cars and tanks and soldiers with automatic weapons patrolling our streets."

"Armored cars and tanks and guns," sang Maura, off key. "Came to take away our sons, but everyman must stand behind the man behind the wire."

"Did you ever hear that one?" asked Patty, poking James in the ribs. "It's about the men in Long Kesh."

"Yeah," said James. He had heard people singing it in the pubs of Dublin. "I know about internment. It's something the Nazis would do."

Mick had told him about the men in Long Kesh who were arrested without charges and held without trial just because they had been born Catholic in Northern Ireland.

"That's what we're fighting up there," said Eamon. "Fascism. Colonialism. We're fighting for self-determination. The right to make our own decisions, to run the country as we see fit."

James nodded. Eamon seemed like someone he could talk to.

"That's something I want to know. What would you do if you did take over? Do you have a plan?"

"That we do, man," said Eamon. "Eire Nua. New Ireland. We want a federal government elected by the people, with one parliament, not two like the Brits. No division between rich and poor. Share the wealth. With the Prods included. We believe in a strict separation between church and state. And more power at the local level. No centralized government like the Russkies have. No big farms. No collectives. Divide up the land, to Irish only. No foreign owners. And free health care."

James was impressed. It sounded good to him.

Eamon raised the cleaned pigeon.

"And enough food for all."

Everyone laughed.

"Do you like to shoot birds?" Patty asked James.

James shook his head.

"Nah. I was a city kid. I never went hunting. I never fired a gun until I went into the army."

"I grew up in the city too," said Patty. "In the Falls Road section of Belfast. One of the toughest city blocks in the world. But I love to hunt: birds and small game. Nothing I like better than to walk the hills with a dog on a nice clear day. We're going up to the mountains now, for some practice. Come with us."

James shook his head. He didn't want to kill anything.

"I want to take a swim. I feel funky."

Patty grinned.

"Good idea. I didn't want to tell you but you do smell bad. How about after that? We'll wait for you."

"That's okay," said James. "Then I'm going to wash my clothes." He didn't want to tell Patty the real reason: he hadn't handled a rifle since he got out of the army and if the truth be told, he didn't want them to know what a lousy shot he was. The only way he had passed the army rifle qualification test was by bribing the scorer to make him an expert. He could fire the big guns, the howitzers and the machine guns but he couldn't hit the broad side of a barn with a rifle.

Patty stared at him, his grin fading.

"Maybe another day, then," said Patty as he climbed the stairs behind Eamon.

James went into the backroom with Mick and prepared a breakfast of bread and cheese and tea. As James ate his breakfast, Mick sucked the bones of a boiled whiting that a neighbor had thrown in the door. He told James about two brothers, Keith and Kevin Littlejohn who had just been arrested in Dublin.

"British agents, mahn. Licensed to kill. Did you hear about the bank robberies and bombings in Dublin last year?"

James said that he had. He had read about them in the Philadelphia papers.

"They were from the IRA weren't they? They wanted money for guns."

Mick waved his hand.

"That's what they want people to believe. They're British agents sent to Ireland to bring on Civil War in the South."

"What? Civil War?" James exclaimed. "How?"

"They wanted to turn the Irish people against the IRA by killing civilians in Dublin. The Irish government in the South, who are, of course, hand-in-hand with the British, would go after the IRA. The IRA would resist. Policemen would be shot. Civil War would erupt. But the Proves were smart: they ordered everyone not to resist arrest by the Gardai. No incidents. The British plan hasn't worked."

James didn't like what he was hearing. It made him feel paranoid. How could he trust anybody? Who knew who was who?

"Those creeps. The British are bad news. Civil War is the worst thing that could happen to a country and they want to bring it on."

"That's right," said Mick. "But it'll have to come eventually. What we have to do is we have to overthrow the government here in the South, a capitalist colony of England is all it is, mahn, and march as an army up to the North and drive the British Army into the sea."

"Really, Mick? You think that'll ever happen?"

"It has to, mahn. Only from destruction can come construction. If you have a bad field of wheat, with too many weeds, the best thing to do is burn the whole lot of it and plant it again."

That made James think. Comparing people to weeds?

Patty and Eamon came into the backroom, carrying the valise full of guns.

"Maura is sleeping again upstairs," said Patty. "That's all she does, now. She's not much good to us anymore. Are you coming, Casey?"

Mick shook his head.

"No, mahn. I have to go up to the confessional box, to call Deirdre."

Patty sneered.

"Forget her. Come and shoot with us."

Mick gritted his teeth.

"I have to talk with her, mahn. I want her to come back."

Patty laughed as he turned and followed Eamon out of the room.

James didn't know what to say. What did he know about these things? It must hurt to lose the woman you love and your child as well. But he had never loved anyone in his life. He didn't know what love was. He remembered what Madeleine had said about the men in Ireland having to change their ways of relating to women. He wished he knew what she meant by that. When Mick looked up, James asked him where Madeleine lived.

Mick stared at him for a moment.

"So she has her hooks in you as well. Be careful, mahn. Madeleine has some strange ideas. Deirdre told me that Madeleine practiced witchcraft, that she and some of her friends had been holding some sort of Black Mass up in the mountains."

James laughed.

"What? What's a Black Mass?"

"I'm not sure, mahn. I've never seen one. It's some perversion of the Catholic Mass."

James thought about that. The Mass was a celebration of the death of the Son, the eating of his body and blood: cannibalism. That seemed like a perversion to him, sometimes.

"They were holding them up in the circle of stones."

"The circle of stones? What's that?"

"It's a sacred place of the druids," said Mick. "You've heard of Stonehenge? There's a smaller version of that up in the mountains. Nobody knows what their purpose was for sure."

James sat silent for a few minutes, thinking of the conversation he had with Madeleine the day before. What had she meant by surrender? Surrender meant to give up. But to give up what? Your life? Your soul? Your gun? He wanted to find out what she meant by that.

"Do you still want to know where she lives, mahn?"

James nodded.

"You have more courage than I do. I wouldn't want to get

involved with her in a love affair; as lovely as she is, she has the devil's tongue and a temper as hot as her hair. It's your funeral, mahn. She lives up the mountain near where you can see the Skelligs Rock. Take the road past the schoolhouse and go for a mile or so to where the road forks, then take a left. The Murphy cottage is about a half mile from there. It's white with green shutters."

James decided that he would go and look for her as soon as had washed his clothes and taken a bath. There was no reason to be afraid. Madeleine was a midwife. She brought life into the world not death. She wouldn't hurt him.

James sat on the crumbling stone wall and looked down into the valley, running his eyes along the stream, but he couldn't see Madeleine anywhere. He heard the crack of a carbine up in the hills. Another bird dead. A vision of Patty prodding Madeleine with a gun flashed through his mind, triggering a wave of panic. He had to find her and warn her. He jumped off the wall and ran a few yards, then settled into a double time. A volley of shots rang through the valley, sending him to a duck walk behind a hedge. Through the bush, he saw smoke over the hills. He turned at the fork in the road and followed it for about a half mile until he came upon a black VW beetle parked in front of a white cottage with green shutters and a wild garden. He knocked on the front door but no one answered, then he peeked in a window but he couldn't see anyone inside. He tried to calm down. More than likely, she wouldn't meet Patty and even if she did, he probably wouldn't do anything to her. He sat on the front steps and looked down into the valley, trying to imagine actually living there and seeing such beauty every day. He could do it. All he had to do was go to Belfast first.

Suddenly, he saw Madeleine rushing towards him, her arms swinging by her sides like a nun chasing a truant child.

"What are you doing here?" she shouted. "Robbing the house?"

"What?" said James, standing.

She screamed, "Leave! Right now!"

"Wait a minute," said James. "What's going on? I just wanted to talk to you."

"There's nothing to talk about," shouted Madeleine. "Go back to Ranchhouse where you belong, with your chum, Patty Byrnes."

James protested, "He's not my chum."

"That's not what I heard," snapped Madeleine. "Someone told me that you and Patty Byrnes were whispering together with your arms around each other in the pub last night."

James almost laughed. He didn't know what to say to her. How could he explain?

She kept her eyes on him as she prowled around the steps like a boxer waiting for the bell.

He came down the steps slowly, trying to find the right words.

"I know what it must have looked like to your friend. But Patty Byrnes is not my chum. I don't even like the man. I came up here because I wanted to find out more about him."

She tilted back her head and squinted at him.

"Who are you anyway?"

James smiled sadly.

"I'm nobody. I don't know who I am. That's my problem."

Suddenly, he remembered that Patty was in the mountains, somewhere. He backed away from her and looked anxiously around him. But he could see no one and he heard nothing but the sound of the birds singing.

"I have to be careful. He might be listening."

"What's going on?" she asked. "I want to know."

James took a deep breath. There it was. If he told her and Patty found out, Patty would be furious. But if he didn't tell her, she wouldn't talk to him anymore. He had to tell her the truth.

"Patty's going to deliver a shipment of guns to Belfast, soon. And he offered me a few thousand pounds to take information to his contacts there, as to when and how and where they are to be delivered."

Madeleine's eyes got wide.

"Your joking."

James shook his head.

"You're not going to do it, are you?"

James shrugged.

"I don't know. I haven't made up my mind."

Her face got tight around the jaws.

"Why would you want to do it? Are you a mercenary?"

James winced.

"No. It's because of Vietnam. I have to do something to make up for it. I feel guilty for going there. I was on the wrong side."

"What do you mean, the wrong side? Would you rather have fought for the Vietnamese?

James rubbed his face with his hand.

"In a way, I guess. I don't know. At least, they were fighting for their country, their people. We weren't. We were fighting for big business, for rich people."

Madeleine smiled slightly.

"You sound like a Communist."

James laughed.

"Me? Nah. I don't know much about Communism to tell the truth. The theory, anyway. Or the philosophy. The only thing I ever read was The Communist Manifesto. And I didn't like it. A specter over Europe. Scary stuff."

Madeleine looked at him, warily, as he continued.

"I only know what I learned in school. That Communism was bad. By the way, I wanted to ask you, are the IRA Communists? Do you know?"

Madeleine shrugged.

"They're not really. Some of them call themselves Marxists, the Officials. And the Provos are nationalists, primarily."

"How about Eamon?" James interrupted. "He told me about their program and it sounded Communist to me."

Madeleine nodded.

"I only met Eamon once. He doesn't seem to be a bad sort. I've read about their program. Eire Nua. It's somewhat socialist. But there's not a word in it about the role of women. In my mind, the first criterion for a good government is one where women's needs get first priority. The IRA opposes abortion. Women need to be in control of their bodies, not men, not the state, not the Church. Abortions should be free and legal. It's true, the IRA does call for birth control and sex education but that's not enough. We need women in positions of power. And there are no women in the leadership."

"How about Bernadette Devlin?' asked James. "Isn't she a leader?"

"But she doesn't belong to the IRA. She's a member of a group called People's Democracy. Some of them are true Marxists, I believe. Trotskyists."

Whatever that means, thought James. He frowned.

"I was afraid of Communism growing up. Communism meant concentration camps. Big brother. No individualism. No freedom."

Madeleine shook her head.

"That's not Communism. Quite simply, Communism means community. That the needs of the community comes before the needs of the individual. That society should be planned around meeting those basic needs. The dictatorship of the proletariat only means that the working people, the masses, have control, instead of what we have now in Great Britain and America: oligarchies, the dictatorships of the rich. Communism is nothing to be afraid of. It's another way of looking at reality, that's all."

James had never heard it put that way before. It didn't sound so bad the way she described it.

"Are you a Communist?" he asked her.

Madeleine smiled.

"I'm a feminist. By that I mean, I want whatever's best for women. But I think that every true feminist finds much to like in Marx and Engels. They admit that women are the first colonized people. Capitalism, patriarchy, began in the family, with the man dominating the woman. That's where it began, that's where it ends."

"Then you wouldn't call Patty a Communist?"

Madeleine snorted.

"No, I don't think so. He believes in dominance. Power. He's a Stalinist. He's no different from the capitalists he claims to hate. Why would you want to get involved with a man like him, anyway?"

James shrugged.

"Like I said, I want to make up for Vietnam. It's the same struggle, isn't it? Against imperialism. I'd be on the right side this time. And my ancestors were driven out of Ireland by the British. I'd be getting even."

Madeleine grimaced.

"Haven't you learned, yet? Violence is not the way. Violence only begets more violence. The pattern must be broken."

"It's easy for you to say," James protested. "You don't live in Belfast. Patty does."

"Yes," said Madeleine. "And it's warped him. Violence is all he knows. Do you want to be like him?"

James shook his head.

"Is that all you can tell me about him?"

Madeleine shrugged.

"I don't know him that well. Don't want to, either, after what he tried to do to me. I met him a few years ago down at Mick's. We talked a few times. He's a great man with the words. He went to the University at Queen's College in Belfast and studied literature. He wanted to be a great writer like James Joyce, his hero. But while he was there, he got involved in the civil rights movement and went on the famous march to Dungannon in 1968. And after he got beat up by the police in the Bogside in '69, he rejected the peace movement. It's all rubbish, according to him. And he joined the IRA."

"I can't blame him," said James.

Madeleine pursed her lips.

"I realize that people have the right to defend themselves. But the IRA has gone beyond defending themselves. They've killed innocent people, too many times. The bombings in Belfast last year and the car bombs in London, for instance. What good did they do? They only turned the people against the IRA and their cause."

James agreed with what she said about that.

"I know. But what can they do? How else can they fight the British?"

"It's a complex problem," said Madeleine, looking at her watch. "There are ways. But who will listen to me? As you said, I don't live in Belfast. And I'm just a woman. But I don't want to talk about this anymore. You must excuse me. I have work to do."

She turned abruptly away from him and ran up the steps. As she opened the door, he called out to her.

"May I see you again?"

She looked over her shoulder at him and said, "I don't know. I can't promise you. If I can, I'll contact you. But please, don't come up here again."

With that, she went inside and closed the door.

As James walked down the mountain road, he listened for gunfire, but he heard only the sound of the wind and the songs of the birds in the hills.

James paced up and down outside the pub. He felt depressed and anxious. He didn't think that he was ever going to see Madeleine again and he was afraid of meeting Patty. He didn't know what to do. He badly wanted a pint, but he was afraid to go inside until he knew who was in there. Finally, one of the local men came out. James asked him who was in there from Ranchhouse. The man told him only Mick and Christy. So James went inside and found them drinking pints in the far corner.

Christy stood and waved his pint.

"Let us welcome the disappearing man. Now you see him; now you don't."

"You're drunk already," said James.

"Why not, mahn? said Mick. "Join us. Where have you been? Of course, you've been with Madeleine."

"I told you, you're wasting your time," Christy sneered. "She's a virgin. In this day and age. Can you believe it?"

James shrugged.

"How do you know, anyway?"

"She told me," Christy snarled. "Never been touched by a man she said. A virgin." He blasphemed the Blessed Virgin and blamed her for all the problems he had with women. "It's all her fault. Madness: A virginal mother. It's impossible. No woman can be that way. The Church made it up because they don't want people having any fun. No sex outside of marriage and then only to have children. No woman should remain a virgin. Sex: that's what women are good for. Every woman should be willing to have sex with any man whenever he wants it."

James thought of what his mother would think of what was just said and he was offended by what Christy said about the Blessed Mother. He didn't believe in the Immaculate Conception and the

Virgin Birth but he didn't like hearing it ridiculed like that.

"You shouldn't be saying things like that. What's wrong with you, man? I don't believe in all that stuff either but have some respect. And Madeleine's a nice person. I'm not trying to have sex with her. And I bet you wouldn't be willing to have sex with any woman who wants it especially if they're not attractive."

Christy laughed.

"What are you, a prude or a faery?"

James clenched his fists. He felt like smashing Christy in the face but he resisted the impulse. That's s all Madeleine would have to hear. He sat next to Mick and asked about Deirdre.

"I couldn't talk to her, mahn," said Mick, his eyes filling with tears. "She's in the hospital and is due to deliver any day now."

James wanted to say something but didn't know what. So he asked Mick where Patty was.

"He's gone with the others to Cork City on business. He should be back soon. He said he'll talk with you when he gets back."

Christy apologized and bought them a round.

James took a deep drink from his pint. He was happy to hear that Patty was gone. That gave him more time to think.

"Mick," said James. "Can you tell me more about Ireland? I want to know more of its history."

"I'll start at the beginning," said Mick, a pleased look on his face. There was nothing he liked to do more than talk about Irish history. "With the Tuatha De Danann, the children of light, who sailed from the Middle East in search of the promised land at the setting sun. They first set up a colony in Spain, but that wasn't close enough to the setting sun, so they set sail again. No one knows for sure when they landed in Ireland. The Dadannans were well known for their skill in magic and witchcraft."

"Witchcraft?" said James, thinking of Madeleine.

"That's right," said Mick. "Witches and leprechauns. The legend of the leprechauns goes back to the Dadannans. They were cobblers by trade, hammering away on the old shoe. They were as green as the land they lived in and were the guardians of the gold and treasure of the land. They were clever fellows and could put you under their spell if you caught them."

"Were the leprechauns male witches?" asked James.

Mick laughed.

"You could say that. I never thought of them that way."

"I read that Ireland was all forest then," said Christy.

"That's true," said Mick. "At that time, you could walk from treetop to treetop from Kerry to Belfast and not touch the ground."

"Look at it now," said Christy. "All bog and seaweed and rock."

Mick gritted his teeth.

"That's because the invaders came in and ravaged the land. The Danes came in the 7th century and they were not defeated completely until 1014 at the battle of Clontarf by the descendants of the Dadannans. Brian Boru. Then in the 12th century, the Normans, led by Strongbow, invaded Ireland. They ravaged the country for years and were infamous for bayoneting babies and saying, 'See how Patty kicks his legs.'"

James winced when Mick said that. Baby killers. Right after he had come home from Vietnam, a college kid had asked him if he had killed any babies. James had only looked at the kid and walked away. What could he say to that? No, he hadn't killed any babies. But the United States had, plenty of them. The realization that he had participated in that caused him great pain. He went up to the bar and bought another round. Only by getting drunk could he forget about it.

When he returned, Mick was talking about Cromwell.

"He's known in Ireland as the great destroyer. His army killed everything in sight. He even killed all the livestock and burnt the crops to ashes. He could kill everything but the puck goat, the only animal that could evade Cromwell's army."

"Puck Fair," said Christy, "That's held up in Killorglin. Reminds the people of Cromwell."

"That's right," said Mick. "The puck goat. A symbol of Irish tenacity. We will never give up the fight, mahn."

"When was the Battle of the Boyne?" James asked. "You mentioned that last year but I forgot."

"We haven't forgotten, mahn. 1690. It was a big battle between the Catholics led by King James II and the Protestants led by William of Orange. King James was a Catholic King of England who was deposed by William of Orange. James came to Ireland to help the Catholic people in their struggle and to regain his crown. But he was defeated by William of Orange at the Boyne River, not too far from Dublin. That defeat spelled the end of the Catholics' hope for freedom for years to come. The Protestants confiscated the land and drove the Catholics off to starve. They've been doing the same ever since, mahn. Starving our children, killing our people, year after year, generation after generation. And they wonder why we are so bitter here, mahn?"

"Let me ask you something, Mick," said James, although he already knew what Mick was going to say. "How does the IRA justify the killing of civilians in England?"

Mick gritted his teeth.

"So they know what it feels like, mahn, to have their women and children killed. Give them a taste of their own medicine. Terrorize them. Maybe then, they'll stop the killing of our people."

James nodded and drank from his pint. Terrorize them. The words echoed in his mind. A lot of people thought of the IRA as terrorists and maybe they were. But what was the killing of a few people in England as compared to the the thousands, the hundreds of thousands of people that the British had killed over the centuries? The British were the true terrorists. But still, it was wrong to kill innocent people. Did he want to be part of that and have that on his conscience? How could he live with himself if he did that? He felt like crying with frustration. He wished that there was some way out of it. The only way, he decided, was to get drunk. He went up to the bar and bought them all another round.

James looked around the back room at the stacks of dirty dishes and the piles of filthy pots and pans. It would take a platoon of soldiers on KP to clean up that mess. But he had to do something or he was going to lose his mind. He was so hung-over, he didn't know what to do with himself. He had been pacing up and down all morning in the back room like a prisoner in solitary. It was raining too hard to go outside. There was no one to talk to. Mick and Christy were still asleep. He couldn't read. He couldn't concentrate. He had to stop drinking. There was no doubt about that. What good did it do? Nothing changed. He still had the same problem, the same decision to make, but now he had a headache and an upset stomach to go with it. And how could he ever do the work that had to be done and drink at the same time? It couldn't be done. He had told Mick about his idea of fixing up Ranchhouse and making it a working farm again and Mick had been all for it. Mick was going to teach him how to farm. They would buy a cow and some chickens and a horse to do the plowing. Mick had even liked James's idea about breeding rabbits. But he needed money to do it and the only way he could get it was by going to Belfast. He had to make up his mind about that soon.

Beside the sink, James saw the cleaned pigeon that Eamon had killed. He put the bird into a large saucepan, covered it with water and put it on the stove to cook. They could eat that for dinner. Then he boiled several kettles of water and began washing the dishes. He did that for a couple of hours. When he was finished, he started on the pots and pans. They had grease so burned into them that he practically had to chisel it out. When that was finished, he cleaned off the table and cut some potatoes, carrots and onions and added them to the saucepan with the pigeon to make a stew. After doing that, he went up the stairs to the front bedroom to find Mick.

Lying fully clothed on the bed, Mick noticed James standing in the doorway and said, "I've been lying here since dawn watching that spider crawl across the window. It's like the title of a story: the man and the spider."

James laughed along with Mick, then walked over to the window, snagged back the ragged curtain and looked out at the rain. The spider panicked along the ledge and scaled the wall to its cobwebbed corner.

"You can see why we drink so much here," said Mick. "What else is there to do? Even the monks communicated through spirits, the same as we do, mahn. Did I ever tell you the story about the monk of Killarney?"

"No," said James. "You didn't."

"Well, it goes like this," said Mick. "One fine summer's evening, a monk was sent out from his monastery to fetch a jug of wine, probably to fetch several jugs of wine, as many as his donkey could carry.

While riding through a glen, the monk heard a bird singing such a sweet song that he stopped his donkey in his tracks and listened for it again. When he heard it repeated, the sweetness of the song caused the monk to leap from his donkey and bury his face in the dirt in prayer and supplication. Then the monk rose to his feet and watched the wood around him transform into a beautiful garden full of exotic plants and flowers and strange fruits. In a trance, the monk rode back the way he had come. Noticing nothing, he knocked on the huge front door of the monastery. It was opened by an enormous mahn, a stranger to the monk. The monk asked the mahn if he had any wine for he had not been able to get any and was thirsty. 'What wine?' the mahn shouted. 'And what are you doing dressed like a monk?' Why, naturally, the monk was surprised by all this, so he asked if this was the monastery; maybe he had somehow stopped at the wrong place. 'Monastery?' the mahn shouted. 'Have you lost your mind, mahn? This is an estate of Queen Elizabeth. You could be beheaded by penal law.' The mahn then told the monk that he had better flee from Ireland before his head rolled. So the monk wisely took his advice and sailed for Spain where he later died, two hundred years after he first set out for the wine. That's a true story, mahn."

It's possible, thought James. Anything is possible in this strange country.

"What was the penal law?" he asked Mick.

"They were laws passed after the Battle of the Boyne to take the land away from the Catholic people and the Church. Under the law, the English could hunt down the priests and monks and execute them. They wanted to destroy the Catholic Church and convert the people to Protestantism."

"Why's that, Mick?" James asked, "Why couldn't they let the people have their own religion?"

Mick gritted his teeth.

"They wanted to make the people over to the image of the English, so that the Irish people, their religion, their language, wouldn't exist at all. Although we certainly could do without the Catholic Church, mahn. Time and time again down history, the priests have sold the Irish people down the river."

James nodded. He could have done without the priests and the

Catholic Church as well. He felt that they had prepared him for war by their insistence on blind faith and obedience. And the sacrifice of the Son by the Father. A bad precedent. It legitimatized victimization.

"Didn't they hound poor Parnell to an early grave," Mick continued.

"Who was Parnell, Mick? James asked. "I remember reading about him in A Portrait of the Artist by Joyce."

"He was an Irish politician, a member of Parliament, in the 1880's who pressed for home rule and land reform. But he got involved in an affair with a married woman and was denounced from the pulpit by the clergy. They drove him from power and ended any chance of real land reform. Land, that's what it's all about, mahn; who owns the land."

"Who owns the land around here, anyway?"

"Some's privately owned," said Mick. "But most of it belongs to the government and the capitalists: Irish, British and American capitalists. Ah, mahn, ifs a cold and desolate Southwest Kerry that I'm looking at today. Everyone's pulling out. Soon, there'll be no one left. Years ago, an old mahn who lived in a thatched hut by the blacksmith's shop, predicted that the entire area from the town to the glen would be one parish. Everyone laughed at him for there were five parishes and schools at that time. Now, there's only one parish, just as he predicted."

"How long ago was that?"

"Around a hundred years ago," said Mick. "They said that the old man was touched in the head and maybe he was, for he started making prophesies after he fell and hit his head one night coming home from the pub."

"Prophesies?"

"That's right, mahn. He predicted that in the future people would speak underground. That baffled the people. The only people they knew who lived underground were the dead."

"What did he mean?"

"Fifty years later, up near the youth hostel, the undersea, underground transatlantic cable was laid down. And sure enough, people spoke underground."

James laughed along with Mick.

"What else did he predict?"

"Headless horses or horses with the heads of men. He said that they would till the land. The people considered him a mad mahn. Then the tractors came. Progress, they called it. But it spelled the death of a way of life. I don't know why I stay. Everyone's leaving."

James looked at Mick's sad face and felt depressed.

Mick's eyes filled with tears.

"I can see it now. A beautiful way of life it was. Living on the land and on the sea. Everyone giving to each other. Give to live. It's a universal law. If a tree doesn't give forth fruit, it dies. So must mahn give or die. Mahn is the only species that doesn't give but only takes. Mahn will become extinct if he doesn't learn to give, to share."

"You make it sound so good," said James.

"It was," said Mick. "I remember as a boy, running down to the strand with the rest of the people in the village when the fishing boats were coming in and we would all help dock the boat and unload the fish. Everyone helped bring in the hay and harvest the potatoes. But that way of life is gone forever, and now, I have no son to leave Ranchhouse to. I should burn the place to ashes."

"What about last night?" James reminded him. "Our plan?"

Mick waved it away.

"A pipe dream, mahn. It can't be done. I don't have the spirit for it. Well, I might as well go up to the pub. Weather like this would drive any mahn to drink."

"C'mon, Mick," said James, feeling desperate. "It's too early. Let's skip the pub tonight. Get a good night's sleep, then maybe we can get some work done in the morning."

Mick gritted his teeth.

"No, mahn. I have to drink. I cannot stop. It's the river of no return. What this place needs is an atomic bomb. We'd all be better off dead."

"No," James cried as Mick walked out the door. "Don't tell me that."

Despair swept over him and he felt the emptiness deep inside of him. He felt like running out into the rain and screaming for it to stop, but instead he found himself on his knees, trying to pray.

Fragments of prayers he used to say flashed through his mind, speeding faster and faster, until he got them right. He repeated them over and over again until he heard no other sound. He knelt there for a long time, with his eyes closed and his face to the floor. He dreamt of a deserted beach, a smiling surf, a blazing fire and a woman with eyes as soft and sorrowful as moonbeams on the sea.

As James slept, the spider startled from its corner and crept along the watery windowpane like a crab scuttling across the ocean floor.

As James walked up the road, he kept looking up and down and side to side and turning around and walking backwards for a few steps, scanning the hills and valleys like a point man on patrol. He hadn't seen rain like this since the monsoon season in Vietnam. It was like walking through a gray waterfall. But he was dry in Mick's old oilskins and rubber boots. He stood and stared out to sea like a lost fisherman searching for his ship. Over the bay, black clouds brooded, pouring rain down in sheets to the sea. He wished so hard to see Madeleine that he almost expected her to appear by his side sparkling like the good witch of the West. His time was drawing near; the day of decision was upon him. Patty was due back tomorrow.

'Stand up and be counted, mahn,' he could hear Mick say. 'You're either with us or against us. Choose which side you're on.'

James had stayed up most of the night thinking about his choices. He could refuse Patty's offer and stay at Ranchhouse until his money ran out. Then he could live on potatoes and Guinness like Mick. A tourist attraction. Let me introduce to you to James O'Rourke, the stereotyped dropout from society, the expatriate, Vietnam veteran, die-hard drunkard and lost soul and listen to his sad story. And buy the mahn a drink. And a pair of shoes, his have gone to sandals. Or he could do what Patty wanted and come back to Ballinskelligs and drink the money away with Mick, then go back and do it again. Run guns and drugs for a living. He spat in disgust. He'd kill himself for sure. There was another option, he thought. Suicide, his old friend. He had thought of killing himself many times. Whenever things got real bad, he would comfort himself that way. But whenever he thought about actually doing it, he would change his mind. He'd probably screw that up, too. He'd wind up a quadriplegic or a vegetable. So that was out. He could stay up in Belfast, live up there, somehow. Think about it, he told himself. Look at it in reality. He wouldn't like it up there, once he was there. There'd be bombings and shootings, helicopters and sirens, screams and shouts in the night. He'd be in the middle of a war. He had to be clear about that.

Those guns were to be used to kill people. Did he want that on his conscience? Did he want to choose the way of violence once again? He had been spared the first time because he knew not what he was doing. But now he knew what he was doing. A feeling of dread came over him and he knew that if he went to Belfast, he would die. He knew it in his bones. What good would that do? He didn't want to die. Not yet. He had come to Ireland because he wanted to live. But how could he do that? He could listen to Dieter and forget about Ireland and forget about politics and go to France and live the life of a gypsy, follow the sun and see the world. But he didn't want to do that, either. What was happening in Ireland was wrong and he wanted to do something about it. But what could he do? The life of a gypsy was a hard one. He saw himself in a few years: his front teeth missing, one eye punched out, a livid broken-bottle scar across his face. He would be out of the world of women forever. And to be out of the world of women was to be out of the world of the living. That's where he really wanted to be: with the women and children. He remembered the time he had spent with Brigid, the third female, on the way to Holyhead.

He lurched through the crowd, trying to get to the front of the train, where he might be able to get a seat. But that didn't seem likely: There were too many people ahead of him. He would have to stand all the way to Holyhead. After landing at Dover Beach, he had taken another train to London where he had to transfer to this train for the ferry to Ireland. Although he had slept for a few hours with the woman on the ferry the night before, he was so tired that he felt like he was dreaming as he walked. A whistle came from above him and he looked up to see a man poking halfway out a window.

'Hey, mate,' the man called. 'Ya looking for a seat?'

James nodded several times and said, 'Are you kidding me? Sure!'

He turned against the flow and struggled through the stream of people like a drowning man being pulled to safety. As he staggered through the aisle, the man waved him into the compartment like a third base coach sending him home. Inside, there were two girls and a woman with a baby at her breast. James stopped and would have backed out but the man encouraged him inside with a pat on the back and a promise of privacy. James took a seat by the window, cater-corner from the mother and her baby. The two girls jumped and tumbled across the seats like acrobats in a circus. The mother smiled and cuddled the baby, who cried like a little kitten.

James put his head back and closed his eyes. He heard snatches of the conversation between the man and the woman, meaningless to him, then the man was shouting at someone; then a fierce argument. James sighed. He hoped that they wouldn't try to involve him in their private lives. He had made a mistake in coming in here. It was going to be a bad trip.

The conductor called, "All Aboard" and the train jerked forward a few times. The man kissed the woman and the children, backed to the doorway with a big grin on his face and said, 'Cheerio. Have a nice holiday at your mum's.' Then he turned and jumped off the train. The children waved at him through the window until he disappeared from view. 'Why not daddy come with us?' they kept saying. 'Where he go?' 'He has to work,' the mother said. 'He'd be with us if he could.'

James couldn't believe it. He had thought that the man would be coming with them. What had he gotten himself into? He was uncomfortable around children, especially when they were little, and especially when they were girls. He didn't know what to say to them and he could never figure out what they wanted. These kids looked wild and smelly, he thought, as he watched the mother change the baby's diaper. But at least he had a seat. The aisles were packed with people standing and it was a six-hour ride. He was so tired.

He closed his eyes and drifted off, but then his head jerked up and he awoke. He looked over to see two girls giggling through their fingers at him. As the train raced through the countryside, he fell asleep and awoke, time and time again, his head snapping up and down and rolling from side to side like a clock hand gone berserk. It was not until the conductor came in to collect the tickets that James finally woke up. He felt as if he were in a trance. One of the girls was standing on the seat across from him. She giggled and stuck out her tongue at him. Without thinking, James stuck out his tongue at her. With that, she jumped from the seat, squealing, and climbed up on his lap. She put her face so close to his that all he could see was her blue eyes. They seemed to swallow him up. Then she pulled back her head abruptly and asked him his name.

'Brigid!' Her mother said, 'Don't be so cheeky.'

'It's all right," James assured her. 'I don't mind. James. That's my name.'

He asked Brigid how old she was.

She held up four fingers.

'Four? No, you're not,' he teased. 'I'm four.'

Brigid giggled.

'No, you're not. I'm four.'

'I'm five,' said the other girl as she climbed next to her sister. 'My name Kathleen.'

'Ah, ya have a way with the children,' the mother said to him. 'Have any of your own, have ya?'

'No, not yet, anyway. Maybe someday.'

It was the first time he had ever put it that way. He surprised himself by his answer. He had never really considered having children. He had enough trouble taking care of himself. He couldn't see himself as a father, an authority figure. And the way the world was, it was no place to bring up a child. There was no country in the world that really cared about children. If they did, there'd be no war. In war, the children suffer the most.

The girls fired questions at him as if they were long-lost relatives at a family reunion. Where was he going? Where did he come from? Where was his mummy and daddy? He answered them as best as he could, then asked them a few. They chattered on for a while about their grandmum's house and the house where they lived and about their family and friends. He couldn't understand much of what they were saying but he didn't care. He enjoyed listening to their voices and their laughs and watching their mouths and their foreheads as they searched for the right words. They had such cute faces.

After they ran out of things to say, he helped them color a few pictures in a book, then he read them a story. To his surprise, they listened and laughed as he read. He felt a curious peace come over him and he wished that they were his family, that they were on a voyage home, back to the farm. He saw a cottage with chickens in the yard and horses and cows in the fields. Smoking his pipe, he walked between the rows of cabbages and spuds, watching the sun set. At night, after a hard day's work, no pub for him, he would sit around the turf fire, reading the children a faery tale from a big book. Before he knew it, they were coming into Holyhead.

When they were in the station, the mother asked him if he would give her a hand with the bags. She smiled as he lifted the largest bag from the overhead rack. Then he knew why the man had wanted him to come with them. He saw Brigid start to run out into the crowd and he grabbed her by the hand. He wasn't going to let her get lost. He followed the mother off the train and onto the ferryboat. He stayed with the family all the way to Dun Laoghaire. At dawn, when they docked, he took Brigid by the hand and walked with her onto the shore. He never could have imagined himself arriving in Ireland that way: hand in hand with a faery, his escort to Ireland.

The rain stopped. Overhead, the wind played a song in the wires and blew the seabirds soaring and whirling above the virgin beach far below. Waves foamed upon fingers of rock greened by seaweed. James stopped walking and looked out over the bay where he saw a small tall island. He stared at it for a few minutes. That was the Skelligs Rock? He couldn't believe it. He hadn't been able to see it before because it had been hidden in a fog bank. But there it was. It looked so different than he remembered. It had lost its halo of crimson clouds. And it wasn't a shaft of stone, a monolith. It slanted and had broad clefts with gashes of grass and trees growing from its sides. He saw the skiff from Valencia, but he had no desire to go out there now. What could he learn from the monks? Misogyny and celibacy? No thanks. He liked women. Transcendence? No. He wanted to live in the world. The thought came to him: He needed to go to the circle of stones. But he didn't know where it was. In a valley, Mick had told him, surrounded by hawthorn trees, a few miles from the Skelligs Bay. But where? He needed a guide. Madeleine. She knew where it was. But where was she? He had listened to her command and had not gone to her house. It had taken all of his strength not to go and knock on her door. He knew that if he did, she would not talk to him. She had to be in control. He looked out over the rolling hills. She was probably out there somewhere, in the wild, gathering herbs and roots. He felt like going out there and looking for her but he knew that if he did, he would not find her. She had to come to him. As he stood staring at the Skelligs Rock, he heard laughter behind him. He turned around and saw Madeleine walking up the road, holding hands with a little girl.

When they got close to him, Madeleine bent over and said something to the little girl, then straightened and said to James, "She thought that you were her father. He has an oilskin just like the one you're wearing."

James laughed and pushed back his hood. He looked down at the little girl and told her his name. She spun away from him and hid behind Madeleine's cape.

"Ah, so you're a shy one," said James. He crouched down and asked her name.

She showed him her eyes and shook her black curls.

James pulled a wild flower that was by his foot and offered it to her.

She reached out a tiny hand to take the flower but James hid it behind his back.

"Not until you tell me your name."

She yanked the cape away like a dancer shedding a veil and shouted, "Maggie."

"Maggie's my favorite name," he said. "Margaret. That's my mother's name. How old are you?"

She held up an open hand.

"Five."

"How about that? I'm five, too," said James.

Maggie stared at him, a puzzled look on her face.

James blushed and handed her the flower like a shy schoolboy on his first date. His face red, he stood and looked at Madeleine.

She was smiling.

"What are you doing out in this weather?"

James shrugged.

"Thinking. I think best when I'm walking. I've made up my mind. I'm not going to Belfast. I'm not going to do what Patty wants me to do."

Madeleine's smile got wider.

"That's good news. I'm glad to hear it."

"Yeah," said James. "I just wanted to tell you."

"So what made you decide?"

James looked at Maggie.

"She did."

Madeleine raised her eyebrows.

"Well, not she, specifically. But it has something to do with children. And women."

Madeleine stared at him for a few moments, her face impassive, then said to Maggie, "Your mother will be looking for you."

"I've been minding her for her mother," she said to James. "And I must be taking her back. You may wait for me if you wish. I won't be but a few minutes."

She pointed at the roof of a cottage that was hidden by trees.

"She lives there, at that farm."

Madeleine took Maggie by the hand and walked down the road, disappearing behind a hedgerow.

James paced up and down, waiting for her to return. He felt as if a weight had been lifted from him. Until he said it, he hadn't known he had made his decision. He was so happy that he felt like shouting. But by the time she got back, he was subdued. He still had a lot to work through.

Without saying a word or looking at him, Madeleine took him by the arm and started down the road.

"So tell me," she said after they had walked for a few minutes. "What did you mean, it has something to do with children? And women?"

James took a deep breath. He hoped that she wouldn't think that he was crazy.

"It's hard to explain," he stammered. "You see, I met these three females on the way to Ireland and they got me thinking and feeling things..."

"Females?" she repeated, testily.

"Well, one was a woman around your age and another one was a teenager and the third one was a little girl."

Madeleine looked at him suspiciously.

"A little girl?"

James smiled and told her about Brigid and how he met her.

"She wasn't afraid of me. She liked me. And I liked just being with her. She made me think that I mustn't be such a bad person after all if she, a child, could feel safe with me. It was a good feeling. For the first time, I felt that it would be nice to have a family. But that's a way off, yet. I have to come to terms with women first. And how I feel about them."

"What do you mean?"

He told her about the woman he met on the train from Luxembourg and how he met her.

"She was the first woman I had been able to talk with in years without feeling guilty."

"Guilty about what?"

"For going to Vietnam. For choosing to go to war. Before I went into the army, I went out with a girl, Laura, was her name. This was in the winter of '68. I was graduating from college in June and my student deferment would be up She knew that I was thinking about going into the service when I was finished with school. She was against the war. She belonged to the Resistance in Philadelphia. She was a demonstrator. She tried to talk to me about the war, how wrong it was. But I wouldn't listen. I was convinced she was wrong. We were right to be in Vietnam. I was a hawk. In 1968. That's how out of it I was. After a while, she gave up and didn't want to go out with me, anymore. When she broke off with me, I got so upset. I felt that there was something wrong with me. She, women, seemed to know things that I didn't...about life. I got so mixed up. I didn't know what to do. When I told my father about her, he said that I was better off away from her. She was a bad influence. She was a Communist or a dupe of the Communists. We were right to fight against them, he told me. So I made my choice. I went down to the draft board and volunteered for the draft. Later, when I realized that she was right, I was ashamed of myself."

She grabbed him by the arm and stopped him.

"Let's sit down for a minute," she said as she led him to stone wall by the side of the road. He sat down next to her and looked at the ground.

"What made you realize she was right?" she asked him.

James grimaced.

"In basic training, the way they were treating us. Like we weren't even persons. I felt like I was in a concentration camp. I had no rights. I was dirt. I had no control over my life. These idiots had power over me. They could send me to my death, some horrible death and I couldn't do anything about it. And the weapons. When I fired them, I could see how lethal they were. This was no game. They could blow a man to pieces, splatter him all over the place. I started thinking about it, in reality. I wouldn't want anyone doing that to me."

"If Patty heard you say that, he say you were just a coward," said Madeleine.

James shrugged.

"He can think that if he wants, but I volunteered for Vietnam."

He told her why he had done that.

"And while I was there, behind the line, I volunteered to go to the field, to go back to the artillery, to combat. But for some reason, they wouldn't let me."

"You confuse me," said Madeleine. "I don't understand. First you tell me, you didn't want to kill anyone and then you say you volunteered for combat. I don't know what to believe."

James shook his head.

"I was mixed-up. It's not easy to change. All my life, I knew that I would go into the military some day. I wanted to be a soldier, growing up. I always thought I would be a good soldier but I wasn't. I smoked dope on guard duty and I went AWOL twice. I'm not proud of those things believe me."

"What's AWOL?"

"Away without leave. It was when I was in Fort Dix in a Holding

Company waiting to go back to Vietnam. I had come home on emergency leave because my brother was sick and my parents needed me. I had applied for a compassionate reassignment because my family was having so many problems that I needed to be near home. To be honest, I don't know how much help I was to them but they wanted me there. But the army said no, I had enough time at home. I had to go back to Vietnam. I only had a few months left in the army. They didn't have to send me back. I wasn't an important soldier. They didn't need me. Since they wouldn't give me any more leave I took off and went home for a few days. When I came back, they gave me an Article 15, non-judicial punishment. They put me on extra duty and fined me a month's pay. They had me working over at Headquarters cutting up the ID cards of guys who had been discharged. Well, I got to be friends with the head clerk there and he told me one day that my orders for Vietnam were coming down. I asked him when. He said either Friday or Monday. I asked him to hold them until Monday so I could go home for the weekend. He agreed to do it but told me that if I wasn't back on Monday, he'd have the MPs after me. I decided that if I had to go back to Vietnam, I'd go but on my terms. I told him I'd be back. I took off again and went home. I came back on Sunday night and snuck into my barracks and went to sleep. I got up early in the morning before everyone else was up and went over to Headquarters and got my orders.

When I got back to the Holding Company, I went to the orderly room to sign out. As I went to do that, the clerk saw who I was and said, ' So you're Specialist O'Rourke. Oh, man, the First Sergeant wants to see you. You're in big trouble.'

As I was going in there, I wasn't nervous or afraid or anything. I was like ice. Later, after it was over, I started shaking. My attitude at the time was: what's he going to do to me? Send me to Vietnam?

The First Sergeant was sitting at his desk when I reported in to him.

He just shook his head and said in a quiet voice, 'I've had enough of you. This is the second time you went AWOL. You got off with an Article 15 last time but this time you're going to the stockade.'

I denied that I had been AWOL. I told him I had been there;

they just hadn't seen me. When I said that, he stood up and he seemed to get bigger and bigger like he was a hot air balloon filling up. I guess that's what the expression 'a towering rage' means. His face got so red that I thought he was going to start smoking. He cursed me out like no one ever had before and that's saying something. He kept shouting, 'The stockade! Over and over again. 'Do you hear me!'

I told him I wasn't deaf but I wasn't going to the stockade.

He talked real slow to me like I was a dunce.

'Oh…Yes…you…are…for…a…long…long…time.'

I replied in kind.

'Oh…No…I'm not…I'm going to Vietnam.' And I threw my orders on his desk.

He picked them up, looked at them for a few moments then threw them at me. He told me that if he ever saw me again, he would beat me to a pulp.

As I walked out of the barracks, in a final act of defiance, I went into my finance records, when you were traveling, we carried all our records with us, and I ripped out the order that had fined me the month's pay. I never paid the fine. I was so mad at the army that I didn't care what they did to me. I felt like I was beyond their control but of course I wasn't. I had to go back. So I went to Maguire Air Force Base and took the plane back to Vietnam."

Madeleine shook her head.

"You were really living on the edge."

I nod my head.

"Yeah, well, thank God, I didn't fall off the edge. The thing is, he could have sent me to the stockade and then sent me to Vietnam but he was probably so furious that he didn't think of it in time. If he had done that, I wouldn't have gotten an honorable discharge and I wouldn't be eligible for any benefits. Look, I'm not proud of doing those things. I never thought I'd ever act that way. In a way, I guess, it seems like a funny story but at the time, I was crazy, really. There's something frightening about being that out of control. I really think that all my bad behavior goes back to something that happened to me when I was a kid. I got thrown off course somehow. I don't know what happened."

"But you don't want to be a soldier anymore?" asked Madeleine.

"No, I think I'm finally being discharged from the army. I don't want to hurt anybody. I don't want to be responsible for anyone dying. I can understand why the IRA does what they do. But I can't do it."

Madeleine put her arm around him and squeezed him

"So what are you going to do now?"

He shook his head and shrugged.

"I don't know. Go to London? Maybe I could find some work there."

Madeleine grimaced.

"You wouldn't be able to get much, temporary dead-end jobs, that's all. And you would need a visa. Which they probably wouldn't give you. The best thing for you to do, James, is to go home. Back where you belong."

James stood and paced before her.

"Uh-uh. No. I can't go back there. What can I do there? I don't want anything to do with the system. What kind of work can you do when you don't believe in the system?"

She observed him for a few moments, her head tilted back.

"I hear what you're saying. But there must be something you can do. What kind of work have you done?"

James laughed.

"I've had a few jobs but I still feel like a student. I'm a college graduate, believe it or not. I have a BA in political science."

He sneered.

"For what it's worth. Nothing. I feel like my whole education was worthless. If I could go to Vietnam with a degree in political science, I didn't learn a thing in school."

"What were you planning to do with your degree?"

James laughed.

"Work for the government. Can you believe it? I actually wanted to work for the US government."

"Doing what?" she asked.

James laughed again, thinking of what Patty had asked him. If he only knew.

"Work for the CIA. Or the FBI. A friend of mine, Moe McDonnell, had a brother in the CIA. Another friend of mine, Eddie Lyons, his brother John, worked for the FBI. I thought they would be good jobs. And I was patriotic."

Madeleine gave him a funny look.

"The CIA? the FBI?"

"Yeah, well, Vietnam changed that. And even if I wanted to work for them after that, which I didn't, they wouldn't have hired me anyway. I was just a peon in the army, a glorified private, a Spec 4. When I got out of the army, I got a job with the State, as an employment counselor. I couldn't find a job, so they gave me one finding them for other people. It was a joke. They only had a few jobs, mostly dead-end, minimum wage jobs in factories and restaurants. And there were very few training programs, with waiting lists for years. I came to realize that the government wants to keep people unemployed, uneducated: a certain amount of them."

Madeleine nodded.

"Capitalism needs a supply of cheap, surplus labor for their armies. And to keep people desperate and divided against each other, so they'll work for nothing."

James nodded.

"You're right. Then my last job was with the VA, the Veterans Administration, as a clerk. I could see myself living the life of my father. Get up day after day and go to the same boring job, then come home and drink beer and listen to the ball game. Trapped. Inside all the time. Away from living things. Pushing paper. I couldn't stand it. Then I got this crazy idea that I would come here and learn how to farm. Doing real work: growing food. Being around animals. Living in a community. But it was just a fantasy, a delusion. I can't turn back the hands of time. But now I don't know what to do."

They sat silently for a few minutes.

Madeleine stood and faced him.

"Go against the system."

James laughed.

"What? Do something illegal? I'm shocked that you would suggest such a thing. Me?"

Madeleine smiled and shook her head.

"No, nothing illegal. I cannot tell you what to do. It has to come from you. The answer is inside of you. All I can do is help you bring it out. Maybe we can do a session together, if you are willing."

She grabbed him by the arm and started walking down the road.

"C'mon, let's go to my house. I'll heat up a kettle of tea and we can talk about it."

James was surprised. He hadn't expected an invitation inside. And he wondered what she meant by a session.

He nodded and went with her down the road and up the path to her cottage. She opened the door and led him through a hall into a small room with a black stove in the center and a settee along one side. There were pictures on the wall turned backwards. He wondered why. He took off his oilskin and handed it to her. She hung it with her cape on the coat rack by the door. He sat on the settee while she made tea in the fireplace. James looked around the room. It was clean and orderly, quite a difference from Ranchhouse.

"This was your grandmother's house?"

Madeleine was busy feeding the fire kindling. She looked up and smiled.

"Yes, it was. My grandmother was a wonderful woman. She lived here alone for years after my grandfather died. She birthed babies until she was eighty years old."

"She was a midwife?" James asked. "Just like you?"

Madeleine shook her head.

"She was a midwife but she didn't have a license. I do. I'm a registered nurse. I worked for a few years on an obstetrics floor, then I went to school for two years to study midwifery in London. My grandmother never went to school for it. She learned her skills from her mother."

"What does a midwife do?" asked James.

Madeleine poured tea into a cup and handed it to James. She poured herself a cup, then sat next to him on the settee.

"Help a mother prepare for the birthing. Monitor her progress, her diet, her weight, her blood pressure. Feel the baby growing inside of her, listen to her heartbeat. Be with her when she goes into labor and stay with her until she births the baby. And for a day or so afterwards."

"I thought that only doctors delivered babies," James said.

"No. Midwives delivered babies long before doctors did, before there were doctors. Doctors, men, didn't start delivering babies until the 17th century. After they burned most of the midwives at the stake as witches."

James felt his mouth go dry as he remembered what Mick had said about Madeleine. He sipped from his tea, his heart pounding. He wanted to ask her if she was a witch, and what she did in the circle of stones. But he was afraid.

Madeleine smiled.

"You seem nervous. What has Mick told you about me? That I'm a witch?"

James grinned.

"He didn't say you were a witch. He said that you practiced witchcraft up in the circle of stones. Black Masses."

Madeleine laughed.

"It's true. I do practice witchcraft in the circle of stones. But not Black Masses. I'm not a Satanist. He's just another male god."

James cleared his throat.

"What do you do?"

"Rituals, hypnosis, healing touch, sing, tell stories, read poetry, play music, dance, dream, pray..."

James didn't know what to say. It sounded strange to him, but not dangerous or threatening, except for hypnosis. He didn't want anyone hypnotizing him, taking control of him.

"This is all new to me," he said. "I never met a witch before."

Madeleine laughed.

"Don't worry. Witches are healers."

James leaned forward as if he had a stitch in his side.

"Can you heal me?"

Madeleine studied him for a few moments, her eyes soft.

"Perhaps. But there are certain conditions that must be met. A covenant that you must agree to."

James swallowed.

"What are they?"

"First, you must realize that there is to be no romantic involvement between us. You must understand that. Have no illusions about it. Also, there is to be a certain amount of touching involved. And touching can create anxiety in some people. So if you want me to stop, say so and I will. And you are not to touch me without my permission."

James rubbed his chin with his hand. He had mixed feelings about what she said. He had the feeling that she would be able to help him. She was a healer, he could see that. But he had to admit he was disappointed about there being no romantic involvement between them. Secretly he had been hoping that she would like him and find him attractive. Christy was right, he did like her. He had been fantasizing about her, making love with her.

"You have to learn, James, that you can't make love with any woman you want to. She has to want to also. If she doesn't, and you go against her will, that's rape. Do you have any problems with what I've said?"

He thought about it for a few minutes. She was right, he could see that. He wouldn't want anyone doing anything to him that he didn't want. As he looked at her face, the thought of violating her in any way made him sick to his stomach.

He shook his head,

"No. But I don't know about being hypnotized. I don't like being under anyone's control."

Madeleine smiled.

"That's not what hypnosis is. It is suggestion. I may, for instance, suggest a way for you to find your life's work."

James laughed.

"What? Find me a job? You'd have to be a magician to do that."

Madeleine smiled.

"Not find you a job. Your life's work. Your calling. Everyone has a calling. And maybe even find out what happened to you as a boy, although that may take some time. You just have to open up your mind to hear the voice."

James leaned back and looked at her.

"You would do this for me? Why?'

Madeleine shrugged.

"You deserve it. You are worthy. You were chosen."

"What?" said James. "Do you mean by that?"

Madeleine smiled.

"You had the courage to come here: to find out who you are. For that, you are to be rewarded."

James was puzzled. Chosen by who?

"What's in it for you? Is there a charge?"

Madeleine shook her head.

"No. But you must promise that you will apply what you learn to your life."

"Okay," said James. "When will we do it?"

"Tomorrow morning at dawn,' said Madeleine. "You must be here at 4 a.m. so we can be in the circle of stones before the sun rises."

Madeleine stood.

"You must be getting along. It'll soon be dark. I will meet you tomorrow at the path to my house. Wait for me there."

James stood and faced her.

"How am I going to see? I doubt if Mick has a flashlight. With batteries."

She looked out the window as they walked to the door.

"There'll be a full moon tonight to light the way. And don't worry about breakfast. I'll bring us food to eat."

"Okay," said James. "It sounds good. I never had a picnic in the morning before."

Madeleine smiled and handed him his oilskin.

After he put it on, he stood in front of the doorway rocking back and forth and looking at his feet. He didn't know what to do: kiss her or hug her, or what.

She took his hands in hers and kissed him on the forehead.

"Relax," she said. "You don't have to be afraid."

James nodded.

"You don't have to either. You can trust me."

"I know I can, fir i hata."

James was startled. Where had he heard that before?

"Fir i hata? What does that mean?"

Madeleine smiled.

"It's Gaelic for the man with the hat. It's the name the village people have for you. Because of that cap you're always wearing."

James tugged at the cap and smiled as he remembered waking up wearing it one morning. So, he had a name in Gaelic. He walked sideways down the steps and turned in a circle at the bottom. He didn't want to leave. He wanted to stay with her forever. But as she closed the door, he remembered his promise. He would not betray her. As he walked down the road, feeling more and more excited, he picked up the pace. By the time he reached the youth hostel, he was running.

As he neared the pub, he saw Mick and Christy pacing in front of it. Mick saw James coming and waved to him.

"What's the matter, mahn? Why are you running?"

James stopped and caught his breath.

"I just felt like it. Trying to get back in shape."

"Really, mahn? Where have you been?"

"Walking," said James. "And talking with Madeleine."

"Really, mahn? Well, while you were up there the Gardai were at Ranchhouse, looking for Patty."

"What?" said James, stunned. "The cops?"

Mick took a hit from his cigarette.

"That's right. They had some civilians with them. Looked like British Intelligence."

James felt the adrenaline rush.

"Is that right? Where are they now?"

"They left about an hour ago, mahn. I just contacted Patty and told him to lay low. They'll be staying the night in one of our safe houses in County Cork."

James didn't like what he was hearing. He didn't want to get involved with the police. Not now. He turned and looked up the mountain. He felt like going up there and asking Madeleine if he could stay with her. But he knew that he couldn't do that. He had to see this through by himself.

"What should we do?" he asked Mick.

"Let's go back to Ranchhouse," said Mick. "And be on guard duty, in case they come back. But I don't think they will."

"We'll tell them where to get off if they do," said Christy, profiling.

They walked out of the circle of light in front of the pub and walked down the dark road to Ranchhouse.

As they walked between the bog fields, Mick said, "Look at the moonbeams on the sea."

James looked out over the bay. It was so beautiful, it made him sad.

"Have you ever heard the poem, The Old Bog Road?" Mick asked James.

"Yeah," said James. "You recited it for me last year. But I'd like to hear it again. It's about an Irishman who immigrated to America. He's always thinking about the old bog road at home."

"Ah, so you remember, mahn. I didn't think you would. You were bolloxed drunk that night. It goes like this:

'My feet are here on Broadway, this blessed harvest morn./But oh the ache that's in them, for the spot where I was born./ My weary hands are blistered, from working cold and heat./ Oh, what it is to swing a scythe today on fields of Irish wheat?/ There was a girl at home who used to walk with me./ Mary Dwyer was her name./ She had eyes as soft and sorrowful as moonbeams on the sea./ She died a year I left her, I building brick and load./ They carried out her coffin, down the old bog road./ Had I the chance to wander back and own a king's abode, I would rather see the old hawthorn tree by the old bog road./ What is the world to any mahn where no one speaks his name?/ I have had my day, and here I am, building brick and load. /A long three thousand miles away, from the old bog road./'"

When Mick finished, James felt a painful sadness come over him, a nostalgia so powerful that he felt like crying.

As Mick opened the door to Ranchhouse, the dogs barked ferociously at them.

"Go to bed." Mick shouted and stomped his foot. The dogs scattered, then crawled on their bellies towards him, their tails wagging. Mick patted them and promised to take them for a walk on the beach later.

The three men went through the kitchen and sat at the table in the back room.

"So you liked that poem, mahn?' Mick asked James.

"Yeah," said James. "I can see how he would miss Ireland. I'd miss it." He almost choked on the words.

"He never should have left, mahn. No mahn can live alone, cut off from his country, his people. He should have stayed and fought, instead of pulling out. Millions of our people are in exile. If they'd stayed, we'd have the manpower to drive the British Army into the sea. But at least, you've come back, James. If only more would do the same."

James grimaced. If Mick only knew.

"How about De Valera, Mick?" said Christy. "There's one who should have stayed in America."

James was puzzled. He thought that De Valera was a hero in Ireland.

"What do you mean by that?" he asked Christy.

"A traitor he was. He turned on the IRA and had them put in jail. Goes to show ya, ya can't trust the Americans."

James looked at Mick.

"It's true, mahn, what he said about De Valera. During the Second World War, Sean Russell was all for making a deal with the Nazis for guns. But De Valera wanted to keep Ireland neutral, so he had the IRA banned. But James is no traitor, no turncoat. He comes from a long line of Irish-American war veterans who have come to our aid. The Fenians? Do you know of them?"

James shook head. He didn't feel like talking. He felt like a phony.

"Fenian is Gaelic for soldier. They were like you, mahn. Many of them fought in your Civil War; that's where they learned to fight. When that war was over, they came to Ireland to fight the British. But they were riddled with informers and were destroyed from within."

Christy sneered.

"I think we have an informer amongst us now. Who told the Gardai that Patty was here? That's what I want to know. Madeleine? Maybe it was her. She hates Patty. Everybody knows that."

"I doubt it," said Mick. "If she were going to do it, she would have done it years ago. She wouldn't inform on Patty, now. Maybe nobody did. They come to Ranchhouse every now and then to look for him. It may have been just a routine visit."

"I don't know," said Christy, looking at James. "I still think that we have an informer amongst us. If it wasn't Madeleine, who else could it be? What do you think, James?"

James stared back at Christy, trying to figure out what was going on. He began to feel paranoid. He shrugged.

"I agree with Mick. But you know what they say, Christy? A fox smells his own hole first. Maybe you're the informer, if there is one."

Mick laughed.

"What do you have to say to that, Christy?"

Christy scowled and muttered something under his breath, then he stood and walked to the back door and looked out it.

"They're out there. I know it. Waiting to rush us when we're asleep."

Despite himself, James felt a stab of fear. He didn't want to get busted now. He got up and walked into the living room and looked out the window. Paranoia, that's all it was, he told himself. Nothing was going to happen. He sat in the darkness for some time, thinking about how he was going to tell Mick about his decision. He hated to let Mick down. Mick had been good to him. But then again, Mick had let him down. And how was Patty going to take it? He would be furious. But so what? He didn't owe Patty anything.

He could just leave. And go where? That was the problem. It was easy for Madeleine to say. She didn't know what it was like living in America. He was a Vietnam veteran: one of the most despised people on the face of the earth. He felt that the people who had supported the war hated him because they had lost and the people who opposed the war hated him because he had gone. He felt like an outsider over there.

"James! What are you doing in there, mahn?"

Startled, James jumped to his feet and went into the back room.

"Christy thinks that we should stand watch for the night," said Mick. "Take turns. We're only three so we can't do all four watches. I don't think It's necessary, but it's better to be safe than sorry."

"Aye," said Christy. "I'll take the first watch. From nine to twelve."

"I'll take the second" said Mick. "I can't sleep anyway. I'll rouse you at three, James."

James didn't know what to say. He thought that it was absurd. But if he waited until six, he would be late in getting up to Madeleine's. And if he refused to do his share, they would be annoyed and suspicious. He would play along with them. Once they were asleep, he leave for the mountain. He would say that he was going to sleep late, so they wouldn't miss him in the morning.

"The last watch," he pretended to complain. "The worst one. All right. What the hell. I'll just sleep in the morning."

It reminded him of the first time he had that watch in Vietnam. He hadn't know what fear was until that night. He had been so afraid that he shook all over. He had never known such darkness. He had been so glad to see the sun come up that day that he felt like standing up and shouting: 'Let there be light! Thank God for the light!'

"Give me an army mahn any day," said Mick.

"I'm going to go up and get some sleep now," said James. "Come and get me at three, Mick."

James went out the back door and walked through the garden to his chalet. He had to prepare himself for what was to come.

The morning star was high in the eastern sky.

Three hawthorn trees stood watch over a bowl of broken white stones scattered in a circle around a small mound of green earth. Madeleine sat on a wide slab supported by two stones, while James walked behind the circle, not wanting to go inside, not feeling worthy enough yet. Sitting on the top of a crumbling shed, a bird sang the same song over and over, a warning or a key. Above, in the low hills, a wild mountain goat nibbled the short grass, pausing from time to time to meditate on the scene. A roofless cottage with gaping windows and open doors testified to the absence of human life. She had brought him to a graveyard.

"What were the stones used for?" James asked. "What was their purpose?"

"There are different theories," said Madeleine. "The largest circle in Ireland is up at New Grange, near Dublin. Some scholars think they were altars. For human sacrifice."

James stopped walking when she said that. He flashed on the knife she had used to cut the bread and cheese for breakfast. She was going to stab him in the back with it. He felt dizzy. He remembered the tea she had given him to drink. It tasted funny. Maybe it was drugged. Grimacing, he clenched his fist and turned towards her.

"But I don't believe it' s true," said Madeleine. "I have another theory. I got it from my grandmother, who got it from her mother. She brought me to this place many years ago, when I was a little girl. Being a midwife, she had a different idea of what the cairn symbolized and what the dolmens were used for."

James took a deep breath and unclenched his fists. He wiped his face with his hand. His legs were shaking.

"Are you all right?" asked Madeleine.

James sat next to her on the stone.

"Yeah, I guess. I just realized that I'm paranoid. For a moment there, I thought you were going to hurt me. I have trouble trusting people."

Madeleine nodded.

"It's understandable. You've been hurt. Your sense of trust has been betrayed. Other people only cause you pain. It is best to stay away from them. Protect yourself. It's you against the world. And that's a lonely place to be, isn't it?"

James gritted his teeth to keep from crying.

"Yeah."

"And you've come here to be healed, have you not?'

"Yes."

He wiped his face with his hands.

"Why here? What kind of place is it?"

"A sacred place," said Madeleine. 'There are sacred places in the world and this is one of them."

"Why a circle of stones?"

Madeleine smiled.

"A circle means continuity, connection, return."

"What were those words you used? Dolmen? Cairn?"

She patted the stone beneath them.

"This is a dolmen. It looks like an altar, probably was one. But I don't think it was meant for sacrifice. Though it may have been used for that purpose by the Druids."

"But I thought that the circle came from the Druids," said James. "That's what Mick said."

Madeleine shook her head.

"It was here before the Druids, before history, before patriarchy.

That's why the cairn."

"What's that?"

She pointed at the mound in the center of the circle.

"It looks like a tomb to me," said James.

"That's what most people think. Apparently the Druids used it for that. But I think it was meant to be something else."

"What?"

"Look at it," she said. "What else does it look like? It all depends on how you see."

James looked at the mound and the small opening at its base. It reminded him of the graveyard down near Ranchhouse, the one with the skull inside one of its crypts. He remembered picking up the skull in his hands the year before and pretending to be Hamlet, much to the shocked amusement of the lads from Dublin. Life or death, that was the question.

"Does it have a head inside?"

Madeleine laughed.

"Of course. It usually has a whole little body."

James looked at the mound again. It was so simple, life.

"A womb," said James. "That's what it is."

Madeleine nodded.

"Yes, that's what my grandmother told me. She told me about the Tuatha De Danann and the triple goddess of Ireland. A time when women had power. A time when people celebrated life not death, as they do today. The mound symbolizes the mother, the source of life."

"The triple goddess?"

Madeleine nodded.

"That's who you met on the way here."

James laughed.

"No, really, I've never heard of her."

Madeleine smiled.

"Have you ever heard of the ancient name for Ireland, Eire?"

James nodded.

"She was one. The others were called Fodha and Banbha."

"Really?" said James.

"Yes. You're her consort, Dagda."

James laughed.

"Dagda. That's a strange name. What's a consort, anyway?"

"A companion, a spouse, a son, a lover, a brother, a father, a friend. Dagda was all men to the goddess and she was all women to him. What men and women should be for each other: everything but enemy."

Madeleine touched her fingers to her forehead, her heart and both her shoulders.

"In the name of the mother and of the daughter and of the Holy Ghost. A woman."

James laughed. He told her the story Patty had told in the pub the other night about being the ghost of Ballinskelligs.

"He's a ghost just like me."

"Speak of the devil," said Madeleine. "Where is Patty?"

James told her that he was due back today.

"What are you going to say to him?"

James shrugged.

"That I don't want anything to do with guns, with violence. That the war is over for me."

Madeleine smiled.

"You are ready to come inside the circle."

She stood and extended her hand to him. He took it and stepped inside the circle. He almost expected something to happen, a feeling of release, a transformation, a bolt of lightning. But nothing did.

He laughed.

"So what do we do now?"

Madeleine led him to the center of the circle. She pointed to a dolmen that was in front of the cairn.

"Lie down on that."

James felt nervous.

"What are you going to do?"

Madeleine smiled.

"Don't worry," she said in a soft voice. "Some healing touch. I'm not actually going to touch your body now, just your energy field."

"My what?"

"That's what we all are: fields of energy. Our bodies don't stop at our skin. I want to assess you. Find any areas of congestion where the energy is blocked."

James started to lie down, but as he did, a feeling of panic sent him back up. He looked into her soft eyes.

"This is too weird. I can't do it."

Madeleine soothed him with her voice,

"Relax. You don't have to be afraid. I won't hurt you. If you don't want to lie down, then just sit there. I'm going to put my hands an inch or so from your body. I'll do it very slowly."

She stood behind him for a few moments so close that he could feel her breath. He turned his head slightly to see what she was doing. Over his shoulder, he saw her hands above his head, moving like a sculptor's molding clay. When she got to his upper back, she kept her hands there for a long time, moving from one side to the other. When she was finished with his back, she came around to his front. He thought about how weird this would look to someone coming upon the scene. He closed his eyes as her hands felt around his face. As she moved down towards his middle, he took a few deep breaths. He didn't want to get excited. She didn't stay there long, however, but moved quickly down his legs to his feet.

She came out of her crouch and said, "I felt a lot of heat just below your right shoulder. Do you have any pain there?"

James was impressed. He grimaced.

"Not any more."

He told her about the knifing and the nightmares.

"How fortunate you are," said Madeleine. "You have knowledge that other people don't. You've already died. Now, you are to be reborn. Lie on your stomach."

He did as she commanded. He closed his eyes, feeling the rough stone on his face. He opened one eye and saw her standing beside him, her arms extended and her eyes closed like a sleepwalker. She stopped at his wound for a few moments, waving her hands in a furious fashion like a mad music conductor. As he lay there, he felt his eyes get heavy. He was so tired. He had only slept for a few hours the night before, pulling that stupid guard duty. He felt himself drift off to sleep. A woman stood over him, a kind smile on her face, her hands raised, ready to stroke. He woke up and saw Madeleine sitting at the entrance of the cairn.

"Come," she said. "It is time."

James felt as if he were in a trance. He got down on his hands and knees and crawled slowly over to where she sat, her back to the opening of the mound.

"I want you to sit, facing my left, " said Madeleine. "I'm going to put my hands on you, one on your back and one on your chest at your heart chakra."

"My what?"

He looked around him at the trees and the grass bending in the wind like eavesdroppers, then sitting upright like an audience at a play.

"Originally, it meant wheel. It's an energy center. There are thirteen chakras in the body. The heart chakra is the center of consciousness. I will transfer energy through there using the chakras in the palms of my hands."

"What's going to happen?"

"Relax," said Madeleine in a soft voice. "Close your eyes and take a few deep breaths. Try to empty your mind. That is very hard, I know. Whenever a thought or a voice intrudes, concentrate on your breathing. I want you to do this so that the energy can flow freely from inside the cairn through me and into you."

James closed his eyes and did as she said. He felt the heat from her hands as they came close to him, touch lightly onto his shirt, then burn into his body. He took a few deep breaths as if he were about to sob.

"I want you to concentrate on the feel of my hands upon you," she said in a soft voice. "That's all you have to do. Feel their warmth."

James felt the energy flow through him, from his feet up to his head, the darkness behind his eyelids growing brighter and brighter until his eyes were filled with a golden light. Like birds gathering themselves for flight, her hands slowly lifted from his body, leaving behind their warmth like freshly laid eggs. He sat for a few minutes with his head back and his eyes closed.

"You will always be able to feel my hands upon you. They will be there whenever you need them."

James nodded. He could still feel her hands upon him

"Now, I want you to tell me how you feel when you think about finding your life's work and what is troubling you."

James swallowed.

"Empty. I feel empty inside"

Madeleine put her face close to his, so all he could see were her eyes.

"You swallowed when you said that. So I want you to tell me a story about a swallow who feels empty inside. By the use of metaphor, you can transfer your feelings into something outside of you, where you will be able to see it and understand it."

James was confused.

"What's a metaphor? I can't remember."

"Something that suggests a likeness to something else. A comparison. Begin it with once upon a time. Every story should begin with once upon a time. You can do it. I know you can."

James laughed. Tell a story about a swallow? A swallow is a what? A bird. How could he do that? But as he sat there, looking into her eyes, he felt more relaxed than he had ever been in his life.

"Once upon a time," he said slowly. "There was a swallow who felt an emptiness deep inside of himself. He felt the need to fill that emptiness, so he ate and he drank all that he could, but it just went through him, leaving him empty once again. Then, one day, he came upon an abandoned nest of tiny swallows who were hungry and thirsty and he fed them, day after day, he fed them and watched them grow, until slowly, the emptiness inside of him was gone and he felt whole once again, as he had been, in the beginning."

When he was finished, Madeleine had tears in her eyes.

"How do you feel?" asked Madeleine

"Good. I feel....full."

"You have such a beautiful golden-green glow about you. You have one more step to take on your journey within. Close your eyes and listen to my words. You are sitting on the strand, looking out to sea. See how green it is, as green as the grass on the hill. The surf smiles at you as it rolls gently upon the shore. Seesoo, hrss, rsseeiss, ooos, you hear it say. The sky is blue, so blue, as blue as your eyes, with faces of clouds floating by: the sun a golden white above - the world at peace."

His eyes closed, James listened to her soft voice and saw the scene.

"Before you is an altar lit by blue candles. Beside it is a blazing fire. On the altar is a child, a young girl."

James took a few deep breaths.

"Take your gun and throw it into the fire."

He surrendered his weapon.

"Pick up the child and hold her to your chest."

He did as she commanded.

"Do you recognize her?"

James nodded.

"She's me."

"Hold her close to you. Rock her. Tell her how you feel about her."

James rocked back and forth like a buddha praying.

"I love you," he said, his voice breaking. "I don't want to hurt you, ever again." He said over and over again until he broke down and cried. When he was finished crying, he heard Madeleine's soft voice.

"Listen to her as she tells you how she feels and what she wants."

"I am you. You are me. We are both together. Be there for me. Don't ever leave me."

When he came back to himself, Madeleine was smiling at him.

"Let's dance."

They held hands and danced in a circle around the mound, chanting until they collapsed in the grass. They lay there, breathing heavily for a few minutes.

"That was fun," said Madeleine, sitting up. "Now, you have the power to do what you have to do."

James shook his head.

"What was that all about?"

Madeleine smiled.

"You'll understand in time. Let's have something to eat, to give us energy for the walk back."

They went over to the dolmen where she had left her bag. She took out the rest of the bread and cheese and put it on the stone.

James took some food and ate it slowly, trying to make sense of what happened.

"So now I'm supposed to know what to do with my life?"

Madeleine smiled.

"Go home, James. You'll know what to do when you get there."

James grimaced.

"I don't want to go home. I want to do something for Ireland, for the Irish people. Do some sort of welfare work, maybe."

Madeleine shook her head.

"It won't happen. You can do more for Ireland in the United States than you can here."

"How can I do that?" asked James.

"The United States is the center of imperialism, of capitalism. It is the same form of government as the English. It's roots are from the English and the Romans, another imperial power. As long as it exists in its present form, Ireland will never be free, the world will never be free. The people in power in the United States support the war. They support any attempt to keep poor people down, anywhere. They are afraid that if the Catholic people take power in Northern Ireland, they would be an inspiration to the poor people in the South and poor people all over the Commonwealth, all over the world."

James didn't understand.

"What are you saying I should do? Go back and try to overthrow the US government? How could I do that?"

Madeleine smiled.

"I don't expect you to do that. Not alone, anyway. And not now. It is not the time for that. Prepare yourself. Join political groups, any that are working for peace or for the working class or for the poor. There are many who are doing it now. We have people in governments, in the schools, in the media, in the corporations, all over the world. Call it the Aquarian Conspiracy, if you will. We're coming out of the Age of Pisces, the Fish, the end of the Christian Era into the Age of Aquarius. Tell your story: what happened in Vietnam, what is happening in Ireland. We need a world - wide revolution. But it cannot be done violently."

"How can it be done?"

"By doing what Gramsci said to do. Slowly, by taking over the institutions. And the way they were doing it in Ireland before the

IRA got involved. Mass demonstrations. Sit-down strikes. By people refusing to pay their taxes and their rents."

"But a lot of people got killed," said James. "And beat up and put in jail."

"That's what happening now," said Madeleine. "But who cares when they're just poor Irish Catholics? But what if there were Irish-Americans with them? That's what you should do, James. Tell them back in the States that if they really want to help the Irish people, they should go to Northern Ireland and stay there, live there for a while. Stand between the British Army and the Catholic people. Be a witness for peace and testify to what they see."

James shook his head.

"How many people would do that?"

Madeleine shrugged.

"Some religious people. Some Internationalists. But once an example is set, others will follow. Education is required. Consciousness needs to be changed. Everything is connected. What hurts you, hurts me. We have to take responsibility for each other. Give up our selfish needs. Care about other people. People are poor in Belfast because they are poor in Philadelphia and vice versa. Our first priority as a society should be satisfying people's basic human needs: for food and shelter and health care."

James sat, thinking about what she said. It made sense to him. Maybe it would work out after all. Maybe all of the fingers pointing at him had been his own.

Going home! When he was in Vietnam, that was all he thought about. He saw his mom's face. She would be so happy to see him. He missed her, he had to admit. And his brother. He wondered how he was doing. And his friends. And his dad. His father was dying. James felt a pain in the pit of his stomach at the thought. His father had been good to him, growing up. He had always been there for him. Now his father needed him. He was sick. That's why he supported the war. He couldn't help it. James felt an overwhelming desire to see his father before he died and forgive him. He jumped off the stone.

"Okay," he said to Madeleine. "You're right. I should go home. I'd be the smart thing to do. But first, I have to go and see Mick and Patty and tell them about my decision. I guess I owe them that."

Madeleine smiled.

"Good. Where will you get your flight?"

"Luxembourg. I flew Icelandic Airlines. It's the cheapest way to get to Europe. I have to go back there."

Madeleine nodded.

"Well, I was planning to leave tomorrow but I could go this afternoon. I could take you as far as London."

"Okay," said James. "It won't take me long to pack. I can be ready by then."

They walked out of the circle together and hiked up the hill, out of the valley. When they got to the top, James looked down over the patchwork quilt of potato fields and pasture and saw the sun flashing on the glass roof of Ranchhouse, sending him a message.

It was high noon.

Patty was back, he knew it. He had to face the man one more time, to complete the circle.

As James walked along the strand, he rehearsed in his mind what he was going to say to Mick and Patty. When he got to the path that led to Ranchhouse, he stood on the small wall and looked out over the bay one last time. He wanted to memorize every detail of it so he would never forget how it looked. He would remember Ballinskelligs for as long as he lived. He turned and walked up the path past the convent to the front door of Ranchhouse. There were two cars parked in the road. From inside the house, he heard voices gargling a litany of violent threats against Ian Paisley. They were going to shoot him early in the morning.

He was in the presence of evil.

James opened the door carefully and sneaked through the kitchen into the backroom. Luckily, the dogs weren't there; they were out back. He duck walked behind the table and looked through the door into the living room where he saw Mick and Christy and Eamon passing around a joint and a bottle of poteen. He heard the violent creaking of bedsprings and a woman screaming upstairs.

Several minutes later, Patty himself descended the stairs, buckling up his pants with a satisfied smile, thrusting out his jaw like Mussolini on the balcony. He strutted around the room, clutching himself and shouting, "All the birds love it. Nothing they like better. You know the story of the Garden of Eden? Let me tell you what really happened."

Patty pantomimed God making a man out of clay, finishing him by forming a huge sexual organ. He lovingly caressed the contours of a shapely woman's body. He stood back for a moment as if admiring his creation.

"It isn't finished. What did I leave out?"

Patty bent over with his fingers stroking his chin and crept in a circle like a mad scientist around his monster. Then he stomped his feet like a storm trooper and balled up a fist with his thick middle finger protruding and uppercut his second creation in the womb and shouted an obscenity. Laughing, he looked around the room for approval.

Hiding beneath the table in the backroom, James watched the men laughing and felt sick to his stomach. How would she feel if she saw that?

"What are you laughing at?" Patty shouted at Christy. "You're no better than a woman yourself. You're nothing but a contrary."

"What do you mean?" asked Christy, his voice breaking.

Paddy stood over Christy and began having his way with him.

James couldn't believe what he was seeing and hearing. He had to stop looking and listening. His first impulse was to take off. He was going to tell Patty that he wasn't going to Belfast, either. Maybe Patty would treat him the same way. He gritted his teeth in anger. Just let him try it, he thought. Visions of violence burned in his brain. As he was about to explode, he remembered what had happened in the circle of stones. Madeleine was right. Patty believed in domination. Either dominate or submit. Be either a killer or a victim. He wanted to be neither. He saw that image of a little girl and he remembered what Madeleine had said to him.

As James stood up, he heard Mick say, "Cut it out, mahn. You're being disgusting."

Patty laughed and walked away from Christy, cursing the hippie mentality.

"Love and peace rubbish. This is our house. Only men live here."

Christy continued crying, his hands over his face.

James walked into the living room.

"He has risen," Mick shouted. "We thought you'd never wake up."

Patty poked James in the chest.

"I was just gonna come and get ya." Patty winked. "But I had to get me some loving first. Didn't have any last night. Had to sleep on the floor in County Cork. Pack your bags, man. We don't have much time. We're leaving for the border and we want you to come with us."

"Up the rebels," shouted Eamon, brandishing a revolver. "If we run into any Brits or the Gardai, we'll blow their brains out."

"Stand up and be counted, mahn," shouted Mick. "Which side are you on? You're either with us or against us."

James looked at Patty and shook his head." I'm not going with you."

Patty looked over at Mick who said, "Why not, mahn? Ah, It's Madeleine, is it? You don't want to leave while she's here."

Patty laughed.

"Ya giving her some loving , are ya? You're quite a man if ya are."

James shook his head.

"No. No man'll ever do that to Madeleine."

"Oh, no?" Patty snarled. "Who does she think she is? The Blessed Virgin? She's like the nuns down the road. It's a bit of a joke. There they are, young women, their lovely bodies just festering, waiting for their Lord Jesus to come down from heaven and give them some loving. A waste of good women. Forget Madeleine and come to Belfast. Meet some real women. Free women."

Patty took a hit from the joint, then pointed at a slogan scrawled on the wall.

"See that? Free Belfacism. That's a word I invented. A little trick I learned from James Joyce: the ability to split words and reunite them to form new words, new meanings. Jesus Joyce. That's what we called him in the university. I used to lecture on him and his works. He knew how to treat a woman: go through her a few times, then give her a slap on the bum and tell her to fix breakfast. Belfacism. That's what we're fighting up there, man. I thought you had your head together. Where's your sense of humanity? You know what's going on up there and you not going to do anything about it?"

"I want to do something about it, Patty," said James. "But I don't want anything to do with guns and killing people. Violence is not the way."

Patty sneered, "What is the way, then?"

James repeated what Madeleine had said.

"We tried that, man," Patty snarled. "It didn't work. And who are you, anyway, man, to tell us what to do? What do you know about it? You're not Irish. You're an American. Mick has you wrong. You're not one of us."

James shrugged.

"That doesn't mean I can't have an opinion. Your way isn't working, either. Maybe you didn't give the other way enough time. Gandhi and the Indians kicked out the British that way, didn't they? Maybe if you had followed him instead of Michael Collins, Ireland would be free right now."

Patty stared at James for a moment, then spit at his feet.

James was silent, his face like flint.

Patty brushed past James and went to the stairs. He shouted for Maura to come but she didn't answer, so Patty went up after her and came down a few minutes later, dragging her after him and threw her through the door into the back room.

Patty pointed his finger at James.

"When are you leaving, anyway, man?"

James looked Patty in the eye and said. "I don't know. When I'm ready."

Patty looked at him for a moment, his shoulders twitching, then stormed out of the room.

Eamon shook James' hand.

"I don't agree with ya. But you're all right with me. Believe me, man. We'd put down our guns if we could. But the British and the Prods won't let us."

James nodded.

"I know. I'll do what I can for you and your cause. As soon as soon as I get organized."

Eamon nodded. He hugged Mick and told him that they'd be back in a couple weeks, then went out after Patty.

Christy jumped up from the couch and ran after Eamon.

"Take me with you. I can do it now. I'll prove to you that I'm a man. I'll do anything that you want me to do. Just give me a gun and I'll kill the first British soldier I see."

"What's all this talk about leaving?" Mick asked James. "Where will you go?"

James shrugged.

"First, I'm going to London with Madeleine."

Mick waved his hand.

"Ah mahn. I don't blame you. I would leave if I could. You can see what a madhouse Ranchhouse has become. By all means, go to London, then. The married life is the best life for those who know how to live it."

James smiled.

"It's not like that, Mick. I'm not going to marry Madeleine. But you're right. If you know how to live it. Maybe someday, I'll get married. But I'm only going to stay in London for a few days. Then I'm going to Luxembourg and get a flight home, back to Philadelphia."

"Really, mahn?" said Mick. "What are you going to do there?"

James thought about the story of the swallow and smiled.

"I don't know, Mick. I'll work it out, somehow. I'll do something. Tell me, Mick. Do you believe in God?"

Mick shook his head.

"No more, mahn. I used to believe in the Lord. I went to church every Sunday. I was a sexton for many years. Helped the priest take communion to the sick. But no more. Why do you ask?"

James shrugged.

"Just wondering. I'm not a Christian either. God can't be an individual person. God is within all of us. And without us. There's something out there, a process, a web, that connects us. There's a new god, now, I believe."

Mick shook his head.

"You really think so, mahn? I wish I could believe that but I can't. We can't depend on God. We don't need a new god to help us. We need guns."

James shook his head and walked out of the room. He went up to his chalet, rolled up his sleeping bag and roped it onto his backpack. He shed his fatigue shirt and left it on the bed. He put on a beat up dungaree jacket that Mick had given him then took off his cap and folded into bag. Looking in the mirror, he tilted onto his head a white wool Tarn O'Shanter he had purchased in Waterville. A touch of the poet. Then he took off his combat boots and threw them into a corner. He strapped on a pair of sandals that he had found in the room. He stuffed the rest of his belongings into his pack and stretched into it.

He found Mick sitting on a chair in the garden.

"You're really leaving me, mahn? I can't believe it. I was hoping that you'd change your mind."

"I'm sorry, Mick," said James. "I can't live here. I wish I could but I can't."

Mick accompanied James to the front door and walked with him onto the path. James turned to Mick and took his hand. They stared at each other for a moment, then Mick turned his head and began to cry. Astonished and moved, James embraced Mick and cried with him. James felt bad about leaving Mick and Ballinskelligs but he had no other choice. He wished that he could live there, that they could all live there, in peace. That was how people should live, close to the land and the sea, surrounded by animals, working together, loving one another. But it could not be, not now, anyway. Maybe someday, he thought. After a few moments, James released himself from Mick's embrace and walked out on the road to wait for Madeleine.

8.

Laughter in the Confessional Box

As Casey walked up Thirteenth Street toward Saint John the Evangelist Church, his pace slowed so much that he felt like he was wading through running water. He had to stop for a moment at the side cemetery to catch his breath. On the wall above its concrete graves, he saw the names and dates of those buried there, some going back to before the Civil War. He could hear the sound of distant music and faint voices raised in song. They were singing a hymn about ashes.

This church was here before his family came to America, he realized. His immigrant ancestors probably came here sometimes. They probably stood right here looking at the church. He wished he could see with their eyes. It looked a lot different then.

As he scanned the tall buildings that were squeezed in around the church - Wanamaker's and a garage across the street, a bank at the corner, a small key shop, a greasy spoon and an empty store - he imagined fruit and shade trees and grass and dirt streets, with horses and carriages instead of cars and buses, men in top hats and black suits, women in hoop dresses. Maybe in the next life, he'll get to see the world as his ancestors saw it and experience life as they lived it, everyone who ever lived, all the way back to Adam and Eve and the Fall.

That reminded him of what he had come to do and a terrible dread came over him. He had to tell the priest his whole sorry story, from the beginning. He had to confess all of his sins. How could he do it? It would take forever. As he stood there, he began to sweat. He felt sick to his stomach. What if the priest wouldn't give him absolution. He had heard of such things happening. What had Jesus said? 'Whose sins you forgive are forgiven and whose you do not are not.' Or words to that effect. What would he do if that happened?

Then he heard the voice again: 'Why do you want to be forgiven anyway? For what? I know: You committed adultery. Once. So you got a woman pregnant. It wasn't your fault she had an abortion. It was her idea. So you went with the ladies of the night, no big deal. Smoked a little pot. Drank some beer. Everyone needs to have some fun in life. So you stole something. Once. Lied a little. Hit a few people. So what? So you got mad and felt like committing murder. Who doesn't? You didn't do it, did you? They hurt you. You're only human. Stop feeling guilty. Go home. Kick back. Drink a few beers. Smoke a bone. Get you some loving. Don't worry about it. Why go back to the Catholic Church? Such hypocrites! Popes with kids. The Vatican. All the money in that place. The Pope living in luxury. Bishops stuffing themselves while the people starve. Priests buggering little boys. Sleeping with their housekeepers. Look at this church: All the money gone into it: gold chalices, white linen, rich robes. And people homeless. What does all that have to do with a poor carpenter? Jesus. A good man, no doubt about it. But that's all he was. He wouldn't judge you. He would understand. He was human. Why go in there and embarrass yourself to another man? That's all he is. How can a man forgive sins, anyway? A man just like Father Wrigley, the one who abused you. Slapped your face so hard that he spun you in a circle. For what? Let me take you back: There you are just a little guy. 15 years old. 5 foot tall. 80 pounds soaking wet. A four eyes. And he was a big man with a loud voice. Liked to intimidate. Put the fear of God into little boys. He storms into class, shouting. He has some important work to do. A big shot. He gives an assignment to the class and sits down and starts scribbling like he was writing some important work. Yeah, sure. Probably a bunch of nothing. You were a good boy. You did the assignment. When you were finished, instead of sitting there daydreaming, you started doing your geometry homework. Made sense. But not to him. He saw you with your geometry book out and asked what you were doing. You told him. He asked why. You said 'because I finished my religion.' He told you to stand up and move into the aisle. Then he walked slowly over to you with his big hands behind his back and whispered, 'Take off your glasses.' When he said that, you knew what was coming. He had beat other boys before. But you couldn't understand why. That's when he hit you. He roared, 'You're never finished with your religion.' Despite yourself, you felt the tears run down your face. He humiliated you. Made you cry in front of your friends. You remember what you said to yourself when you sat down. 'Ain't I, Father. I'm finished with my religion.' And here you are, going back to that religion. No!'

As Casey stood there paralyzed, a tiny, hunchbacked old woman carrying several carryall bags and wearing a tan raincoat and a black bandana walked by the steps of the church and made the sign of the cross. Casey tried to imitate her but his hand felt like it was holding a fifty-pound dumbbell. Slowly, with great effort, he forced his arm up and with his fingers touched his head, his heart and his shoulders. With that the voices were struck dumb.

In fear and trembling, he opened the door of the church and began his descent. From the back of the church, he saw a golden object standing on the center of the stone altar in the sanctuary. As he walked up the aisle toward it, he couldn't take his eyes off it. He could see a white disc with golden spikes radiating around it like rays from the sun. He got down on his knees and bowed his head.

He was in the presence of the Lord.

He knelt there for a few minutes then got up and knelt in the pew. He fixed his eyes on the golden object. He hadn't seen one of them in years.

What did they call it? It had a strange name.

He racked his brain.

'Monstrance, that was it. Probably from a Latin word. What did it mean? Monstrance. Demonstrate. To show. To show what? To show the Truth. That's it.'

He stared at the white Host inside of the disc.

'That is Jesus Christ, the Son of God, the second person of the Blessed Trinity. What a strange thing to believe: that God could be in a piece of bread. Strange as it was, though, it was true.'

He knew it now. He had never really believed before but now he did. He remembered what the priest had said on Sunday. He couldn't understand all of it. It was still a mystery but now it made more sense to him. Something happened. Something was communicated last Sunday at Mass. When he saw the priest raise that Host and say 'this is Jesus', in that instant, he believed. The theology behind it didn't matter. How it happened didn't matter. What mattered was that it was the Truth and the Truth was a Person, someone he could talk to.

Behind him, he heard the clatter of jackboots. A tall, bearded black man dressed in a tight black leather jumpsuit and a do-rag, with roller blades wrapped around his neck, stomped up towards the front of the altar. As he went past, Casey saw the man scowling, with sweat running down his face, looking like a man who had just fled the scene of a crime. He wondered where the bloody knife was. He could see the man grabbing the monstrance, tearing out the Host and spitting on it. Casey stood and saw himself throwing his body in front of the Lord to protect him but before he did, the man blessed himself, got down on his knees, took off his roller blades and placed them before the altar. He prostrated himself, his arms extended, in front of the Blessed Sacrament. He laid there as rigid as a man on a cross.

Relieved, Casey took a few deep breaths, shook his head and smiled. That was the last thing he expected to see.

It was time to confront the enemy.

He looked around him and he saw a scattering of people kneeling in the pews. Along the side walls, under the Stations of the Cross, he saw lines of people waiting for confession. He had to make up his mind. Who should he go to? He started toward the one which had the shortest line but then changed his mind and went to the one with the longest line. He wanted to rehearse what he was going to say to the priest.

He remembered the introduction, 'Bless me, father, for I have sinned. It's been eighteen years since my last confession.' But after that, he didn't know what to say. Where to begin? Everything blended together until it seemed as if it were all one big sin: No! He wished he could go in and say, 'Forgive me, father. I was nothing but a no good selfish creep.' And that would be it. But he knew he had to be more specific than that.

As he waited, he felt his anxiety level rise. He wished that he could pace instead of just standing there. He studied the other people in line. Most of them were women. They didn't look like real wrongdoers, not like he was. He wished that he could announce to them that he was the worst one there and ask them if he could go to the front of the line. He was that desperate. He had to get it over with. He looked over at the other line. There were only two people in that line and there were about seven in the one he was in. He had made a mistake. He should have gotten in the other line. He decided to quick shoot over there. He made his move before anyone else got the same idea and got behind a teenage boy, who was praying the rosary while he waited.

Casey was surprised. He didn't think teenagers today went to confession or prayed the rosary. He admired the kid's courage. When he was that age, he wouldn't have been caught dead doing that. But now, he wished he had prayed the rosary every day. If he had to do it all over again, he would have never left the Church. He would have never left home. He would have gone to confession every Saturday and to Mass every Sunday, every day if he could have.

An old man went into the confessional box and was out in just a few minutes, then the boy went in. Casey was next. He wiped his hands on his pants and took some deep breaths. He figured the boy would be out fast like the others, but he wasn't. He took a long time. Casey wondered what the boy could have done to be in there that long. He was just a kid. What sins could he have committed? But then he thought of his life and he wished that he had spent more time in the confessional. He had plenty to confess back then. Casey could hear the boy and the priest laughing. He couldn't believe it: laughter in the confessional box? Finally, the boy came out and smiled at Casey. The boy's face seemed so happy and innocent that Casey envied him. He wished he could have been like that when he was a boy.

As Casey opened the door, he saw a sign with 'Visiting Priest' on it, instead of a name. He went inside and closed the door. Through the screen, he could see he image of a face.

As he knelt down, he heard the priest say, "Welcome to this most wonderful sacrament. Thank you for coming."

Casey was tongue-tied. He hadn't expected to be thanked for coming.

"Uh, I, Uh, I, Uh. I don't. I don't know where to start, Father. It's been so long. Eighteen years. I just know I, I wanna come back to the Church."

Father Michael McDonald laughed. It made him so happy when people came back to the Church. He needed to be very gentle here.

"And what brought that about? May I ask?"

Casey hesitated. How could he explain? He would have to write a book to explain it all.

Finally, he blurted out, "It was my mother praying for me every day."

Father Mike laughed.

"Ah, that'll do it every time. I want to assure you: There is nothing to fear. The purpose of this sacrament is to take away guilt. God is very pleased with you. He loves you very much. God knows the sins you've committed and Jesus has already confessed them for you on the Cross. He is the one who forgives your sins, not me. I represent Jesus here in this sacrament. I give you absolution through the ministry of the Church which is the Body of Christ. I'm sure you remember the parable of the prodigal son. Surely, you remember the words of the Father: 'Now, we must celebrate and rejoice, because your brother was dead and has come to life again; he was lost and has been found.' This is a great day for you and for the Church. As Jesus says, There will be more joy in heaven over one sinner who repents than over ninety-nine righteous people who have no need of repentance.'"

Casey felt his eyes brimming with tears and flowing over. He let them run down his face. This was not what he expected. 'God was very pleased with him?'

'Thank you, Father," he squeaked.

"Since this is your first confession in a long time, you can make a general confession. I'll take you through the commandments.

Don't worry at this time about details. As time goes on, whenever something bothers you and you want to confess it specifically, then do it. I recommend that you go to confession frequently, at least once a month, weekly if possible. Saint Vincent de Paul, a saint, went to confession every day. Scripture tells us that the just man is his own accuser."

"Okay," Casey squeaked again.

He bowed his head and watched images of himself flashing before his eyes like mug shots from rogues' gallery: his face sneering and leering, a cigarette in his mouth, a beer in his hand, snarling and shouting, his eyes cold and full of hate, his mouth twisting with lies, ridiculing others, condemning and berating, his finger pointing, blaming others for his problems. He was repulsed by his ugliness. He saw every sin he ever committed. He felt like sin itself.

"Did you ever deny the existence of God? Or worship a false god, other than the God of Jesus Christ and the Catholic Church?"

Casey saw an image of himself shouting in a barroom, echoing Feuerbach, 'Only fools believe in God. There is no God. We invented Him. He's only a projection of ourselves.' Then nodding his head as he read Karl Marx, 'The opium of the people. That's all God is,' he heard himself saying, 'A construct of the ruling class, to keep poor people down, by putting their hope in the next life.' He remembered exulting with Nietzsche, 'God is dead! We killed him! Earth is all!' Then agreeing with Mary Daly, 'If the God is male then the male is God. Nine million women burned at the stake.' He saw himself sneering, 'God the Father is a male fantasy, a bloodthirsty war lover. A father who would send his own son to die so that fathers would then send their own sons to die in war.'

He said softly, "Yes. Both."

Father Mike thought about pursuing this further, but he knew that many people denied God and followed false gods: themselves, sex, money, fame, drugs, Satan. All of these were very common, always were.

"Did you ever use the name of God thoughtlessly, in cursing or blasphemy, or spoken irreverently about the Mother of God or the other saints?"

Casey's face flamed as he remembered the foul language he had so often used. He had even been proud of his ability to curse, to make up or repeat new phrases and combinations of curses as if it took a special talent to use such words.

"Yes. Many times."

"Now," said Father Mike, "During all these years, did you go to church at all?"

Casey shook his head.

"No, Father. As I understand it now, it was a gradual process. It started when I was a little boy." He told the priest the sins he had committed as a boy and about the insight he just had about what had happened after the car accident.

"They were all like thin threads wrapping around me, paralyzing me. I first started skipping Mass when I was in high school. I went to church off and on in college. Then I went in the army. The only time I went to Mass in the army was when I was in basic training and I only went then because it was an opportunity of get out of the barracks and away from the drill sergeant. After that, I might of went a couple times but I wasn't into it. I didn't even go the whole time I was in Vietnam. The only time I went after that was a few years later when I went to confession and communion for my father's funeral in 1974 but I haven't gone since then. But today, when I was on my way here, I saw what happened when I was a boy."

He described what happened after the car accident.

"Who is this 'other self?" This 'imposter?"

Father Mike shrugged.

"It may be just your own sinful nature. Or it may be just what some theologians call the Law of Desire. A law within us that drives us to do the opposite of what we truly want to do. Paul mentions it in Romans. 'For I do not do the good I want, but I do the evil I do not want.'"

"Could it be the devil?"

Father Mike sighed.

"Perhaps. We don't want to make the mistake of seeing the devil in everything. That's as bad as those who deny that he exists. But you could probably call what happened to you satanic bondage. I'm no authority on Satan although I certainly believe that he exists. The devil's existence is one of the truths of our faith. Pope Paul VI wrote one time, 'that one of our greatest needs is defense from that evil which is called the Devil.'"

Casey shook his head.

"I can believe that there is a devil. But bondage? You mean I was possessed by the devil? I never thought I was possessed. I remember that movie **The Exorcist** and I was never anything like that."

Father Mike shook his head.

"No, I wouldn't say possessed. True possession is rare and can only be healed by exorcism. But there are degrees of bondage which over time can dominate a person's life. The devil gets a foothold in our lives through our weaknesses, in our imagination, in lust, in utopian logic and in disordered relations with other people. From what you told me it seems as if he got a hold on you through your sexual fantasies and then he tempted you after that accident in your strength which was your mother's love for you and your love for her. Once he undermined that, he had you firmly in his grip."

"Will he ever go away completely?"

Father Mike smiled.

"As you progress in the spiritual life and go further into the interior castle where God lives within you, this 'other self' will no longer have power over you. As Saint Paul said, 'For he, Jesus Christ, is our peace, he who made both one and broke down the dividing wall of enmity, so that he might create in himself one new person in place of the two, thus establishing peace.'"

Casey was happy to hear that. But there was one more incident that he had to talk about. He realized how he still had deeply rooted resentment and anger about it.

"I also stopped going to church because of something that happened to me in high school."

He told the story of how a priest had slapped him around.

"He should have been stopped," said Father Mike. "He probably had some psychiatric disorder. They must of known he was acting like that."

"He wasn't the only one," said Casey. "Most of the guys I know got paddled. I only got paddled once and that was when the whole class got it. But that wasn't as bad as getting smacked in the face. And unjustly. That's what angered me the most. I'm not blaming a priest for me leaving the Church but it didn't help. I know that they had to do something to keep us in line, otherwise, we'd have ruled the school not them, but they should have done it differently. I know that there are other guys who resent what was done to them and I would bet it affects their attitude towards the Church today."

"I'm sorry that happened," said Father Mike. "It shouldn't have. It's true that years ago, we used corporal punishment in our schools but it's wrong to hit children. It's more important to show children love than to control them by fear, because when you rule by fear, they may be behaving but inside are seething with hatred. But when they know you love them, they feel safe. We, too, need God's forgiveness. We ask for it every day at Mass. Remember: You must also forgive, to be forgiven. There is no doubt that there are many people who feel betrayed by people in the Church. It's the weeds and wheat. It's not the Church itself. The Church is holy. It is holy because it is the body of Christ, the people of God. You must remember that the Church spread throughout the world because of the way the Christian people loved each other. The prohibition against divorce helped protect women from being abandoned by their husbands, which was done routinely. Also, the Church was instrumental in stopping the practice of exposing babies, usually girls, who weren't wanted. The Church was responsible for the establishment of poor houses, orphanages and hospitals and universities. Despite all the wrongs and sins that have been committed by people in the Church, and there have been many, the Church has always provided the people with the means of sanctification, with the Word and with the Sacraments. You must forgive them for your own good. We have all sinned. We need to forgive each other."

Casey agreed.

"It's good that I came here today. In addition to getting a lot off my chest, I'm finding out how wrong I've been about a lot of things."

Father Mike smiled.

"How wonderful God is. What grace God has given you, to bring you to this sacrament. How much He wants you for His own. God showed us at Calvary how much He loves us. Even though we put Him to death, He will still redeem us. Despite ourselves."

Casey rubbed his face with his hands as if he were wiping off makeup. Despite himself, Casey laughed.

"I went to church last Sunday," said Casey, smiling. "Fighting it all the way. I don't know what happened at Mass but when I saw the priest raise the Host, it was as if a light beam came from it and went into me and I knew, knew, that it was Jesus Christ, himself."

'That happens more often than you know." said Father Mike. "Jesus Christ is truly present in the Eucharist: Body and Blood, Soul and Divinity. Most of us know this by faith and by trust in the teaching of the Church, handed down to us from the Apostles, but others, like yourself are blessed by God and experience the Divine Presence. One famous example is that of Andre Frossard, a Communist and an atheist. He happened to go into a chapel where there was exposition of the Blessed Sacrament. He had no idea of what he was looking at, when suddenly, he was overwhelmed by the presence of the supernatural. He left that chapel a Catholic. It was so unexpected that he said that it was as if he had gone to the zoo and come out a giraffe."

Casey laughed. If someone had told him that he would be going back to the Church, he would have said: 'Yeah, sure. And I'm going to be a child again, too.'

"I don't understand, Father," said Casey. "Why would God do that? Why would He come to me in that way? Why not to people who are good?'

"God's ways are not our ways." said Father Mike. "God loves sinners as much as He does the faithful. It's not because of anything you did. None of us deserve to be saved. It's not because you deserved it because you don't. Saint Paul says 'Where sin increased, grace abounded all the more.' Does this mean that we should sin so we could get more grace? No, of course not. It is better not to have sinned at all. We need the saints to pray for our sinners, so that God will send us His grace. You said yourself it was your mother praying for you that brought you here."

Casey nodded.

"I remember once years ago, when I considered myself an atheist, I told someone it had to be my mother praying for me that got me through Vietnam because I was the kind of soldier who should have died there: I was such a lousy soldier, inattentive and incompetent. I was amazed myself when I said that. Did I really believe that? I guess I did."

"What about your parents?" continued Father Mike. "Have you been good to them?"

Casey sighed.

"Not really, I'm sorry to say. I know I caused them a lot of problems, especially when I was a teenager. But I'm doing better. I'm looking after my mom now. My father's dead. When he was sick, he asked me to be there for him, but I took off and went to Europe, instead. I came back before he died and we reconciled, but I regret not doing more for him. I'm truly sorry about that."

"It's good that you're helping out your Mom," said Father Mike. "We have an obligation to our parents, especially when they're old. People don't seem to realize that this is a commandment of God. And this refers to all parents, not just good ones. Even if they were bad parents, we need to show them respect."

"Yes, Father," said Casey. "But I had good parents. I went to Catholic schools and yet, I still went wrong. How did that happen?"

"Original sin," said Father Mike. "G.K. Chesterton once said that original sin was the most obvious truth that the Church teaches. All you have to do is read the paper and see that there is something fundamentally wrong with the human race. Some believe that the first sin was the lie: If we disobey God's commandments, we shall not die. But we will. Our spirit will die and we will be wanderers upon the earth. It stems from the fact that we are born free and are able to choose. Do we believe in God or ourselves? Our first parents chose themselves and so it is in our nature to choose ourselves first."

Casey nodded when he heard that. Babies and young children are so selfish. When they want something, they want it: now. And their favorite word is No!

"Baptism purifies us," continued Father Mike. 'The soul is changed from sin unto grace. But we are still weak. That's why we need the other sacraments to strengthen us especially the sacrament of reconciliation. It also changes us from sin unto grace. The more we avail ourselves of them, the stronger we become. So even if you are brought up in a good family and taught the faith, if you allow yourself to fall into repeated sins and do not properly confess and repent of them, you can fall. And when you fall from grace in the Catholic Church, you fall hard. So much has been given to you, so much is taken away."

As he listened to the priest, Casey saw how it happened. For the first time, he understood what had happened to him. Finally, his life was beginning to make sense.

"Now," said Father Mike, "I have to ask you: Have you ever committed violence against yourself or against others, in word or in action?"

Casey closed his eyes and confessed as best he could of the fights he had been in and the violent thoughts he had against so many people, all of the mean and nasty things he said, including the times he made racist remarks. He knew now that it was only the grace of God which prevented him from being a murderer. He remembered all the times he had driven his car, drunk and high on pot. He could have killed people with his car. He asked for forgiveness for those actions.

"And I also did violence to myself by getting drunk all those times and doing drugs, marijuana mostly. I just stopped smoking a few months ago. Believe me, that stuff is not benign like some people say. It distorts your mind. They don't call it the devil's weed for nothing. It affects the thought patterns of your mind so you can't think with your reason. I don't think you can really be a Christian if you're smoking marijuana. I'm sorry I ever smoked it. I wish I never did."

"Did you ever participate in an abortion?"

Casey felt tears come into his eyes.

"Yes. I got a woman pregnant and she had an abortion. She did it without asking me. I didn't even know she was pregnant until afterwards. But I was also responsible. I shouldn't have had sex with her. We weren't married. We didn't love each other. She hurt me. I hurt her. I even hit here a couple times. I don't want to do anything like that again. I'm ashamed of myself."

Father Mike sighed.

"You poor man. What you did was wrong. No question. But what she did was worse. It was your baby too. You were the father and she totally disrespected you and the baby. She had it sucked from her womb like it was a piece of garbage."

There was a moment of silence.

"So, obviously," said Father Mike when Casey finished his sorry story, "You have sinned against chastity?"

"Yes," he said, "many times. All my life, in every way, except homosexual. I never did any of that."

As Father Mike went through the rest of the commandments, all he could do was say, yes, to every question. He had lied. He had cheated. He had coveted. He had done it all. He had broken all the commandments: each and every one, in one way or another.

Finally, it was over.

When he was finished, Father Mike said, "For your penance, say ten Hail Mary's and ten Our Father's. Now, say a good Act of Contrition."

He heard the penance but couldn't believe it.

'Ten Hail Mary's and ten Our Father's?' he thought. 'That's all?'

He felt like he should be in sackcloth and ashes. He tried to remember the form he had used as a boy, but couldn't.

"How do I say it?" said Casey. "I'm sorry. God, please forgive me. I don't want to do those things anymore, commit those sins."

"That's a good act of contrition," said Father Mike. "But let me take you through the one I like to use. Say it along with me. 'Oh, my God, I am heartily sorry for having offended you and I detest all my sins because I dread the loss of heaven and the pains of hell but most of all because they offend you my God who is all good and deserving of all my love. I firmly resolve with the help of your grace to avoid the near occasions of sin and to sin no more.'"

After they were finished, there was a moment of silence.

Casey closed his eyes and waited for absolution.

Father Mike raised his hand over Casey's head and said, "God, the Father of mercies, through the death and resurrection of his Son has reconciled the world to himself and sent The Holy Spirit among us for the forgiveness of sins; through the ministry of the Church may God give you pardon and peace, and I absolve you from your sins in the name of the Father, and of the Son, and of The Holy Spirit. Amen."

As Casey made the sign of the cross, he felt like a load had been lifted from his shoulders. He felt years younger.

"Remember, now," said Father Mike. "All of your sins have been forgiven. All of them. The prophet Isaiah tells us, 'Though your sins be like scarlet, they may become white as snow.' Now, your soul is as white as it was the day you were baptized. God bless you. Welcome home."

"Yes," said Casey, "Yes, thank you, Father, yes. What do I do now? I want to be a good person from now on."

"It's not that difficult to be a good person," said Father Mike. "Many people are good because they have been blessed with a pleasant, easy going disposition. Others are too timid to do anything wrong; they are afraid of getting into trouble. We are called not only to be good but to be holy. 'Be holy as I am holy.' We are all called to be saints. There are more saints than most people realize. The Book of Revelation tells us they are a great multitude which no one could count, from every nation, race, people and tongue."

Casey almost laughed out loud at the idea that we are all called to be saints. How could he ever be a saint? How far fetched was that? He wasn't ready to buy all of this.

He felt his other self creeping back up inside of him.

"How about the Popes?" he sneered. "They were as corrupt as could be, even had children. I thought that the Pope was supposed to be infallible."

Father Mike sighed.

"Being sinful has nothing to do with infallibility. When we say that the Pope is infallible, we mean that when he speaks on matters of faith and morals in the name of the Church, he is prevented by the Holy Spirit from teaching anything contrary to the deposit of faith. In other words, the Pope could never come out and say that adultery is permissible or that we do not have to believe in the dogma of the Trinity. Infallibility has nothing to do with the Pope's personal conduct. And despite the fact that there have been corrupt and immoral Popes, not one of them ever said that it was permissible to be that way. And over the history of the Church, the vast majority of Popes have been moral men."

As the priest was speaking, Casey made the sign of the cross and he felt his other self recede into the darkness. He had just received absolution and he was still in the confessional and he was already under temptation. He told the priest about it.

Father Mike nodded.

"We have to be constantly on guard. Saint Peter tells us in his first letter, "Stay sober and alert. Your opponent the devil is prowling like a roaring lion looking for someone to devour, Resist him, solid in your faith.' We do that, first, by keeping the commandments and we can only do that with the grace of God. We have to recognize that. We can't do it on our own. Prayer has to be our first priority in life. We need to humble ourselves before God. And we must give of ourselves. Think of others first. If we do these things, God will give us the grace that we need."

"I'll try," said Casey. "But I don't know if I know how to pray."

"The Mass is the most powerful prayer," said Father Mike. "Make sure you go every Sunday, more often if possible. I know there are people who say that you don't have to go to church to pray. That God is everywhere. That you can pray by the ocean or in the woods, and while certainly this is true, God is present in a special way in church, in the Blessed Sacrament, and in the community. God wants us to pray together. The rosary is also a special form of prayer. Try to say it every day."

"I'll try, Father," said Casey. "But I don't understand how it works. I mean, how does God hear what I say, when I pray? I know that they say God is omniscient, that He knows everything. But how?"

Father Mike smiled.

"We cannot totally understand God. If we could, He wouldn't be God. Much of the life of God is shrouded in mystery and we are in darkness. Aquinas teaches us that we can know more about what God is not than what He is. But in Christ we see a great light. Jesus tells us 'If anyone loves me, he will keep my word, and my Father will love him, and we will come to him and make our abode with him.' When we live the Christian life, God dwells within us; we call it being in the state of grace, and so when we pray, it is easy for Him to hear our prayer. That is why the saints are often able to do great works; they are filled with the presence of God."

Casey thought of the healings he had done at Seaside House.

"But is it possible for people who are not in the state of grace to do good things?"

"It would seem not to be so," said Father Mike. "For without the Spirit we can do nothing. But Saint Augustine teaches us that 'God's mercy and graces goes before us so that we may be healed and follows us so that once healed, we may be given life.' Many nonbelievers do good works. There are good Buddhists and good Moslems and Hindus. They are hidden saints. People who take care of their families, who take care of the poor and the sick. They are doing God's will. I'll even grant you that some of the things that Socialists, Communists have done are good. But they take credit for it themselves, instead of attributing it to the grace of God, working within them."

Casey agreed with that. When he was down in Nicaragua with the Sandinistas, he had met many people who were Communists who truly cared about the poor, who were against war. People from every country, from all walks of life came to Nicaragua to cut coffee, to give a helping hand.

"But we also have to remember that Communism has two faces," said Father Mike.

Casey nodded. He remembered when he was in Nicaragua with IFCO, a Christian organization, they met with Tomas Borge, the top cop of the Sandinistas. He talked with them in his office the walls of which were covered with crucifixes. He found out later that when Borge met with Communist groups he met them in another office, the walls of which were covered with pictures of Lenin, Che Guevara and Castro.

"We can't forget the Gulag," said Father Mike. "And the millions of people murdered by the Communists in the Soviet Union and China and the vast number of human rights abuses in all the other Communist countries: the tortures, the persecutions, the unjust imprisonments."

As he heard that, Casey felt his face flush with shame.

It was true. He had put all that out of his mind. It was as if he had been brainwashed. Hitler is always portrayed as being the epitome of evil and yet Stalin and Mao were responsible for millions of more deaths than Hitler was.

Casey was silent for a few moments, shaking inside as he thought of how lost he had been. He had been on the verge of becoming a communist himself.

"God is present in all people and things," said Father Mike. "Even in Stalin and Satan and in hell itself. If he wasn't, they wouldn't exist. God holds all things in existence."

"One more question, Father," said Casey. "You mentioned the rosary. How does it work? Could a mother praying the rosary for her son who was in danger, prevent him from doing something that was wrong, that would get him in trouble if did it? And if so, how?"

Father Mike smiled.

"Of course, the rosary has saved many people's lives. We usually see the Rosary as a vocal and a meditative prayer: something that we do, which it is. As we pray, we meditate on the mysteries and we enter into them as Mary did and Jesus comes into our very being as He did with Mary at the Incarnation. 'Hail Mary, full of grace, the Lord is with you.' Because the rosary is also a contemplative prayer: something that God does, He infuses his presence into us. We have no control over this. We can't make it happen. It is a free gift from God that he gives to those who love Him and keep His word. And I would venture to say that your mother is a friend of God and His Holy Mother. So when praying the rosary, your mother would have been infused with the presence of Jesus just as Mary was. They would hear her prayer and go to the person that your mother was praying for: you."

"How?" asked Casey.

"It wouldn't be in any dramatic way, necessarily," answered Father Mike. "Although sometimes it is. But usually in the person's thoughts or imagination. Saint Joan of Arc said that the voices she heard were in her imagination."

Casey needed time to take all of this in. It was too much for him now.

"Thank you, Father," he said and left the confessional box. He went into the nearest pew and knelt down. He looked up into the sanctuary and saw that the man was still prostrate before the Blessed Sacrament. He didn't look like he had moved at all. Casey wished that he had the courage to do that. Suddenly, the man rose to his feet, made the sign of the cross, picked up his roller blades and got in the line for confession.

Casey began saying his penance, but it had been so long since he had said the Our Father and the Hail Mary that he could only remember fragments, but finally, after a few attempts, he got the words right. When he was finished, he decided that he had to do more penance than that. Tomorrow was Ash Wednesday, the beginning of Lent. He decided that he would go to Mass tomorrow and then every day for Lent. He was working evenings, so his mornings were free. He promised the Lord that he would do it and this time he would keep it.

He sat down, bowed his head and closed his eyes, holding his hands on his lap. He took a few deep breaths, trying to clear his mind. As he did so, he felt his arms raise and his hands open as if he were about to do therapeutic touch with a sick child. He could almost feel Andrea and Neil on his lap. No, not Andrea, just Neil. He had to tell the truth, now.

"So, it was you," he whispered, "who healed those children. It wasn't energy. It was you."

He could hear a tiny whisper in his mind's ear.

"Yes."

With that, Casey opened his eyes. He was beginning to see clearly now. When he got home, he would call Father Gal again and set up an appointment to see him and the priest who was reading his books. Then he decided to stay for a while and pray.

9.

Effigies in Ashes

Casey got off the bus and looked at his watch. It was high noon. He sprinted towards the church. Mass was to begin in a few minutes and he didn't want to be late. He extended his legs like a hurdler and took the large stone steps two at a time. He stopped for a moment at the door to catch his breath and then entered the church. He was surprised. There was a good crowd.

He paused for a few moments, awed by the beauty of the church: the stained glass windows with pictures of the saints, the statues, the intricate detailed patterns and symbols that adorned the walls and arches of the nave. High above in the apse was a painting of a woman seated on a throne: Mary, Mother of the Church, looking like a queen. Hail, Holy Queen.

He looked towards the altar to see if Mass had begun. The candles were lit but there was no one in the sanctuary. He breathed a sigh of relief. He didn't want to be late for his first Holy Communion in eighteen years. As he walked up the center aisle, he saw a golden tabernacle behind the altar with a large candle burning before it.

He was in the presence of the Lord.

He went up to the first pew, genuflected, bowed his head and made the Sign of the Cross.

As he knelt in the pew, he noticed three large paintings on the walls of the sanctuary behind the tabernacle: a nativity scene; one of a young girl kneeling, with an angel behind her; and, one of a woman in the sky, standing on a globe, surrounded by angels. On his left, above a side altar, he saw a large picture of Christ crucified; cater-cornered to it, another picture of Christ being lowered from the cross into the arms of his mother.

He took out a pair of rosary beads and a little booklet that his mother had given him. He looked at the instructions. Wednesday: the Glorious Mysteries. But today was Ash Wednesday. It seemed more appropriate to pray the Sorrowful Mysteries. But then again, he didn't feel sorrowful. He had never felt so happy in his life. He felt like praying the Joyful Mysteries. Then he had a happy thought. He would pray the entire rosary, all fifteen decades. Out of the corner of his eye, he saw a vision of beauty. In an alcove to his right, above an altar, there was a statue of the Blessed Mother standing on a globe with her arms extended down and her palms open. As he looked at the statue, he had the feeling that he had seen that image before, somewhere.

A bell rang.

He saw several priests come out and process towards the altar. He put the booklet and the rosary back in his pocket. He would pray it later.

He stood with the rest of the congregation and made the Sign of the Cross.

He studied the priest as he welcomed everyone to the Holy Sacrifice of the Mass and to the great season of Lent. He was tall and stooped with a shock of white hair, combed straight back, his face as creased and gray as an old map of Ireland.

'So that's Father Mike McDonald,' thought Casey.

He had talked with Father the night before and Father had told him he would be saying Mass this afternoon. It was weird. The priest's voice had sounded so familiar.

Father opened his arms and prayed: "Father in heaven, the light of your truth bestows sight to the darkness of sinful eyes. May this season of repentance bring us the blessing of your forgiveness and the gift of your light. Grant this through Christ Our Lord. Amen."

"Amen," said Casey as he sat for the readings. He was struck by the relevance of the prayer to his own life, thinking of the insight he had received the day before of what had happened after that car accident.

He listened to the readings and to the Gospel with special attention. After hearing them, he promised God again that he would go to Mass every day during Lent and to fast and to do penance in every way he could.

After the Gospel, Father Mike began his homily.

"My dear brothers and sisters in Christ. As you know, today is Ash Wednesday, the beginning of the great season of Lent. The Church gives us this season as an opportunity - as the prophet Joel tells us - to return to God with our whole heart, with fasting, and weeping, and mourning. We do not like to fast and to weep and to mourn. They are not pleasant things to do, not pleasant but necessary and they are necessary because we have sinned. All of us. Everyone except me, of course, because everyone knows that I am practically a saint."

Casey laughed along with the others.

"It is good to laugh during Lent, along with our fasting and weeping and mourning. For we must always keep in mind what Lent is preparing us for: Easter, a time of rejoicing, a time of celebration. But in order to arrive at this time of celebration, we must do what Our Lord did. We must be put to the test. We must go out into the desert for forty days and there we must decide which side we are on: God's or Satan's. Are we moving away from God or towards Him? We must stand up and be counted! Remember the words of Our Lord: 'He who is not with me is against me.'

I know that some of you are thinking: Go out into the desert? What does he mean by that? In Biblical terms, it means a deserted place, a wilderness, a reminder of danger, hardship, and death, a haunt of demons and wild animals. In our world today, it means: There is no God; there is no right or wrong; it is all relative; truth is what we make it. It means people getting drunk and taking drugs because they have lost who they are and have no faith, no hope; it means people picking up guns and settling disputes with violence; it means children dying young, being killed in the womb even before they are born; it means the elderly being left isolated and alone, tormented by predators who want what little they have; it means families breaking up; it means children having sex with adults, men having sex with men, women with women.

This is the desert that we are living in today. It is there where God comes to meet us. It is there where we are put to the test.

In order to pass this test, we must be strong. We must be able to say what Jesus did: 'Bygone, Satan! For it is written, you shall worship the Lord your God and Him only shall you serve.'

How do we do we become strong?

By fasting. By not allowing ourselves to be attached to the things of this world, whether they be food, or possessions, or how we spend our time. By weeping, in sorrow, for the times we have offended God by our sins. By mourning, not only for the ones that have gone before us, but for ourselves and for our neighbor, for the times when we have been lost in the desert and away from God.

The prophet tells us that we must do these things with our whole heart. What does he mean by this: our whole heart? In Hebrew, in Semitic thought, it signifies the entire interior life of a person. It signifies the essence of a person as he actually is.

This raises the question: Who am I, really? I think I can safely say that all of us have asked ourselves that question. Saint Paul tells us in his letter to the Romans, 'I do not understand my own actions. For I do not do what I want, but I do the very thing I hate.' We think we know who we are but then we do something or say something that surprises us, that causes us to question: Was that me who did that? Was that the true me? Or a false image of myself, an effigy, if you will. If this be the case, then, how do we know who we truly are? How do we turn to God with our whole hearts?

We do this by uniting our hearts with the Immaculate Heart of Mary and do as she did and let God be born within us. 'Hail Mary, full of grace, the Lord is with thee.' Let our heart beat as one with His Sacred Heart: the heart of Jesus, the true God and true man.

He is who we all should be.

Then, once our hearts are united with His, what must we do?

First, we must do as Jesus did: We must confront Satan and reject him as Jesus did in the desert. We do this first of all at our baptism when we reject sin and Satan, the father of evil and the prince of darkness. But because we are still weak, we must meet with Jesus in the Sacrament of Reconciliation and together with him confront the enemy and reject him again and again, whenever we sin.

Then, when we are worthy, we eat the Body and Blood of Our Lord Jesus Christ in Holy Communion and thus become one with Him again. We must do this as frequently as we can, at least once a week on Sunday, but more often if possible.

Shortly, you will be receiving on your foreheads the Sign of the Cross in ashes and you will be hearing the words: 'Repent and believe in the Gospel.' These are among the first words spoken by Jesus in the Gospel of Mark.

To repent means to ask for forgiveness, to change our hearts. To believe in the Gospel means believing in the Good News: that God is with us, that we are not alone, that we are not orphans, lost in the cosmos, just dust blowing in the desert. The Good News is that, if we repent, our sins have been forgiven, that we can cast off the false images of ourselves and become new men, new women, in Christ.

When we do this, these false images, or effigies of ourselves, are cast off and are then burned in the fire, the fire of love or the fire of loss, and it is the ashes of these effigies that we receive today on our foreheads as a reminder, as a symbol, of what we once were, but are no longer.

And so my dear brothers and sisters in Christ, let us begin this great season of Lent by turning to God with our whole hearts with fasting and weeping and mourning so that we can enter into Our Father's House, the Kingdom of Heaven, and become who we truly are: sons and daughters of God.

God bless you."

As Casey watched the priests prepare the ashes, he meditated on the homily, especially on the words: Our Father's House.

'So this is the third house,' he thought. 'I knew that there had to be a third house. I went from Ranchhouse to Seaside House and now I'm in Our Father's House. That does it. I have come home.' But then came the thought: 'but not yet. Not all the way. That only comes with death.'

Casey got in line with the rest of the people and received his effigies in ashes on his forehead. The ashes would be a sign to everyone of who he was: a son of God, a Christian, a Catholic, a

Roman Catholic. As he knelt, he touched the ashes with his finger and looked into them as if into a mirror, darkly. He saw in it all the false images of himself. They were dead and gone. Finally, he was who he was supposed to be.

During the consecration of the bread and wine, he was overcome by feelings of gratitude for the Church for continuing on, for keeping the faith. All the years he had been away, it had been doing this over and over again, as they had done for centuries, for almost two thousand years.

Suddenly, he saw Jesus on the mountain, feeding the people: 'Take and eat. This is my body."

Casey felt overwhelmed. His head was reeling.

'It's the multiplication of the loaves. Every day for two thousand years, in all the churches, all over the world; sometimes, several times a day. That's what was happening here. How many times has this been done? How many people have been fed? It's astronomical. All life is gift.'

"Lord, I am not worthy to receive you," said Casey, his face flushing as he remembered saying that the Mass was a perversion, that it was cannibalism. What a foolish and ignorant person he had been.

"But only say the word and I shall be healed."

As Casey said these words, a feeling of well-being flowed through him and he realized he had been healed. He was not sick anymore.

When it was time for Communion, Casey stood in front of Father McDonald, cupped his hand into a cradle and took the Body of Christ into his mouth, and into his heart and soul. As he chewed the Bread of Life, he felt faint for a moment and envisioned himself falling onto the floor, blinded by the light that was flowing around him, and for the first time, he understood what had happened to Paul on the road to Damascus.

He knelt in his pew, thanking God for creating him, for bringing him into being, for saving him from danger and death, but most of all, for bringing him back into His Church and into communion with the Father and the Son and the Holy Spirit. When Mass was over, he stayed in the pew, praying.

Epilogue

Epilogue

When he finished his prayers, Casey genuflected in front of the tabernacle and walked over in front of a side altar. There it was right in front of his eyes: the key he had been looking for. He stood for a moment in front of the large painting of Christ crucified and vowed never to forget what Jesus had done. The creator of the world had come to suffer and die with us so that we might live. 'Must Christ die every day to save those with no imagination.' The meaning of that statement continued to elude him. He wished that he knew where it came from. A Protestant? He remembered that some of them believed that the Catholic Church taught that Christ died every day at Mass. Not true. Christ died only once, not every day. Why those with no imagination? As he looked at the painting, he heard Jesus say, "Father, forgive them for they know not what they do." His killers had no imagination. They could not imagine that Jesus was God. Then he remembered what the priest had said in his homily on Sunday: that every time we receive communion we become Christ and that Christ is united with every person, no matter who they are. So that every time we kill another person we kill Christ? We are made in the image and likeness of God. As persons. Is that what it means? Casey took a deep breath. Father forgive us for we know not who we are. He opened the door and went into the sacristy. He knew that Father McDonald would be waiting for him. He saw the priest standing in the middle of the room.

He went over and introduced himself.

"Ah, so you're Bill Casey," said Father Mike. "You don't look anything like James O'Rourke."

Casey smiled as he stroked his clean-shaven face.

"He's not me. He's an effigy of me."

Father McDonald laughed and motioned towards some chairs by the window.

"Let's sit and talk for a few minutes."

Casey nodded and sat beside the priest.

"I don't have too much time, Father, I have to be at work at 3 o'clock."

"Do you still work as a nurse?" asked Father Mike. "I see you're wearing whites."

Casey nodded.

"Yes. At Children's Heart Hospital. I work four days a week, so I have some time to write. It's the same work I did at Seaside House. It's the same kind of kids. I've been there eight years now."

"God bless you," said Father Mike. "You seemed so angry at hospitals in your book that I thought maybe you weren't working in one, anymore."

Casey nodded.

"I said some things that I shouldn't have. Seaside House and 'The Holy' do a good job for the most part. So does MHP. And most of the doctors and nurses really care about the children. More that I do if you want to know the truth."

"Do you still think we need National Health Care in this country?"

Casey shrugged.

"I don't know. We need some way to control the costs so that everyone gets good care. But I really don't know how that can be done."

Father Mike nodded.

"I'm not sure either. But I don't think we want the government controlling health care. Then they would be able to decide who lives and who dies. It would open the door to euthanasia. It seems to me that the best way to go is to allow the people to decide what type of insurance they want and how much money they want to pay for it. And let there be more care done at home."

Casey agreed.

"I did home care for a while. As long as the insurance will pay for quality home care, that's the way to go. People are better off out of the hospital. But I missed being with the nurses and I missed the children. Taking care of them is what I do best. That's what I was called to do."

Father Mike smiled.

"I've always believed that nursing was a vocation. What made you decide to become a nurse?"

Casey smiled.

"It was that woman: the Blessed Mother. Though I didn't know it was her at the time. When I was finishing **The Circle of Stones**, I didn't know where to go from there. I knew I'd never be able to make a living on my writing and I needed to do something. Then I heard that voice saying to me that I should become a nurse. My first response was: 'What? A nurse? Me?' I wasn't a caring type of person. I didn't know anything about what nurses did and it's a good thing I didn't because if I had, I don't know if I would have done it. I didn't like hospitals, being around sick people. I was in the hospital only once in my life when I had my tonsils out when I was a boy. I was in the Emergency Room a couple of times but I wasn't admitted. But since I believed it was that woman again, the one I had talked with in Ireland, and she had given me the right advice there, I decided to do what she asked. I went to nursing school at MHP on the GI Bill. Thank God, I got an honorable discharge. I wouldn't have been able to do it otherwise. Becoming a nurse changed my life for the better. ."

Father Mike smiled.

"You've become a caring type of person. Do you still do those things that you describe in your book **The Story of a Swallow**? therapeutic touch?"

Casey put his head down and shook it.

"No. I lost....faith in it. I couldn't believe it was me who was doing those things. Who was I to think I could heal anyone? And if it wasn't me, then who was it? Energy? That seemed absurd to me."

"All healings come from the Lord," said Father Mike. "All life, all health comes from God."

Casey nodded.

"Yes. That makes more sense than believing that mindless energy did it."

Father Mike smiled.

"So it's true? Those children were healed?"

Casey nodded.

"Yes. I took care of the boy with seizures and it happened just as I described it but the girl Andrea was actually a boy named Willie. He was taken care of by a friend of mine: Danny Stein. He was a nurse over at 'The Holy,' and he came over one night to see Joanne Ruth, one of the nurses at Seaside House. She was Willie's nurse. Danny did therapeutic touch on him, out of the goodness of his heart, for no other reason. Willie started tracking the next morning and by the time he went home he was eating by mouth and was trying to talk. I don't know how he is now. That's why O'Rourke didn't want anyone to know about it and wouldn't take credit for it. When I wrote the story I didn't want to complicate it by bringing in Danny and Joanne and to be honest, I figured people who read it would think that I was O'Rourke and it would make me look good. I don't think either Danny or I really knew what we were doing."

Father Mike smiled.

"You didn't know it but both of you were working for a Jewish doctor by the name of Jesus Christ."

When they stopped laughing, Casey said, "But you know, some children did get better in other ways: with medicine and surgery and good care. Though many of them don't get better. They just suffer and suffer. It's so sad."

Father Mike put his hands together as if he were praying.

"When Jesus walked the earth among us, he didn't heal all the sick. Why he didn't is a mystery. Something that is difficult for us to understand. Miracles are a sign of the kingdom, of what is to come. 'The sufferings of this time are as nothing compared with the glory to be revealed for us.' But Jesus suffered with us, so that our suffering would have meaning. It is not a waste. 'They complete what is lacking in the sufferings of Christ for the sake of His Church.' Those children are suffering souls. They are innocent. They are like Jesus. They help to save the rest of us. In fact, Jesus tells us that they are Him. He says in the Gospel, 'I was sick and you visited me.'"

"Well, then, I guess I'd better be good to those children."

Father Mike smiled.

"I'm sure you will. You certainly seemed to care about those children in Seaside House. I found the story very moving. I have to admit I was in tears over the death of that boy Billie. Was that based on a true story?"

Casey nodded.

'The whole story is true, essentially. But Billie's death is a composite as is the whole **Story of a Swallow.** It's not the depiction of an actual night. It's not like I came home one morning and sat down and wrote about it. But while we're on the subject of death, I have a few questions for you that you probably can't answer. What's it all about?"

Father Mike smiled.

"'In God's good time' as Dilsey the black woman cook in Faulkner's **The Sound and the Fury** said. All questions will be answered. She's the most humane character in that tormented world of Yoknapatawpha county. The Queen of the South. She's good to Benjy, the 'idiot' of the story . She takes him to church on Easter Sunday when his own family won't. She keeps the family together in very difficult times. As you know, the South in those years was not a safe place for the blacks; their condition was not much better than it was during slavery. As I'm sure you know, the narrative is broken and told out of sequence because it reflects a sinful, fallen world, the South after the Civil War. But once you realize that the book is structured around the Tridium and it is not 'a tale told by an idiot, full of sound and fury, signifying nothing.' It does signify something: that through all the noise and confusion and sinfulness, there is the decency and kindness of the mother, symbolized by Dilsey, who restores us, protects us and intercedes for us. Catholics see this mother, the valiant woman, as Mary and the Church. Faulkner, being brought up as a Protestant, could not see that, of course. The Protestants are blind about the Mother of God. It's because she's so connected to the Church. She's the Mother of the Church. Faulkner was conflicted about Christianity and that's understandable when you consider the state of Christianity in the

South at that time. They were more like Old Testament Jews that Christians, selective Old Testament, of course, with slavery and an eye for an eye and a tooth for a tooth but no Exodus and no Let My People Go. They had Jehovah, the Lord of Armies morphed with a bearded Confederate Colonel on a high horse, its hoofs pawing the air like a bear and then roaring off in a cloud of dust to fight the blue devils of the North. Faulkner was more of a philosophical Christian. He believed in the Beatitudes, blessed are the poor, for they are his most humane characters. He was good to children but he rarely went to church and he was a drunk and an adulterer and a habitué of brothels. "

Casey put out his hand and touched Father Mike on the arm.

'Excuse me but what's the Tridium?"

Father Mike smiled.

"I'm sorry. I tend to digress. But I'm not totally off point here. The Tridium is the three days of the Death and Resurrection of the Son of God. And we were talking about the dying process, weren't we?"

Casey nodded.

"Yes. What's it all about?"

Father Mike smiled.

"A few years ago, I read an outstanding little book by the philosopher Josef Pieper entitled **Death and Immortality** which I found helpful. As you know, philosophy comes to understand life through reason. I hope I can explain this right: Pieper says that since we are beings capable of recognizing the truth as such and truth is nothing but reality being known and because we are capable of this act-the apprehension of truth-which by its essence goes beyond every conceivable material construction and remains independent of it, we must be beings independent of the material body, an entity that persists through the dissolution of the material body and beyond death."

As Father Mike talked Casey had to keep his eyes wide open to take it all in. He remembered thinking the other day that what was the point of learning if there was no truth.

"So this guy Peiper says that by the fact that there is such a thing as truth and we can get to know it means that there is life after death?"

Father Mike nodded.

"From Revelation, we know that the Truth is a person: Jesus Christ and he was raised from the dead. As Saint Paul said, 'Death is swallowed up in victory.'"

Casey held up a finger.

"Does that apply to everyone?"

Father Mike nodded.

"Yes, but not everyone will be with him in paradise, only those who are worthy. Those who have fed the hungry, welcomed the stranger, clothed the naked, cared for the sick, visited those in prison."

Casey took a deep breath. At least, he had done one of those things.

"What about those who died very young and those who were aborted or miscarried, do they go to heaven or do they go to Limbo? Or what?"

Father Mike smiled.

"Limbo was never a dogma of the faith. It was an attempt by some to reconcile, on the one hand, the words of Jesus that we need to be baptized to enter the kingdom of God and on the other hand with the mercy of God who would not deprive innocent children the joys and happiness of heaven. The space between these hands is Limbo. Others, some saints and mystics tell us that in heaven all lives are shared and each of us will receive in heaven, through the communion of saints, all the earthly experiences of love and learning that were denied on earth. We'll be able to meet our ancestors and see what they experienced all the way back to the Fall and forward to the last day."

Father Mike stopped for a moment.

"I bet you're thinking of your children, aren't you? If you get to heaven and that's a big IF...

Father Mikes laughed at the expression on Casey's face and then continued. "You'll get to know them and you'll be able to tell them about your life and what you've seen and learned. If they don't know about it already."

Casey shook his head.

"But they weren't even born."

Father Mike smiled.

"Don't you listen to your characters? Didn't Katie answer that question already? They're persons once they've been conceived and are persons for all eternity."

Casey took a deep breath.

He was happy to hear that. He could never have imagined someone telling him something like that. He'd be able to meet and get to know his own children! It didn't seem possible. But as Father Joe said the other day: anything is possible with God."

Father Mike continued.

"Now, atheist materialists do not accept any of this. They believe that we return to matter. 'Thou art dust and to dust thou shall return.' Eastern religions believe that we go back into being itself. Christians believe that Being itself is God: I am who Am.'"

Casey interrupted him.

"Didn't you just say that's what the Eastern religions believe."

"Yes," said Father Mike. "But they believe that we lose our individual personhood when we die. As Christians, we believe that God is a person, three persons in One God. And since we too are persons, we remain persons after death. The entire person: body and soul. Not just the soul. In Western Philosophy, going back to Plato, people have believed in the immortality of the soul but not the body. But we believe in the Resurrection of the Body, the person. It is a dogma of our Faith. I remember talking about that in class one day and the students laughed. They thought it was absurd. They brought out the age-old objections: how about those who were burned into ashes or those lost at sea and torn to pieces by fish or by explosions in war. But of course, we do not mean the body we have now. Saint Paul calls it the glorified body. The body I have today is not the same one I had as a boy or yesterday or a minute ago for that matter. Our bodies are constantly changing. Jesus rose in his human body and he took that body into heaven. And our bodies will be raised up on the last day. We base our belief in life after death because of revelation as well as reason. There should be no conflict between faith and reason. God created the universe, the seen and the unseen, out of nothing and God created everything good. And since death is bad, it cannot be the end. Your character, Katie, talks about death being a punishment. The Book of Wisdom tells us that God did not make death. He created all things that they might exist.

Death came into the world because of sin. So in that sense, death is a punishment. But Jesus came to undo the punishment of death by dying on the cross. He is the Way, the Truth and the Life and He will raise us up on the last day."

Casey sighed deeply.

"This is deep stuff. So we aren't reunited with our bodies right after we die? What are we until then and where are we?"

Father Mike smiled.

"It's impossible to say exactly. Sleeping in Abraham's bosom, as Our Lord puts it or watching in the Beatific Vision, seeing what God sees. The dogma of the Assumption teaches us that Mary, the Mother of God was assumed body and soul into heaven. Christians who scoff at this dogma should read the Old Testament a little more carefully. Enoch and Elijah were both bodily assumed into heaven. Mary's Assumption is a sign and a type of the general resurrection of all mankind."

Father Mike stopped talking for a moment.

"I don't usually discuss the Marian dogmas but your character, James stated in **The Circle of Stones** that he didn't believe in the Immaculate Conception."

Casey shrugged.

"Yeah, I know. I hadn't thought about it in years. I forgot what it meant, if I ever really knew. In all the courses I took in theology, I don't remember studying it at any length. I got it mixed up with the Virgin Birth."

Father Mike nodded.

"That often happens. We believe that Mary was immaculately conceived, that is, she was born full of grace, without original sin. She is the Second Eve as she was called by the Fathers of the Church and so wonderfully explained by John Henry Newman. We believe that back in the beginning of time, something happened, that there was a primordial sin, a falling away from God, the famous story of Adam and Eve. They were immaculately conceived but they sinned. We inherit from them, not the actual sin but the state to which their sin reduces us. It is a deprivation of that super-natural unmerited grace which Adam and Eve had on their creation. Mary was conceived as was Eve in the state of sanctifying grace and she had this special privilege in order to fit her to become the Mother of her and our Redeemer, to fit her mentally and spiritually for it. We believe that Mary reversed the choice made by Eve and she committed no sin in her life. From the beginning Mary did the will of God. and since death and decay are the result of the Fall and sin, she would go straight to heaven.

The Book of Revelation indicates that the martyrs also are united with their bodies before the Last Judgment. 'Each of them was given a white robe and they were told to be patient a little while longer until the number was filled of their fellow servants and brothers who were going to be killed as they had been.' They were given robes because they had bodies.

The Church believes that most of us are in Purgatory, the Church Suffering, being purified. Which stands to reason. Most of us are not evil but we're not pure either and no one can be in the presence of the All Good God unless they have been cleansed of all impurities. That's why we pray for the dead. If there was no purgatory, there would be no reason to pray for them. 'Judas Maccabeus prayed for the dead that they might be delivered from their sin.' As Saint Paul says in 1 Corinthians: 'If any man's work is burned up, he will suffer loss, though he himself will be saved, but only as through fire.' But the fire of purgatory is the fire of love. The fire of hell is the fire of loss."

Casey sighed.

"I have so much to learn. I'm so ignorant. There were times over the years that I made fun of the teachings of the Church. I remember saying that the Church was irrelevant and obsolete. I'm ashamed of myself."

Father Mike nodded.

"You not alone, believe me. Anti-Catholicism is the last acceptable prejudice and some of the worst perpetrators are fallen-away Catholics. The Church is still called the Whore of Babylon and the Pope is denounced as the Anti-Christ in some circles. Others believe that the Church is a fraud, that the priests and the bishops know what the Church teaches is a myth, that is, a lie, but they promulgate it just so they don't have to do any real work or have to live in the real world."

Casey shook his head.

"No. I now believe, know, that everything the Catholic Church teaches is true because of what has happened these last few days. Now, I can see what happened to me. It all means something. My life makes sense. If I had stayed in the Church, if I had kept going to the sacraments, what happened to me as a boy could have been avoided."

He told Father Mike about the insight he had received the day before.

Father Mike smiled as he listened. It is a small world.

"That's what happens to all of us in one way or another. Every person is subject to temptations, although most people don't recognized temptation at all. In fact, they don't believe in the reality of sin much as less the devil."

Casey nodded.

'I know. I remember laughing when I heard people talking about sin and the devil. I thought they were religious fanatics. But that's why I started drinking when I was a boy. The devil put it in my head that my mother didn't love me and that there was no God. It made me feel empty inside. All my life I would get that empty feeling whenever I didn't feel loved or I felt lost so I would drink all that I could until it went through me leaving me empty once again. There was no love. There was no God. The world was **The Wasteland** with no way out."

Father Mike smiled.

"That poem by Eliot has been misinterpreted for years. If you remember, in the final section: 'What the Thunder Said,' we see that everywhere there is no giving, no compassion and no self control: the world is a wasteland. But then at the end of the poem we are given the way out in three commands from the mountain: give, have compassion and self control. If we all did that, the world would be a better place."

Casey shook his head

"That's not the way the poem is taught in school. They say that there is no way out of the wasteland."

Father Mike smiled.

"That's because they're secularists and the interpretation I proposed suggests a Deity and redemption. One reason I had to leave Niagara was because I refused to teach deconstructionism. So I was sent into retirement. Politely. For my own good, of course. Deconstructionism is the literary theory that there is no objective reality. Everything is subjective. Once a person believes that, he's finished as a moral person because then we create our own reality, our own morality. It's the Fall, the original sin. We decide what is right and wrong. Books, even the Bible, are whatever the reader makes them. What the author intends is meaningless. Because ultimately, there is no author, there is no truth, there is no God."

Casey shook his head.

"In my books, I wrote for a reason, to show that my life had meaning, that what I did was part of a plan. It seemed to me that my stories were part of a pattern that already existed somewhere. They signified something. I just had to find out what it was. I came to believe that I had a mission. That was what that woman, the Blessed Mother told me. I just didn't know what it was. My original title for **The Circle of Stones** was **Redemption.** I thought that I had redeemed myself for going to Vietnam. It was as if I had been given another chance to make the choice again: life or death, that Mick had taken the place of my father and McCann was the military recruiter and I had to decide again whether or not to go into the army. I thought that was my mission: that if one person could reverse the decision, to choose life instead of death, peace instead of war and that it could be symbolized in literature, it would transform the world."

Father Mike shook his head again.

"I have to stop you there. That's quite a mission. I believe that literature can tell us where we've been and where we are and where we going, if it's literature. But are your books literature? I have to be honest with you: they're not, not in this form. They might be if they were part of a larger story. Art is the universal in the particular. But no one can redeem himself. We need to have the humility to admit that we need a Savior. Our Redemption took place at Calvary and cannot be repeated, not even sacramentally. It is not applicable to individuals but for the whole of mankind. But you could say you were protected in Ireland. As we say in the memorare: 'Remember, O most compassionate Virgin Mary, that never was it known that anyone who fled to your protection....was left unaided.'"

Casey took a deep breath.

"Yeah, I can see that now. I was mixed up. I was in way over my head, trying to figure out what had happened in Ireland. I was such an amateur. I also thought that my mission was to promote healing between the sexes because that was where the war really takes place. That's why I had James give birth to a little girl who was him."

Father Mike smiled.

"'Bone of my bones,'" said Father Mike, "'and flesh of my flesh.' That's what the biblical author of Genesis was saying. I read it as a midrash on the second story of creation. With a different twist: a girl instead of a wife."

"A what?" asked Casey.

Father Mike explained.

"A midrash is a reconstruction of a biblical scene for contemporary interpretation. You had Patty do the same in that infuriating parody of the first story of creation."

Casey shrugged.

"I don't know anything about midrash. McCann actually told that story as a joke, so I used it. I saw it as an expression of his contempt for women."

Father Mike nodded.

'To be more exact: for the mother. Remember who was the woman he was molding: Eve, the mother of all the living. The precursor of Mary, the mother of all Christians. The theologian Henri De Lubac in his book **The Motherhood of the Church** wrote that if the Church is Mother than each Christian is also a mother. Our Lord said that whoever does the will of God is his mother and his brother and his sister. And Paul says in Galatians somewhere, 'my little children, I am like a mother giving birth to you, until Christ is formed in you.' And didn't Christ compare himself to a mother when he said, 'Jerusalem, Jerusalem, you who kill the prophets and stone those sent to you, how many times I yearned to gather your children together as a hen gathers her brood under her wings, but you were unwilling.' I hear its echoes in your little fable the story of a swallow."

Casey sat shaking his head. Had he really done all of this in his little books? How? It didn't seem possible. He hadn't thought of those quotes from the Bible. He couldn't remember ever hearing of them.

"Maybe you were just trying to say that 'Unless you be converted and become as children, you cannot enter the kingdom of heaven.'"

Casey smiled.

"I think you're giving me more credit than I deserve. I really wasn't thinking of the New Testament when I described the birthing scene in the circle of stones."

"Is that why you made Madeleine into a midwife?"

"Yeah. So that she could deliver the child. A child born without sex."

Father Mike laughed.

"A Virgin birth."

Casey smiled.

"Yeah, I used to laugh about that as well. Look, ma, no man. It's a miracle! God forgive me. I was such a dope. I was making fun of realities that were way beyond me."

Father Mike nodded.

"You weren't alone. They made fun of the Virgin Birth from the beginning and people still do today or they believe it is mere legend or myth or some theological construct. But it stands to reason that if God was going to become one of us, he would do it in an extraordinary way. Anything is possible with God. He is the creator of the universe. If he wanted to bypass the natural order, He could do it. The Fathers see in the virginal conception the sign that it truly was the Son of God who came in a humanity like our own. It's a divine work that surpasses all human understanding and possibility."

Casey nodded.

"But what I was imagining was impossible, totally out of the natural order, a man giving birth. I was imitating James Joyce, a renegade Catholic if there ever was one. He had Leopold Bloom give birth in **Ulysses.** I did a paper in graduate school on the **Movement towards Androgyny in Ulysses**. I bought into that nonsense for a while, I'm embarrassed to say. You can say that we all have male and female traits but I don't have a woman inside of me. I'm a man, a true man now. Men and women are different. I guess I was just trying to say that we men have to identify with women, that even though we're different, we're both persons. We have to reject the Patty Byrnes that is in all of us."

Father Mike nodded.

"But rejecting Patty wasn't where you went wrong in the book, was it? You told Father Joe that **The Circle of Stones** was a lie. What did you mean by that? I hope you're not going to tell me that it's a fiction you've created as a cover for your crimes. You weren't running guns and slitting throats were you?"

Casey shook his head.

"No. I didn't do what McCann asked me to do. The character Patty Byrnes is based on James McCann. He was a Provo from Belfast who had escaped from Crumlin Road Jail in 1969. I did meet him in Ballinskelligs and he did offer me money to take information about them to Belfast. I refused to do it."

"Why?" asked Father Mike. "I mean, I'm glad that you did and you certainly made the right decision. But that's not where you went wrong, is it?"

Casey shook his head.

"No. I always felt that was the right decision. If I had done what he asked, I would have wound up either dead or in prison."

Father Mike nodded.

"He reminded me of what Saint Cyril of Jerusalem said: that all of us have to get past the dragon before we can enter the kingdom. But I have to say that I wondered why Patty, McCann would recruit James, you, for the IRA. It seems to me that he would have been more careful. How could he know who you really were?"

Casey nodded.

"I know. I've wondered that myself, sometimes. I always felt it was because of Mick, that he vouched for me. For some reason, Mick seemed to think that I was special in some way. I don't know why."

Father Mike nodded.

"Don't be so hard on yourself. It saddened me to see you so demoralized. So broken. Alienated. Sin alienates us, first from God and then from ourselves and then from our community. But you are a brave man. You volunteered to fight against Communism, against Evil. You were willing to lay down your life for your brother. There is no greater love than that. Mick recognized those qualities, I'm sure."

Casey shrugged.

"Maybe. But Mick didn't know me that well either. Who knows? Maybe he just wanted to use me, too. Then, last night when I was re-reading my books, it occurred to me for the first time that maybe McCann wasn't asking me to help with the shipment of guns at all but with drugs."

'That's another question I had," said Father Mike. "Is the IRA involved in drugs?"

Casey shrugged.

"I don't think the old-timers are. But the young Turks? I think so. Some of them are anyway. McCann was."

"It's a shame," said Father Mike. "But that's what happens when you cut yourself off from your roots. You lose who you are. The Irish have done this before, you know. Mick was furious with Pope Adrian for sending the Norman King of England Henry II to Ireland. He sees it as an English invasion but it was actually a Norman invasion, Norman meaning Catholic, supported by the Pope to help restore Christianity to Ireland. Some of the Irish princes and chieftains had begun imitating the barbaric practices of the Danes and were burning down churches and monasteries. The Pope was attempting to protect the Church. And today, the snakes are back in Ireland. Again, some of the people are attacking the Church, calling her misogynist and homophobic. Vocations to the priesthood are at a record low. Mass attendance is down dramatically. Politicians speak of post-Christian Ireland. I understand that most of the IRA are atheists, practical atheists, anyway. Their cause may be just and certainly the Catholic people have suffered much up in the North but as the Holy Father said when he was in Ireland: 'The Troubles' are a struggle between haters and Christianity forbids hated and murder and terrorism. And the sale of drugs. The ends don't justify the means."

Casey nodded.

"Well, McCann was a murderer and a terrorist and a drug dealer. The newspapers over there called him 'The Scarlet Pimpernel' because he evaded capture for so long: ten years. He was finally rearrested in 1979 in County Kildare for the possession of thousands of pounds worth of marijuana. The IRA beat up him in jail after he got arrested, probably because he got caught. He made the IRA look bad. They didn't want to be identified as drug dealers."

"How do you know all this?" asked Father Mike.

Casey shrugged.

"I read about it in a book on the IRA by Tim Pat Coogan."

"But you actually met this guy, McCann?" asked Father Mike.

Casey nodded.

"It was a hairy time, Father. He was really angry when I told him no. He wouldn't have made the offer if he hadn't thought I was going to do it."

Father Mike's eyes got wide.

"Did you actually consider doing it?"

Casey nodded.

"It's a miracle I didn't. I thought I really wanted to live in Ballinskelligs. I needed money and it was something I was capable of doing. I went up there last year: to the North of Ireland, to Derry, not to Belfast."

Casey stopped talking for a moment. Some of the few people who had read **The Circle of Stones** saw it as a putdown of the Irish people. That was not his intention.

"I just want to say that the people in my book don't represent all of the Irish, most of whom are good, hardworking, faithful people. Just like my family was. When I did genealogical research on my family, I found out that they had come from County Derry and County Donegal, in the 1840's so I went there, looking for my roots. I took the bus up there like I would have in 1973.1 had no problem crossing the border. We were stopped by British soldiers with rifles and one of them got on the bus, but they didn't even look at me. So I could have done it. But after I turned McCann down, it's a miracle I got out of there alive. I knew the kind of car he drove, the people he was with. I could have dropped the dime on him, easy. I never had any intention of going to the police or the British but he didn't know that. He was really mad at me. But he didn't do anything when I said no."

Casey shrugged.

"I have to admit that I was afraid of him but after the army and after being knifed, what could happen that was any worse? Thank

God, he didn't try to do anything to me because if he had, I would've killed him. I would have broken one of those Guinness bottles and slashed his throat with it. You remember that line, 'Visions of violence burned through his brain.?' That's what I was thinking. I mean it. I would've done it. I wasn't going to let him or anyone hurt me again."

Father Mike shook his head.

"The British would have probably given you a medal for doing it but his pals would have killed you first. You must have had all the saints and angels in heaven looking after you."

Casey nodded.

"I know it. But they were looking after me, I can tell you that. When I left there, I didn't leave with Madeleine. I stayed a week after I turned McCann down. I wasn't going to let him run me out of town like I was some punk like he did the others. I left with his brother, Jerry. He was Eamon in the book. He took me on the most harrowing ride I ever had in my life, packed in his little car, zooming at top speed on those narrow roads with him talking and shouting and singing all the way to Dublin. He took me to one of his relatives' house there and they put me up for a couple of days. But every time I went somewhere, a young guy there, one of his nephews, tagged along with me. I got tired of that so I ditched him. I walked and walked around Dublin until he got too tired to stay with me. I was in great shape from all the walking I did in the mountains. I tried to get a room where I had stayed the year before but they were booked. I guess it was a good thing since the guy that owned the place was a Irish cop. That would have made the boys suspicious. So I took another bed and breakfast near the Dollymount Inn. The next day, as I was walking down O'Connell Street, who do I run into but a guy whose name was Patty Something, I don't know his last name. He was also there at Ranchhouse but he wasn't in the book. Him and a lot of other IRA guys. They were in and out of Ranchhouse all the time. I cut them down to three so it wouldn't be too confusing. He was a bank robber. He was one of the ones who did that job in County Tyrone."

Casey laughed at the expression on Father Mike's face.

"That's the company I was keeping in those days. He seemed

surprised to see me. Very friendly. He asked me where I was going to next. He was real interested. I had intended to go to London to see Madeline Hancock but something, someone, the Blessed Mother? told me that would be a big mistake. So I made up my mind right then and there to go to France instead to pick grapes like that guy Dieter was going to do. If I had said London, Patty might have thought I was going to the British and rat on them. The next day, I went down to Rosslare to get the ferry for France."

Father Mike's eyes narrowed

"And you just happened to run into an Irishman who just happened to be wearing a Vietnam veteran's shirt. A sign that they knew you would see and that you would probably talk to him. Was he also IRA, do you think?'

Casey laughed.

"You know, it never occurred to me. I don't think so. He was just a young guy, but then again, the IRA were usually young guys."

Casey had to digest that for a few moments, then he shook his head.

"I would have to say no. But you never know. I spent a few weeks with him and he never said anything or did anything that would make me think he was IRA. He was more like a guardian angel. He got me to the vineyards."

"Interesting," said Father Mike. "I'm curious. Did McCann actually brandish that revolver around like some two-bit hoodlum?"

Casey grinned.

"Yeah, he did but not in that circumstance. He put a gun to the head of one of the lads from Dublin who came down one weekend with a whole truckload of lads and lassies. They were there off and on the whole time I was there, sleeping all around the place, getting drunk and high. It was a madhouse. Total chaos. I reduced them down to one person: Christy. He was a representative character. But anyway, one of the lads foolishly made a pass at McCann's girl friend and McCann told him he would blow his brains out if he ever did it again. That kid was shaking all over after that. His girl friend was this voluptuous blonde from Amsterdam. She was Miss Holland of 1968 or something. Legend has it that she was arrested in Germany one time and McCann threatened the German police that if they didn't let her go he would bring the bombing campaign to Germany so they let her go."

Father Mike shook his head.

"Then he wasn't traveling around with an Irish woman? Maura?"

Casey shook his head.

"No, I transformed the girlfriend for the sake of the theme. McCann didn't treat her the way Patty treats Maura in the story but he could have or he might have but I didn't see it. It typified his attitude towards women in general so I described it that way."

Father Mike smiled.

"This story gets more amazing all the time. It also amazes me that you were able to describe Ballinskelligs and Ranchhouse so well. And McCann and Mick and the other characters. It was very detailed. How did you do it? If I may ask. Did you take notes or keep a journal?"

Casey laughed.

"No. Not when it was happening. I didn't go there to write a book. I remembered some things, but a lot of the details about the place: the flowers and the layout of the land, and the poems recited by Mick - Mick Murphy was his real name by the way, I got them when I went back there, in the winter of 1975."

"You went back there again?" asked Father Mike.

Casey laughed.

"Yeah, looking back, it was the most dangerous thing I ever did but I really wanted to write about that experience and I couldn't do it without going back. When I got there, I told Mick that I was writing a book about what happened in '73 and that I was going to use the money that I got for selling the book to restore Ranchhouse. I meant it at the time and I guess he believed me because he gave me what I wanted. I stayed there for three weeks that winter and not a drop taken. I wasn't going to drink that time. I realized the danger I was in. I didn't know what I was going to tell McCann when he showed up again: 'Yeah, I'm back, again. I'm writing a book about when I met you before. Remember, you offered me money to help you run guns to Belfast and I refused. I'm going to tell everybody about that. Don't worry, I promise, I won't tell them the kind of car you drive and its license plate number. Or where you sleep at night.'"

Casey laughed.

Father Mike's eyes got wide.

"Did you see him again?"

Casey kept laughing.

"No. When I got there, Mick told me that McCann was due to come back in a few days. When I heard that, my first thought was to pack my bags and get the hell out of there. But then, I felt this calming sensation come over me. It was that woman again. She let me know that nothing was going to happen to me. I was doing what God wanted me to do. McCann didn't come. And I got what I needed to write the book. Of course, I failed to make any money on it. But maybe that's because I got it wrong. I didn't tell the truth of what really happened there. Why I turned McCann down."

Father Mike sat back in his seat.

"I can believe that something happened. As I read your books, I was struck by the change in James. It was hard for me to believe that he was the same character in Ireland as he was in Seaside House. It was like the transformation in a faery tale. What did happen?"

Casey sighed.

"It wasn't anything dramatic. I met a young woman there: Madeleine Hancock. She wasn't anything like Madeleine Chadwick in the book except that she was a virgin."

"How did you know?" asked Father Mike.

Casey shrugged.

"She told me. She was there with her parents visiting her grandmother. She was a grade school teacher in London. We met in the pub. We talked and walked along the beach. It was a very romantic place. We starting making out. I wanted to have sex but she didn't. She was saving herself for marriage, she said. She was a good Catholic girl. I respected her. I backed off. Then I told her about what McCann wanted me to do. She was horrified. She told me in no uncertain terms that there was no way I should do it. That I would be contributing to people getting killed and I wouldn't want that on my conscience."

Father Mike smiled.

'That was why you decided not to do it? Then what makes you

think that it had anything to do with the Blessed Mother?"

Casey laughed.

"Maybe because she was a virgin. But it wasn't Madeleine alone who convinced me not to do it. I used to take long walks in the mountains, thinking about what was going on. The whole process took longer than it does in the book. I was there for about six weeks. I shortened it for dramatic effect. And I cleaned up the language as best I could. It's a good thing you didn't hear it in real life: it was really foul."

Father Mike nodded.

"Foul language is the language of hell and I would say that James was in hell then."

Casey nodded.

"Yeah. You can be in hell in this life. I know. I was there. What does it say in the Apostles Creed ? 'He descended into hell.' I never really understood that before. Is being in hell not the same as being damned?"

Father Mike smiled.

"I think so. Some theologians believe that hell is not only a place but a state of being. Our Lord loves us so much that He will go even into hell to save us. Damnation is the second death. 'If we sin deliberately after receiving knowledge of the truth.' It's for people who once they know that the Church is necessary for salvation reject it and go their own way, alone. I had the sense when reading **The Circle of Stones** that Christ was there with you. You just couldn't see him. He can only be seen with the eyes of faith. The book seemed like a palimpsest or an allegory, that there was another story behind the surface. The Blessed Mother was there too: the morning star. An ancient symbol of Mary."

Casey smiled.

"It's strange. I didn't know why I used that image. But I had the sense that someone was with me. After Madeleine went back to London, I continued the conversation in my mind with her, but over time she seemed to become someone else. It was like I was talking to a universal woman. It was her: the Blessed Mother. I know that now. Sent to me by my mother's prayers."

Father Mike smiled.

"Mary is the mother of us all. She brought Jesus into the world and she brings Jesus to each one of us. As Bishop Sheen said, 'She's the one woman that all of us can love.'"

Casey smiled.

"I knew some day I would come to love a woman. I love the Blessed Mother. And my mom. In some way, she's like the Blessed Mother. She's not perfect. She gossips. She loses her temper. But I don't think my mom ever committed a mortal sin in her life. With my mother as an example, I don't know why I never thought that woman could be the Blessed Mother. I guess it was because of those three females that I met on the way to Ireland."

Father Mike shrugged.

"I have to tell you that they are least believable parts of your book."

Casey laughed.

"But they were true. I did meet them on the way to Ireland and I met them pretty much as I described but when I think about it, I have to admit that I fictionalized parts of my encounter with the woman on the train from Luxembourg. She was actually a practicing catholic and didn't believe in any goddess. I made that up because I was trying to do what Joyce had done in **Ulysses**: to construct a myth as the structure of the story. Because that's all the triple goddess is: a myth. But the other two happened pretty much as I described. The one on the ferry boat, she did put her head on my lap and I did land in Ireland holding hands with a little girl. Then when I read about the triple goddess in a book by Robert Graves, **The White Goddess**, I imagined that they were a manifestation of her. Nonetheless, it was strange how it happened. If I hadn't gotten on the wrong train from Luxembourg, I wouldn't have met the other two. I wonder who they were?"

Father Mike smiled.

"Belloc might call them the three graces. Dante named them Beatrice, Lucia and Rachel. But above them was the Blessed Mother and above her was the Father. If it wasn't for the father on the train, you wouldn't have met the little girl. And if you hadn't met her, you wouldn't have seen the three females."

Casey sat back in his seat.

"You're right. And if I hadn't met them, I wouldn't have discovered the triple goddess. She was the myth before the reality, the Blessed Mother. I didn't think of that. It amazes me that out of all the people on that platform that man picked me out to go with his family to Ireland. I wasn't the most reputable looking person at the time. I was dirty and my eyes were burning; they had to be red. I needed a shave and a haircut. I looked like a bum. But yet, he picked me. Amazing."

Father Mike smiled.

"He knew what he was doing. He made the right choice. You were a big help to his family, weren't you? He was like God the Father choosing you out of all the people in the world to tell this story. He's the one who's behind everything. He's the author of the story, the director of the drama."

Casey nodded.

"So it was the Father who was behind it all. Of course."

Father Mike smiled.

"You say in **The Story of a Swallow** that the search for the father is one of the major themes in literature but that's because he's never there. But He is there and always has been since the beginning. Many religions invoke God as "Father," the God above all gods, the Great Spirit in the Sky. In Israel, God is called Father inasmuch as He is Creator of the world. He is Father but not male or female, although he has the attributes of both mother and father. He is the Father of the poor, the orphaned and the widowed.

But your books are also about the search for the mother. That's a theme that began with the pagans who believed that since all human life came from the woman, it meant that the creator of the world was a mother, that god was immanent or part of this world: Pantheism, in other words. And if you believe that all creation comes from a sexual act then it becomes the liturgy or the way that god is worshipped. That's why we read about orgies and temple prostitutes in the Old Testament. Then along came the Israelites. God was revealed to them as transcendent or outside of the material world, not immanent. The goddess religions were abhorrent to them and they believed that Yahweh wanted them destroyed. That was what was behind the wars that you see in the Old Testament.

But then Jesus of Nazareth was born of the Virgin Mother. He is 'our peace, he who made both one and broke down the dividing wall of enmity.' He was both God and Man, without confusion as the Council of Chalcedon decreed. Jesus is both transcendent and immanent. Jesus revealed God to us as Father, in a way not understood before. God is not alone. He is a family, a community, a Trinity.

The Church from the beginning was always aware that Jesus was born of the Virgin Mary by the power of the Holy Spirit. The early Church knew that she was special but they weren't totally aware of who she really was. Who was that woman? Saint Louse de Montfort tells us that Mary was called Alma Mater-Mother secret and hidden. Cardinal Ratzinger in his book **Daughter Zion** shows the figure of the woman who is seen typologically, beginning with Eve and proceeding throughout salvation history with the great women of Israel: Rachel and Sarah and Hannah and Esther and Judith and Sophia until she finally emerges with a name: Mary, the Mother of God. And even though anyone who reads the New Testament should be able to see her importance in the main events of Jesus' life: at his birth, at his presentation at the temple and at the marriage feast of Cana where he works his first miracle, at the cross where she witnessed his death and in the Upper Room at Pentecost when the Church is born, her significance continues to be hidden from many Christians who see her as an incidental person who just happened to be the person who gave Jesus his humanity. The Catholic Church believes, however, that Mary is present even before the creation of the world as the one whom the Father has chosen as Mother of his Son in the Incarnation. The early church knew that Mary was special. She was definitively called the Theotokos or the Mother of God at the Council of Ephesus in 431.

The search for Mary, the Mother of God continued in Christian literature. **The Divine Comedy** by Dante is the archetype. Beatrice brought him to the Blessed Mother who brought him to the Father. As I'm sure you know, in the classical tradition, a comedy is a story with a happy ending. Being in the Church Triumphant in heaven is the happiest ending there can be and being in the Church Militant here on earth is a foretaste of heaven. Many of the saints like Saint Louis de Montfort and Saint Bernard of Clairvaux also spent their lives searching for the Blessed Mother."

There was silence for a few moments as Casey digested what had just been said. Father Mike couldn't have been comparing him to Dante. No way. His talent was too small. And him a saint? Not likely. He was too sinful. He have to be martyred for that to happen. Otherwise, he'd be fortunate just to squeeze through heaven's gate, after centuries in purgatory.

"Was there a circle of stones?"

Casey shrugged.

"Yeah. But it wasn't like I described. Ballinskelligs was where the monks lived centuries before. It's a sacred place. The Skelligs Rock that I referred to is actually called the Skelligs Michael, an island off the coast where the monks lived before moving to the mainland. Now, I realize, it is a symbol of Christianity. As I wrote the book, I had O'Rourke constantly looking for the Skelligs Rock. I wasn't sure why when I was writing it. It was as if what he, I, was looking for was there. Which it was."

Father Mike nodded.

"Yes, O'Rourke tells Madeleine that he was looking for peace. Jesus is our peace. As we say in the Mass every day: I leave you peace, my peace I give you'."

Casey agreed.

"I know that now. Unfortunately, neither one of us, O'Rourke or I, actually went to the Skelligs Rock. The circle of stones that I went to was really a wall of stones in a circle. I went there once with Mick. It was up on the mountain. It was a ruin of an abbey, a place where the monks used to pray."

"An oratory," said Father Mike.

"I guess," said Casey. "I transformed it into a stone circle because of the witches' circle I had been in Vermont."

"A witches' circle?"

Casey laughed.

"Yeah. It was called **The Art of the Possible** by Dawna Marcova. That's where I learned about chakras and auras. That was when I composed the story of a swallow."

"Is that right?" asked Father Mike. "I wondered where you got that. What's the story behind that?"

Casey laughed.

'That's a long story, not worth telling in its entirety. Let me just say that Dawna asked everyone in the circle to tell her what we wanted her to do for us. I said that something happened to me when I was a boy but I didn't know what it was. She said, 'how does it make you feel.' I said, 'Empty.' She said, 'You swallowed when you said that, so tell a story about a swallow who feels empty inside.' That's how I composed the story of a swallow."

"Were you working as a pediatrics nurse, then?" asked Father Mike.

Casey nodded.

"Yes. It reinforced to me that I was doing the right thing, that in some way, by becoming a pediatrics nurse, I was reversing the curse I was under. But I still didn't know what happened to me until Our Lord revealed it to me yesterday. When I wrote **The Circle of Stones,** I transferred the story of a swallow to Ireland. When I did it, I wasn't sure if people would believe all that really happened."

Father Mike shrugged.

"I was always skeptical about the circle of stones so I read it as fantasy."

Casey grinned.

"As I was writing the book, I was trying to describe what really happened in Ireland, based on my experience with the real Madeleine, Madeleine Hancock and I wasn't getting anywhere. One of my roommates Meredith Allen read one of the first drafts of **Redemption** and she told me that it was a very catholic book. Well, I didn't want to hear that. I couldn't accept the fact that I was writing a catholic book. Then all of a sudden this other Madeleine, Madeleine Chadwick appeared and the book took off it another direction."

Casey stopped talking.

"That's where I went wrong in the book. It was her. Tell me Father: is it possible for a demon to come into a fictional character?"

Father Mike sat back in his chair.

"I never thought of such a thing to be honest with you. Are you saying that your character Madeleine was demonic? But she hated Patty. And she was against terrorism. She seemed like a good character to me."

Casey shrugged.

"But the Devil comes to us in our imagination, doesn't he? And she was for abortion. Liberated women usually are. That's what being liberated means: to be free of the bonds of childbearing. It seems to me, now, that abortion is a manifestation of the demonic. The circle is a symbol of radical feminism, and radical feminism is a totally different form of religion: pagan, with roots in the occult. Take my word for it. I read their books."

Father Mike nodded.

"I have to disagree with you about the circle. The circle is also a symbol of Christianity, the larger circle that encompasses all the smaller circles. We start out in life when we're born and we return back to God when we die. But I agree with you about radical feminism. But your character, a demon? She may have led you astray to some extent, but in the end, she brought you to the right place."

Casey shook his head.

"But none of what is described about her is real. I made it up. She didn't lead me to the truth. That's why the book is a lie. She led me away from the truth into a pagan explanation of what happened there. That's what makes her a demonic character."

Father Mike shook his head.

"I missed that about abortion. Maybe you're right. The devil often comes disguised as an angel of light. But don't be too hard on the pagans. They were trying to find the truth about God and were doing it without the benefit of revelation. Some of the great thinkers of antiquity were pagans: Plato and Aristotle, for instance. And you can see the triple goddess of Ireland as a glimpse of the Trinity and the Blessed Mother. They didn't get it right but they were on the right track."

Casey shook his head.

"You may be right about the pagans but the character Madeleine got a hold on me. She became a creature of my imagination who lived inside of me. You see, I came to identify so much with her that it was like she took over my very self. Up until then, I hadn't been going to Mass and I was very critical of the Church but I never had any problem with Jesus Himself. But then, I turned against Him and denied Him. I saw him as weak, a victim. I even saw myself as superior to Him. After all, I told people, I had lived in my confrontation with evil and he had died. That attitude had to make Satan proud.

I saw Madeleine as a radical feminist so in order to understand her, I went down to Giovanni's Room on South Street, a gay and lesbian bookstore and bought all the books I could on radical feminism. I remember reading **Beyond God the Father** by Mary Daly, **Of Woman Born** by Adrianna Rich, **Sisterhood is Powerful** by Robin Morgan, **Against Our Will** by Susan Brownmiller. I even read books by Andrea Dworkin and Shulasmith Firestone. Et al. Boy, did they mess me up. I started thinking like a radical lesbian feminist. I even started going out with lesbians, nurses that I met, to dinner and the movies with them. Nothing ever happened between us. How could it? They liked women and I was still a man. Normal women didn't know what to make of me. I was like some strange being to them, not male, not female, not gay. What was I? I didn't know myself. One night, I went to a concert by Chris Williamson. She's a lesbian singer and songwriter. There were about a thousand women in the place and I was the only man, the invisible man. Not one woman looked at me or talked to me the entire night. I tried to talk with the woman next to me but I was like a dummy with no ventriloquist. I'd open my mouth to speak but no words would come out. The only sound I made all night was like a man with a tongue depressor in his mouth."

Casey started to laugh and then stopped.

"It's funny in a pathetic kind of way. I thought my mission was to promote healing between the sexes and I couldn't even talk to women anymore. I was a total failure in my relationships with women. I knew I had to re-think what my mission was but by then I was totally lost."

Father Mike shook his head. He didn't know what to make of what he had just heard: a man who sees himself as a radical lesbian feminist. That's why the Church used to condemn certain books; they can be too dangerous and that's what happens when a person loses who they are, especially if they are not deeply rooted in the teachings of the Church. They can become anybody.

"So what would you say that your mission is now?"

Casey shook his head.

"I'd have to re-write my books again. I don't know if I can do it. I've written them over and over again already. It's like I'm an illiterate. Until I set out to write the story of what happened in Ireland, I had never written anything, other than a few term papers in college. Who am I to think I can write a book, especially one that is concerned with salvation. I'd have to go back and study theology again. How can I do that. I don't even know where to start."

Father Mike smiled.

"You couldn't do it on your own. Saint Louis de Montfort in his book **True Devotion to Mary** will teach you how to do it. Read it. I highly recommend it. He says that we give to Our Lord, by his mother's hands, all our good works, that the good Mother purifies them, embellishes them and makes them acceptable to her Son. It is as if a peasant, wishing to gain the friendship of the king, went to the queen and presented her with a fruit in order that she might present it to the king. The queen would place the fruit on a beautiful dish of gold and would present it to the king. Then the fruit, unworthy in itself, would become worthy because of the dish of gold and the person who presented it. If you make your story that fruit, our Holy Mother will make it worthy for the king."

"I'll try," said Casey. "Maybe my mission to be is to tell the world that God is truly with us especially when we are in great danger of losing our souls, that prayers are answered, especially a mother's prayers, that miracles do happen and that even in the worst of sinners, you can see the face of Jesus Christ.

The two men were silent for several minutes.

"Very good. Okay, then Bill," said Father Mike. "I have other comments and disagreements with some of what you, or your effigy said. I'll print them out and get them to you, if you want."

Casey nodded.

"I'd appreciate it. I disagree with him myself now. You mean, what he said about abortion and the Church and the Eucharist?"

Father Mike nodded.

'Those, of course, but also his politics. He seems like a socialist to me."

Casey nodded.

"I regret to say that I did become a socialist. I lost who I was. I'm beginning to see how it happened. I was weakened by sin. Then I met a woman in college, Laura, who was a Communist. She had a great influence on me, I'm sad to say. She was the one who put the germ in my head that we were wrong to be in Vietnam. Growing up, I knew about the Gulag and the millions of people Stalin and Mao killed. But I allowed myself to be brainwashed into thinking that we were the bad guys. I became a fool. A dupe of the Communists. I'm ashamed of myself. My father was right about Communism and I was wrong."

Pain stopped Casey from talking for a few moments.

"I used to blame him for my going to war but it was me who wanted to go. He wanted me to serve my country but he didn't want me to die over there. When I was in college, I wanted to drop out of school and go in the marines but he talked me out of it. He was upset when I volunteered for the draft. He was my father not Mick. Mick could never take his place. I wish my dad were still alive so I could tell him that."

Father Mike smiled.

"He knows. From what you told me, he was a good father so you can rest assured he is with the Father now, watching in the Beatific Vision so he can see you as you are now. Aquinas tells us that at the very least the blessed perceive those things that concern them."

That comment made Casey very happy.

Father Mike sighed.

"The Vietnam War was very confusing to everyone. It's no wonder you lost your bearings. I remember telling my students at Saint John's to go there, that we were fighting atheism there: Evil. I didn't realize at the time that they never intended for us to win that war."

Casey's eyes widened.

"What? Who didn't?"

'The people in power. The elites." said Father Mike. "The Conspiracy."

Casey smiled.

'The Aquarian Conspiracy, you mean?"

Father Mike shook his head.

"You mean the New Age? That's part of it: the spiritual element.

As you know now, it's based on the occult. I mean the people who are really pulling the strings behind the scenes: the monopolists, the elites of the world. The money behind it. The Communists, the Socialists are also part of it. They provide the ideology. Communism is atheistic materialism. We have to stop thinking of Communism as being for a sharing of the wealth, or for being for the welfare of the common man. That's a lie. They want to control the wealth, just like the corporate capitalists in the West, who are also atheistic materialists. They consider themselves Internationalists just like the Communists. The Vietnam War was like a big war game: both sides controlled by the same people."

Casey shook his head.

"What are you saying? That the Communists and the US were on the same side? That doesn't make sense. We destroyed Vietnam. Why would the Communists agree to that?"

Father Mike put his hands together as if he were praying.

"I'm not saying the US, only some of the people in the country and the government. And remember: Both the Soviets and the Chinese Communists murdered millions of their own people. Why would they care about the Vietnamese? As you said, 'they don't care about the little people.' Think about it. How else can you explain our strategy there? You know that we traded with all the Communist countries during the War. Joe McCarthy was right. There were many communists in the our government. That's been proven since the fall of the Soviet Union. They were responsible for all the absurd restrictions that were placed on our troops: don't shoot first even if they're preparing to attack, don't bomb anti-aircraft sites until after they've fired first, don't shoot stationary trucks on the Ho Chi Minh trail etcetera, etcetera, etcetera. Our government supplied the communist countries in Europe with material that was used to kill our soldiers. We could have ended the war in no time. If we had put a division of troops on the Ho Chi Minh Trail and blockaded Haiphong Harbor and not allowed the Soviets and the Chinese to send in arms and ammunition, the war would have been over in months. The North Vietnamese themselves admit that now."

Casey shook his head.

"So you're saying we deliberately lost the war in Vietnam?"

Father Mike nodded.

"I'm sorry to say. You were the fall guys. They put our military in a no-win situation. General Westmoreland broke all the rules of how to fight to win a war. He didn't take ground and hold it. He sent our troops on search and destroy missions in the jungle, instead of defending the cities and villages. Then, after taking ground, he pulled the troops back and let the Commies move back in. Doing exactly what General Giap, the Commander of the North Vietnamese Army, wanted him to do. A coincidence? I don't think so."

Casey put up both hands in front of himself like he was trying to hold back a falling wall.

"What are you saying? That Westmoreland was a traitor?"

Father Mike shrugged.

"I don't know. Maybe he was just what the Communists call a useful idiot. Westmoreland made it a war of attrition, making killing people more important than defending territory. Remember how important was the body count. He put our troops in atrocity producing situations, knowing that would cause guilt feelings and demoralization and drug and alcohol abuse. You can vouch for that, can't you, Bill?"

Casey closed his eyes and nodded. Even though he had not participated in them, he knew about innocent people being killed, the crimes that had been committed: The Serious Incident Reports. They were the things that had turned him against the war. Then suddenly it occurred to him: those reports were proof that the military took seriously crimes committed against the Vietnamese. Soldiers were punished for violating the rules of war. He remembered what he had learned in college: the US was a country ruled by laws not by people, different and better than communist countries who were ruled by dictators: Stalin, Mao, Ho Chi Minh. Mass murderers all.

Casey did have a caveat.

"Maybe Westmoreland was a failure as a general but he was a soldier. He was under orders. I think it was more the policy of McNamara and the rest of the so-called best and the brightest than that of Westmoreland."

Father Mike shrugged.

"Perhaps. And McNamara went on to be the CEO of the World

Bank. That and the IMF are part of the whole deck of cards. They want to control all of the world's money."

Casey shook his head.

"How do you know this stuff?"

Father Mike smiled.

"I read a lot. And one of my confreres at Saint John's, Father Joe Symes, a professor of history and a brilliant man, clued me in. He was influenced by Christopher Dawson and his theory of meta-history and what Hans Urs von Balthasar called theo-drama: that history can only be understood if we realize that above the surface of events there is another level of activity. As Father Joe said,' we have a choice: we can believe that history is a series of accidental misfortunes, violence and horrors, with no one in charge or else we can believe it is a war between good and evil, between God and the Devil: the Prince of the world.' As the Psalmist said, 'Princes plot against the Lord and his anointed.' That's who's behind the movement towards World Government, the New World Order. This is a struggle that has been going on since before time began. It started when Satan rebelled against God and has continued throughout history. As Paul said, 'We are not contending against flesh and blood, but against the principalities, against the powers, against the world rulers of this present darkness, against the spiritual hosts of wickedness in the heavenly places.' Remember: Jesus was a victim of a conspiracy. The Jews and the Gentiles, all of us, in other words, put him to death."

Casey took a deep breath.

"Are you saying that the US Government plotted to lose the war in Vietnam and destroy its own Army?"

Father Mike shrugged.

"Not everyone in the Government was in on it. Only the elites."

"Why?"

'To discourage other people who were fighting against Communism around the world. So that they would believe the Communists were so powerful that even a tiny country could defeat the US. That Communism was so right that it couldn't be stopped."

Casey had to think more about this. It seemed so far out, so extreme. Wasn't it more likely that people like Westmoreland were just inept. But it did make some sense. Otherwise, the Vietnam War was a mystery, inexplicable, but then again, all of life is a mystery.

Father Mike continued.

"They wanted the American people to think that we couldn't stand alone, that we had to unite with other nations."

"So who are these people?" asked Casey

Father Mike shrugged.

"It's difficult to know for sure. They are masters of deceit. Like the Masons, there are different levels of complicity. A pyramid. Most people are like you: dupes and fools. It's the weeds and the wheat. The bad is mixed in with the good."

That reminded Casey of something Mick had said.

"So what do we do? Destroy the whole field of wheat?"

"No," said Father Mike, "because we would destroy the wheat as well as the weeds. That's a job for the Lord to do. We have to leave it in His hands."

Casey took off his glasses, rubbed his face, then put his glasses back on. He felt like he was home from a masquerade and was peeling off the mask he had been wearing: the rebel. He had never felt comfortable in that role. He had always felt like an impostor.

"I don't understand," said Casey. "If what you say is true: What's the purpose of it all?"

"Control of the world," said Father Mike.

"How?" asked Casey.

"Through the United Nations," said Father Mike.

Casey laughed.

'The UN? Is a joke. Whenever the UN sends in troops, it's really the United States Military. And nothing good is ever achieved by it."

Father Mike nodded.

'That's right. Remember who sent US troops into Korea: The UN. And into Vietnam: The UN. Under the auspices of SEATO. The UN is no joke. Behind it is a deadly deception. It is a pagan, socialist organization. And so corrupt. It sounds so innocent to most people. What's wrong with all of the nations uniting to keep the world free of war and injustice? There's nothing wrong with the idea. But the UN is not a peace organization. It's a war organization. God has already given us the structure that we need for peace. It's called the Catholic Church. So we can be one as the Trinity is one. The UN is a counterfeit Church. Ruled by an anti-Christ."

Casey started to laugh but stopped. Father Mike was a serious man and no fool.

"An anti-Christ?

Father Mike nodded.

"'Whoever denies that Jesus is the Christ. Whoever denies the Father and the Son, this is the anti-Christ.' Today, the Conspiracy is expanding its influence more and more. There are different levels of involvement, as there are in the US Government. Think about what happened after Vietnam. Communism spread throughout the world: into Cambodia and Laos, into Africa and Latin America. And here in this country, we've become more and more like the Communist countries. The role of Government in our lives has expanded enormously. We've put God out of our schools and out of our homes. The State is God. They know that the way to destroy society is to tear apart the family and that's done by loosening the sexual mores. Remember the Sexual Revolution? The 60s? The same time as the Vietnam War. Look at the rise in premarital sex and illegitimate children. And divorce. Homosexuality is rampant. Abortion is the law of the land. All of which are supported in the UN. When was Roe vs. Wade? 1973. The year we pulled out of Vietnam. A coincidence? I don't think so."

Casey had to think about this. So many people believed in conspiracies that were absurd and then there were others who scoffed at the very idea of conspiracies. And yet, people conspired with others every day to commit crimes. Maybe what he was talking about was the ultimate one. But he wasn't sure how it all fit together.

"But the Berlin wall is down and the Soviet Union and the communist countries in Eastern Europe are gone."

Father Mike smiled.

"Yes, it seems that way. The Pope was very influential in bringing that about as well as all the faithful praying their rosaries and all the masses that were said over the years."

"And Reagan had a lot to do with it," said Casey. "I think I'm going to have to reevaluate my opinion of him. I used to hate his guts."

Father Mike smiled

"Ronnie Raygun. Yes. Somehow, he got in there and it doesn't seem like he was one of them. But you never know. The communists are still lurking offstage, in disguise, biding their time. Then there's Red China and North Korea and Cuba. And the Islamic countries. They seem to be the wild card. They've been enemies of the Church for centuries. Islam is a heresy, a strange mixture of heretical Judaism and Christianity. In the **Summa Contra Gentiles,** Aquinas points out that Mohammed seduced the people by promises of carnal pleasure: multiple wives, the 72 virgins in paradise and the 21 beardless boys; let's not forget about them. Whatever truths Mohammed taught were mingled with many fables and false doctrines. He didn't bring forth any signs like Jesus did that were produced in a supernatural way. Mohammad said that he was sent in the power of arms which are signs not lacking even to robbers and tyrants. Those who believed in him were brutal men and desert wanderers who forced others to become his followers by violence. That's where all the hatred comes from. Remember the book **The Satanic Verses**? Its thesis was that Mohammad was inspired by Satan. They reacted by condemning the author, Salmon Rushdie, to death. It makes me think he was on to something. Muslims are even more dangerous than secularized Jews and fallen-away Catholics and that's saying something."

"Whew. This is so strange." said Casey. "It's like I'm just waking up from a spell that I was under, a trance of some kind. They had me brainwashed."

"Who are they?" asked Father Mike.

Casey shook his head.

"I don't know. The anti-war movement. The left. My effigies. The Devil?"

Father Mike nodded.

"So what do we do?" asked Casey. "How do we fight them? You're not going to tell me to pick up the gun, are you? I laid down my gun in Ireland."

Father Mike sighed.

"It seems so simple. Everybody should just put down their guns and the world will be safe. That's what the people who run UN and their ilk would have us believe. That's what they want. Then only they will have the guns. We will be under their control. And they are no friends of Christians. They will imprison us, torture us, kill us, indoctrinate us. Just as they did in the Soviet Union and in Red China, Vietnam, Cuba. All the Communist countries. And the Islamic ones as well. Make no mistake about it. It is not time to lay down the gun. Maybe some day. 'When we form that perfect man who is Christ come to full stature.'"

Casey shook his head

"But Christ allowed himself to be crucified rather than resort to violence."

Father Mike nodded.

"Not everyone is capable of being a martyr. Of going all the way to Calvary. The Church permits us to fight in self defense. An armed citizenry is the best defense against tyranny."

"But didn't the early Church follow the example of Christ?"

Father Mike nodded.

"Not everyone, only some. The Church decided that we had to give people the option to defend themselves and their loved ones. Love toward oneself is a fundamental principle of morality. You must understand: The Church has the authority to interpret the Scriptures and the teachings of Christ and what they mean in our lives. The Church recognizes the evil of war and violence but does not require that everyone be a pacifist. We have to trust the Church on this."

Casey remembered the insight that he just had in front of the crucified Christ and he told Father Mike about it.

Father Mike sighed.

'The great Polish writer Henryk Sienkiewicz in his novel **The Teutonic Knights** tells how the Polish King Jagiello before the battle of Tannenberg cried many tears over the thought of shedding of so much Christian blood. But the Teutonic knights, even though Christian, would not listen to reason or the Church and continued their wars of aggression. Their killing and raping had to be stopped and the only way to do it was by fire and sword. Sometimes, even Christians have to fight and kill and hope and pray that we can do so in a honorable way and not allow the violence to consume us."

Casey closed his eyes. He could see the logic in the argument.

He had been wrong again. No more rebellion. He would listen to the Church and follow its lead.

"So what do we do now?"

"Evangelize," said Father Mike. "Lay people like yourselves need to bring Christ to the workplace. Despite its faults, the United States is still the best country in the world. Work within the Constitution, by electing to Congress good Christian people, especially to the House of Representatives. That is where we can take control, especially of the money. It is easier for the Conspiracy to control one man: the President. It's more difficult to control the entire Congress. But the first step is getting the US out of the UN."

Casey smiled.

"Anything else?"

Father Mike smiled.

"I have a long laundry list. Most importantly though, we need prayer. At Fatima, Our Lady told us that was the way to fight Communism: by all of us praying the rosary every day. Not enough of us have done so."

Casey nodded.

'The rosary saved my life. I'm convinced of it now. Just by the fact that I'm here, at this Shrine, right now, and that I came back to the Church against all odds. It's a miracle, really, that I'm here, that I'm healthy, that I'm solvent, that I'm not dead, that I'm not in prison, or lying drunk in the gutter somewhere."

Father Mike nodded.

"Miracles happen every day. Most people when they think of miracles think of extraordinary physical healings, but most miracles are spiritual: sinners coming back to God. We call them favors here at the Shrine, done through the intercession of Mary. She is the mediatrix of all graces: They come through her from Him. She receives her power from Jesus. She is not God. She is human. Jesus is God. He is the one who saves us, at Calvary and through the Mass. During the Mass, our hearts are lifted up into eternity and it is there where the war is won. Remember: we have already won the war. Christ won it for us on the Cross where he defeated the Devil. God is in charge. But the battle continues."

Casey nodded.

"I'm back in the battle now. But this time, my mind is clear and my eyes are open. But I have a lot of questions I'd like to ask you about the Faith. I've forgotten so much and I know so little."

Father Mike smiled.

'The best place to start is the with the Gospels. Read them. We'll talk again, I'm sure."

Casey nodded then looked at his watch.

"I wish we could talk some more, now. But it's getting late. I'd like to go over and visit with Father Gal before I go to work. I want to thank you again, Father, for reading my books."

Father Mike smiled.

"It was my pleasure. It's quite a story."

Casey shrugged.

"For what it's worth. I failed."

"Some say ,wrongly, that so did Jesus," said Father Mike. "He was deserted by his friends. He was tortured. He was executed as a common criminal. But he was raised from the dead. And so were you. Metaphorically speaking of course."

Casey opened his hands in front of him.

"Yes, I was. But I didn't realize it for a long time. When I came home from Ireland, I went to Confession and Communion for my father's funeral. I was back in the Church. I was where I should have been. But I was too weak, too stupid. I stopped going to church again and my behavior got worse. I became a monster, a Patty Byrnes. Even after seeing him for what he was, I became like him anyway."

Father Mike put his hand on Casey's arm.

"You poor man. Jesus tells us that when an unclean spirit has gone out of a man, he returns to the house from which he came and brings with him seven other spirits more evil than himself and the state of the man becomes worse than it was. I would say that you were like him in kind but not in degree. But you're a new man, now, a new creation in Christ. You must always keep close to Our Lord and His Holy Mother."

Casey nodded.

"I know that now and I will. I should have stayed in the Church then. My life would have been totally different. I would have been fighting Evil, instead of contributing to it. I might have gotten married. Had children of my own. Instead, I lost eighteen years. I ruined my life."

Father Mike shook his head.

"No. No. Don't be so hard on yourself. The purpose of life is to attain salvation, to be in communion with God. To love and be loved. If you do that, your life is a success. As we pray in the novena, 'O Lord Jesus Christ, who for the accomplishment of your greatest works, have chosen the weak things of the world.' Whatever failures you've had in life become learning experiences. You have to see your life in its totality, as God sees it: from the eternal. It would have been better if you had stayed in the Church Militant but those years weren't a total loss. You look after your mother. You worked as a nurse, taking care of the sick. That's doing the work of God. You made the right choice in Ireland. It's a choice we all have to make: to dominate or to serve. To choose our will or be like the Theotokos, to do the will of God. People like McCann are an example of what Nietzsche called the ubermensch, the overman. I prefer that translation to the more common one of superman. I don't want the overman to be confused with the comic book character who went around helping the weak. Nietzsche despised the weak. He wanted to be over man. Like you, he came to hate Jesus Christ. But thank God, you've repented. It's been a long road for you but now you're home. You've been forgiven. 'God has cast all your sins into the depths of the sea.' Don't torture yourself. Of course, you need to do penance for your sins, but penance is prayer and good works, not self-torture; that's the work of Satan. Certainly, you're going to feel pain when you think of the times when you've offended God, but you must never forget that you've been forgiven."

Casey nodded.

I'll try, Father. Thank you, again."

Father Mike and Casey stood on the platform that connected the Shrine to Saint Vincent's and to Saint Catherine's. Father Mike told Casey about the history of the three buildings.

'The first Vincentians came to this country in 1818 from France."

Casey interrupted him.

"I'm sorry. Who are the Vincentians?"

"Our order was founded in France by Saint Vincent de Paul in 1625. Our official title is the Congregation of the Missions: C.M. Our mission is to preach the Gospel to the poor, although we are also involved in teaching: at Saint John's University and Niagara in the Eastern Province, DePaul in the Midwest. Back in the 1800's North America was a missionary country and our priests and brothers and nuns - the Daughters and Sisters of Charity - came here from Europe. To this day, we have missionaries around the world: in Panama and Africa and Asia. We first came to Germantown in the 1860's. First we founded Saint Vincent's parish on Price Street. Soon after, we began building our seminary here on this site."

Father Mike pointed to the parking lot in front of them.

"When I was here in the 1940's, this was a baseball field and a tennis court. Saint Catherine's Infirmary wasn't built until 1980. More and more of our priests and brothers were getting old and infirm, so we felt the need to build a larger infirmary than the one we had in the Seminary building. The Infirmary was built, in part, from money we got from the Chinese Communists."

Casey laughed.

"What do you mean?"

Father Mike smiled.

'The Vincentians had been sending missionaries to China since the 17th century. Our province sent some there in the 1920's. When the Communists took over in 1950, they expelled our people and confiscated our property, property that we had brought from donations made by our Catholic people to the Central Association of the Miraculous Medal. In the 1970's when Nixon reestablished relations with China, one of the stipulations was that China had to reimburse those from whom they had taken property. We were one of them. We used that money to help build the Infirmary and to renovate the Chapel."

'The Chapel we were just in?" asked Casey.

"Yes. It was originally called the Chapel of the Immaculate Conception. It was built in the 1870's. Now, most people call it the Miraculous Medal Shrine."

"The Miraculous Medal?" asked Casey. "I remember hearing something about it, but I don't know what it is."

Father Mike unbuttoned his black shirt and took out a medal he wore around his neck and showed it to Casey.

'This image of the Blessed Mother was manifested to Saint Catherine Laboure in 1830. It was originally called the Medal of the Immaculate Conception, but over the years, so many miracles were attributed to it, to those wearing it, that the people called it the Miraculous Medal. Of course, the medal itself has no power. It's the faith of the people in Our Lord and his Holy Mother that brings about the miracles. There's a statue of the image in the Chapel, in the alcove on the right-hand side."

Casey nodded.

"I saw it. And I saw this medal before, somewhere."

As Casey looked at the medal, a memory so powerful flooded through his brain that he had to close his eyes and bow his head.

"Now I remember where I saw this: at Fort Bragg, North Carolina. That's where I did my basic training when I first went into the army. As I was unpacking my bag that I had brought from home, I found a medal tucked away in the bottom. My mother had put it in there before I left home."

Casey felt tears filling his eyes.

"God forgive me, but I don't know what I did with that medal. I probably threw it away."

"She didn't throw you away," said Father Mike. "Remember what I just said: The medal itself has no power. It was your mother's faith and the intercession of the Blessed Mother that protected you. We'll get you another one. We have plenty of them here."

Casey nodded.

"I'd like that. But we'd better get going. I want to see how Father Gal is doing before I go to work."

As they walked up the ramp to the Infirmary, they discussed Father Gal and his health problems.

"He's doing well," said Father Mike. "He gets good care here at the Infirmary. His foot is healing. He's in good spirits."

When they walked into his room, Father Gal was sitting in his recliner. When he saw his two visitors, he put down the book he was reading and welcomed them.

"I'm happy to see you two have met.""We had a good talk," said Father Mike. "I told him how impressed I was by his books."

"I'll have to read them sometime," said Father Gal.

Casey shook his head.

"No. Don't bother. Maybe sometime, but not now. They're fatally flawed. They have to be rewritten. Father Mike has pointed out to me that they have to be part of a larger narrative. I have no idea of what that is. But it's not that important. I found what I've been looking for: who I really am as a person. That's the important thing."

Father Gal nodded.

"I see the sign of who you are on your forehead. Welcome home."

Casey smiled.

"It's also the sign of who I'm not."

When Father Mike saw the puzzled look on Father Gal's face, he mentioned briefly his homily on effigies in ashes.

"I had help from the mystic, Adrienne von Speyr. It was she who said that whenever we become a new person in Christ, our false selves, or effigies, are what are cast into the fire and burned. I took it from there."

"So, how's your foot?' asked Casey.

Father Gal smiled.

"Healing. Father Mike told me about your abilities. I was going to ask you if you could heal my foot, but it's almost healed now."

Casey smiled.

"I have no more ability than anyone else does. We can pray but it's God who heals. You're in the best place here. You're surrounded by prayerful people."

"Give me your blessing, Father Joe," said Father Mike. "I have to be on my way. I'll let you two talk."

The two priests exchanged blessings and then Father Mike shook hands with Casey. They promised to stay in touch with each other. With that, Father Mike left the room, closing the door behind him.

When they were alone, Father Gal said, "I've been thinking about that discussion we had about God approving of war."

Casey held up both hands.

"Hey, you don't have to get into it. I know the difference now between God and the Devil. I've been wrong about so many things in my life, especially about God and the Church and that's one of them."

Father Joe smiled.

"The Scriptures are very complex. A library. Complex but simple. I remember one of the saints saying that all of Sacred Scripture is but one book and that one book is Christ. But there are many different types of stories in the Bible : told in the form of history and poetry, drama and prophecy. And the gospels. They're in a category all their own. The book of Genesis, for instance, is poetry and is not to be read literally. The book of Job is a type of drama. What we call the historical books are not history as we think of history, that is, an accurate account of factual events. Although archeologists and scientists are beginning to discover that books like the Exodus for instance are based on fact not fiction. Even if they are embellished somewhat it doesn't mean they're not true, because they are: they're spiritually true."

Casey nodded.

"Like in literature. The story can be true, but didn't happen exactly as described."

Father Joe agreed.

"As we find in the gospels. Where much of the stories about Jesus are rearranged for the different audiences. Written in the light of the resurrection, under the inspiration of the Holy Spirit, with a fuller understanding of what Jesus said and did and who He was. But then there are stories in the Bible that may not have happened at all in reality, but nonetheless tell the truth about life. The book of Esther, for instance. And Tobit. The authors use literary techniques to tell the story just as writers do today: metaphors and hyperbole and parables. And other techniques that were used in ancient times that we don't use today: midrash and panegyric, for instance. We need to know what was the intent and purpose of the writer when he wrote the book. For instance, when we read about God telling the Israelites to kill all the people of Canaan it was because their gods were demons. It was to keep the Jews from being spiritually contaminated that God ordered the destruction of those people. Today, the Church would interpret it in a spiritual sense: that God hates sin so much that He wants it to be totally destroyed. So that

God's people could live in peace. Which we now know will only come in the next life."

"How can someone like me find out these things?" asked Casey. "I never learned any of that in college."

Father Joe nodded.

'There have been some recent developments in the Church in biblical exegesis. We have to read the Bible through the mind of the Church. There was a Church before there was a Bible as we know it today. The Catholic Church gave us the Bible. Saint Charles Seminary has courses for lay people, in scripture and theology. You might want to take some classes there. They're the same courses the seminarians take. Very soon, there will be a new Catechism of the Catholic Church. I've haven't read it myself yet, but I've heard that it is very good. I'm sure you will be able to learn much from it. But the simplest answer to your problem comes from Jesus. He says in the Gospel of John: 'I and the Father are one. Whoever sees me, sees the Father.'"

Casey smiled.

"And Jesus allowed himself to be crucified rather than to commit violence. I see the truth now. Jesus showed us who God really is. He showed us, all of us, the way out of the circle of violence two thousand years ago. We've just haven't taken it to heart, not enough of us, anyway."

Father Gal smiled.

"So true. But we're human and God loves us, anyway."

Father Gal opened both hands and raised them slightly as if calling them to prayer.

"So. How's your mother doing? God bless her. My mother said that they talked on the phone last night. They had a good cry together."

Casey smiled.

"I know. Mom was so happy I came back to the Church. My Godfather, Dimmo McCann told her it was a miracle."

Father Gal showed him the cover of the book he was reading: **A Key to the Doctrine of the Eucharist.**

'The author of this book Abbot Vonier says the same thing in a paraphrase of Aquinas. That a person who is in a state of mortal sin can come back to the state of grace through the normal process of supernatural life, through sacramental confession, but once a person apostatizes, as I'm afraid you did, it takes a miracle to bring him back."

Casey closed his eyes and took a deep breath. It frightened and sickened him to think how close he came to being lost forever.

"So your mother's doing okay."

Casey nodded.

"Yeah. She has arthritis and it causes her pain, but overall, she's healthy. She's reaping the benefit of having led a sensible life. She never really smoked or drank and she worked hard all her life. She told me that your parents are doing well."

'They are," said Father Gal. "All my family is well. Thank God. How about your brother? How's he doing? I know he's had some problems."

Casey shrugged.

"I don't know how he's doing. He's alienated. Estranged from Mom and me and from the Church. We don't hear from him or see him very often. The same thing happened to him as happened to me. A demon got into him when he was a boy. In a different way than me. Deeper. Probably because my brother was a better kid than I was. He had the potential to be a saint, I think. He was a gentle, sensitive kid. Unlike me. Even as a young boy, he cared about others in ways that I never did. He was nice to Annie Morrison, the old lady who lived across the street. I remember him befriending Bobby, a retarded kid from the neighborhood. The kid's parents even named their youngest son after my brother. It's a shame. We had a good family life until the late 60's then it all fell apart. I don't know what happened. My family was a good one."

Father Gal sighed.

"Saint Therese of Lisieux, the Little Flower, may give us some insight into this. When she was a young girl, she got very sick and came close to death from a mysterious disease which she believed was a virulent demonic attack that left her extremely weak and despondent. She was cured by the Blessed Mother. Therese attributed this attack to the Devil because he realized the danger her family could do and did do to him and his minions. Any family that is good is going to be under special attack by Satan. What happened to your brother?"

Casey shrugged.

"It's a long story. And it's his to tell, not mine. He needs to do what I did: go to confession and receive the grace he needs for his eyes to be opened, so he can see what truly happened to him when he was a boy."

"We'll pray for him," said Father Gal as he reached for a small book he had on his desk. "Here's a copy of our novena prayers. Say them for him. And come over on Mondays for our perpetual novena. We pray it every Monday. The schedule is inside the book."

Casey took the book and studied the picture on the front. It was the same as the statue he saw in church and on the miraculous medal.

"I will. And maybe I'll be able to see you then as well."

"I'd like that," said Father Gal.

Casey looked at his watch.

"I got to go. I have to be at work at 3. But before I go, would you give me your blessing, Father?"

Casey knelt on the floor in front of the priest like a knight kneeling before his king.

Father Gal raised his hand over Casey's head and made the sign of the cross over him.

"May the blessing of Almighty God descend upon you and remain with you forever and I bless you in the name of the Father and of the Son and of The Holy Spirit. Amen."